THE HAND PUPPET

WILLIAM MARTEN

A Lucky Bat Book
The Hand Puppet
Copyright ©2022 by William Marten

ISBN: 978-1-939051-16-5

Cover Artist: Nuno Moreira
Published by Lucky Bat Books
10 9 8 7 6 5 4 3 2 1

"Freedom is what you do with what's been done to you."
– Jean-Paul Sartre

NOTE FROM THE AUTHOR

THE BDSM PRACTICES AND EXPERIENCES MENTIONED or described in this work, though they may appear realistic and are drawn from activities that do exist, are fictional. The author and publisher accept no responsibility for injuries and damages incurred in discussion of them or in practicing them. The opinions expressed in this story are those of the characters and not of the author.

1

The Hand Puppet

AT AGE THIRTEEN, A BOY DOESN'T need a best friend. He actually needs several. Leaving adolescence and exploring the possibilities of adult life are much easier when doing them with a pal, and there's one for each adventure. Sam figured this out right away and made good use of it.

He and his friend Roger learned the entrepreneurial world together with daily newspaper routes. For Sam, that meant rising at five in the morning; riding his bicycle through the dark, rain, snow, and slush; and making sure each paper made it to a dry spot on the porch. Roger delivered the evening paper after school with similar challenges. Their camaraderie was needed most when going door to door trying to collect money from stingy and evasive subscribers.

Sam and his friend Charlie strengthened their throwing arms and hitting eyes with endless games of catch and practice shagging fly balls. Sam was not the power slugger that Charlie was, but he was quick on the bases and could field. Both made it onto the same little league baseball team.

And Jeffrey, who was hampered by congenitally bad eyesight and would never participate in either of those prerequisites of youth, showed Sam (or tried to) how to grow one's brain with a chessboard.

But Sam's friend Benny was interested in none of those conventional boyhood pursuits. The avenues Benny was keen to walk bordered on illegal, forbidden, and unhealthy—even better if they involved all three. One such activity was smoking, an adult affectation and therefore irresistible. Benny introduced Sam to cigarettes one Saturday afternoon behind the movie theater, where the boys had just seen *Creature from the Black Lagoon*. Benny withdrew a wrinkled pack of cigarettes from his back pocket and pulled one out. He furtively looked around the alley, a clear advertisement for impending mischief, and put the bent cigarette to his lips.

"Is that a cigarette?" Sam asked, a bit shocked.

"No, you moron, it's a donkey turd." Benny lit the cigarette, cupping his hand around the match like any seasoned smoker, then inhaled deeply and blew out the smoke in one long and apparently satisfying breath.

"Aren't those supposed to stunt your growth?" Sam asked.

"Nah. Both my parents smoke, and they grew up fine. These are Camels, my dad's. Mom smokes Parliaments with filters. Only pussies smoke filtered cigarettes. Camels are great. Dad smokes three packs a day, so he never misses a pack or two. Here, you try it."

He passed the cigarette over. Sam regarded the burning object like it was filled with poison, then tentatively took a drag. After hacking out what seemed like a chunk of his lung, he could not understand the appeal. Benny laughed and shook his head. He was not yet hooked and had no idea what awaited him.

Drinking was also a tempting pleasure restricted to grown-ups. To that point, the only way a boy could get high was on a roller coaster or by hyperventilating. Benny, naturally, had discovered another way in a bottle of bourbon he'd smuggled from his parents' liquor cabinet. After his recent experience with smoking, Sam began to suspect that any Benny-generated thrill would come with a price. True enough, one swig turned his throat into an incinerator flue and his stomach inside out.

"This is supposed to feel good?" Sam groaned when his guts finally untwisted.

"The boy just can't hold his liquor," Benny said, greatly amused by Sam's peristalsis and feeling quite inflated as the self-appointed guide to the promised land of adult vice.

Despite the assault on his vital organs by these common teenage rites of passage, Sam remained a steadfast friend because Benny seemed able to ferret out minor sins from places Sam didn't know existed. He couldn't quite put his finger on why Benny's shady proclivities felt so seductive, but he was always eager to see the next one. That happened one day after school in Benny's bedroom, when Benny showed Sam where to put his fingers.

"Hey, you wanna do something really cool?" Benny said.

"Sure," said Sam, thinking about an air rifle or firecrackers or anything else that Benny might use to tweak convention and propriety. Sunlight poured into the bedroom, with the liquid amber glow only a clear September afternoon could distill. Benny walked to the window and closed the curtains.

"Watch this," he said with a sly grin. He dropped his pants and underwear, flopped back on his bed; closed his fist around his small, limp penis; and began to stroke.

"If you do this for a while," said Benny, "your dick gets hard and white sticky stuff shoots out the end, and it feels really, *really* good."

Curious and a little dubious, Sam watched Benny grip his penis tighter, saw it swelling larger, and then Benny started to pump faster. Sam knew Benny was a joker, frequently pulling pranks on anyone he considered prankable, and this odd scene had the makings of another.

Benny closed his eyes and began to moan. The moans became groans, and then louder. Benny's act looked so ridiculous Sam assumed he was faking going crazy. But after one loud cry, Benny's hips arched and, sure enough, white fluid erupted from his penis with such force and velocity it hit the opposite wall. Astonished, Sam watched the viscous glop dribble down.

"What *is* that?" he asked.

"Jism," Benny said, trying to catch his breath. "Your balls make it. It's called jerking off. It's really the best. Now you try it."

Sam was now very intrigued but uncertain what to expect. He dropped his pants, lay down next to Benny, and imitated the procedure. His penis remained soft.

"Keep at it," said Benny.

After five minutes, Sam gave up. Benny shrugged.

"Don't worry about it," he said. "It took me a few tries. You're supposed to think about girls when you do it. Think about putting your dick in their crack."

"Their crack?"

"Where else, you turkey?"

Sam knew about sex the same way he knew the moon orbited the earth: it obviously happened, but the mechanics remained unknown and unknowable. Sex was still an entrancing, intangible activity none of his friends had actually done or seen but had lewdly discussed in locker rooms and on baseball fields as if they had. Sam always joined in the laughter, but he didn't get the joke.

"Hey," Benny said, "maybe this will help."

Benny opened the bottom drawer of his bureau, rummaged beneath the clothes, and withdrew an envelope. It contained a black-and-white photograph of a naked woman. She was sitting outdoors against a brick wall with her knees drawn to her chest, just barely covering the tips of her large breasts. She was blonde, pretty, and smiling at the camera. On one hand she wore a little clown puppet. The clown was also smiling (as well he should be, impaled on the fingers of a beautiful bare-naked woman). But it seemed such a sad smile, so close to sex but so impossibly beyond his reach.

Sam could relate. He stood and gaped at the photograph, transfixed. His groin, not feeling much a minute ago, was suddenly caught in the grip of a powerful force, a suction he didn't know could exist. A suction that quickly seized the rest of his body, stopping his breath, dilating his eyes, purging his mind of all else, and doing something very strange and exciting to his penis. He truly believed if he wished hard enough and long enough, the pretty lady would move her knees and reveal everything.

Sam found himself staring at the hand puppet as much as the woman's naked body, adding confusion to his enthrallment. Her being naked outdoors and unprotected intensified her eroticism. *Eroticism.* Sam had heard the word before. It was flavored with seduction and mystery, an adult thing and just beyond his capacity to sense. Now he did, and exultantly so.

He had to do something about this, something new, daring, and soon, and he knew what it was. His penis did not share his stupor. It began to swell of its own volition with an unexpected ferocity and hunger. The organ seemed to no longer belong to him; it now obeyed an imperative far beyond his sovereignty. To what, he wasn't sure, but the picture was getting clearer.

"Now try jerking off while looking at the picture," urged Benny gleefully.

Sam again imitated Benny's protocol, but despite his penis's tumescence, it was to no effect. He suspected there was a torrid link between his trance, its perplexing immediacy, his new penis, jism, and the photograph, but he couldn't connect the dots. He watched Benny grip the photograph with one hand, stroke his erect cock with the other, and within a minute a second line of jism slowly ran down the wall.

"Can I borrow the picture?" said Sam.

"Not a chance!" Benny laughed like a drunken donkey and wiped his semen off the wall with a T-shirt.

That night in bed, Sam's hand slipped to his groin to try again. In his mind, the pretty naked woman and her sad little clown were still fresh and glowing with that word: eroticism. Sam imagined himself as the puppet and felt the woman's fingers gently slide into him and rub him over her breasts and thighs—she knew exactly where she wanted him. His penis got the message. His groin involuntarily jerked with a new kind of electricity, his skull bones exploded, and a sticky puddle blossomed into his hand. The dots got connected in one searing flash.

But not a minute into wafting through his first post-orgasmic cloud-bank, Sam thudded back to earth. He felt like he was standing on the edge of a wide, abyssal chasm that seconds ago had not been there. Girls were on the other side, now having acquired a fierce allure he could not ignore, nor did he know how to consummate it or whether this was even possible. And this new stuff, jism, was involved, like gasoline poured on open flames. The sex playground he had only just discovered was, just as suddenly, off limits to him. How could an orgasm infuse him with such pleasure one minute and make him feel so powerless the next?

Besides watching their bodies begin to change, Sam knew something else was up with the girls—something that only widened this bedeviling chasm. He remembered one day in sixth grade, when all the girls were sequestered in an adjacent classroom to watch a movie made especially for them. In compensation and as a distraction, the boys were shown their own movie, a safety-patrol-boy recruitment plea. That movie failed both missions, as the boys' attentions were solidly focused on what was happening in the next room. The subject of the girls' movie was a source of constant speculation, and the girls were not talking... except one.

"Cindy said it's about some kind of cycle they have," Benny said.

"Like a bicycle?" Sam couldn't imagine why that would be such a hot secret.

"No, more like, um, it has something to do with their bodies and the moon."

"The moon? Right. Cindy's yanking your chain, Benny."

"I don't think so. I once heard Mom say something about her moon time."

"Moon time? That's crazy!"

Sam had to declare moon time crazy because he detected a grain of truth hidden within that strange phrase—a truth imbued with mystery and which smacked of a conspiracy between girls, their mothers, and female teachers. This mystery frightened him, though no threat was visible. That chasm was wide enough, and thinking about moon times made it more so. What was his mystery? Where was his special movie? Who would tell him about what was happening to his body and this new urge that both so transfixed and troubled him?

Neither Sam, Benny, nor the rest of their newly horny crew at school knew the word *pornography*, but they sure knew what they liked and wanted more of it. The little clown and his beautiful naked puppeteer visited Sam every night, sometimes dropping by several times. Other racy photographs surfaced in the school hallways and locker rooms. Like ravenous seagulls around a morsel of fish, all the boys scrambled for a peek. It didn't matter if the pornography lived in the real world or not, only that it did its job: grab a boy by his penis and fling him on a long, wild trajectory into orgasm. And then do it again an hour later.

Photographs of naked women entered the body through the eyes, but words claimed the mind, turning it into a far more exciting and fertile playground. A paperback novel called *Lydia's Lust* appeared in the school's clandestine smut corridors, animating the boys' two-dimensional fantasies and confirming that sex was indeed possible, and then showing how it was done.

The book had been torn along its spine into three sections to make circulation among the seagulls more efficient. Sam got his hands on the last part, which made understanding the plot a problem. But the plot was not the point of the book. Lydia, the blonde, beautiful, melon-breasted protagonist was. Lydia was also possessed by an insatiable sex drive, and her condition was documented in lurid detail every four or five pages, thus demonstrating that boys weren't the only ones with drives.

Besides being a sex maniac, Lydia was also a murderess, and Sam suspected the two conditions were somehow linked. Her modus was to seduce some horny guy she'd just met, shoot him in the groin while he lay in postcoital bliss, and then move on to her next victim. Why she did this was probably explained in the first part of the book. But what mattered most were the dog-eared passages of Lydia tearing open her blouse and spilling her melons into the hands of her unknowing, doomed prey. The book ended with Lydia being cornered and shot to death by an army of policemen, supposedly as a lesson to all girls thinking about becoming sex maniacs.

Then Sam obtained a copy of *Lady Chatterley's Lover* in its entirety. The book was on the banned reading list, and he quickly found out why. But scant few of the pages were dog-eared, and there was a catch: he had to wade through something called literature to get to the sex, which perhaps had been Lawrence's plan all along. Instead of reading repetitive accounts of blouses and melons, Sam discovered richly detailed scenes of texture and tenderness that framed sex in unimaginable ways. For the first time, the allure of romantic love licked at his body. More than anything else, he wanted to weave tiny wildflowers into a pretty girl's bush.

D.H. Lawrence, Lydia, and Benny convinced Sam that what girls had under their dresses was the whole point of life, and Sam was growing more frantic to get it. That's the merciless tyranny of testosterone—it demands a boy comply with its mandates but won't tell him how to do so, or even how to find out. But what did the prize actually look like? Sam's family's encyclopedia showed the insides of a woman's reproductive system, but there was frustratingly little information about the outside. Marble statues of Greek goddesses, the closest the encyclopedia came to pornography, were not much help. Thank heaven for the toilet stall walls in the boys' locker room.

At that time, and not having a special movie, the locker room was the only place a boy could get any form of sex education. There Sam learned that boys had boners, cocks, dicks, rods, wieners, whangers, peckers, and pricks. Girls owned tits, boobs, bazoombas, melons, jugs, hooters, honkers, and knockers. Down below were their pussies, cunts, beavers, nookies, holes, muffs, and twats. And boys were supposed to fuck, lay, hump, pork, screw, bang, and boink the aforementioned. Apparently, that's all one needed to know about sex. Sex, aside from being an elemental force of nature, also sprouted euphemisms like mushrooms on a cow flop.

One afternoon in the locker room after gym class, Gary, a ninth-grader, still naked from the showers, took a condom out of his locker and held it aloft like a medal he'd just won at a track meet. None of the other boys knew what it was, but the display smelled of intrigue and suggested this was an adult thing, a secretive and sexual thing.

They were right. Gary rolled the condom onto his penis.

"What *is* that?" asked Benny, just as transfixed as Sam and everyone else.

"It's called a rubber," smiled Gary as he massaged his wiener into a boner.

"Does it feel good?" asked Benny.

"You're not supposed to feel it at all."

"Well then, what's it for?"

Sam was astonished to see Benny caught at a loss.

"I can't believe you morons!" Gary said. "It's for fucking a girl. You feel her pussy through it. It's almost as good as her naked pussy, but you won't knock her up."

"Knock her up?" asked another boy.

"Get her pregnant, Dork," Gary said. Dork was actually the boy's nickname, not by his choice.

Sam and the rest of the dorks now paid close attention to Gary and his spellbinding toy. The locker room smelled of sweat, chlorine, spray deodorant, and gym shoes. The faint latex odor of condoms added to the mix became the early scent of sex to Sam. He thought about the adjacent locker room filled with wet, naked girls. He wondered how it smelled and why, and whether the girl's plumbing fixtures were any different from or stranger than those of the boys.

Gary continued, "You see, there's sperm in your jism and eggs in her cunt. When you fuck her, the sperm and egg make a fetus that becomes a baby. Then you have to marry her, leave school, and work as a janitor for the rest of your miserable life to support the kid. And all because you didn't wear a rubber. Get it?"

"So how do you get rubbers?" Benny asked. Count on Benny to ask the questions they all had but were reluctant to voice.

"At a drugstore," Gary said. "But you have to ask for them because they keep them hidden behind the counter. And their real name is pro-phylactics, not rubbers."

"Pro what?" Benny seemed to be taking mental notes.

"Get a clue, misfit," said Gary. "And some rubbers have little rubber spikes on them. Those are called french ticklers. It drives the girls bonkers and they'll beg you for more."

This was utterly fascinating to Sam. An entire industry devoted to sex.

"Then, like, how do you get a girl to fuck you?" Dork bravely pressed on.

Gary laughed. "There's ways, but you have to figure it out for your-selves. I did."

That's not what the crowd wanted to hear. "That sounds like bullshit," Dork said, very un-dork-like.

"I'll tell you one thing that's not bullshit," Gary said. "Girls have been warned by their mothers that we want to fuck them. And they've been told to never, ever let that happen."

"Why not?" cried Dork, incensed. "Don't girls get horny, too? How can they not want sex when it feels so great? That's crazy!"

"It's just how it is," Gary shrugged. "Sex is supposed to feel good, not make sense."

Gary, as it happened, also sold rubbers for a dollar each, no doubt on his way to becoming a drug dealer. Afraid or unable to buy rubbers legitimately, the boys had no choice but to patronize him. Benny bought one. Gary took out his wallet and showed him where to put the rubber so the ring impression would show through the leather.

"Show this to the girls," he said, "and they'll really get turned on. Then they'll know you're experienced and that leads to an instant fuck, guaranteed. Especially if she's a nympho."

"Nympho?" Sam asked.

"Nymphomaniac," Gary said. "It's a mental disease some girls get. It makes them want to fuck everything they see. All you have to do is ask. It's true."

Dork thought hard about this incredible new information. "Well, then," he said, "doesn't that make us nymphomaniacs, too?"

"No!" said Gary. "We're guys!"

"So how do you find a nympho?" Benny chimed in, asking the obvious follow-up question.

"You just have to get lucky," Gary laughed. "There's a few of 'em in school, this I know."

2
GOBLINS

THIS WAS MOST FANTASTIC NEWS. NYMPHOMANIACS like Lydia the serial killer were not just fiction. Sam now scanned every girl in the school hallways and classrooms, trying to identify anything in her dress or behavior that might reveal her secret. A positively guaranteed fuck—all you had to do was ask! Sex truly was mystifying, so unbelievably complicated and utterly simple at the same time. The possibility of a serial-killer-to-nymphomania link made him a little uneasy, but hormones had a way of keeping one's intention on course.

Sam arrived at a sobering conclusion: if he did manage to find an agreeable nympho, he'd be disqualified by not having a rubber. Without one, sex with any girl, nympho or not, would be impossible and risky, if not illegal. Benny's rubber was getting a workout without ever having to leave its package. The ring impression in his wallet fooled no one and taught him that girls, besides having melons and muffs, also had brains and could use them. He didn't get any of his guaranteed fucks, only several offers from other boys to buy the rubber. Gary had also warned that some rubbers had pinholes in them as someone's idea of a joke. Surprise! A baby!

"How do you know if that's true?" the boys fretted.

"You have to wait and see," laughed Gary. No one else thought it was funny.

Benny's rubber now was suspect. He couldn't see any pinholes, but why take a chance? Sam and Benny discussed their options. Neither boy had an older brother or a more courageous friend who could keep a secret. Asking a parent was unthinkable. Gary's prices were extortion, not to mention the terrifying possibility of pinholes. But need always conquers embarrassment, and after several days of perseverating, the two best friends ventured forth.

Benny went into the drugstore first and Sam followed, pretending they didn't know each other. That way, they previously agreed, if one got arrested, the other could escape. Benny wandered among the aisles of beauty aids, shampoos, and notions, orbiting closer to the pharmacy counter. The druggist watched both boys with understandable suspicion. Sam drifted over to the magazine rack, fearing to see what might happen to Benny.

Sam eyed the detective magazines. Cops, robbers, and murder mysteries held little interest for him, but he picked out a magazine at random and leafed through it. Nestled among the ads for bodybuilding courses, X-ray glasses, and elevator shoes was a story unashamedly called "The Torture of the Bound Nudes." The front illustration showed a beautiful naked woman with her arms pinned behind her by, of all things, goblins with bulging eyes and slobbering maws. One goblin had withdrawn a red-hot skewer from a glowing brazier and made ready to thrust it into one of her huge, cartoon breasts as she looked on in horror.

The picture shot straight into Sam's groin like a poisoned arrow fired by the Anti-Cupid. He slipped behind the magazine rack, where he could investigate this fascinating and forbidden discovery in private. The plot of the story was basically its title: a cult of crazed, murderous goblins tortured nude, bound women for their own and the reader's pleasure. In explicit detail, each paragraph documented the goblins' escalating ingenuity and brutality. The story concluded with one bound nude finally expiring from the excruciating pain.

The story threw Sam into a paralyzing thrall. The magazine rack, the drugstore, and even Benny vanished. There existed only the goblins' torture chamber and its mesmerized voyeur. Neither the goblins nor the author explained why this horror was being done in the first place, although their reasons were very clear to Sam's erection.

Sam knew the story was fiction, but he wouldn't accept that. Somewhere goblins were torturing naked women, and he was frantic to see it. But no, this was wrong, deplorably wrong, prison and gas chamber wrong. Sam had no place to put this, no way to explain how this unholy union of excitement and cruelty could so instantly invade, bewitch, and possess his genitals. Forget Lydia and her nymphomaniac sisters. All Sam could think of was that coming night when the lights would go off and those goblins would come out.

Sam nervously put the magazine back on the rack, but he knew it wouldn't stay there. Once certain things are seen, they can't be unseen. He felt his old life disappearing, like dirty bathwater swirling down the drain into the stygian depths of hell. He saw a new life, alien, obsessed, and diseased, with bulging eyes and a slobbering maw, crawl out of the drain to take its place. He became very, very frightened.

After his pulse rate returned to normal and he precipitated back into the real world, Sam took inventory. He felt basically the same, but not quite. He felt this alien thing, this goblin, roaming around inside his body looking for a place to live. Then Benny appeared in front of him, empty-handed and downcast.

"I asked the druggist for some prolifics," Benny said, "and he said, 'what size?' Then I chickened out. Let's get out of here."

The boys walked out of the store together.

"Hey, what's with you?" Benny asked, seeing Sam's ashen face.

"Nothing. I'm fine. Never felt better," said Sam.

He'd never felt worse. He'd never felt more savagely aroused. That night, he threw Lydia to the goblins as punishment for murdering all those men, never mind that they weren't real. Then the goblins tortured that pretty naked woman with her hand puppet, and deservedly so for tempting Sam with what he'd never get. Cindy was next; her crime was joining a secret moon-time conspiracy whose sole purpose was to keep him out.

His favorite victim was Ginny from homeroom, who had gone from beanpole to voluptuous overnight and would not say a word to him. Beautiful, bosomy Ginny, who was destined to be a prom queen, never knew of her other fate in Sam's bedroom. Her aloofness no longer mattered because soon she'd be screaming for mercy and getting none. The highlight of Sam's days became his nights.

After every climax, Sam slid into guilt and shame for what he'd done to these women, fictitious or not. And every climax nourished that goblin within, which now demanded more victims and ever newer atrocities to use on them. The more nights he let the goblins loose, the further away from himself he felt. Had he known about such things, Sam would have witnessed the beginning of dissociation. He also didn't know that once a split occurs, it only grows wider. But he knew enough to uneasily suspect this might be the onset of mental illness.

Sam's view of the mentally ill was forged by the intelligence and sensitivity of the time: lock the loonies up and be darn glad you're normal. He recalled one odd-looking girl in class who would occasionally burst into tears for no reason. She always sat in back of the classroom, would never participate, and rubbed snot into her hair. The teachers knew not to call on her. One day she was gone, taken to a special school, everyone was told. Everyone also knew that "special school" meant "funny farm." That's what mental illness looked like to Sam.

Now it looked like a horde of slobbering goblins rampaging through his crotch. He tried to exorcise the goblins by not thinking about them, which of course increased their appeal. He tried goblin abstinence. He imagined Cindy and Ginny naked and kissing their breasts and weaving tiny wildflowers into their pubic hair. But that didn't work, not even for one night, because thinking about naked girls meant acquiring them, and that possibility was as remote as walking on the moon and just about as feasible. What did work were naked girls screaming in the goblin dungeon, and he just could not stop.

But it had to stop. Sam genuinely feared being sent to the funny farm with snot-girl. Solutions to his problem were becoming fewer, more unreasonable, and then nonexistent. There was no one he could talk to, not even Benny, who seemed equally possessed by his penis and his unopened rubber. Sam finally decided if he didn't tell anyone about the goblins and didn't rub snot into his hair, he could pass as a normal guy with a normal penis and no one would ever suspect differently. But he knew better, and so did the goblins.

The Anti-Cupid was not yet finished with Sam. His parents' bedroom was a place he'd never explored. The invisible fence of adult privacy had been established since childhood, and he'd always respected it without a problem. What that fence protected concerned him little, as there were plenty of other rooms, inside the house and out, that provided all the mystery and mischief a lad could want.

Sex was not discussed in Sam's household; his parents seemed to have decided there was no need. There wasn't. He'd already learned the essentials in the boys' locker room, where the mechanics of the sex act had been vividly, if not accurately, detailed. But he suspected that vital information had been left out or ignored. Did girls get turned on? Did they have orgasms like boys? What did they like about sex? And why did they want to avoid it so much? These were questions that Sam could not ask his parents, particularly his mother.

When he was seven, Sam had approached her with The Big One. It was in the late afternoon. She was lying on the sofa with her forearm draped across her eyes, which she seemed to do every day at that time. "I have a headache," was the reason she always gave him. She assumed he wouldn't understand the term *chronic depression*. She barely did.

"Mom, where do babies come from?" he asked.

It was the question all parents dread, the last one his mother expected, and it came at a very bad time. She sighed, sat up, and just looked at him with her brow in a knot. From her concern and hesitation, Sam wondered if she even knew the answer herself.

"Well," she finally ventured, "when a man and a woman get married, and *only* after they're married, then a baby comes."

Sam found this conceptually baffling. "So how does the baby know they're married?"

"It just does," she sighed and laid back on the sofa, forearm in place.

Back to the question. "Yeah, but the baby comes from where?"

"The husband gives his wife a seed and puts it in her belly."

"A seed? What kind of seed? And how does it get into her belly?"

"You'll learn about it later," his mother said.

"Later? When's later?"

"Later."

"Mom!"

"Leave me alone, Sam."

That was the only conversation about sex Sam would ever hear in that house.

But later had arrived. The mysteries of sex had been replaced by fascination and obsession. Now fourteen and a veteran explorer of the land between his thighs, Sam eyed his parents' closed bedroom door. He knew what had happened in there, twice at least, considering his younger sister, although imagining it made him queasy. He didn't exactly know what lay hidden behind that door, but it called out to him with a distinctly feminine voice that hollowed out his stomach and tickled his groin.

Sam was alone in the house. His father was at work as a lab technician, his sister was at a friend's house, his mother at her bridge club. Sam stood at the bedroom door and hesitated. He could hear cicadas chirring in the summer-parched maples and elms, their crescendo rising and falling in a rhythm only they understood. Had he known the purpose of their singing, he would have appreciated how appropriate their music was to the moment. He slowly opened the bedroom door.

He found nothing of interest in the chest of drawers, only underwear and intimates. Having never touched a bra, he picked up one of his mother's. The cups were huge, which was not a great surprise. He expected some sort of thrill from it, quickly decided he didn't want it, and replaced the bra, trying to remember how it was folded.

The drawer in the bedside table contained facial tissue, vials of aspirin, nail clippers, and other instruments for hygiene and grooming. The only unexplored territory was the large walk-in closet. Sam entered apprehensively. The closet was filled with what one would expect to find in a bedroom closet: clothes, shoes, linen, towels, and plastic storage bags filled with the same. Quilts and blankets were stacked on the upper shelf. He was both disappointed and relieved to see that uncovering mysteries here might come with a price.

But he'd already crossed the line and was committed, so he might as well be thorough. He reached high and groped past the blankets on the shelf. His fingers touched a book and he carefully withdrew it. The book was hardbound and would have been taken for an ordinary school textbook, except for the title on the drab dust jacket: *Variations in Human Sexuality.*

Now this is more like it, he thought.

Sam sat on the closet floor with the book in his lap and leafed through it—a textbook, it seemed to be: all words and no photographs. The headings in the chapter outline were dry and filled with unfamiliar technical jargon: voyeurism, fetish disorder, auto-eroticism, pedophilia, obsessive disorder, nymphomania—

Nymphomania?

Hurriedly, he turned to the chapter and read with growing interest. Again, and alas, no pictures, just a compilation of case histories of females afflicted by the condition. One case was a girl who fantasized about being raped by a gang of faceless men. Another found such a reality in a motorcycle gang and contracted two strains of gonorrhea. The symptoms of nymphomania were presented with disappointingly scant detail; most of the chapter discussed the psychology and the causes of the disorder, which Sam found as arousing as a brick.

Another chapter title caught his eye: "Sadomasochism." Sam didn't know the word but felt strongly compelled to find out its meaning. He read that it was an amalgam of sadism, which meant finding sexual release by causing someone pain, and masochism, which was when someone loved receiving pain. The goblins' puzzling motivations now became clear: they were sadists. And like when he had discovered that magazine story, Sam was instantly entranced.

The cicada din permeated the bedroom and its closet, but Sam didn't hear a note of it. Possessed, he read the entire chapter, psychological drivel and all. The few details of the case histories were like confections. One girl pleasured herself with anything of any size that would penetrate and hurt. Another cut her breasts and forearms with razor blades and masturbated. Until now, goblins slicing bound nudes with razors had lived in the two-dimensional world of fiction. This new third dimension, the real world, ramped up the eroticism to unbearable heights.

Sam continued reading with growing hunger and dread. The chapter turned to the boys. One boy fantasized about being spanked by his female teacher in front of the entire classroom. Sam imagined Miss Miller, his English teacher, pulling down his pants and going at his butt with a ruler while the class watched. To his surprise and distress, that woke up his cock. Another boy pushed straight pins through the skin of his penis and scrotum as he masturbated, claiming this intensified his orgasm. Another could climax by simply pressing rose thorns into his testicles. An even more adventurous case history told of a boy who had driven a large sewing needle through head of his penis. It seemed that goblins could torture boys as well as girls, with even more malice, as his erection attested.

Sam shut the book, terrified to read any further. His hands trembled, and astonishingly he could not steady them. Like that boy's sewing needle and the goblins' razor blades, another poison arrow pierced his genitals, injecting an erotic venom that infused every cell in his body, changing everything it touched. A wet spot appeared in his pants without him touching himself. After reading *Bound Nudes,* Sam had feared he'd never be the same. Now he knew that for certain. The discordant symphony of the cicadas became almost hypnotic. Sam thought this must be how madness would sound.

He shelved the book in the exact position he'd found it and swore never to open it again. He wished he'd never seen it. He couldn't bear thinking about *oh my God* whose book this was and *oh my God* why it was there. But pins, needles, and rose thorns would not leave him alone, pricking him the rest of the day and well into the night. The book didn't look like pornography, but not all pornography did—as long as it worked.

Sam rigorously kept his vow of closet celibacy until the following afternoon, when he was frantic to break it. His father was again at work, and his mother and sister were preparing to go shopping with infuriating leisure, as if deliberately keeping him from his secret pleasure. Finally, the house again deserted, Sam slunk back into the bedroom closet, now with his private sex palace looking more and more like the goblins' subterranean torture chamber.

He scoured the textbook, searching for more case histories of erotic pain and torture. He found none but learned another word: paraphilia, defined as the love of the abnormal and classified as one form of mental illness. Sam suspected this diagnosis now applied to him, and he worried himself sick about it. *Am I becoming a snot-boy?*

Sam tried, really tried, to masturbate while thinking about normal sex, hoping his new bent desires would eventually disappear like a plantar's wart. Cindy and Ginny and all the other pretty girls in school looked so sexy walking down his imagination's runway modeling low-cut blouses, strapless gowns, and skimpy underwear. But they looked so much sexier naked, tied up, and screaming, and he could not restrain himself. This was no wart.

One night, as another goblin scene unfolded with lovely Ginny getting her umpteenth maltreatment, Sam was struck by an intriguing and convenient solution to his moral dilemma. Since torturing girls was so atrociously wrong and sick, there was someone he could torture and it would be perfectly okay: himself. That book in the closet had showed him how.

He sat up in bed. It was brilliant. There would be no shame, no remorse, and no fear of ending up institutionalized or in prison. And the best part was he could do anything he wanted, any time he wanted, and didn't need the consent of Ginny or anyone else. He was already becoming a paraphilic case history, so why not enjoy it?

"And besides," he said to himself, "I deserve it."

The knot of anxiety in his guts untwisted and disappeared. He lay back down, feeling cradled in the soft bosom of relief. *I deserve it.* Curiously, he heard a distant voice, a comforting voice and distinctly feminine, agreeing with him. Although the window was closed, he felt a cool, invigorating breeze wash over him, and he fell into a deep sleep.

If dreaming about goblins was a descent down a dungeon staircase, Sam was now in unrestrained free fall. His mother's sewing basket became his favorite sex store, as did his father's workbench. The case-boys were right. Anything that could cause pain greatly inflamed his orgasms, sometimes three or four in an afternoon of solitary exploration. Sam played with any object that would bite, pinch, pierce, clamp, or abrade. Nothing seemed to hurt enough. How he avoided infections, septicemia, or permanent mutilation was a miracle. Sam thought if he had a guardian angel, she must surely be lobbying for a transfer.

At night, he transgendered the goblins into girls, each wearing the face of one of his pretty classmates. Ginny was their leader, and a merciless one, as she had just cause. She used the weapons Sam gave her with a ferocity and determination that frightened even the goblins. Although he'd be spared an eternity in hell for his brutal misogynist fantasies, Sam wondered if he was now committing a sin far worse.

3

MISS MILLER

SAM NOW KNEW THE WORDS *SADISM*, *masochism*, and *paraphilia*, and dispiritedly accepted he was infected with all of them. He hadn't yet heard the word *dominatrix*, but he had one. Miss Miller taught eighth-grade English literature. She was around thirty, petite and pretty, exquisitely proportioned, and had bewitching hazel eyes and rich auburn hair that swirled about her shoulders. On the first day of class, she wore a crisply ironed white blouse with the top two buttons undone, challenging the school's dress code and the modest fashions of the late 1950s. Her bright plaid skirt had a hemline that committed the same misdemeanors.

But it was her smile—sweet, alluring, slightly asymmetrical, and not needing a trace of lipstick for enhancement—that maintained her magic and mastery over the class. A smile that could melt a glacier and rip one's heart from its aortal moorings. The first time Miss Miller smiled at Sam, he shot straight into the stratosphere and wafted about there all day long. Whenever she'd smile at another boy, his guts rumbled with jealousy. Sam did not recognize the symptoms of a nascent infatuation, though there was little he could do if he had. Eliciting Miss Miller's smile now rivaled obsessing on what lay beneath those open blouse buttons.

Sam wasn't alone with his blouse fixation. After her first class was over and the bell rang, liberating her captives, Benny took Sam aside in the hallway. The corridors, completely vacant and tomb-quiet just fifteen seconds ago, were now swarming with a chaos of students trying to find their friends amid the mob and sidle and shove their way to their next classes.

"So whaddya think?" Benny shouted over the commotion.

"About what?" Sam yelled back.

"Miller, dummy! Is she wearing a bra or not? Wow. What bazoombas!"

Sam was loath to reveal his newfound affection for Miss Miller to anyone, let alone Benny. He certainly enjoyed watching the gaps in Miss Miller's blouse, but calling her breasts *bazoombas* seemed like defiling them.

"I hadn't noticed," said Sam.

Benny pushed Sam into a zone of relative quiet behind a bank of lockers. "You hadn't noticed? What, are you dead or something?"

Of course, he'd noticed. Sam, like boys of all ages, had female breasts under constant surveillance, although he was usually too entranced and too dense to survey them discreetly. Tight sweaters, sleeveless blouses, and two-piece swimsuits suggested an infinite variety of bosom shapes and sizes, and he appreciated them all. Most of his female teachers wore bras that looked like traffic cones or as if they'd stuffed newspaper wads down their blouses, and therefore were of zero interest. Perhaps that was the idea.

Sam had found Miss Miller's breasts especially entrancing for two reasons, the primary being that they were on her. The second was how delicately they bounced beneath her blouse as she walked around the room. He had assumed the bouncing was a characteristic of her bra, and certainly an attractive one, but he hadn't considered there wasn't a bra at all. The possibility of just a naked breast under a scant millimeter of fabric made him lightheaded.

"I say there's no bra," said Benny, determined to keep this conversation on track. "Roger and Carl say yes. Jeffrey can't see a damn thing anyway but said no. And Sammy, the nutless wonder, hasn't noticed?"

"I'll think about it," Sam said.

"You toad! It's not about thinking. Tomorrow, how about opening your eyes?"

The first day of Miss Miller's class had been untaxing and relaxed—a good way to ease her boisterous wards out of their summer indulgences and into the proper business of learning English literature. The students had drawn their seat assignments and introduced themselves. Miss Miller recounted her own education and teaching history, artfully punctuated with stories and humorous anecdotes. The hour was essentially a party.

The following day Miss Miller wore a beige skirt that barely covered her kneecaps, and to make Sam's reconnaissance mission easier, a light blue blouse with the top *three* buttons undone. Whether this was accidental or a deliberate attempt to boil over the fifteen simmering cauldrons of testosterone sitting before her, Sam wasn't sure. But he did know if blouses could go on, they could also come off, and any hint of that, as those three errant buttons suggested, staggered him. Benny, sitting a row behind, bounced a spit wad off Sam's neck. Sam turned. Benny undid his top shirt button and winked.

"Today," said Miss Miller, walking around the room and bouncing as she went, "please share with the class a book you read over the summer. Tell us what you liked about it and why. For those of you who don't know what a book is, this will be a good time to learn."

She smiled and laughed. The students laughed as well, albeit a little nervously because it was rumored that, despite her comely face and radiant smile, Miss Miller ruled her class just as strictly as a drill sergeant—the main differences being she wore a uniform no sergeant would be caught dead in, and she had a softer, though just as intimidating, voice. Each student prayed it would be another who'd find out whether the rumor was true.

Sam was exuberant about the assignment, for he actually had read a book that summer, a rare achievement, and he looked forward to impressing Miss Miller. But today, making impressions was not his top priority. He began to scrutinize her chest with determination and focus that a tiger stalking its prey would envy. The bouncing was absorbing but inconclusive. Then she dropped her pen. When she stooped to pick it up, her blouse's neckline parted, giving Sam a clear view of not only her bra strap but also the top half of her left breast. *Her actual breast!* Sam sat back in his chair, stunned.

But tigers have the sense to stay hidden while hunting. And teachers have the ability to see everything that goes on in their classroom. Miss Miller stood and looked squarely at Sam. He froze, as if caught stealing with the goods still in his hand. The thrill of the voyeurism was quickly replaced by stark fear of her reprisal. And rightly so, as he had stolen a glance at nine square inches of skin from her body, glowing with forbidden intimacy, which he'd add to the cache of other erotic treasures he used at night.

The look on his face must have told Miss Miller exactly what had happened, he assumed. But to his astonishment, she just smiled at him. He could breathe again. His mission had been accomplished, but barely. *Did she know?* But another question arose and grew in importance: was her smile an invitation for him to peek some more, or was it incidental? Sam did not like mysteries like this.

"Who wants to begin?" Miss Miller asked the class.

Patty, the insufferable class brain, raised her hand right away, as she was always the first to do.

"My book was *Jane Eyre*," Patty said proudly, "by Charlotte Brontë."

"That's very good… Patty," said Miss Miller, consulting the seating chart. "What did you like about it?"

"Oh, the way Jane endured those awful things those people did to her and finally found her strength and happiness," Patty replied. "That makes me feel I can do the same in my life."

Sam looked back at Benny, and both rolled their eyes. Miss Miller glanced at the chart.

"Yes, we all can," said Miss Miller. "That's the empowering gift of literature and—"

"And it was a courageous book for a woman to write," added Patty, feeling on a roll. "Especially in that place and time."

"Thank you, Patty. That's called a hero's journey, or heroine's journey, in Jane's example. Would you agree with that, Sam?"

Sam felt like he'd suddenly been slapped to attention. "Yeah, I guess so."

"What book did you read this summer?"

"Well, um…"

"Stand, please."

He did, certain the class could see the red handprint on his face. He was convinced Miss Miller had found him guilty of theft, and his punishment was coming due.

"It was called *The Terror Beneath Our Feet*," Sam said with growing apprehension.

"What a dramatic title," Miss Miller said. "Who's the author?"

"Um, I don't remember." He didn't bother to look.

"What's it about? Does it have a hero's journey as well?"

"Well, sort of. It's where they find this underground city of giant mole people at the center of the earth who live in tunnels and, ah, have these tunnels they dig."

Sam's voice went flat. He suspected his book review, the rest of the hour, the day, and possibly his life, were not going to end well.

Patty snorted, which initiated a cascade of tittering throughout the room.

"Tunnels?" said Miss Miller. "Does the hero make his journey through these tunnels?"

"Yeah. He invents this special ray gun that can, um, shoot through rock and…"

Now Sam's voice completely died, as if the power cord to his mouth had been yanked. He thought the story was actually exciting, especially when they went into the dark labyrinth of tunnels to battle the giant mole people. Giant mole people, once a terror beneath one's foot, now threatened to flay Sam alive in front of Miss Miller and everyone he knew.

"Do you think that fighting mole people qualifies as English literature?" Miss Miller said, like that drill sergeant waiting for the signal to attack.

"No. No, ma'am. I guess not. I'm sorry."

Miss Miller had another weapon of control, one that sergeants didn't have. She always carried it with her: her smile. The smile was not the actual weapon, but rather its stark, chilling absence, and Sam was its first casualty. Her stony face felt like a crowbar to his gut, and he shrank into his seat. Miss Miller looked away and did not see him for the rest of the hour. He wanted to crawl down a mole tunnel and disappear forever.

"Great job, Sammy," smirked Benny after the class bell. "Giant mole people."

"You're the one who gave me the book, asshole!"

"Well? What do you think? Is she wearing a bra or not?"

"Yeah, she is," Sam said quietly, still reeling from his brutal fall from Miss Miller's grace. "I saw the strap."

"Way to go! What color was it?"

"Pink."

"Pink? Oh yeah! Sammy, you are the hero!"

He didn't feel like one.

A week after the mole-people/bra-strap debacle, Miss Miller's smiles returned to Sam, her point having been made. His rapturous flights into the stratosphere resumed. And a good thing too, as he found her English class agonizingly tedious and a complete waste of fifty-five minutes—a huge expanse of time to a bored boy. The assignments seemed senseless and useless. For example, the entire class had to memorize the first forty lines of Chaucer's *The Canterbury Tales*, and in old English, no less. The only possible benefit, Sam concluded, might be if he wound up on *Jeopardy* someday.

Mercifully, he was spared reading about poor Jane Eyre, but not the rich Jay Gatsby, whose life had little to do with Sam's or anyone else's in the room. He tolerated poetry because there wasn't much to read, and despite having even fewer words, haiku was weird and unfathomable. The worst torture was *Moby Dick*. Why say something in a few sentences when you can say it in five pages? Sam considered reading Melville death by literature. Only Patty read and seemed to understand every one of the novel's two-hundred-six thousand words. Sam and the rest of the class settled for failing grades. That left Miss Miller as the only subject of real interest, but as he and everyone else were discovering, a potentially dangerous one.

Despite Miss Miller's frightening Miss Hyde persona, Sam's infatuation with her thrived. He'd had a crush on Cindy since second grade, but this was much more. This was adult love with an adult woman, and he assumed his desire would prepare him for the challenge—and a challenge it would be. He had little to offer Miss Miller as a boyfriend. He wasn't even half her age; was six inches shorter; had no money, job, or driver's license; still lived with his parents; had no idea what sex was about; and was still in the eighth grade. Not very impressive credentials for sparking the attentions of a sophisticated and urbane woman like Miss Miller, and Sam grudgingly accepted the folly of his daydreams. But at night anything was possible.

Indeed, Miss Miller intersected Sam's sex life like an arrow through a balloon. One night as Ginny and her girl-goblins had him again stretched on a rack and were joyfully administering mayhem on his tender parts, he looked to the side of the dungeon and got a surprise. Standing in the shadows, enraptured by the scene and playing with her blouse buttons, was Miss Miller. The girls instantly vanished, leaving him naked and helpless before his beautiful, cold, and unattainable paramour.

Miss Miller was no longer a public educator but now a private disciplinarian who came to punish him for his shoddy classroom performance and, most of all, his relentless voyeurism. Humiliation and disempowerment, so unbearable in the classroom, became an aphrodisiac in his private dungeon. He had no idea why, and the moment discouraged inquiry.

Miss Miller did not smile in this fantasy as she so beguilingly did in her classroom. Sam did not want her smiling in the least. She undid her remaining blouse buttons, leaned over him, looked deeply into his eyes, and skewered him with that icy crowbar glare of hers. Then she went to work with every terrible tool in the goblins' arsenal. After that night, the goblin-girls did not return; they had lost their jobs to a professional.

4
NYMPHS

IN HIGH SCHOOL, EVERYTHING WAS BIGGER: the building was bigger, as was the homework, the student body, and especially the girls' assets. So were the girls' boyfriends, who would pound any boy into pudding who tried anything funny with their steadies. Sam was easily poundable. He was one of the smallest and youngest boys in his class, having been stupid enough (or smart enough) to be booted up from fourth to sixth grade.

That qualified him to be a Brain. Among the castes of high school society, which thrived on stratification and popularity rule, the Brains actually hovered near the bottom of the food chain. The top tiers were occupied by the Jocks, the Cools, and the Babes. Below them were the Coins, Bitches, and Greasers. Nerds and Skags came next. Nerds were Brains who had the ambition to do something with them, like being in the chess club or knowing how to run a movie projector. Skags were female Nerds. And at the bottom, just below the Brains, were the Corpses—kids who, though not actually dead, might as well be considering their social deficiencies.

Brains had their flings with popularity during midterm and final exam weeks, when members of every stratum solicited their help. It was a heady time for Sam, especially when being pursued by the Babes and Cools, but he kept forgetting that fame is fickle and temporary. After exams, he was back on the bottom, holding a hard truth: brains were useful only for achieving long-term goals, such as getting an education, a good-paying job, and a comfortable retirement. But they don't count for shit about getting a date for Saturday night, which is what life is really about.

To Sam it was clear: something was missing from his being, something really important, that was causing his involuntary celibacy. But what? Everyone else seemed to have worked it out. He assumed that Cindy, his longtime crush, would be his girlfriend in high school. But she had grown a tall, firm body and lush breasts while he wasn't looking and immediately was swept into the social scene, then wound up dating a Greaser from another school, which Sam felt was an utter outrage. Dork's nickname had changed to Klutz, as his brain couldn't keep up with the location of his hands, thanks to his fast-growing bones. When it finally did, Klutz became The Man—he was the center of the basketball team, a position that automatically came with a cheerleader girlfriend. Even Benny had managed to find a paramour because if it involved sex of any nature, Benny was there.

"It's great, Sammy," he crooned. "It's better than we ever thought. You've got to try it!"

"So the rubber in your wallet worked?" Sam asked, now thinking to revisit this silly ploy.

"Nah. The package split open and there was some kind of goo inside that leaked all over everything. And besides, you really don't need a rubber. You just pull out before you shoot. They say it works great."

This eased the rubber-buying burden for Sam, but he still needed a girl to shoot into.

"Hey, Sammy," Benny smirked, "why don't you try for Ginny? She's a total babe, she's hot to trot, and besides, and she ain't seeing nobody. Go figure that one out."

It was true. Ginny, easily the most beautiful girl in the school and on the planet, was, inexplicably, without a boyfriend. She just hung out with her coterie of girlfriends, aloof and inaccessible. This gave Sam everlasting hope, as a thread of a chance was as good as a ladder. Although Ginny often starred in his private midnight movies, he'd never seriously considered her becoming anything more than a dream.

Sam couldn't keep his eyes off her in homeroom. Once, she caught him looking and gave him a shy smile, which fueled his fantasies for weeks. Ginny often wore sleeveless blouses, some with wide-open necklines, providing great peeking opportunities. Over the term, Sam compiled a mental montage of how much of her breasts he'd actually seen. It capped at around seventy-five percent, he reckoned. Although this furtive, remote intimacy with her was tinged with guilt, it was the only intimacy he had, and it had to do. And it did, until Benny opened his big mouth to suggest otherwise.

Now Sam had to ask Ginny out. Maybe Benny was right about her and maybe he wasn't, but Sam couldn't rest not knowing for sure. The more he thought about how to make his move, the greater grew the risk and anxiety until it gave him stomach cramps. He grasped at any excuse to avoid the moment: he felt a cold coming on; it was Wednesday and those were bad luck days. Or Ginny was talking with girlfriend A, then girlfriend B. All were reprieves, but only temporary, and his mission still loomed, massive and daunting.

Sam had another excuse, but this one was unwanted. He didn't really understand why, but his mother was determined to keep him home as much as possible and out of harm's way. This not only made a date with Ginny problematic, but also squashed any bit of social life he might have scrounged up.

"Mom, can I go to the movies with Billy Friday night?"

"How are you going to get there?"

"Uh, Billy has his dad's car."

"How long has Billy been driving?"

"I don't know."

"No. This is too dangerous. I can't allow it."

Even coming home an hour late from school would earn him a grilling, no matter if the crime was as innocent as a pick-up game of football. There was nothing about his incarceration that suggested family life was any different for anyone else, so Sam just gave up and accepted this unreasonable and arbitrary injustice. Trying to battle his mother over any issue was futile, as she would never back down on anything.

His father was of no help. "Whatever your mother wants goes," was his usual response.

"But why?" Sam couldn't understand his father's unconditional surrender to her.

"The number one rule in this house," his father once said when Sam kept pushing on him for support, "is do not piss off your mother. Under no circumstances. You got that?"

Sam had never heard such conviction—or fear—in his father's voice, and suspected his emphatic warning to Sam held a clue. Sam didn't know the origins of what seemed like an endless war between his parents, nor what had caused their latest skirmish, but he always felt tension between them. It hung thick in the air like the ubiquitous blue cloud of their cigarette smoke. It was mostly a cold war: long stretches of strained silence occasionally broken by harsh words they fired at random at each other and everyone else. Whenever Sam came back after going out, he knew instantly that his father was home just by the expression on his mother's face. It was the face of someone who had just stubbed her toe and was determined not to scream.

Pissing off his mother came as naturally to Sam as breathing. She was always unhappy and complaining about something—or everything. It seemed he could do nothing right around the house; he heard nothing but her barbs and insults. At times he felt like he was tiptoeing through a minefield, never knowing what would set her off. But what else could he do? He lived there. Even worse, no matter what he was doing or where, he could still feel her presence hovering around him and hear her biting criticisms.

Although Sam's bitter domestic oppression did let him off the hook with the Ginny-risk issue, he could not let it ride. He needed a good cause to fight for his liberation, and Ginny would be it. One afternoon after school let out, an opportunity presented itself. Only a few students were in the hallways—some going to band practice, running cross country, or going to some other extracurricular activity they could enjoy without being chastised at home.

Ginny and one of her friends, Marcia, were talking in the hall beside the Coke machine. Each girl had a can. That ruled out buying Ginny a Coke, a prerequisite for a boy making a move. *Darn.* Now what to do about Marcia? As if on cue, Marcia kissed Ginny on her cheek and left, leaving Ginny squarely in his sights. The omen could not be ignored. It was now or never.

"Hi Ginny."

"Oh, hi Sam. How are you?"

This was now the longest conversation he'd ever had with her. Another good sign.

"Oh, just fine. Um, and how are you?"

"Fine," said Ginny, smiling and brushing a few strands of hair from her goddess face.

She was wearing a close-fitting red sweater. Sam battled every eye muscle in his head not to stare at the swells beneath it. Ginny just stood there, giving no sign of revulsion or flight. This was unbelievable. Emboldened by his newfound resolve, Sam took the plunge.

"Um, Ginny, you know, *West Side Story* is playing downtown," he said, "and I thought maybe you'd like to see it with me."

There. It's out. It's done. I'll hire a fucking cab if I have to.

Ginny's smile remained on her movie star lips, giving Sam a microsecond of hope.

"Oh, that's so sweet of you to ask," she said, "but I don't date boys."

The microsecond ended. *What? She doesn't date boys?* Looking like a nerdy fifth-grader, dressing like a dweeb, and being a complete social cipher were understandable and familiar reasons for rejection, but this new one stunned him. What qualified him to be a man, and man enough to date Ginny? Age? Height? Having a car?

Ginny just sipped her Coke and looked at him with her liquid brown eyes.

"I thought you knew. It seems like everyone else does," she said with a touch of acid. "See you in homeroom, Sam."

Ginny walked away, leaving Sam with another hole in his life, and a mysterious one at that. But at least he had dared, scant comfort as that was. That night he tried taking greater comfort in bringing Ginny back into the goblin's chamber, the only place he could win. But after she screamed once on the rack, his vengeance began to wither. He cranked the winch tighter, which shrank his penis even smaller. Feeling thoroughly brutish and foul, Sam freed her, angry at his impotence in both the real world and the goblin's. He saw that little clown puppet smiling at him.

But then there was Jill, a tall, pretty, flaxen-haired senior who also worked in the school cafeteria on Mondays serving lunch. Although she was not as fatally beautiful as Ginny, Sam was smitten. The fact that Jill was a Babe, and a hot one, and two years older made a romance with her so far beyond the limits of possibility that he was happily content to moon at her from across the cafeteria and daydream.

At night the dream continued. He and Jill would hold hands and walk closely together through a sunlit meadow. They'd lie down on the grass in a secluded grove. Jill would slowly remove her clothes, then his. She'd brush her breasts against his body, and that was as far as he usually could get. Unlike his friends, Sam didn't dread school Mondays; he looked forward to them because they were also Jill days.

That all changed when the rumor mill, terminating at Benny, hinted that Jill was a slut, a.k.a. a nymphomaniac. From his earlier reading, Sam knew such girls were real and not just a hopeful adolescent fantasy. He and Benny were standing on the curb one afternoon after school had let out, waiting for their bus. Other students hurriedly brushed past, looking for their bus zones. Sam waited until they cleared.

"So you're saying Jill's a slut?" Sam exclaimed, indignant about his dream lover being sullied.

"Certified and boner fide," assured Benny.

"How do you know that?"

"Just look over there," said Benny, nodding to the school parking lot.

Jill was at the far end of the lot, gaily talking to three guys wearing shiny black leather jackets and sitting on motorcycles. They were big guys, older guys, guys certainly not from his school, or from any school at all. Big guys with big cocks who probably got Jill naked every night and fucked her, Sam icily presumed. Jill was standing very close to them. Way too close.

"There's only one way a chick can attract all those guys," Benny said knowingly.

"No fucking way," Sam blurted out. He felt like a knight with a limp lance, trying to defend the virtue of his beloved, who in all truth neither knew nor cared if he existed.

"Every fucking way," Benny laughed.

Sam immediately hated these guys. He hated them because they were defiling his fantasy—now in the parking lot and then later on a filthy mattress in some grimy garage. He hated their nonchalance, their confidence, their casual ease with Jill, and their urban outlaw charade. Mostly he hated them because a big guy with a big cock on a big motorcycle was the exact opposite of a Sam, and that would never change.

He did not like this at all. The dangerous, captivating reality of Jill, the motorcycle gang nympho, had hijacked his cock and chased fantasy Jill, his safe, meadow-sex lover, from his bed. Now that he knew the difference, he could not call her back. Worse, as with Ginny, he was seized by the compulsion to act on this, making him no better than a gang member. But unlike Ginny and her puzzling rejection, Jill actually dated boys, and he definitely qualified as one. That would have to do, as acquiring a motorcycle and a leather jacket was out of the question. He hoped that wouldn't matter to Jill.

This now uncomfortably complicated Mondays, and one was less than a week away. Sam had to say something to Jill, but what? Does one talk to a nympho like any normal girl? Should he just simply ask her out? Of course he should; that was how you treated a normal girl. But he didn't know how to treat normal girls either. They were all... girls.

Sam was vexed. This shouldn't be all that difficult. Everyone else managed to get dates, so why not him? He ran through all the possible opening lines and finally settled on, "Hi Jill, I'm Sam. I'd really like it if you'd go out with me." That was it. Simple, straightforward, honest, and not suggesting a hint of his agenda. He rehearsed it.

But what if she said yes? What would he do next? He couldn't just say, "I heard you were a nympho, and would you please fuck me?" She'd likely kill him. And the idea of waiting in line behind a big guy turned his stomach. Was that the price he'd have to pay for sex? And getting gonorrhea as well? But Sam could think of nothing else all week, and each thought was more nerve-racking than the last.

Monday finally arrived. Sam inched through the lunch line, his guts knotted and throat dry. Sure enough, there was Jill, tall and willowy, standing behind the counter and ladling steaming swill onto heavy white ceramic plates. Her long brown hair was hastily gathered in a swirl atop her head, with loose strands framing her elfin face. The top three buttons of her dress were undone, revealing her bra strap and a triangle of her chest shiny with sweat from the steam tables. She seemed unconcerned by her disheveled appearance and casual exposure, which confirmed to Sam his vulgar assumptions.

There were three students in line ahead of him. The knot crept into his diaphragm as he stared at Jill and that triangle. Jill the nympho, just two feet away, with her body naked beneath the thin cotton veneer of her dress. A body covered with greasy biker fingerprints. He had to revive himself and soon. What was his line? He'd forgotten his line! Two people in front of him. Panic arrested his breathing. All he could do was gaze at Jill. Now one person ahead of him. He was next. His brain felt like it had seized up and cracked open. Then—

"Tuna casserole or mac and cheese, honey?" Jill asked brightly and smiled.

Honey? Sam became so lightheaded he almost tipped over. *She called me honey and smiled at me!*

Twit! Then say something!

Jill just smiled and awaited his decision.

"Tuna," was all he could sputter out.

"Tuna cass it is, hon," Jill chirped. She smiled again and handed him a platter.

Sam sat quietly by himself at a food-splattered table in the far corner of the cafeteria, trying to swallow the boulder of his retreat. He stared down at his lunch and poked at the congealing mass with his fork. The lumps under the yellow-white sauce could have been tuna or gravel; his twisted stomach would prevent him from knowing. He turned to look at the lunch counter. Jill was still there, ladling, smiling, and probably calling every boy in line honey. Sam imagined them all in motorcycle leathers.

Jill, his gentle, meadow-sprite lover, was dead. She lay entombed like a tuna flake smothered under the gelatinous glop on his plate. Jill, the nymphomaniac gang slut, was all that remained. He could see her jump on the back of a motorcycle, let her long hair fall free, wrap her arms around a big guy's waist, and massage his crotch.

But Sam was not finished with her, not in the least. He feverishly planned his revenge for that night and all the nights to follow. He'd throw her to the goblins to suffer the worst they had to offer. Jill had been indicted, tried, and found guilty, and now she would pay dearly. Her only crime had been to smile and call him honey.

Would you rather she scowl and call you a twit?

In the turmoil of his misery, Sam didn't think to question this odd inner voice, or where it came from. It was just another echo, one of many that comprised the chaotic array within his mind, especially when he was confused and angry. Which seemed to be most of the time.

5

BASEBALL

SAM HAD BEEN ACCEPTED INTO A sprawling midwestern mega-university that was home to a first-class curriculum, a world-class faculty, and a skunk-class football team. It was essentially a diploma factory that assumed its students were there to get theirs and would know what to do with them. There was never a question about Sam's admission. Having been a Brain in high school, he coasted by on a minimum of studying and effort. But that had been a handicap—brains were linked to ineptitude with girls. Perhaps getting a college brain would fix this.

The week before classes was an ongoing party. For many students, this was their first time away from home and parents and a superb opportunity to take advantage of it. For Sam, this meant acquiring an expanded vocabulary of profanity, learning to smoke cigarettes and keep the smoke in, and, of course, how to drink—which, encouraged by the other neophyte libertines in his dormitory, Sam immediately did to blind excess one evening with a fifth of contraband gin. This resulted in alcohol poisoning from not knowing how much booze to drink to get drunk. His strained dry heaving broke so many capillaries in his face he looked like a human beet. Adding to the misery were the hole burned into his only dress shirt from a cigarette ember and the stern reprimand from the dormitory's house mother for his excessively blue language.

Sam was puzzled by an all-male dormitory needing a house mother. Her name was Mrs. Pittston, often irreverently called The Pit; she was a widowed grandmother of sixty who lived in a small suite on the second floor. Her door was always open, she said, for any homesick boys who might need a surrogate parent during their lonely and disorienting new life. Sam thought of her as an institutional, unarmed babysitter. And another mother was the very last thing he wanted, as he was still aggravatingly tethered to his first one.

The only occasions that could entice Sam to walk through The Pit's open door were football Sundays because the dorm's only television set resided in her living room. Sam, along with thirty other unbathed dormies, would moan, groan, and politely swear over another Detroit Lions loss. Robbie, Sam's roommate and newest best friend, was from Chicago and wisely kept his enjoyment of the rout to himself. Mrs. Pittston seemed to genuinely enjoy these Sunday afternoon parties, despite what her overcrowded apartment smelled like, and the cookies and lemonade flowed freely.

Aside from learning how to moderate his newly acquired vices, Sam discovered that a real college education occurred not in the classroom, but in late-night dormitory bull sessions. Most of these occurred in Greg's room, just down the hall from Sam and Robbie. Greg was a junior who, for reasons he never revealed, chose to remain in the dormitory rather than move into an apartment or a fraternity house as most boys eagerly did at the end of their first year. By virtue of his age and the fact he'd smuggled his girlfriend into his room for entire weekends, Greg was considered to be the local authority on sex—a status he savored.

At one o'clock in the morning, there in Greg's small, cluttered room, its walls lined with *Playboy* foldouts, the wastebasket overflowing with empty pizza boxes and soda cans, and the air thick with cigarette smoke, Sam's sex education took a quantum leap sideways. Sam, Robbie, and three other boys were there, most of them sitting on Greg's bed and stretching its springs almost to the floor. A bra hung from the overhead light fixture and several packages of rubbers lay on the bedside table. Benny would love this, Sam thought. In the summer, Benny had enlisted in the Navy, to see the world and no doubt visit its brothels.

The Greg-hosted bull sessions commonly began with a discussion about the foldouts.

"What's wrong with her tits?" asked Lester, pointing to Miss August. "She has no nipples."

Sam had noticed this as well. Miss August was a dark-haired, sloe-eyed beauty who certainly complied with the magazine's requirement that each month featured large, firm breasts. And yes, she had no nipples, just fuzzy, brown smears on the tips. Sam thought it was a strange, unfortunate birth defect, and he admired Miss August for displaying her bosom so proudly.

"You dumb shit," Greg said to Lester. "They've been airbrushed out."

"Well, the rest of the months all have nipples," Lester protested.

"Maybe she doesn't want to be recognized," laughed Robbie.

"No, she's obviously a prude," Howard said, not getting his gaffe.

"Well, I sure wouldn't kick her out of bed," said Sam, as if she were already in it.

Greg laughed. "In *your* bed? Hah! Dream on, pudwacker. You want to know how to get Miss August into your bed?"

"Yeah, just rip her out of the magazine!" Robbie said.

"No way is it that easy," Greg snorted. "You see, you have to turn on a chick's head before her bod can turn on. That's just the way they're wired. And it takes a lot of patience and skill."

"Well, do you know how?" Robbie asked.

Greg pointed to the bra. "What do you think?"

Robbie shrugged.

"Okay," Greg said, "pay attention, all you hopeless virgins. Since you haven't asked, I'll tell you how to cure that. First, you got to show a girl you've been around the block a time or two. Buy her a fancy drink, like a sidecar or a pink grasshopper. And chicks really dig guys who are deep thinkers, so you gotta have intelligent opinions on everything, especially politics."

"But what do you do if she has her own opinions?" Lester asked. "Or she hates politics?"

Greg regarded Lester as he would a squashed cockroach. "Anyway," Greg continued, "you also gotta have a career plan. Tell her you know exactly where you're going, what you want to do, and that it will bring in the dough. Big bucks is one of their turn-ons. Make up anything you want and she'll buy it. I've never had a chick frisk me for my transcript."

"What's a pink grasshopper?" Sam asked.

"Rum and something," said Greg. "Shit, I don't know, but it doesn't matter. Girls don't know booze either, so just buy them anything and they'll drink it. And here's the most important thing to know about girls: they think you're only after their bodies, so you have to sincerely convince them otherwise. That skill is what really separates the men from the pudwackers."

Everyone nodded in agreement. Greg's admonition chilled Sam to the core, as the only thing he knew was pudwacking. He remembered a similar lecture by Gary in the boy's locker room a few years before, the difference now being the foldouts and the fact that everyone knew what a rubber was for. Still, he thought he'd do well to pay attention.

"The bottom line," Greg continued, "is that chicks are basically obstacles that you have to fool, finesse, and manipulate around to get to their bodies. Agreed?"

More nods.

"Since chicks don't hand out manuals on how to score, here's how it's done. Think of having sex with a girl like running around a baseball diamond. If you're kissing her, then you're on first base. Got it? That also means frenching her."

"Frenching?" Lester repeated.

"Yeah," Greg said. "French kissing. You know, with your tongue. You stick it in, play around with her tongue, maybe suck on it a little. Oh, they love that. They think it's a safe little dick they can play with."

Sam thought this unsanitary and a bit repugnant, but if it was necessary, so be it.

"In France it's called English kissing, you know," Howard said.

"Bite me, Howard," said Greg. "Now, getting to second base means feeling up her tits. There's an important progression here, and you got to get it right. You just can't go and grab it. First, you have to be firmly on first base, frenching included. Now here's where it gets delicate. She knows what's coming and she'll be ready for it. Girls assume that guys assume that feeling her tits means a fuck is a done deal. That is *so* not true. Chicks have this stupid, stubborn obsession with self-respect and will battle you until doomsday to protect it."

"But why?" asked Lester. "Don't they like sex, too?"

"Yeah," said Greg, "they like sex all right, but they'll never admit it, and they'll make you work for it. It's that damn respect thing."

Greg opened his drink cooler and pulled out a can of beer.

"That's a beer!" said Lester, a bit shocked.

"It is! Give that boy an A for asshole," Greg said. He opened the can with a church key.

"But that's illegal!" Lester cried.

"It's only illegal if you're underage and on university property," said Greg in all sobriety. Then he laughed and gave the beer a long pull. Lester just sat there bewildered.

Greg looked into the cooler. "There's two left. Anyone want them?"

"We'll take them," Robbie quickly said before anyone else could. Sam's near-fatal bout with liquor was still fresh in his memory, and he winced at Robbie's presumption. Greg gave Sam and Robbie each a can. Sam took a tentative swig and thought it tasted like horse urine—not that he had a basis for comparison. But being given a free beer meant you'd better drink it, no matter what its source. Robbie apparently had a taste for horse piss and chugged away.

"Okay," Greg went on, "back to baseball. Where was I?"

"Second base," said Robbie and Howard.

"Oh, yeah. So you slide your hand slowly down her shoulder or up her belly, or wherever she lets you put it. If she pulls it away, which she will, keep frenching her and try again a minute or two later. Notice how close you get to her boob before she stops you. If you sense you're gaining a little ground, keep at it."

"Will frenching her faster help?" Lester asked.

"You moron," Greg said. "You can't french faster. Look, girls have things they want too. Like a husband. Why do think they're up here? Campus is hubby city. They know they have to give something to get something, but they do it slowly, to keep your interest. If she makes it too easy, she thinks that you'll think she's a nympho and she's blown it."

Greg snickered at his own pun.

"What's a nympho?" said Lester.

"Nympho is short for nymphomaniac," Sam said, happy to contribute some worldliness. "It's a mental disease that some girls get. It makes them want to fuck every guy they see."

Greg eyed Sam. "Are you speaking from experience, Sammy?"

"Well, sort of."

"You *sort of* fucked a nympho? How does that happen, exactly?"

Sam shrugged, swigged more beer, and struggled to keep it down.

"Okay, you're on her tit, but only sort of," said Greg, glancing at Sam. "That's because you're on her sweater. The next step is to get under the sweater to the bra. Next is under the bra to the actual tit. And finally, the bra comes off."

"You make it sound easy," Robbie said.

"It most definitely is not," said Greg. "It happens over four or five dates, if you're lucky. The real skill is unhooking her bra smoothly and quickly before she can recover her decorum and change her mind. And you gotta do it using only one hand, in the dark, and without looking. If you dick around too long, that'll give her time to back out. Or she'll think you're a clueless dweeb and the ball game's over. At least for that date."

Greg pulled down the bra from the overhead light.

"The size of a girl's tits is rated by how many hooks or snaps her bra has." Greg held up the lacy beige bra. "As you can see, Suzanne's a three-snapper," he said proudly.

"So what's third base?" Lester asked.

"Ahh," Greg said as if he were reliving a fond memory, "third base is a finger-fuck. Anyone here not know what that is?"

Lester opened his mouth and then closed it.

"Forget going to third if you haven't made it to second," Greg said. "You see, a girl's cunt is guarded by enormously strong thigh muscles, so she has to cooperate. If you've done a good job at first and second base, she will. You place your hand on her knee and slowly slide it north. She'll immediately know what's going on and then third base will either open up or it won't, and if it won't, there's nothing you can do about it so don't even try."

"So you stick your finger in there like a dick?" Robbie said. "In and out?"

"Yeah, basically," said Greg. "And there's something else down there called her clit."

"Clitoris," said Barry, who until now had been silent.

"Yeah, clitoris," Greg said. "It's also called her fuck button. Pressing it turns her on like nothing else. It's like magic."

This was astounding news and everyone eagerly awaited details. But Greg seemed concerned about something.

"Well, where is it?" said Lester, eyes wide.

"It's kind of hard to find," Greg said. "It's very slippery and there's all these folds of skin and bumps and things. It's somewhere in there."

"Somewhere in there?" Lester cried. "And you can't find it? That's crazy!"

Greg was silent for a moment. "Yeah. Ain't that just like a chick?"

"Well, what's it look like?" Robbie asked.

Greg shrugged.

"Haven't you seen it?" pressed Robbie. "Doesn't Suzanne have one?"

"Of course she has one!" Greg roared, startling everyone.

Now Sam was really paying attention. To this point, Greg's discourse, although engaging and illuminating, still had the feel of theater. Now the real world of sex and its intimate secrets had crept in. Sam knew that world well. He was both heartened to think that someone else had something to hide and yet was troubled to see Greg and his bravado deflating.

The room was silent, waiting on Greg, who just stared at the beer can in his hands.

"She doesn't want me to, ah, look at her," Greg said. "She likes it to be dark."

"Maybe she doesn't want you to get too close," said Barry. "Maybe she's self-conscious about something."

Greg looked up at Barry. "Yeah. I suppose she's got her reasons."

"That's bullshit!" Howard erupted. "She's got this magic sex button and you don't know where it is or what it looks like and she won't show it to you? That's crazy! That's not fair. Why don't you just turn on the goddamned light?"

Greg returned to examining his beer can.

"Fair to who?" Barry asked Howard. "What about being fair to her?"

"Hey, man," Howard said to Greg, ignoring Barry. "Didn't you just say you have to, what, finesse the bitch? So finesse her."

"Howard, you really are dense," Barry said. "Did you ever consider that girls might be finesse-proof? And they're more than just sex objects for playing baseball, you know. Maybe she'll see you're nothing more than a pecker-pusher with a one-track mind. Maybe she'll outfinesse you and walk away with your balls in her purse."

"Kiss my ass, Barry," said Howard, disregarding the fact that Barry was four inches taller and forty pounds heavier than he.

"Hah! That's likely the only kiss you'll ever get!" Barry laughed.

Howard sat back and scowled.

Greg drained his beer and stood up. "Okay, gents. It's been fun. Time to hit the hay."

"But what's a home run, Greg?" Lester asked.

"What do you think, limp-dick?" Howard said as he was leaving.

"A magic fuck button," Robbie said to Sam back in their room. "I just don't believe this. Can you believe that shit?"

Sam was silent and thinking. He suspected that foreplay wasn't as organized and tidy as Greg's baseball diamond and women weren't really that naïve to play along. It was reasonable that women should be seen as more than just sex objects, as Barry had admonished. But to Sam, when sex was the object, nothing else seemed to matter. Seeing women any other way felt laborious and threatening, and what would be the point? And besides, being unattainable sex objects meant they wielded enormous power and control over him. It was just a more complicated game of baseball. So like all information about females that he'd heard and didn't understand, Sam disregarded it. But Barry's discourse remained on his mind, disquieting and nettlesome.

Sam's sophomore year began with two pivotal events. The first was a letter from the dean's office informing him he was on probation for his abysmal grades. Another semester like that, scolded the letter, and his ass was out (although it had been phrased more politely). Sam's impressive Brain grade point average in high school had been inflated by all the honors classes he took, which resulted in a fatal overestimation of his abilities. He was now up against the best brains in the country, and he vowed to study more and party less.

And second, he joined a fraternity, which was designed to take him in the opposite direction.

Sam was fundamentally an introvert. Most of his friends were also introverts who, united by their shared condition, reinforced each other's dysfunction with grim reliability. At a high school dance, for instance, Sam and his herd of fellow Nerds lined one wall of the gymnasium, with their female counterparts crowding the opposite wall. The two groups enviously watched the cool extroverts on the dance floor and cautiously checked to see who was checking them out from the far wall. If eye contact was made, it was immediately broken before the two eyers mentally electrocuted each other, as all introverts know well could happen.

"Hey, Sam, there's Linda," Benny said at one such ordeal. "Why don't you grow a pair of balls and ask her to dance?"

"Why don't you, Benny?"

"Nah. She's a Skag."

"Well, how about Sally?"

"No way. A real bowser."

"What about Marianne, Cynthia, and Patty?"

"Nope. Cow, dodo, and man-eating robot. Hey, Sammy, isn't that Alicia standing over there all by herself? Wow, she's absolutely gorgeous, got killer boobs, and no boyfriend. And she's been watching you all night. Go ahead, ask her to dance."

Everything Benny said about Alicia was true... except the part about her watching him, which Sam knew was pure Benny bullshit. In the absence of a better explanation for his social cowardice, Sam convinced himself he broadcasted highly toxic geek rays or something equally offensive that would surely send Alicia or any other girl in the target zone running for the door. Which meant never having to leave his nice, safe niche on the wall.

Not much had changed since then, and Sam believed that joining a fraternity would cure that. Besides providing an ad hoc family away from home and a safe harbor in the turbulent ocean of a monster university, a fraternity also offered an instant social network to hopefully offset the crippling effects of introversion. Sam and Robbie were both accepted into a Nerd fraternity, which actually was a recognized category in the Greek system, joining the Jock, Brain, Money, and Animal houses.

At age nineteen, Sam was still a virgin, a shameful rarity among his lothario frat brothers, whose exploits he heard with depressing regularity in the fraternity's version of the bull session. These were similar to Greg's soirees but with the addition of more beer. The main topic was still sex: how to get it, get more of it, and get it more often. Sam had nothing to contribute to these conversations; it seemed sex was happening everywhere, all the time, and to everyone else but him. He often thought of himself as a starving street urchin with his nose pressed against the window of a closed candy and sex store. He'd rejected Gary's screwball locker room advice and considered Greg's baseball diamond as equally suspect, which left him without much.

Not that the opportunities weren't there. A fraternity indeed supplied them, as Sam had hoped they would. One was the TGIF beer keg mixer that was prearranged with a sorority of equally shy and withdrawn women hoping to change all that. A mixer was the college version of a high school sock hop, except the walls sheltering the opposing Nerd and Skag flocks were closer together, cheap draft beer provided the social lubricant, and one had to be careful not to slip on the spills.

Mixers occurred in the dining room of the fraternity house. Tables and chairs were piled up against one wall, clearing the space for the band, dancing, and large aluminum beer keg nestled in a washtub of ice. Framed portraits of the fraternity's founding brothers ringed the dark wood-paneled room, solemnly watching over their legacies' juvenile antics, having survived their own. Adjacent was the large living room, whose four couches and six wing chairs would soon be occupied with newly acquainted, alcohol-emboldened couples necking and groping their way toward a temporary future together.

Sam gravitated toward the mousier-looking girls at the mixers, as he was no lion himself. This was in part a standard introvert response, as he assumed he'd be snubbed by the rare hot number in the room or elbowed aside by his less insecure brothers anxious to get to her. The other part being he was basically too chicken.

At one mixer Sam caught the eye of a somewhat pretty, short-haired blonde with stick-like arms and a small chest, which mattered not because she eyed him back and smiled. That gave him a jump. With his courage inflated, he approached her, assuming that his virginity was finally destined to die. Beer makes sketchy logic jumps like that possible.

"Hi! I'm Sam," he yelled over the din of the atrocious dance band the fraternity's social director had scrounged up that had substituted decibels for talent.

"I'm Barbara," she shouted back.

"Would you like to dance?"

"Sure," she yelled, smiling.

Sam placed their paper beer cups on the floor, and the pair merged into the crowd. The band amped up a ragged rendition of "Louie Louie," everyone's favorite because it was all about sex and had somehow slipped past the FCC's stodgy censors. Sam had taught himself to dance by imitating the moves of those around him. That wasn't difficult as there were no moves, only spasmodic jerking and twitching to the drumbeat. At an earlier party, Robbie watched Sam dance and asked if he were having a seizure. Sam, self-conscious enough, left the room in a huff.

Barbara, however, loved to dance and it showed. Her thin, stork-like body, so unremarkable and inert in stasis, became hypnotically fluid on the dance floor. Her eyes were closed as in a reverie, her lips parted in a half-smile, and her upraised arms embraced the beat and extruded it throughout her body in one seamless, sinuous wave. Sam ceased his clumsy gyrating and stared at her, held rapt by her performance, proud and ecstatic that this lissome blonde Salome was dancing with *him*.

The band segued into a slow but equally loud number, which Sam and Barbara mutually agreed was not appropriate for them at this stage. Sam retrieved their beers, now gone warm and flat, but the line at the keg was long. They sipped and smiled at each other. He imagined Barbara naked and dancing in front of him. (That's beer again.)

"What's your major?" Sam shouted at Barbara.

"Sosh," she yelled back into his ear.

"Sosh? What's sosh?"

"Sociology! What's yours?"

Sam hadn't yet declared one, and trying to belt out "environmental sciences" or "liberal arts studies" would not be possible. The band's noise was beyond intolerable, and in the living room it wasn't much better. In the low lamplight, Sam could see most of the sofas and chairs were already being wantonly used. He pointed to his ears and shrugged. Barbara nodded, smiled at him, and sipped some more beer.

"Great party!" she screamed into his ear.

Sam was done with shouting. He leaned toward her ear, intoxicated by both the beer and her delicate perfume. "Would you like to go up to my room?"

Barbara stared at him aghast, as if he had just offered to saw off one of her stick arms.

"No!" she yelled into his face. "*No!*"

Barbara wheeled around, dropped the dregs of her beer cup on the carpet, and left the fraternity house in a storm.

Sam just stood there, struck stone cold dumb. He'd been rejected before by girls in his few courageous and awkward attempts, but never so abruptly and vehemently. Worse, he had no idea why. With his tepid flat beer still in hand, he wandered upstairs and found Robbie and a group of other dateless drones watching a baseball game on television, the default alternative to partying.

Sam sat to the side and stared at the TV screen. A cheer went up; a late-inning home run gave the Tigers a hard-earned lead over the hated New York Yankees. Sam didn't notice.

Robbie looked over at him. "Sammy, you look like shit. What's up?"

Sam told him.

"You unbelievable asshole!" Robbie said. "You only say that after you've groped her for an hour. What a Romeo!"

How was I to know?

Sam imagined Barbara calling a special meeting of her sisters to warn them about Sam the Letch. Scratch Barbara. Scratch that sorority. Scratch everything. Humiliation burned down to his bones. He felt something inside him lie down, curl into a ball, and just give up. He found sweet comfort in that hole and decided there he would stay forever.

And he did until he met Amber.

6

AMBER

IT HAPPENED A MONTH LATER AT a Saturday night toga party.

Running a girl's bases, Greg had said earlier, was a hell of a lot easier if you first got her stone-plastered drunk. Which was the purpose of a toga party. The costumes were cheap and easy to make. With some ingenuity and a few safety pins, a partygoer could turn a bedsheet into an almost-authentic Roman toga. This showed off some skin, provided easy access to more, and prevented any worries about ruining one's wardrobe with booze, barf, and body fluids. According to honored Roman tradition, everyone gets hammered on cheap red wine, stuffs themselves to their gastric maximums, dances, drinks more wine, fucks, vomits, then repeats the procedure, preferably in the same order.

Sam's toga was hastily thrown together; his chances of scoring were minimal, so he didn't care how he looked. There at the punchbowl stood a pretty girl dressed like a goddess. She'd turned a humble bedsheet into a designer gown: it was sleeveless, cut low in the front and back, with a gold braid that trimmed the bodice and accentuated the swell of her breasts. Even her long brown hair was swept atop her head and tied with ribbons, as was the style of Roman women. She was drinking gin-spiked punch like a dehydrated camel. She saw Sam staring at her and gave him a warm smile that knocked him loopy. His legs motored him toward the punchbowl.

"Hi! I'm Amber," she said cheerfully and extended her hand.

"Hi. Um, I'm, yes, my name is Sam, um, Sam." Sam was to smooth repartee as an eel was to figure skating. "Would you, ah, Amber, like to have some punch?"

Amber smiled and held up her full cup.

"Would you like some pretzels?" Sam asked just before realizing he'd not seen any.

"No, thank you," said Amber.

"How about some cheese and crackers?"

"No, thank you." Amber gulped down some more punch.

"Would you like to dance?"

Amber gulped again and shook her head.

"Well, what would you like to do?"

Amber gave Sam another smile, took his hand, led him to a dark corner of the party room, and gently placed it on her breast.

"This is a toga party, Sam," she said.

Sam had never before touched a girl's breast. He stared at his hand as if it were glued to her bodice, more astonished by the act than what he was actually feeling. Amber delicately removed his hand and took it in both of hers.

"Do you have a room upstairs?"

Sam could only nod, still in disbelief. No hour of prerequisite sofa groping needed here.

"Let's go then." Amber smiled and led him out of the ersatz Roman orgy and into some authentic contemporary decadence.

Apparently, Amber had never been to a baseball game. As soon as Sam closed the door to his room, she pushed him onto the bed, climbed on top, held his face firmly, and kissed him, deep and hard. He'd also never been kissed before and fortunately didn't have to do much other than just lie there. Amber started sucking and nibbling his lips. She sat up, smiled, and traced his lips with her finger. "You've never kissed a girl before, have you?"

"Uh, no. It shows?"

"Yup. Don't worry about it. Here, I'll show you how. Open your mouth. Just slightly."

Sam did. She kissed his upper lip, then lower, then both, deep and slow. She traced his lips with her tongue and found his tongue with hers, probing and exploring. Sam remembered his earlier apprehension about tongues; now his had just become his newest genital.

"Is this called french kissing?" he mumbled.

"Uh, hmm," she mumbled back. "Now, do the same to me."

Sam did as he was told. She could feel him stirring beneath her crotch. Amber sat up, loosened the cords of her bodice, and let it slip off her shoulders. Her bra was pink. The mounds of her breasts were there for the looking; no peek-stealing was necessary. A miracle!

"Do you know what to do next, Mister First Kiss?"

Sam did, sort of. Greg had advised the guys to buy a bra and practice unhooking it with one hand and as quickly as possible. Sam's best time was two minutes, and he needed both hands—not the way to succeed in girl baseball.

Amber loosened her hair and let it brush across Sam's face, her perfume adding to his escalating sensory inundation. She leaned closer and he reached around to remove her bra. It soon it became clear he'd need ten minutes and three hands. Amber pulled his away, reached behind her, and two seconds later cast the bra aside. It had four hooks.

Still sitting astride him, Amber lowered her breasts to his face. They were full, firm, and pendulous, and Sam went after them like a man possessed.

"Oh my God, oh my God," he kept saying, as he stroked, caressed, fondled, kneaded, squeezed, kissed, sucked, nibbled, bit, and licked the soft flesh until he ran out of verbs.

"First time for this, too?" Amber whispered, melting into his hands and lips.

"Oh my God."

Amber closed her eyes, her hips rocking, nipples stiffening, and softly sighing while Sam continued to devour her chest. He placed his hand on Amber's upper thigh as one might pet a feral cat, not sure if it would purr or claw him. This one did both. Amber hastily stripped off her toga and threw it on the floor. Her soaking panties were next. She unpinned and discarded Sam's toga and slowly pulled his underwear over his erection and down his legs, her fingernails lightly scratching everything she touched. She sat back and looked at him with a smile he'd never seen on a girl's face before. Sam looked back at her, still dazed by what he saw.

A naked girl. Right here and right now and she's for me.

"A naked girl," he said.

"A naked boy," Amber echoed. Her smile grew even more entrancing.

Amber lay down beside him and inserted two of his fingers into her sopping vagina, then placed them on her clitoris, gently moving them around then on top of the bump. Sam got the idea but kept losing the slippery button among the folds of skin as Greg had warned. Amber guided him back and he lost it again. Then it seemed not to matter. She rolled on top of him.

"Do you have any protection?" she said.

"Protection?"

"A rubber, you silly!"

Despite Sam's longing for this very moment, he'd assumed it would never come and was moronically unprepared. But he knew where Robbie hid his rubbers and stole one, immensely grateful that someone less moronic had rescued his magic evening.

Sam tore open the packet and didn't know what to do next. Amber did. She unrolled the condom over his deflating erection and squeezed it back to life. He didn't want to know where she'd learned this. She lay on her back and guided him in. Within seconds he climaxed, so ending his protracted virginity and those many nights trying to imagine the sensation. The real thing surpassed his dreams by orders of magnitude. A half an hour and another stolen rubber later, Sam made sure his virginity was thoroughly, completely, and irrevocably dead.

At evening's end, they stood at the front door of her dormitory, kissing as if they'd die if they stopped. The October night turned biting cold but neither of them noticed. That was remarkable seeing as Amber's underwear was in her purse and all that remained under her coat were the tatters of her toga. A co-ed walked by and giggled. Amber pulled away.

"I don't want to be late," she was able to gasp out. "I'll be grounded."

"Grounded?" Sam asked, surprised a university was allowed to wield parent-like power.

"Yeah. Curfew is eleven during the week and midnight on Saturday. Isn't that just so generous of them? They know they can't stop all the sex, but they think this will slow it down."

Sam thought on it. "So how can they keep you inside? Armed guards?"

"Hah! Surprise room checks by the housemother and the curfew Nazis. We could get expelled if we break it too much. Here's the crazy part: if you're late for curfew, you're actually better off staying out all night. They have no reason to suspect that you're gone unless you got a fink roommate. You know what that means, don't you, hmm?"

Sam did but dared not say it. "Can I see you next Saturday?"

"So long? How about Tuesday night? At your place?"

It could have been anytime and anywhere. "Absolutely."

Another embrace and a quick, ravenous kiss, and Amber darted into the dormitory. Sam's body walked him back to the fraternity house, though he was elsewhere, reliving every naked, fleshy, and turgid moment of the most incredible evening of his life.

But with a nympho.

Sam startled. He looked around but saw no one nearby. The voice was familiar, but he couldn't place it. He grew uneasy. Not as much by this sudden, spooky, and intrusive voice but more by what it had said. *Nympho.* The word seemed like a cancer, metastasizing into the luminescent memory of his evening. Amber was no nympho. Amber was going to be his girlfriend.

A girlfriend! At last, I have a girlfriend!

But as he walked home, *nympho* lingered and troubled him, as would a snake hidden somewhere in the weeds. He didn't care where the word had come from, but he had to purge it from his mind. Like a drowning man desperately thrashing toward a life preserver, he invoked Amber: her smile, full lips, and large breasts with their hard, brown nipples and the wet enfolding softness of her vagina. All the while praying this would chase *nympho* away. And since he couldn't explain that puzzling voice, he disregarded it.

I have a girlfriend!

Indeed, Sam was ecstatic to have finally joined the brotherhood of ex-virgin studs, although he chose not to advertise it. He'd finally passed through that well-defined but elusive gate to become a man, a real boner-fide man who could order pink grasshoppers, chug down three horse-piss beers in a row, smoke unfiltered cigarettes, and, above all, fuck.

And fuck Sam and Amber did, as often as school classes and her menses would allow. Tuesday night was followed by more Tuesday nights, then Saturdays, and every day in between. They lived in a carnal playground. Sam tried to keep count of his orgasms, as each still seemed like a miracle, until he lost track after one long weekend in which the two lovers never left his bed. This was much to the irritation of Robbie, who begrudgingly accepted his exile to another brother's couch and finally guessed why his rubber stash was dwindling.

Sam felt like he was making up for lost time. What Amber was doing had never crossed his mind, but the word *nymphomaniac* still did, and it wouldn't go away. He grew more concerned. This had happened too fast and too easily, his first kiss to first fuck, all in one evening. Hitting a home run with a girl was supposed to be a triumph, the essence of male achievement, according to Greg's rules of baseball. But Amber had done it for him. He felt like a fraud. *Amber is no nympho, period,* he repeatedly said to himself. He was worried by how often he had to say it.

He had to know. Nearing the end of another long, sweaty, and predominantly naked weekend, he and Amber lay nestled in his bed in a cave of quilts and pillows, with their hands into each other's business. A heavy snow was falling, muffling all sound and activity outside, making their nest even warmer and cozier. A perfect time for some intimate nuzzling.

But not for Sam. He had been waiting for the right moment to ask, but there was no right moment for a question like this. "Um, Amber, how many guys, have you, you know…"

"Jesus, Sam! What a thing to ask! And what a time to ask it! A girl has to have some secrets, you know."

"Yeah, that was dumb. I'm sorry." He retreated, justly reprimanded. "But you know all about my first time. What was yours like?"

Amber was silent for a few moments. "I was twelve," she said quietly. "It was with my stepfather. On the kitchen table. He was drunk."

"Twelve?"

"Yeah. He raped me."

"He raped you?" Sam knew what rape was, but it was a remote, improbable, and evil thing found only in newspapers and fuck books or in crime dramas on television. Not in his life, not in his love nest—a nest starting to grow chilly.

Amber began to softly cry. "At first, I didn't know what was happening, only that I was terrified and couldn't stop it. He smelled awful and it really hurt. Afterward he said he'd kill me if I told anyone. Especially my mother."

"Oh, God, I'm sorry."

"God didn't care. Nobody cared. He did it again a few weeks later. The next day I ran away to a girlfriend's house, but her parents sent me back. I ran away again, this time to the bus station. I didn't have any money but I didn't know where else to go. The cops found me. I told them what happened. They didn't believe me, so I started screaming as loud as I could, right there in the bus station."

At age twelve, Sam had been playing third base and earning Boy Scout merit badges. His greatest worries had been zits, science quizzes, and being out of fashion in school. A nightmare world like Amber's would have been inconceivable to him. Now, seven years later, it was here in his bed. He held Amber close. After a few minutes she stopped sniffling.

"They put me in this kind of hospital," she continued. "It had bars on the windows. Some hospital! My mother picked me up the next day. I told her what happened. I told her he was going to kill me if told anyone. 'That's nonsense,' she said. Can you believe that bitch? 'Nonsense' is what she said. She knew! She had to know!"

Her crying resumed, now gasping sobs. Sam kept holding her, not knowing what to say or do. Although they were as close as two bodies could be, he saw Amber standing on the far edge of a deep chasm a mile across. He could hear and feel her perfectly well, but she was no longer part of his small, safe, violence-free world. She felt remote and tainted, as would be a convict paroled from an unfathomably strange prison. He knew this was small-hearted and shameful, but he couldn't shake it.

He had to bring Amber back across the chasm. "Did he ever do it again?"

"Not for a while. A woman from the county came a few times to talk to him and my mother. He left me alone after that, but not for long. He'd, like, touch my breasts and put his hand down there when he could get away with it. One time I tried to pull away and he hit me. Then he did it again, when he was drunk again. He even tried to tie my hands so I couldn't claw his goddamned eyes out."

"What happened after that?" Sam asked, though he was afraid to know.

"They put me in a foster home with an older couple. They were great. But it was only for a few months until Mom could divorce the bastard and he had to move out."

"That's awful," he said, having no idea what awful really was.

"Yeah, it was." After a few moments, she asked, "Does all this make any difference, you know, like with us?"

"Of course not," Sam said, feeling a frozen lump growing inside his guts. Amber hugged him fiercely, then kissed him, and the lump in his guts melted. Almost.

A week later, on another steamy evening, they were play wrestling on the sofa, naked. Sam had pinned Amber on her back with her hands behind her. He stopped and looked at her apprehensively, thinking he might have just crossed a line. But Amber shrugged and smiled up at him. He had an idea.

"Stay there and don't move," said Sam, holding down her shoulders.

"Yes, sir."

Sir? That gave him a thrill. The thrill burrowed into his being and woke something up.

Sam got up, withdrew the belt from his bathrobe, raised it up, and looked down at her. Amber gave him another shrug and a smile. He rolled her over on her belly. She kept her hands in place. He tied her wrists together and rolled her back. She allowed this with feigned protest.

Amber tested the bond and realized she could not free herself. It was a precarious moment, and Sam watched her carefully. Then he either imagined or felt something crouching in a dark corner of the room, also watching. It frightened him. But Amber smiled and relaxed and brought him back to her. Emboldened by his uncharacteristic nerve, Sam ran his hands all over and into the bound girl, as if not knowing which part to devour first—perhaps everything at once. He began on her breasts.

"Pinch my nipples," Amber said softly.

Sam could now feel the thing in the corner paying close attention. He knew what it was. He'd once read a story about them.

He pinched one nipple. "Like this?"

"A little harder."

He was not sure he'd heard her correctly, but tightened his grip. This had to be hurting her.

"Harder, please. Both nipples."

Sam did. Amber was staring intently into his eyes, breathing fast and hard. He stared back, again seeing her on the far edge of that chasm. He could hear something in the darkness breathing heavily.

"Now," said Amber, "pinch as hard as you can."

"What?"

"Please!"

Sam looked at her nipples, like two tiny erect penises quivering atop the enormous swells of her breasts.

"This may hurt," he said, as if needing her final permission. The darkness now seemed to be behind him, crouching, waiting.

"Do it, Sam! Do it!"

Sam pinched both nipples as hard as his thumbs and fingers could manage without tearing their ligaments. Amber shrieked, leaped off the sofa, and collapsed on the floor, still with her hands tied behind her, her breathing rapid and ragged. Sam quickly untied her and helped her onto the sofa. He kissed and massaged her nipples back to life and apologized nonstop.

"It's okay," Amber said and smiled. "I'm okay. I really am."

He wasn't. His cock was rock hard and growing harder. That surprised then alarmed him. Sam felt that thing in the corner, the goblin, retreat into its cave somewhere deep within his body. Amber led him into the bedroom by the pole of his penis, and they fucked like they'd just discovered it. Spent, he lay close beside her, gently stroking her breasts and nipples.

"Do they still hurt?" he said.

"Yeah," smiled Amber. "But it's a good kind of hurt."

Sam knew exactly what she meant, and that disturbed him. But that loose goblin disturbed him even more.

A week later, Amber and Sam were once again on the sofa, naked and play wrestling. She managed to grab his testicles and tightened her grip.

"Uncle! Uncle! Uncle!" Sam cried. "You win!"

Amber relaxed her hold but did not release him.

"Do you remember what we did last week?" she said. "You know, with the belt from your bathrobe?"

"Yes. Of course."

"Can we do it again?"

Sam hesitated, growing uneasy as to where this might lead and still unsettled by it. Amber lightly squeezed her fist.

"Yowch! Yes, yes! We can do it again."

Amber smiled and let go of him. "Did you like that? What I just did to you?"

"It hurt."

"Yeah, but did you like it?"

Yes, I liked it. He absolutely craved it, but he couldn't answer her truthfully. His secret, dying to reveal itself, fled deeper into hiding.

Amber took his face in her hands and kissed him. She then crossed her wrists together and held them up as an offering. Sam turned her over on the sofa, bound her hands behind her back with a necktie, and rolled her back. Amber remained still and cooperative. Again, he had the run of the table and caressed every inch of her breasts, thighs, and vulva, now heavily seeping with fluid. Amber returned to her inner boudoir, sighing and rocking her pelvis.

Sam then tried to bind her ankles together with his belt. To his surprise, Amber fought him, kicking and flailing. But he was strong and determined, and after nearly getting kicked in the face twice, finally managed to corral her legs and tie her ankles together. Amber relaxed and smiled. Her nipples were erect.

"Pinch me," she said.

Sam did, hard and then harder. Amber cried out but ordered him not to stop. He could again sense the goblin in the room, now much closer.

Later in bed, after another body-mauling round of coitus, they lay close together, lightly stroking each other's faces.

"Wasn't that technically a rape?" Sam asked. "You know, what I did to you tonight?"

"Yeah, maybe, technically," said Amber. "But I liked it and I wanted it."

"But how can that be, after what your stepfather did to you? Even tying your hands?"

"Yeah, it's weird. I haven't figured it out. I think my turn-on is that you want me so much you'll take me down like that. You'll force yourself on me. It's very sexy."

"You didn't like it when you were raped at home, did you?"

"Oh, God no. I hated it."

"Then why is this any different?"

"Because *you* are."

"I don't understand."

"I don't either."

"But aren't you bothered by wanting this… violence?" Sam asked cautiously. "Don't you ever think there's something wrong with you? Something unhealthy?"

"Yeah, at first I was bothered a lot. Girls shouldn't want to be hurt and raped. But I did, and I didn't know why something so scary and abusive could also be so sexy. Maybe my brain's wires got crossed that time when it first happened. But I figured I've already suffered enough because of my screwed-up family, so why punish myself and suffer more? I deserve to feel happy and enjoy sex, and not crawl down some hole feeling sorry for myself."

Sam remained silent.

"Don't you have anything unusual that turns you on?" she asked. "Something you can't tell anyone about?"

He paused for a long moment. "No." He felt like he'd just swallowed an open safety pin.

The next weekend was their standard date: they got drunk at the party downstairs and, groping each other every five feet, made their way up to Sam's room. On the sofa, Sam started to pull off Amber's sweater.

"Not yet," she said.

Amber opened her purse, larger than her usual one, and withdrew two objects wrapped in tissue paper. She smiled at Sam and slowly opened one package, as if mimicking a striptease. It was a pink rubber dildo the size of a normal erect penis. Sam had seen dildoes before but had never touched or closely examined one. It looked like it had been cast from the real item, with detailed vasculature, curves, and ridges. Amber handed it to him.

At first, he was reluctant to hold it, it being another man's penis, sort of. But he took it, feeling the rubbery bumps and its heft. He pointed it at Amber's groin. She smiled and nodded. He didn't understand the appeal of a fake penis when a real one was so easily within her reach. Then she carefully and even more seductively unwrapped the second, larger package. It was another rubber dildo, but this one was shiny black, twice as long, and twice as thick. A grotesque thing, it was covered with bumps, ridges, and small spikes—someone's fanciful idea of what might hang beneath a centaur.

"Is this a joke?" Sam asked, assuming it had to be.

"No," frowned Amber. "It most certainly is not."

Sam didn't know what to make of that. Amber took the centaur from his hands and set it down. She wrapped her arms around his neck and whispered into his ear.

"I want you to do something," she said. "I want you to take me down and tie me to your bed and make love to me with these."

Sam heard her words, but they didn't make sense. He again felt the goblin in the corner, watching, listening, and rapt by her request.

"Please," she said. "Will you please do it?"

He nodded, feeling as if he'd just agreed to step in front of a bus. He peeled off Amber's sweater and skirt but was too tipsy to manage the hooks of her bra. *The hell with it.* He ripped the bra apart and tore off her panties. Amber responded with a sharp cry and a flurry of wild, passionate kisses.

"Take me down, Sam," she breathed. "Take me down hard!"

Sam looked around the room and found two neckties and two belts. He grabbed Amber by her breasts, dragged her onto his bed, and tied her wrists and ankles to the four corners of the bed frame. Amber did not fight him. She became very quiet and passive, intently watching everything he did.

After he tied and stretched her tight, Sam stood aside and looked at his lover… or was she now his victim? Although he now knew what to do with a lover, and what he fantasized about doing to a victim, in that moment, he couldn't do anything to either. Alcohol, confusion, and apprehension befogged him. Amber pulled and twisted at her bonds. After seeing she was truly captive, she relaxed and looked up at him.

"Are you okay?" she asked.

Sam couldn't answer because he didn't know who he was, how he was, or even where he was. In the harsh yellow light cast by a single overhead bulb, he looked around his bedroom. Faded rock concert posters on the walls, a dingy thrift store bureau, a hamper overflowing with dirty laundry, and a naked girl tied down on a blue-and-white-striped mattress with her arms and legs spread wide. *Whose room is this?* He felt paralyzed.

"Sam?"

"I'm okay."

That was not true. Sam felt the distinct sensation of something somewhere inside him splitting apart. Abruptly, he was in two places at the same time: standing beside Amber with a growing and savage intent, and also wedged into the corner of the room, fascinated, frightened, and barely able to breathe. He could no longer feel that goblin watching him, and he knew why.

Sam watched himself strip off his clothes and climb on top of Amber. He mauled, bit, and pinched her breasts and nipples with abandon, ignoring her cries and struggles. He kneaded her vulva squishy and entered her, not bothering with a condom and not gently, humping away, like a bull possessed in a rutting frenzy. Amber met his thrusts with her pelvis arched, her limbs twisting, and straining at her bonds. He was too hard to come.

"Use the small one on me," Amber said.

Sam picked up the dildo. She was soaking wet. It easily slid in.

"All the way," she said. "In and out."

He complied, slowly at first and then faster. Amber's hips wildly gyrated despite their restraints, making her vagina a difficult target to hit.

"Now the big one," Amber gasped after a few minutes of wild, synthetic penetration.

Sam in the corner said, "The big one? That's not possible!"

"Yes, it is. Please!" Her eyes were wide and glassy.

The Sam who was on the bed picked up the huge rubber dildo. He sized up its girth and then the width of her vagina.

"Do it, do it," Amber pleaded.

He placed the bulbous head into her vagina and pushed. It wouldn't go in. Corner Sam was afraid to hurt her. The other Sam was not.

"Rub the end with your spit and my juice," she said, "and push."

He did but it wouldn't go in.

"Push harder!" she cried.

"Jesus, be careful!" yelled Corner Sam.

Sam gave the rubber monster a mighty shove and it slid into her vagina, hard and deep. Amber screamed and twisted at her restraints.

Instinctively, Corner Sam started to withdraw it.

"No!" Amber cried. "Fuck me. Fuck me, hard!"

Sam watched his double ram the dildo into her, pounding it and twisting it without remorse or restraint, like a robot run amok. Amber cried out and struggled against her bonds and the impalement. Her eyes were tightly shut and she gasped for breath. Sam knew that terrible damage was happening, both to him and to Amber's distended vagina, but the pounding continued. He feared he would never be the same.

Amber shuddered, then lay motionless, shiny with sweat and softly sobbing. Sam came out of the corner. He withdrew the monstrous dildo as gently as possible but she still screamed as it slid out. He easily unbelted her ankles, but the necktie knots on her wrists gave him trouble. She gazed up at him as he picked at the knots, her face pale and blank. Finally freed, Amber sat up in bed, dazed and exhausted. She tried to smile, then she swooned and fainted.

Terrified he'd somehow killed her, Sam felt for, and *thank God* found, a pulse. He covered her with a blanket and sat there beside her, not knowing what else to do and still immobilized by his own trauma. The goblin was gone, but in its place, Sam felt an alien, sinister future coalesce around him like a swarm of biting gnats. A minute later, Amber opened her eyes, turned over the side of the bed, and vomited Coke and cheap whiskey onto the floor. She lay back, covered her face with her hands, and cried.

"I don't feel so good," she said.

"I don't either," he said.

They slowly dressed, and Sam walked her unsteadily back to her dormitory, neither of them saying a word. The chasm had returned, with

Amber on the other side and now a thousand miles away and barely visible. They gave each other a brief, desultory hug and, without looking at him, she disappeared into the building. Sam staggered home through the sleet and snow to clean up the mess in his room. He had no idea how to clean up the mess in his mind. It raged like a cyclone filled with glass shards, its winds sounding like the din of a million cicadas.

Did you like that, Sam? Was it good for you?

Sam startled and stopped walking. He looked around him. No one was there. Of course, no one was there—it was that freakish voice again. Then he noticed the cyclone was gone. All was quiet, tomb quiet. The eye of the storm.

Oh my, what a sex drive that girl has, and lord, those boobs!

He knew that voice. He remembered Jill and that humiliating day in the cafeteria, and those caustic words that had chastised him. It was the same voice. Of this he was certain. He was still woozy from the alcohol and dazed by his unearthly dissociation and the violence it wrought. *That must be it.* The wind and cold made his nose run. Sam wiped it and looked at the smear on the back of his hand. It was the hand of a snot-boy. He stared at it, seeing it as someone else's.

The cloud of gnats returned, their mad buzzing growing even louder, keeping this baffling, schizoid voice in line with the rest of the unnerving evening. Insanity was now becoming a very real and very frightening possibility, and growing more real by the moment. Because two hours ago Sam had known what sanity felt like, and it sure as hell didn't feel like this. Or sound like it.

Did you enjoy that as much as I did?

What? Who are you?

His throat tightened—he was actually responding to this... thing. *Snot-boy. Crazy.*

You didn't answer my question, Sam.

Who are you, goddammit?

Maybe I'm a what, not a who. Maybe I'm that missing piece you worry about so much. Do you think that little chasm of yours is empty?

That really scared him. How did this thing know about the chasm?

"Oh my God, I *am* going crazy," he said out loud, not caring who heard him. He spun around to see if anyone had. No. "Crazy! Crazy! Crazy!" echoed off the darkened class buildings.

A couple hurried past him on their way to beat the dormitory curfew. They couldn't have heard him or they would have reacted. That was good. He was safe. He was crazy but had to be very careful not to show it. He looked around, then kept walking, but slowly and quietly as if not wanting to disturb anything—or wake it up. The snow turned to sleet. He was freezing and he didn't care. He was really liking not caring. His nose kept running. More snot for the snot-boy.

"Then crazy it shall be," he said to himself. That resignation became a dark, grim resolve that spread throughout his body like the biting wind in the street. He had good reason to be crazy. He cradled the word in his mind. It offered a strange kind of warmth that sheltered him not only from the storm around him, but from the one within him as well. Protection from what, he wasn't certain. He stood there in the cold sleet, trying to think what to do next until the need to survive prompted his body to take him home.

He didn't call Amber the next day, or the next, because he had a chaotic, hallucinatory, glass-shredded mess for a mind, and he wouldn't know what to say anyway. He'd fallen into that chasm between them and was flailing around for a handhold, desperate to find a way back into himself. But maybe there wasn't a handhold. Maybe this was how insanity happened. This confounding, inexplicable voice was proof. It hadn't returned. *Maybe it won't.* He grew terrified that it would.

Late that evening, exhausted and distraught, he finally hit bottom with a thud. At least he was no longer falling. The bottom looked like his old life, his old familiar and safe life, but something was still not right, something really important. The next morning, he called Amber, still not sure what he'd say to her. He didn't have to say anything, as her seething roommate did all the talking.

"She's in the hospital," she spat, her words like razor blades.

"Oh my God," Sam said. "What happened?"

"You happened, you asshole! Last night she cut her wrists with a nail file. A goddamned nail file! She's in the psych ward at student health."

"Oh Jesus. Is she all right?"

"No! She's not all right! She's in the hospital! Amber told me what you did to her. This all your fault, you sack of shit." She hung up with a bang.

Sam took it. He deserved it. He knew the roommate was right, but not entirely, and there was no way to tell her. He knew whose fault it was, but that didn't leave him off the hook.

He went to visit Amber that afternoon. He approached the hospital's information desk. The woman sitting behind it looked to be about twelve.

"I'm, uh, where's the psych ward?" he asked.

The young woman regarded him for a moment. "Are you wanting to check yourself in?"

Sam almost said yes. "No. I'm looking for a... someone."

"There isn't a psychiatric wing. What's your someone's name?"

Sam found the room. Amber was sitting on the bed doing a crossword puzzle. She seemed bright and cheerful, despite where she was and why. To his astonishment, she was genuinely happy to see him.

"Sam! Oh jeez, I thought I'd never see you again. Look!"

She held up her wrists like they were trophies. One wrist bore a single wide bandage, but the other was swathed in gauze and tape.

"It took a while, but I finally got the vein," she said.

Sam didn't know what to think about that, or this thoroughly bewildering scene, only that he was frightened to the bone.

"I'm sorry, Amber. Oh God, I'm so sorry."

"Don't be sorry," she said. "I'm not."

Amber was still on the far edge of that chilling chasm. He could see her clearly, but it wasn't Amber. It looked like her, but something else was in her body. The chasm widened.

"You did this because of me?" he asked.

"What? No, I did this because of me. You know why."

"I don't understand. Your roommate said—"

"Forget that. Come, come to bed. Let's have sex. The hospital won't mind."

Amber loosened the ties of the hospital gown and let it fall. Her breasts were covered with scratches, probably from the same nail file. Sam slowly backed away from her. She just gazed at him, smiling and expectant, completing this bizarre inversion of a young woman who once had been Amber.

Without saying a word, Sam bolted from the room and ran nonstop back to his house. He collapsed on the sofa and started shaking, too stunned to do anything else. After almost two hours, exhausted, inert, and feebly wishing for the oblivion of a coma, he rebooted himself.

He picked up a photograph of Amber taken at a recent party. She was bright and pretty, dancing and smiling back at him and looking like any normal girl at a normal party. Then he saw her sitting on the hospital bed with her bizarre smile, bandaged wrists, and disfigured breasts. He could not resolve the two pictures into one. He tore the photograph to shreds, hoping that would somehow change something. It didn't.

Of course it didn't.

Oh no, oh God, you're still there.

Absolutely. You seem upset, Sam. Do you want to talk about it?

Sam struggled to get a grip on this. He'd always known about people hearing inner voices and talking back to them. He'd seen them on the streets, carrying plastic bags filled with more plastic bags, wearing everything they owned, and hurling paranoid rants at everyone and no one. Those people were called schizophrenics. *Schizo.* That meant split apart. That was exactly what had happened to him. He was now among them.

Have I gone crazy? Am I a schizo?

What? Because you're hearing me? I'm insulted!

Sam was now more confused than frightened. This was no clichéd demonic voice urging him to gather plastic bags and start screaming at pigeons. And it was distinctly female and seemed to care about him, which added another layer of mystery. There was no other conclusion: his mind had simply cracked open, and this was what crazy looked like.

Yeah, that's what happens when you tie girls down and fuck them with giant dildoes.

No, Sam, this happened to you long before that. Don't you remember?

He did and didn't want to. Craziness was now bigger than him, growing bigger, and he was too wasted and wretched to continue resisting it anyway. And this intrusive voice, this *thing*, clearly was not going away either. Maybe it did have something to say. He was certain he'd already lost his mind, so what was left for him to lose?

Why are you doing this to me?

What else have I got to do?

Okay. Right. Then what was that... thing in the hospital?

That thing is a frightened girl who needed to find and feel something solid in her world. Something she can get whenever she needs it. Last night it was seeing her own blood. And what do you need tonight? Seeing your blood? Or maybe more snot on your hand?

That stunned him. Were all schizoid inner voices just as perceptive and intelligent? His confusion ebbed. This might be crazy, but it was also becoming intriguing.

How do you know all that?

Because I was there and listening. Do you really believe purging Amber from your life will purge you of your sickness? Is your goblin gone? Do you feel clean and healthy now?

No. I feel sicker than ever.

Big surprise.

Go away. Please, just go away and leave me alone.

I'm sorry, Sam, but that is not possible. And even if it was, I wouldn't.

THE SERIAL KILLER

SAM FELT LIKE HE WAS PAINTING himself into a corner, in a room with no doors. The possibility of finding a similarly "paraphilic" sex partner was remote, and he'd probably end up fleeing as he had with Amber. Normal dating and sex were now becoming more feasible for him, though these were still fraught with insecurities and fear and always made exasperatingly complicated by the goblins in his mind. And the appearance of this troublesome, disparaging other voice in his head fueled a growing anxiety about his mental health. All seemed hopeless.

To make matters worse, the Summer of Love had arrived, bringing flocks of winsome, long-haired, bare-footed hippie chicks to make all the love happen. It seemed these free-spirited girls would eagerly fuck anyone who was also a hippie, male or female, without the risk of being tagged as nymphomaniacs. Also, unknown to all the free spirits and their lovers, venereal disease was becoming just as prevalent as the sex. On the streets and in the parks, promiscuity had been blessed and renamed "free love," but to Sam it was just as dishearteningly expensive as ever.

He thought he knew the reason: he wasn't a hippie and knew he'd make a pathetically bad one. His hair was short, his beard was peach fuzz, his wardrobe was shopping mall chic. He couldn't afford tie-dyed clothes, had no idea where to get pot, and hated vegetables, organic or not. Political and spiritual correctness and their vocabularies flew right over his head as well. Although he could parrot "right on" and "off the pigs" in unison with the rest of the chanting, rioting masses, he still felt like an imposter. That's because he simply wasn't hip—wasn't even hip enough to see it but suspected that hipness should have motivations more elevated than his own.

Amid the war protests, drug usage, vegetarian restaurants, and flaky cults, Sam felt like he was drifting around in interplanetary limbo. Indeed, the long-haired, long-bearded, tie-dyed, and bead-draped young men and their similarly attired girlfriends seemed like gentle aliens from a more evolved and civilized world who had come to earth to show it a better way. A popular song lyric kept worming through his thoughts:

> *Because something is happening here*
> *But you don't know what it is*
> *Do you, Mister Jones?*

Mister Sam could relate.

Sam's fraternity brothers despised hippies. They thought of them as lazy, drug-addicted, draft-dodging, Commie cowards, and as for their girlfriends, they were all sluts. Sam remained silent on the subject, all the while planning his defection to the strawberry fields and dreaming of braless hippie chick breasts in his hands. Indeed, bras had become the defining element that separated the women in Sam's life into two camps. In his crowd, the proper sorority girls always wore bras, which made their breasts look like lumpy, quilted pillows and possibly concealed layers of padding. Some girls even wedged themselves into tight, spandex girdles that also served well as chastity belts. Getting both garments off required investing a lot of time, money, and chivalrous attention and still didn't guarantee a thing.

In the other camp, the hippie chicks were the exact opposite. Bras were symbolic of female sexual repression and uncomfortable to boot and thus taboo among this group. Unconfined breasts implied their owner was uninhibited, slightly feral, and perhaps available for a good time. It also meant there was one less layer of protective fabric, which made the breasts more accessible... if access was granted. Sam reasoned that the lack of a bra made access more grantable. Screwy times called for screwy thinking.

So Sam tried testing the counterculture waters. His single concession to a trendy wardrobe was a pair of daring open-toed sandals he'd found in a shopping mall bargain bin. It would be a clear signal of his commitment to ending the war and offing the pigs. *Right on, dude.* He cruised city parks, bookstores, head shops, and cafés that were rumored to harbor hippies and their free-loving chicks. His disguise didn't fool anyone, and all he ended up getting was dirty feet. Another piece seemed to be missing.

The real hippie chick bonanzas were the music festivals. Sam would stand entranced on the shoreline of a sea of bouncing, supple, tanned bodies, with their swirling long hair; loose, flowing robes; acres of feminine skin; and a seemingly limitless number of braless breasts. This mirrored his high school dance experiences: standing and watching, envious and miserable. But when this party was over, unlike those high school dances with their restrictive chaperone rules, the celebrants would retreat to their unsupervised pads to crash, where, Sam assumed, everyone got stoned and naked and chaperoning would be a crime. *This is just not fair.*

Fair? Who says getting laid is supposed to be fair? Fair is an issue only for the losers, like you, twit!

Oh, shit. It's you.

Of course it is. You'd better get used to it.

I suppose I have no choice.

You never did.

Sam cautiously glanced at the people standing around him. No one seemed to notice anything unusual going on with him. That was good. But how long could he hide this… *thing* before it got really bad? He decided to rationally examine the situation and figure out a way to deal with it. Then maybe, just maybe, it might go away. He knew that was sloppy logic but it was all he had.

He looked at the facts. One: this other voice, this inner mental she-demon, apparently could come and go at will, and he couldn't prevent it.

That's right. You can't, Sam. Good call.

Shut up.

I will not shut up.

Fact two: he couldn't shut her up either.

Three: she somehow knew things about him, important and personal things. Things he should have known about himself but for some reason didn't.

The reason being you're a clueless twit.

Four: she wasn't urging him to freak out or do anything sick and stupid.

You're doing that already without my help.

Five: she—it—was just… really mean. That's all.

Mean? Me? You haven't seen mean.

Six: he seemed to be stuck with her anyway. And besides, in an odd way, right now, he needed an odd friend.

Is that all I am? Just an odd friend to you? Ha!

What else can you be?

You'll find out.

Sam sighed and returned to his music festival misery. There was one hippie chick in particular who caught his eye and ire. She was tall and lithe, an auburn-haired beauty, dancing barefoot in the grass by herself. Her loose, white, gauzy dress threatened to unravel with every move. Her braless breasts swayed beneath her low-necked peasant blouse. Her navel was pierced, adding to her exotic appeal. She danced freely and wildly, flying in her own skies with the beat of the drums and the thrum of the crowd. Sam could not look away from her. She would never look at him. He had never felt so small, unattractive, unhip, and *defective*.

That's because you are.

Jesus! What's with you? Why are you being so shitty to me?

Because you deserve it. What's the matter? Don't you like my dress and the way I dance?

Who the hell are you? You tell me right now, goddammit!

Who would you like me to be? And who would you like me to be tonight, hmm?

I want you to be gone!

Sorry, no can do.

Okay, he decided. *What the fuck? Let's just see what this nasty bitch can do.*

Nasty bitch, am I? That works for me. Bring it on, baby.

All right, I'll tell you what's not fair. Just look at them, damn it! With their sexy dresses and their bouncing tits and nipple bumps and pierced navels and smooth legs and long hair and tight asses and pretty faces, and their flirting and posing, and they say yes when they mean no, and they act like they really want you and then they yank it all away!

Oh, stop your damn whining. What are we supposed to do? Wear burlap sacks, live like nuns, and waddle around like penguins just so poor, horny little Sammy won't get hot and frustrated and risk being a fool?

That one struck home. *Why do I need this?*

Because you're Sam, Sam. Anything else I can do for you today?

Sam turned and walked away from this ocean of joy and celebration, pretending it had never existed. Fact seven: he would never pass as a cool, laid-back, long-haired, pot-smoking, war-resisting, free-loving, festival-dancing hippie dude. And there weren't enough open-toed sandals in the world to help him wangle a bare-breasted hippie chick into his bed. The sandals went into the garbage the next day, and he felt like jumping in after them.

Sam gave up pursuing hippie chicks (they were sluts anyway) and cast about looking for women more his speed and style. He found himself attracted to geeky, moody, and depressed women—not surprising, as like attracted like. Unfortunately, unlike him, their primary need was for commiseration, not sex. These women were also highly intelligent, which meant Greg's advice to finesse and finagle would not play well here. That was good, as Sam was not proficient at either.

But Barry's discourse on women and intimacy still kept gnawing at him. Barry had suggested there were pathways to intimacy other than running a girl's bases, but, unfortunately, he had left out the details. Maybe he didn't know them either. Despite the absence of instructions, Sam decided to explore on his own. After all, things couldn't get any worse.

Is that so?

There's worse? What is it?

I could tell you, but then I wouldn't get a chance to see it.

Sam quickly learned this alternate path was a far more complicated game of baseball played by different rules—women's rules. There still was a progression, but it was convoluted, laborious, and most of the time completely mystifying. To begin, an unspecified number of lengthy and often tiresome coffee date conversations were required, the quality and sincerity of which were were nearly impossible to finesse or fake. Dishonesty, hiding defects, and manufacturing assets wouldn't work either—a relief, as this was another thing at which he was terrible. It took two brains for this kind of intercourse, and fortunately his still worked.

Sam's busiest genitalia were his ears, and the more he offered them, the more desirable he became. His skills were impressive: an ability to listen, the willingness to do so, the intuition for when listening was needed, and the stamina and patience to do it all. He learned this at home, where he'd had to develop a radar for detecting his mother's moods and either tactfully negotiating them or avoiding them altogether.

After many dates and interminable sessions of verbal foreplay, Sam finally concluded that intelligence and melancholy in females must be genetically linked. He also discovered a discouraging pattern on this road to intimacy. The more a girl talked about her issues and angst, the more attentively he'd listen, which provided incentive for her to become even more anxious and despondent, and soon both of them were so profoundly depressed that even the idea of sex was unimaginable.

When geeky girl sex finally did happen, it was always normal sex. Kissing, frenching, fondling, fingering, and, after the appropriate number of dates, rubber-mediated intercourse. He was also introduced to oral sex, which he surprisingly liked and had a knack for, and it gave his tongue something more constructive to do. This was followed by (immensely appreciated if not required) postcoital snuggling, in which past sexual experiences were reviewed, the present moment savored, and future plans proposed and excitedly discussed.

But as Sam lay in bed, gently entwined with either Bonnie, Joanie, or Beverly, he kept thinking about Amber, naked, tied up, and straining against her bonds. (He chose not to remember her strange smile in the hospital and her clawed breasts.) In moments of extreme horniness and stupidity, which seemed to occur together, he thought about calling Amber to perhaps make things right, and then make it wrong all over again. That was ill-advised, if only for its sheer idiocy and base motivations; plus, he had no wish to tangle with her enraged roommate again.

"What are you thinking about?" Bonnie whispered into Sam's ear one evening while they lay in bed after both had come.

"Us," said Sam, immediately jumping from Amber to Bonnie in the nick of time.

Bonnie smiled and nuzzled against his side. "I'm glad."

Sam hated that question, though he knew it was an essential one for establishing intimacy. But it was also a dangerous question because it could also have many different answers—all of them could be true, but only one answer was right, and it had better be answered promptly and convincingly.

Sam was certain Bonnie would not appreciate hearing the truth: how cute she'd look all tied up and helpless. No matter how good the petting, sucking, and fucking, the goblin was always hovering nearby with its usual agenda.

A few weeks later, he and Beverly lay coiled up next to each other after a long evening of sex, sweet and slow. But normal sex was becoming unsatisfying, even to the point of boredom, just a job to do.

"What are you thinking?" Beverly asked.

That damn question again.

The truth or another lie?

Jeez! You're even here in bed?

Especially here in bed.

"Then good! Enjoy yourself."

"I *am* enjoying myself, Sam," Beverly said, a bit puzzled.

Oh, shit.

You need to be more careful, twit. Pay attention to whom you're with. Sheesh!

Beverly awaited his answer. Sam gently traced his fingertip around her nipples. "Okay. Do you remember when I held your hands above your head and kissed your breasts?"

"Oh yes."

"Did you like that?"

"Mmm."

"Would you like it if I tied your hands that way?"

Beverly hardened. "Is *that* what you were thinking?"

"Well…"

"That's sick and creepy. Jeez, Sam."

Good job, twit. Scratch Beverly. Scratch another one.

But it was Sam who always ended the relationships with Bonnie and Beverly and everyone who came after. The reason was always the same: sexual dissatisfaction, not clearly stated as such but couched in an excuse that made him the bad guy and protected his secrets and his shame. "I'm just not ready for this. I have serious issues about relationships. I have a problem with commitment." And so on.

That evening Beverly heard, "You're right. I guess I am sick and creepy. I'm sorry."

Sam believed all these women saw *potential partner* written on his forehead. They did not see *pervert* or *dead end* but soon figured out that he was these things. What he saw written on theirs was *salvation*. With enough healthy, normal sex, he believed, he'd be cured of his goblins. Apparently not so. That left his former lovers confused, even angry, but none of them protested. And that left him in an oubliette of despair with no exit or chance of rescue. Why begin dating a girl when it was sure to be doomed? He was wasting everyone's time.

Sam found that managing the goblin was difficult but not impossible, despite its maddening persistence. Ignoring it, he'd repeatedly learned, was futile. At least he knew when and where the thing would show up. But managing this vexing voice in his head was another matter because she was basically unmanageable. Trying to ignore her was not only impossible, but it seemed to strengthen her resolve to be heard. No matter how vigilant he was, her appearance was unpredictable and seldom appreciated.

He discovered this one evening in a local beer hall that catered to the just-barely-above-drinking-age crowd. In a passable imitation of a German *bierstube,* long wooden tables sat in the center of the room, covered with pitchers of cheap draft beer, enormous bowls of pretzels and peanuts, and overflowing ashtrays, surrounded by booze-saturated college students who were learning how to have a good time. Keeping with Oktoberfest tradition, full-bosomed waitresses in low-cut peasant blouses navigated the tables with two full pitchers in each hand and crunched peanut shells wherever they walked.

Sam was sitting with his drinking crew next to a pretty ash-blonde who drank with him pint for pint. Conversation was impossible over the loud oompah band, so they toasted the tuba player and sang "Roll Out the Barrel" with the inebriated chorus in the room. Their elbows touched on the table, and she didn't move hers. That electrified him.

The band took a break. Sam leaned closer to the blonde.

"I'm Sam."

"I'm Beth. You come here often?"

"Yeah. My grades prove it."

Beth laughed and pulled a cigarette from her purse, and Sam lit it. He'd been advised to always carry a cigarette lighter, and now he knew why. Beth blew smoke away from his face, then offered him her cigarette. He didn't smoke but could now fake it. He inhaled and tasted her lipstick on the filter, a sweet if not tar-soaked, ersatz kiss. The electricity stayed on.

Beth sipped her pint and smiled at him. Sam smiled back. The figure-skating eel flailed about in the beery fog, trying to think of what to say next.

How about this: Hey, Beth, would you like to see my new machete?

"Hey, Beth. Would you like to come back to my place and see my machete?"

Beth's smile dropped. "What? What did you say?"

It's very sharp and never been used.

"It's really sharp, urp, and I haven't used it yet," said Sam.

Beth said not a word. She frowned at him, turned her back, and started talking to the guy on her other elbow.

Why the fuck did you make me say that?

I didn't make you say anything. You were drunk, acting like a jackass, and not paying attention. And besides, you figured she'd reject you anyway, so what the hell?

How about helping me out for once? Give me some good lines or something.

I was helping you out. I was saving you from making a bigger jackass out of yourself.

Sam suspected he was heading for real trouble. He knew it for certain two weeks later at the wedding of one of his fraternity brothers. The ceremony was traditional and very expensive, held in a huge church in the suburbs. Six of Sam's frat-brother ushers in rented tuxedos stood on one side of the altar, mirrored by six sorority-sister bridesmaids in expensive, nonreturnable gowns on the other. The congregation pushed two hundred, including Sam, and was watched over by a doddering, white-haired minister. Everything about the venue said, "If you get married here, you're going to damn well stay married."

The ceremony was long and tedious, punctuated by psalms and tiresome sermons, and the pews were very hard on everyone's butts. Sam was growing anxious. The line he dreaded was fast approaching, and he prayed he'd survive it.

"If there be any here among you," droned the minister, "who hath just cause why these two should not be wedded..."

Sam held his breath.

"Let ye speak now or forever hold your—"

The bride is a sleazy, clap-ridden nympho bitch! She's fucked every cock on campus!

He gritted his teeth and said nothing. The moment passed. He breathed again.

You goddamned monster.

At your service, twit.

This was not the end of it. Being haunted by this voice was bad enough, but now she was becoming deliberately perverse, goading him into recklessly profaning authority and propriety, just to see what would happen. Sam still worried that this was a crazy person's deportment, which edged him toward his uneducated diagnosis of mental illness. Fortunately, he was getting better at predicting when she'd most likely surface and usually could restrain himself before the unthinkable would happen. But sometimes it wasn't easy and rarely with time to spare.

During an ingratiating interview for a summer job as an office assistant: ***Kiss my fucking ass, you sleazy corporate cocksucker.***

The interviewer asked Sam why he had suddenly gone silent. He didn't get the job.

Upon meeting the condescending and reproving mother of his date for the first time: ***I'm going to fuck the stuffing out of your bitch slut daughter, you shit-ugly snob.***

If he'd spoken the words, he would have received two vicious slaps.

When stopped by a fat and imperious traffic cop for making an illegal turn, Sam came close to prison with, ***Fuck off, pig, or I'll blow your ass away with my Uzi.***

The officer let Sam off with just a warning. Afterward, he sat behind the steering wheel and trembled, reluctant to go anywhere lest another cop see and stop him.

My God! Why the hell are you doing this to me?

What's the problem, twit? You wanted to say all these things anyway, didn't you?

From now on I'm going to ignore you.

That won't work. Sorry.

Why not?

Must I explain everything? In order to ignore something, you have to acknowledge it's there, right?

Yeah, I suppose.

Which means you're not ignoring it, right again?

I'll ignore that, too.

Despite his recent disastrous flings with romance, Sam still wanted one badly but faced some grim choices: suppress the goblin and continue with his charade of penis normalcy until it once again fell apart and he lost; find a girl like Amber, with sadomasochistic proclivities (as if girls like that advertised themselves as such), invite in more misery and insanity, and lose again; or simply give up and return to Fantasyland, the only place where he could rule and be happy, though it was the consolation prize for losers.

Sam was tired of losing. For the present, he decided his best move, even if it led to terminal corruption, was to give the goblin something. Whereas most hale and hearty fraternity men found their inspirations in

Playboy, Penthouse, and their lesser clones, Sam discovered his porn in the university's undergraduate library, the last place one would think to look.

While studying there one evening, Sam came across a book titled *The History of Torture.* He quickly flipped the book face down and secreted it into a study alcove, thinking about that seminal book he'd found in his parents' bedroom closet. This one was similar, a scholarly retrospective of various torture techniques throughout Western civilization. *Some civilization.*

Sam quickly leafed through the pages, randomly scanning the passages. It made him very glad he didn't live in medieval Spain. He saw that most torture techniques were pretty basic and straightforward although some ventured far beyond the limits of sadistic ingenuity. Like that closet book on sexual variations, Sam was most drawn to accounts of genital torture. Except the goal here was pleasure for the torturers, not their victims. The sensitive body parts of both sexes were abused until the poor souls confessed their sins or revealed names of other witches and heretics, or the inquisitors had their orgasms (or their religious equivalent). The book's woodcuts and engravings, although blocky and crude, still showed enough detail to more than meet his need. He had to have this book.

The young woman at the checkout desk presented a problem. Sam was positive she'd intuit his intention and call campus security. He considered stealing the book, but committing one sin was bad enough. He nervously circled the study room with his prize, waiting for the right moment and the courage to step forward. He would repeat this little agony many times in the future when buying certified pornography. Finally, he took the risk.

"It's for a term paper," he said. "About torture. About how really wrong it is."

She didn't look up at him and stamped the book like it was a cockroach, seeming to know full well what the book was for. And that's how he used it.

That book was followed by *Torture Devices of the Inquisitors, Techniques of the Witch Hunters,* and *America's Unsolved Sex Crimes.* They all worked exquisitely well. Sam couldn't decide whom he envied more: the sadists, their screaming victims, or both. He pored over the volumes, devouring every word with stellar comprehension and retention. *Imagine my grades,* he lamented, *if only I applied the same effort to my schoolwork.* He also knew he was adding more material to his paraphilic case history file, and he just didn't care. The goblin was happy.

MURDERING WOMEN, WHETHER THEY WERE GUILTY of witchcraft or not, was not just confined to the Dark Ages. That summer, a serial killer of women was on the hunt in the area. Eight bodies had already been discovered, and now another young woman had disappeared. The victims were all single, attractive college students. Their naked bodies were usually found in the woods or in an isolated roadside ditch. Some had been sexually assaulted, some had been tortured, and all had their futures suddenly and brutally annihilated.

The state, county, and local police were stymied. They had no clues, no leads, and no suspects but were convinced the same person was responsible. At one point, the police were so desperate they semi-officially consulted a renowned psychic, who predicted more murders to come, perhaps committed by a satanic cult of killers gathering sacrifices. People remembered the horrific killing of eight student nurses in Chicago a few years earlier, and now this.

According to witnesses, some of the murdered women had last been seen in or outside of singles' bars talking with a young man (the whole point of going to singles' bars). There was no reason why a young woman would mistrust another horny college boy on the make—until his real motive emerged. When these accounts surfaced, singles' bar businesses in particular and student dating in general tanked.

Understandably, the women on the three nearby college campuses were very nervous. Co-eds were discouraged from dating people they didn't know, which was the purpose of dating, and from hitchhiking, which was how everyone, men and women, got around. Women were also advised not to walk alone, especially at night. Ad hoc escort services sprang up: chivalrous college men who volunteered to walk the women to and from their destinations. *What a brilliant idea,* thought the guys; *what a great way to meet chicks. What a fucking idiotic idea,* thought the women; *what a great way for the killer to find victims.*

Sam was deeply conflicted by these events. He was genuinely appalled by the gruesome murders, yet, given his predilection, he was turned on by the whole business as well. He scoured the newspaper articles looking for details of the crimes and guiltily thrilled when he found one. Sometimes he believed he was no different from the killer. Outrage and shame, decency and depravity were escalating to total war inside him—with him being both the battleground and the spoils. Sam knew this was nourishing his conflict, but he could find no truce.

The battle reached its height when a national tabloid ran two photographs of the latest victim, a twenty-year-old woman. One was a portrait taken from a school yearbook. She was blonde, pretty, and had an infectious smile. In the second picture, she was naked lying face down in a stand of tall grass and weeds. Both pictures took Sam's breath away, never mind the woman was dead. Sam knew he was now in serious trouble. He sat on his bed with the newspaper, staring at the two grainy photos—all that remained of a once-vibrant young life—and wept.

God help me. I just don't know what to do.

You called for help? God's out today. I'm in. What seems to be the problem, twit?

The problem? The murders are abominable, horrible, but the pictures turn me on. How do I live with that? Now do you see the problem? I'm no better than the goddamned killer!

Killers have to come from somewhere, so why not you?

Are you serious?

Maybe this is how it begins. All it might take is one tiny missing piece, you know.

I'm not a criminal! You know that. I'm just... just a little crazy, that's all.

And the killer's not?

What should I do?

Don't kill anyone.

Don't kill anyone? You call that help?

Would you rather have me encourage the opposite? Some voices do that, you know.

Like the sensitive, compassionate men the college boys were, Sam's fraternity brothers complained about how hard it was to get a date that summer. None thought about what hell the murdered women had gone through or what hell the living ones now faced. Some of the guys speculated how to catch the killer and what they'd do to the bastard when they caught him. One forensic genius came up with a bold scheme to use his girlfriend as bait. She'd be seductively dressed and hitchhiking late at night while he and his buddies crouched behind the bushes, lying in ambush with baseball bats. The girlfriend declined the offer.

Sam had to do something about this, if not to save the twenty thousand young women in the county who were at risk, but to atone for his shame and derail a possibly ominous future. And late one evening, something presented itself. He was driving back from a party and saw a young woman hitchhiking alone in the other direction, the very thing she wasn't supposed to do. He thought she might as well hold up a sign reading "Stupid Bitch. Murder Me."

"Stupid bitch," he muttered and drove on.

Hold on here, twit. What if the killer saw her hitchhiking, picked her up and killed her? Then you'd be responsible, you coward, because you saw her and did nothing.

That's bullshit. That's total, paranoid bullshit.

Is it? It's happened before and could happen again, right? Then you'd have to live with it. Could you live with it?

Shit! Shit! Shit!

Sam abruptly braked, made an illegal U-turn, and drove back. Thank God she was still there and alive. Sam stopped alongside her.

"Do you need a lift?" he asked.

"Oh, yes," she said and hopped in the front seat. "Gee, thanks, you're a lifesaver."

If you only knew the truth, you stupid bitch.

Oh please, not here! Not now!

"I'm Sam."

"I'm Diane," she smiled.

Diane was slim and very pretty.

Very pretty murder fodder, isn't she?

Shut up!

I told you I will not shut up.

Okay, then, will you please be quiet?

Never.

"Are you a co-ed at the U?" Sam asked.

"Nope, I go to Mercy."

You'll get no mercy from me, bitch.

"Mercy? The girl's college?"

"The women's college," she smiled again.

Sam liked her smile. He wondered what Diane looked like naked.

Imagine her tits naked and bloody.

Please, don't do this.

You know you want it.

No! Not like this. Please!

"What about you?" Diane asked. "Do you go to the university?"

"Yeah. I'm a co-ed." Trying to stay focused was getting more difficult.

She laughed. "A co-ed?"

"Um, no, I'm a student, not a co-ed. A guy student." Sam winced at his eloquence.

"What's your major?"

Murdering stupid bitches like you.

"Biology," Sam said, the moment forcing him to pick one. He was gripping the steering wheel so hard his knuckles turned white. Diane didn't notice.

"Biology?" she replied. "Really? What a coincidence! So's mine. I'm studying to be a science teacher, maybe high school. That's why I'm at Mercy. It's the best teacher's college in the state. So what are you going to do after you graduate?"

I'm going to the gas chamber.

"Maybe graduate school," said Sam, trying to stay focused on both his driving and stability. "Actually, I'm thinking about teaching, too."

"Hey, that's really cool. Now that you're a co-ed and all, have you thought about switching to Mercy?"

"Not until now."

Diane gave him a sly smile.

Grab her now. Grab her when she's least expecting it.

No! No!

Go ahead, grab her and strangle her!

"Goddammit! Will you just shut the fuck up!"

Diane jumped in her seat. "What? What did you just say to me?"

Sam just stared at her, dumbstruck. "I, uh, jeez, I'm sorry—"

"Stop the car!" she screamed. "Stop the car right now!"

Diane had pressed herself tightly against the door, as far away from Sam as possible. He abruptly braked by a closed service station. She bolted from the car, leaving the door open, and disappeared into the darkness.

God Jesus! What the hell do you think you're doing?

What I do, twit. Jesus, you really, totally screwed that one up. I told you to be careful. Now she'll give the cops your description and license plate.

Oh no! Did she get the number?

Who knows? Hey, wouldn't that be ironic payback for your heroism? Imprisoned for a crime you tried to prevent.

You'll be in jail, too, you know.

I already am, in a way.

Sam made another U-turn and was able to drive home, somehow, though his mind was not on his driving but on its unhinged state and its increasingly ungovernable inhabitant. Now he was really worried. Worried about Diane and what she may do. More worried about going to jail, and worried crazy with fear for himself.

Adding to the serial-killer-obsessed, delusional drama already fomenting in his mind, Sam gave himself another problem. In his psychology class, he learned about a condition called dissociative identity disorder, commonly known as a multiple personality disorder. It was typically caused by a serious trauma in childhood and resulted in the person fragmenting into one or more distinct personalities, each having its own name, history, and behavior.

Even more curious, each personality was unaware of the others, although one usually emerged as dominant. Sam read that both psychologists and law enforcement agencies were still debating the legitimacy of the condition. There was no debate within him; he thought back to that schizoid conversation with Diane that had frightened the wits out of them both.

A little knowledge was a dangerous thing, especially to a brilliant guy like Sam. Given this new information and his attraction to deviance, he concluded that it was highly improbable, but still possible, he harbored multiple personalities, and one could be this serial killer. Why not? He'd had plenty of childhood traumas—it was just a matter of choosing which was the culprit. He already housed an intractable, capricious voice and a sadistic, insatiable goblin, so who knew what else lurked within?

Following a promising lead on the latest disappearance, the state police detectives descended on Sam's fraternity house. But they found the lead to be a dead end, concluding it was a case of mistaken identity. But the detectives were nothing if not thorough and planned to interrogate everyone in the fraternity on the slight chance the killer might be hiding among the brothers. After all, according to their latest reports, he looked just like one of them.

Sam grew increasingly nervous. The fact that he'd killed nobody proved nothing because multiple personalities have no memory or knowledge of the others. He reviewed the past few months searching for unexplained missing stretches of time. He found none, but it was possible that Killer Sam was out strangling co-eds while Normal Sam thought he was sleeping. But he didn't recall seeing any suspicious evidence, like blood under his fingernails, bites, scratches, and claw marks on his face—all the things that women did while being murdered. But maybe Killer Sam took painstaking care to clean everything up. He looked at his fingernails; they were freshly clipped, and, to his horror, he didn't remember doing it.

Now the police had found him. His paranoia ran amok. He felt the noose of circumstantial evidence tighten around his neck. Diane's eyewitness account must have been responsible. Maybe Amber had decided to offer her story as revenge. And now he duly regretted scaring that beer hall crumpet Beth with his machete gaffe.

The library! Suppose they discovered his check-out history and those books. *Shit!* Had he returned the latest book, *The History of Sex Murders*, or was it still in his desk, broadcasting his deviance like a radio station? The police were no dummies. They'd find out what he liked. They could smell a murderer a mile away. How could a mere nerd hide his sweating guilt from trained detectives desperate for a suspect? *It's over, case closed.*

Sam ran through the horrors of the impending calamity. Should he make a fast break for the back door and Canada? Should he first grab some food because who knew when he'd eat again? Where would he stay? How would he get money? Did Michigan have the death penalty? He'd never see another football game again. But wasn't there television in prison? Would any inmates be Lions fans? Would they sodomize him after the game and every night afterward?

Oh God. I promise I'll never wank off to goblins again.

Wanking is a little different from killing, twit. Don't make promises you can't keep, and don't make them to me. I'm not the one holding the gavel.

By the time they called Sam's name, he was ready to confess everything. Two detectives waited for him in the fraternity's den, a small, richly appointed room with plush sofas and dark wooden paneling. Photographs of the graduating classes of brothers lined the walls, seemingly eager to witness Sam's confession. It was far from a concrete interrogation room with a chair and a single harsh bulb, yet Sam worried himself into a frenzy, fearing an incriminating outburst similar to what had happened with Diane. It would be a fight to the death—his gas chamber death.

The detectives were polite and even seemed bored.

"Sam, do you remember what were you doing the night of May 24?" one asked.

I was out murdering co-eds, you dickhead, because I'm a multiple personality freak. See? Look how clean I got my fingernails afterward.

Please! Don't do this. Not now. I beg you!

Oh, I just can't help myself. And what better time than now?

"I'm sorry, but I don't remember," Sam said. He knew this answer hardly exonerated him, but at least it was honest. He didn't offer an explanation as to why he might not remember.

"Have you ever seen anyone in the fraternity act strangely?" the detective asked.

Everyone in the fraternity acts strangely, especially that deranged sex pervert Sam.

"No," Sam said, holding himself steady.

"Have you ever found anything unusual in the garbage?"

You bet. I dig through the garbage every night to hide the bloody bras and panties.

"No," Sam said.

"Does anyone ever come home late at night?"

Sam does, all covered with blood.

"Sometimes," said Sam.

"Does anyone ever take showers unusually late at night?"

Sam does, to wash off the blood, you fucking moron.

"Sometimes. It's a fraternity house," said Sam, his voice as dry as the Sahara.

"Sam, is there anything else you'd like to tell us?"

Sam froze. The second detective stopped taking notes and looked at him.

Tell them. Tell them the truth.

I can't!

They're not going to stop until they get it, twit!

"Sam?" said the first detective.

Sam could barely speak. "I didn't do it."

"Do what?"

"Kill all those women. I really didn't do it. I just…" *Oh shit. I'm dead.*

No, you're not. It'll just be life without parole.

Stop fucking with me, goddammit!

"You're just what, Sam?"

"It's just that, I know this is sick and wrong, but I think it's, um, kind of…"

"Arousing?" offered the detective.

Sam looked at his shoes and nodded.

"This is not the first time we've heard this," said the detective. "We know you didn't do it. You don't match the description we have. But we thought you might know something helpful. Do you?"

Sam shook his head, still looking down.

"Thank you for your cooperation, Sam. We're going to fingerprint you now. Don't be concerned, it's just a formality, part of the investigation, and then you're free to go."

Free to go. He was free to go. This nerve-racking, Kafka-esque nightmare was over. If the killer truly was him, they would have arrested him, right? But they hadn't and he was free to go. Sam's life came flooding back in one exhilarating whoosh. Multiple personalities, bloody bras, and crazy voices evaporated into the night like remnants of a bad dream. Sam looked at the photographs on the walls. One day his would be among them. He walked out of the den reborn.

Good job, twit, damn good job. You've earned your sanity merit badge.

Are you satisfied now? You almost got me thrown in jail.

No, I didn't. And I'll never be satisfied. And don't get too relaxed, either. They now have your fingerprints on file, as you know.

Oh, shit. What will they do?

Whatever they want, of course.

Sam's relief wasn't complete until they caught the real killer six months later. He was a college student like Sam, and the same age. In fact, their birthdays were just two days apart. Those who knew him thought him shy, quiet, and well-mannered. He was linked to fifteen of the murdered women, probably killed nine, definitely killed seven, and was imprisoned for life for killing one.

But they didn't really know him, did they? No one really knows me either.

I know you, Sam.

Am I crazy?

No more than I am. Think about what that means.

8

ADDICTION

ALTHOUGH HE'D BEEN ONE MOST OF his life, Sam could never call himself an artist. That's because in his dictionary, an artist is someone who perceives the world and projects it through his passions, skills, and paint, so the world could see itself in a new way. Or the artist stands before his easel and let his spontaneity and joy run free, so the world could see the artist view the world in a new way.

But Sam was neither of those people and harbored a massive grudge against those who were. He considered art a self-absorbed indulgence by self-deluded narcissists who called their vanity a thousand different names except the true one. And "art for art's sake" was just a slick slogan created by the marketing department of some art supply company.

Sam's cynicism did not arise from an exhaustive study of art and the human condition, but from knowing *real* artists were much better than him—were getting better every day—and he'd never catch up. That was an intolerable situation for anyone's art, or vanity, or whatever it was called. He also knew he'd have slim chance of becoming recognized and experiencing all the treasures that vanity in particular was famous for dishing out, so what was the point of doing art? The fact that he even asked that question confirmed his delinquency.

He hadn't always felt that way. His first drawings were gleefully birthed on the margins of his middle school notebooks. Whereas most boys drew rocket ships, jet airplanes, superheroes, and unreasonably vicious military ordnance, and the girls sketched horses, Sam was attracted to the possibilities of the morbid and macabre. Comic books were his first form of art education. Super-, Bat-, and Aquaman were studs all right, but being heroic and studly were just not enough. *Tales of Horror* was more his speed.

Aided by *Tales*, his imagination, and the anatomical drawings in his family's encyclopedia, Sam depicted in explicit detail all the ways a human body could be deconstructed, specifically without anesthetics. Most of his victims looked like him, which curiously didn't concern him. His artistic joy arose not from the act of creation, but from the uproar it would hopefully cause. If he'd known to ask why, Descartes would have given him a clue. *Exterreo ergo sum.* I shock, therefore I am.

Soon his notebooks contained more drawings than class notes. With each new work, he tried to strike deeper into the heart of decency, and to his mind—and satisfaction—he always succeeded. He acquired a following of boys in his classes who were eager to see what atrocity he'd come up with next, and he always delivered. He became known as the class ghoul—his first taste of fame, and a sweet one. After all, being a ghoul was better than being a nobody.

Sam's gory masterpieces also attracted the attention of several teachers (including Miss Miller), his parents, and eventually the school district psychologist, who sought to understand why such monstrosities would dwell inside this kid. Having no benchmark for normalcy, artistic or otherwise, Sam couldn't imagine what the problem was but accepted there must be one and sullenly complied with the battery of tests and evaluations he was given. After being thoroughly shamed by the adults, he continued decapitating and eviscerating his teachers and classmates on paper but wisely kept the art to himself, a bitter consolation.

In high school, Sam gave up the ghoul and turned to more conventional art. He learned mechanical drafting, followed by scientific illustration in college. Soon after graduation, he found his niche as a freelance illustrator. The jobs were plentiful, the money was okay, but something vital was missing, like owning a car without an engine.

He knew what it was. The ghoul kept pacing the floor of his cranium without rest, giving him no rest either. He remembered his middle school monsters with fondness and the notoriety they'd earned for him. Drawing hydraulic systems and extinct mollusk shells for a living, he realized, would never take him where he desperately wanted to go. But becoming a fine artist would, as it should.

That's when the trouble started. Sam launched into his new art career by handicapping himself with two burdens. One, he rejected the importance of practice. Whether that arose from laziness or impatience was unimportant. He was not willing to pay his dues, and his artwork showed it. And two, he opted to be self-taught. Art school, he rationalized, murdered one's initiative and creativity, and he would not become the clone of some failed artist-turned-art instructor. Instead, he'd define his art on his own terms, as all true genius artists did.

As had been the case for artists throughout the millennia, Sam found his inspiration in nature. Everywhere he looked he saw a painting: from the cosmic to the mundane, from etheric tableaus of sunset-lit clouds to the wondrous miniature worlds under a leaf on a forest floor. Long walks in the woods and shores with his camera filled him with awe and reverence for the natural world, and in response Gaia shed her vestments and let him behold her bounty.

And that was fine until he tried to replicate on canvas what his camera and heart saw; he failed with reliable regularity. That's because his genius art education was limited to the tried-and-true trial-and-error method, followed by the let's-paint-and-maybe-something-good-will-accidentally-happen method. That was like learning how to operate a car by flipping every switch on the dashboard until the engine started. What to do next would presumably be taught the following semester.

But art cannot be ignored. Using this haphazard approach, Sam experimented with media and techniques, always hoping for a breakthrough in style and a doorway to fame. Occasionally a successful painting would randomly emerge, but the problem would then be that he had no idea how he'd done it. Many of his paintings were aborted in fits of brush-snapping, profanity-hurling, foot-stomping rage, to the distress of his religious neighbor downstairs, who wondered what kind of soul would pray to Jesus Fucking Christ.

Soon Sam dreaded going to his easel for fear of confronting his inadequacy. He finally acknowledged that paintings would never magically drip from his brush as they so easily did in animation studios. No, they had to be carefully and mindfully constructed—a practice he was reluctant to embrace. The real world could sure be a pain in the ass. At times the only reason he endured the misery of working at his easel was because he felt more miserable avoiding it. Making art was not supposed to feel this way. What was wrong?

The answer came one cold, rainy, and dreary Saturday night that once again found Sam dateless, lonely, bored, depressed, and horny—the basic ingredients for another session of erotic fantasy and whatever happened next. But that prospect saddened him even more, and he found himself once again staring at his empty easel with hard loathing. Easels were supposed to be portals into joy, not walls to bash your head against. Anger joined his hatred. Anger at his incompetence, his impotence, and his utter lack of drive.

Sam knew about the muses of Greek myth, and the inspiration and torment they traditionally visited upon artists. Even if muses weren't stories, he'd never considered that he'd ever had one, assuming no muse in her right mind would abet his twisted artistic shenanigans.

What the hell, maybe I do need a muse. I need something, damn it!

"Fuck!" he screamed at full volume, because screaming was the only thing it seemed he could do at the moment. He knew this probably wasn't the best way to summon a muse. He also knew his downstairs neighbor was not home. "Fuck! Fuck! *Fuck!*"

No muse showed up, but at least the unhinged screaming made him feel better. Then a startling thought occurred to him: *why not use the best of my abilities to animate the hottest of my sexual fantasies?* Sam could feel the fires of his creativity being stoked. He remembered the monsters in his middle school notebooks. Definitely portals to joy, as he recalled. Why not give them tits and genitals and let them have some fun? Fun art, not great art, for a blessed change. Oh, hell yes. *Muse? Who needs a muse?*

The idea worked. Fun art. And first-rate fun art, not the crude, furtive scrawls that had adorned the toilet stall doors in high school. Carpe diem, it was called. Seize the day. Why not? He could always seize the dick later. Fueled by this intoxicating brew of possibility, erotic spice, and daring, Sam set out to carpe some diem.

He didn't have to look far for inspiration, only back in time. One day, at age six, he had been perusing his family's newly purchased encyclopedia, each page being a wondrous revelation. He had the world at his fingertips, and the world could work in mysterious ways. Encyclopedias brim with information on every subject; that's their job. Nothing was meant to be overtly erotic, especially in the sexually repressed Fifties, yet no one could have predicted the book's potential for creating trouble.

In *Volume N-P*, Sam came across the myth of the Greek titan Prometheus. According to this version, Zeus, king of the gods, sent

Prometheus and his brother, Epimetheus, to the earth on a mission: to bestow upon each creature a gift that would enable it to survive and prosper. The tortoise got its shell, the hare its swiftness, the tiger its teeth, and so on. But their gift bag was empty when the brothers got to the humans. "Tough luck, folks," said Zeus, as the supreme god was not famous for his charity.

Not so with Prometheus. He took pity on the shivering, defenseless people and gave them fire. This absolutely enraged Zeus. As punishment, Prometheus was chained to a high mountain ledge where Zeus, in the form of an eagle, would descend upon the titan, tear open his belly, devour his liver, and fly away. At night the wound would heal, only to be ravaged again the following day. The length of the sentence was eternity. But Hercules, who happened to be passing by, took pity on the suffering Prometheus, shot the eagle with an arrow, and freed him. Zeus had his own plans for Hercules, which could be found in *Volume G-I.*

The myth was irrelevant; the illustration was the hook, instantly igniting a spark in Sam's preadolescent groin and fertile imagination. He could not peel his eyes from the naked and magnificently muscled Prometheus straining at his bonds, his face contorted in agony while the eagle tore into his flesh. Sam became indelibly entranced, inexplicably aroused, and utterly envious of the titan's predicament. If his tiny testicles had been up to it, he likely would have come. He was puzzled by the tassel on the tip of Prometheus's penis, as his own had none, and wondered why the eagle didn't chew on that.

The magnetism of that illustration drew little Sam secretly back to that page many times, never failing to induce a proto-erotic trance. Time had not diminished its erotic stranglehold, and it still served as the template for many of Adult Sam's fantasies. On this bleak Saturday night, he decided to blatantly sexualize the myth, as this was his party. He taped a drawing board to his nemesis easel and then just stared at it.

Giving yourself another problem, twit?

This is wrong.

Everything you do is wrong, so what else is new?

It's about sex.

Sex is wrong?

Mine is.

And you think you can make it right by sitting there and staring at your easel? Now this should be interesting.

Okay. Sam changed the eagle into a winged woman, as uncompromisingly sadistic and vindictive as Zeus, who coveted Prometheus' penis instead of his liver, naturally. Sam restrained the titan more comfortably and blessed him with an enormous erection. In Sam's myth, the woman-eagle would fly to Prometheus's mountain ledge, hump his priapic cock to ribbons, and, satisfied, she'd fly away. Every night his cock would heal and grow hard. She'd return the next morning and shred away all day long, for eternity, with no Hercules to spoil the fun. *Oh my, yes.*

Sam also shared Prometheus's boner and struggled to keep his left hand from his crotch as he drew with the right. He had what could only be called a sustained hour-long dry orgasm and was rewarded with a fine piece of artwork instead of a sticky puddle. Who needed a date on Saturday night? She was right here on paper and would do anything he wanted.

So what about me? I'll do anything you want. Anything. You know that.

Yeah, but here I'm *in charge.*

Are you really? Then go ahead and charge. Are you ever in for a surprise!

Sam knew he was onto something, but he didn't know what or where it would take him. Even if he had known, it wouldn't have mattered. Let the other fine and talented artists paint masterpieces of ineffable beauty and wonder. He had bigger, sexier fish to fry and he knew just the pond in which to fish.

The following night he painted a portrait of his penis. It was the ultimate vanity and he didn't care. Although his cock had been the main focus of his life for sixteen years, he'd never looked at it closely. Now he did so with the eye of an artist. The organ was truly a beautiful and miraculous thing, a natural architectural wonder of curves and swells covered in venous parchment. The creature subtly shifted beneath its skin, as if it were breathing and had a life of its own.

But Sam needed to make this beautiful thing suffer for causing him such grief. In the next portrait, he chained up and imprisoned the engorged flesh in the Dungeon of Eternal Pain, now his second most favorite playground. And again, the act of drawing it turned him on, not only for its eroticism but also because it was flavored with the thrill of challenging the forbidden.

Sam liked where this new adventure was going. In the third painting, he pierced the miraculous thing's head with a gold ring and made it scream. Although he didn't know it at the time, he'd drawn a popular male genital piercing called the Prince Albert, named after Queen Victoria's royal consort. According to the story, Prince Albert needed a way to affix his member down his pants to keep it from springing up whenever he saw the lovely monarch, although being affixed like that probably made it much springier.

Then Sam went after the women. A bound maiden lay on a red velvet pillow, entranced and excited, as she awaited a serpent's invasion of her sex and her initiation into womanhood. The next piece showed a woman tied to a post as a huge python approached with the same agenda. For every piece he completed, several more ideas popped up, each more salacious than the previous. He had to make a list. Without realizing it, Sam had strolled into the goblin's torture chamber and was taking pictures.

The possibilities sent him reeling... until one day when he drew a bound and gagged woman hanging from an iron rack with her legs spread wide, helplessly watching an improbable, sinister machine chew into her sex. He looked into the frightened eyes of his victim, trapped and suffering on paper for all time, and was taken aback. This was still wrong, very wrong.

Sam finally admitted he didn't know how to make this kind of sex right, but at least he could stop making it wronger. He stuffed his new art into a folder, taped it shut, and put it in the back of the coat closet, the traditional prison for anything sexually anomalous. He then turned his focus back to nature, hopefully seeking a return to her graces. To his relief, he discovered that nature could be infinitely forgiving, and this time he'd be worthy of her benevolence. And to his surprise and elation, his dip into the sex pond had dramatically improved his artistic skills. The disparity between what he saw in life and what appeared on canvas was growing smaller, and the five-to-one failure-to-success ratio had been reversed.

Mountains became massive, glittering crystals thrust up through the green loam of their forested foothills. Colossal, towering banks of cumulus clouds collided with each other in an aerial lover's embrace of majestic proportions. A rhododendron flower blossomed into a pink and crimson boudoir for a honeybee. The signs couldn't be clearer. Sam felt endowed with a special gift, an ordination from a higher source for some grand design in the universe. The way was open and the shining path led to fame, fortune, and, presumably, redemption.

A special gift from the universe? Oh, please, spare me. This is why you call artists narcissists. Specialness can sure be a powerful narcotic, can't it?

Well, my ideas come from somewhere.

And you think this universe of yours gets off on drawings of sex machines? Does the universe know what goes on in your bedroom at night?

But my new work has transcended all that. It's about spirit, not sex.

Oh? There's a difference? And it's absolutely fizzing with sex! Thrusting mountains, pink rhododendron boudoirs, and clouds groping each other. Open your eyes, twit!

Why are you making this such a problem?

You're the one making it a problem. I'm simply pointing it out.

There is no damn problem!

Indeed. Why don't you ask that chained-up lady of yours if there's a problem?

I just may do that.

Listen, Sam, I know what goes on in your bedroom at night, and I don't care.

Sam stared at the closet door, fearing what waited inside and fearing more what it might have to tell him. He had to know. He retrieved the folder from its prison. The sex-machine-ravaged woman was still there and suffering. He removed her gag.

"You scum!" she screamed. "You evil, corrupt, degenerate bastard! You get turned on by seeing me helpless and crying in pain? What does that do for you, you chicken-shit sexist bully?"

The gag immediately went back on.

This wasn't what he'd expected or wanted to hear. He looked through the artwork, scenes of the goblin's torture chamber, with growing apprehension. It was clear his victims had things to say to him—things that did not speak well of him or his diseased ambitions. He remembered how his first dip into the pond filled him with such joy and possibility—not to mention the fiery eroticism. Somehow, it all had been shunted into the sewers. He resolved the issue by shoving the folder back into its prison cell. *Art can be ignored—at least, some of it.*

Art now comprised Sam's entire world, and he could ignore none of it. His day job was freelance illustration—doing any odd job he could scrounge up, like drawing circuit boards, ketchup bottles, and diagrams of prairie dog burrows. At night, he threw himself back into his mainstream art like a fire tearing through a tinderbox. His once-dormant easel now birthed majestic cloud massifs, magic crystal mountains, and ghost-like cranes dancing under a fluorescent full moon. After a while, he could draw circuit boards and prairie dogs with his eyes closed—and some looked like he had—but at least they paid the bills. In compensation, the moons and mountains fed his dreams, but soon those dreams turned into nightmares.

One reason for that immediately became clear: he was an authoritative, merciless, and unmitigated prick to work for. Boss Sam allowed no weekends, no vacations, no breaks, no benefits, and, of course, no money. Nothing he painted was good enough, and if he did manage to occasionally satisfy Boss Sam, Boss Universe took over, who was just as displeased, harsh, and critical. Making matters worse, Sam attended an exhibition of visionary artwork that made his best work look like a child's finger painting. Both bosses landed hard on his ass for that one. *Some life as an artist,* he sulked.

The other reason for his self-inflicted torment was just as clear—and exasperating. A naked pixie, eager to be tied up and mistreated, was constantly sitting by his ear whispering, "Draw me! Draw me next!"

"I'm sorry," Sam said, "I've got more important things to do."

"Aren't I important?"

"No! You're about lust and sex and perversion."

"What's wrong with that? Jeez, dude, that's all you think about day and night."

"Go away and don't bother me!"

"Come on, just draw me and I promise to leave you alone," wheedled the pixie. "Please draw me, *pleeeeease*?"

"Then you'll go away?"

"Sure. For at least twenty seconds."

Okay. Sam quickly drew a woman, arms bound behind her, straddling a rough fiber rope that sawed into her crotch.

"Oooh, that felt really good!" the pixie cried. "I love it! What's next?"

This was not right. Sam started painting a magical crystal mountain, but another pixie and then a goblin showed up in the waiting room, and they did not like waiting. He drew them doing unspeakable things to each other. Now, back to the mountain.

"Not so fast," said more pixies and goblins as they elbowed each other to be next in line.

"Hey! You can't serve two masters," Boss Sam said to the oppressed Minion Sam.

"Then serve us," said the pixie. "We give you a better time, don't we?"

The thing had a point.

BUT LURKING JUST BEHIND THE PIXIE was a different kind of goblin, not one of Sam's but belonging to another artist, and it promised thrills far more exciting. When he was fourteen, after *The Torture of the Bound Nudes* had been etched into his soul, he didn't suspect there were more bound nudes out there. But as an adult he knew differently, and he knew just where to find them. All it took was resolve, money, and courage—resources not abundant in his world.

Two other obstacles blocked Sam from buying pornography. One, he assumed he'd have to devolve into a degenerate creep to buy porn because that's who bought porn. He envisioned himself and his fellow creeps wallowing in the fetid backwaters of the city, scuttling from one porn shop to another, always with one hand in their pocket fondling away. And if they weren't creeps to begin with, porn would soon make them that way. Sam wasn't quite ready to accept this fate, as if anyone ever was. One day you just found yourself there.

The second obstacle: Sam feared that once he started consuming porn, he'd never stop.

It would prove to be true. In that day, pornography was not a simple mouse click away. One had to hunt for it on foot, and the forests could be dangerous. Sam discovered a seedy-looking adult bookstore in the seedy part of town, and a quick, furtive peek inside set the hook. He knew right away he could not unfind what he'd just found. The naked porn maidens on the magazine covers became the sirens on the rocks calling out to his Odysseus. Their enchanting songs plagued him day and night, and he knew he'd have to return.

But when? When he grew the courage. But when would that be? When he decided, he decided. After a week of perseverating and being unable to mute the sirens' songs, he finally set a date for a porn raid for the coming Saturday morning. That entire week he could think of nothing else. He swore his body was growing more nerve cells just for his anxiety to fry. To settle them down and allay his wickedness, he decided to solidify his intention.

Your intention? I see. This is now in the name of self-examination?

Ah, well, I...

Or to convince yourself that porn is ultimately corrupt and not fit for consumption?

Well, I, ah...

Or how low can you go?

I, ah, well...

So much for rock-solid intentions. Logistical problems had to be addressed. That was the easy part. As if he were planning a bank heist, Sam made meticulous preparations. He'd already scoped out the parking options to minimize the distance he'd have to carry the booty on foot. He bought a full tank of gas to cover the six-mile drive. Then he had to justify the expense, figuring an average porn purchase would equal two restaurant dinners. He could live with that.

Or a movie date with a chick?

Yeah! Except now I can have all the dates I want, and sex is guaranteed!

You bet it is. In fact, you now have a choice of dates: left hand or right.

Leave me alone!

Absolutely. I have no intention of watching this.

On the morning of the designated day, Sam was too jittery to eat breakfast. He hadn't been struck by lightning nor hit by a bus during the week, so he assumed God had given him the green light, was too busy, or didn't consider the matter worth worrying about. He headed to the bank for cash, as checks and credit cards were traceable. As the teller counted out the bills, her frown seemed to say, "Only men needing cash to buy pornography would come in so early on a Saturday morning, sir."

Sam found a parking space, but a block farther away than he wanted—not a good omen. Heading for the store, he was certain his intentions were clearly visible to all passersby who would mistake his anxious skulking for nothing else. Heart aflutter, he walked into the store holding his breath as if entering a fouled bathroom. Once inside, he instantly saw the reason for the whole ordeal: shelves and racks filled with luscious, forbidden, naked sex of every quirk, flavor, and description.

Sam resumed his normal breathing. He was vaguely aware of the other men perusing the magazine racks, hovering like ghosts before their particular curses. Everyone kept to themselves, preserving the anonymity that veteran porn browsers afforded one another. He wandered the aisles, pretending to be interested in the racks of skimpy lingerie, displays of male masturbation contraptions, and a locked glass case filled with dildos and anal toys looking like a platoon of little rubber-armored aliens, all mustered up and ready to dive into action.

He finally settled before his real objective: the nudie magazines. They were encased in plastic sheaths to discourage browsing and prevent the pages from becoming stuck together. The covers showed variations of skanky, naked women doing skanky things to themselves and each other. He soon found it boring; if you've seen one naked boob, you've seen them all, but you keep looking anyway.

What caught Sam's eye like a fishhook was a magazine subtly titled *Big Tits in Bondage.* The model on the cover, naked from the waist up, her lips frozen in a posed grimace of pain, was bound to a chair, arms behind her, with rope tightly coiled around her large, pendulous breasts, proving the title of the magazine did not lie. Sam paid for the magazine without looking the clerk in the eye, and scurried home with his precious cargo, immensely pleased with himself to have pulled off the entire escapade.

Once safely in his apartment, the door locked, deadbolt thrown, window shades drawn, and phone unplugged, Sam feasted. The innards of the magazine were variations on the cover with the same model, not that it mattered. In one pose, she agonized over clothespins on her nipples. He savored every photograph, paragraph, and punctuation mark.

At day and night's end, his penis looked like a kielbasa that had been left on the grill too long. He came at least five times—he'd lost count, amazed that his balls had been up to the task. Then, overcome with self-loathing and disgust, he stuffed the rumpled magazine into the garbage can, covered it with detritus from the refrigerator to discourage snooping trash collectors and the vice squad, and vowed never again. He kept that vow until the following Saturday morning. He was hooked.

On the next raid, Sam brought home *Beavers in Bondage,* the exciting sequel to *Big Tits.* It was a different model, though with the same poses and same enormous breasts, giving the same results, and then into a different bag of garbage. Next, he sampled something more elevated: literature. *The Chateau of Cruel Bondage* was a profusely and amateurishly illustrated story about men and women held captive as sex slaves in an isolated mansion run by a cadre of beautiful, sadistic dominatrices. Their victims were subjected to a whole catalogue of humiliations and tortures, each clumsily documented and accompanied by an equally tacky drawing. The most outlandish showed two harnessed male slaves pulling a carriage driven by a snarling, whip-wielding dominatrix; their efforts were compensated by huge, spurting erections. This was erotic? Something about *Chateau* made Sam feel small and cheap.

Another novel, *Sin Sisters*, told of a secret sorority that kept naked college boys chained up in its basement dungeon to service the girls' desires. Padlocks around their balls kept the guys captive, and tough shit if they missed a class. This book got Sam hot because it was not that far removed from possibility—or so he needed to believe. He fervently longed to find these isolated chateaus and licentious sororities and stay there forever. But in the clarity of mind that usually followed an orgasm, he'd see the vapid and phantom promises of pornography.

Because once a photograph has been seen or a story read, its erotic power inevitably fades, which means the consumer has to keep buying more porn, as the publishers were well aware. Sam had become enslaved by the classic addictive cycle: indulgence, shame, and then more indulgence to alleviate the shame. After devouring all the magazines and books he could afford, he still needed more fixes. His binge drove him to visit the few remaining porn theaters in town, a vanishing venue due to the advent of VHS tapes. Any movie suggesting it contained scenes of bondage and sadomasochism caught his immediate interest.

One such film he couldn't resist was an adaptation of the popular and seminal novel about sadomasochism, *The Story of O*. The book's beautiful heroine, known only by her initial, surrenders herself to a dominant gentleman in a large country mansion maintained for those pursuits. This was no cheap fuck book but a legitimate erotic novel, one of the few with an engaging plot and, more astonishing, competent writing. But the movie version told a different story, one with minimal plot and zero cinematic merit but lots of whip-reddened skin. Cruelty never looked so staged.

Sam was one of about a dozen men in the theater, each choosing his seat to maximize the distance between one another for privacy while masturbating. The floor was sticky, and he knew it wasn't chewing gum. Sam found nothing about the movie arousing, and he almost fell asleep. What woke him was his row of seats shaking in time with the stroking being done by the fellow at the far end. Back home, Sam threw his shoes into the garbage.

After his long, sweaty, sticky journey into the palaces of pornography, Sam returned to the place from which he'd started, just as frustrated and empty as when he'd left. The addictive cycle seemed to have finally burned itself out as well as burning up his bank account, leaving him sexually bereft, exhausted, disillusioned, sorely blistered, and with no remaining viable or reasonable options.

"Psst," whispered that pixie into his ear. "Remember what you decided about doing fun art for a change? I'm still here, hot, horny, and waiting."

Why not? It had been a while since he had indulged the pixies on paper, and he had lots more paper. What had really bugged him during his tortured odyssey into pornography was how bad the art was, and he'd seen enough to know. He knew he could do much better.

This was excellent news for the pixies and goblins who buffed up their bodies and waited impatiently for their numbers to be called. It was a brilliant plan. Unlike his first venture into the sex pond, which had birthed some remarkable paintings, this trip would have no such lofty ambitions. He would become his own custom pornographer, applying his skills to animating his most depraved fantasies. He had a bottomless pit of them, and boy would he ever cream! Not to mention all the money he'd save.

So began *Sam's Chateau of Cruel Bondage.* He became like a tyrannical god of antiquity: sadistic, capricious, and corrupt, and subjecting his terrified subjects to every whim and want without mercy. The men got the worst of it, because that's what they deserved, that's what Sam liked, and a model was always available in the mirror.

Drawing women was more problematic as no woman in her right mind would pose for such scenes. Sam used sketches from the few life drawing classes he'd taken to cut and paste body parts to fit the desired scenes. At this he completely failed, though; the lifeless ladies looked like they'd been cut out and pasted together. All Sam got was remorse for what he was doing to these poor women who didn't deserve it. Shamed by his own cartoon victims—how sad was that?

But art could not be ignored. One drawing begat another and the floodgates opened, disgorging a steaming effluvium of kinky sex onto paper. But Sam ran into an unexpected and puzzling snag: his new custom porn didn't steam him up in the least. Although birthed in erotic fire, the images lay there: flat, flaccid, and taunting him with their impotence. He'd come over far cruder drawings in magazines, so why weren't these working?

Had Sam attended art school, he would have learned that the power of art rests not in what it shows but what it suggests. The best example was

Leonardo da Vinci's *Mona Lisa*, perhaps the most entrancing painting of our time and for that reason. Sam's masterpiece was a little different: his Mona was tightly bound with clothespins on her nipples, suggesting nothing and showing everything. She was also smiling, albeit for other reasons. But she did absolutely nothing for Sam because there was nothing left to imagine.

"That's exactly right," she said. "In your mind's eye you tied me up, tortured me, and then drew me. The eroticism can never be more than what you visualized, only less. It can't cycle back on itself. I can do nothing more for you. But if another artist draws my big tits in bondage, you get to see something new, no matter how crudely it's done. The scene gives you the thrill, and the artist gets nothing but his pitiful commission."

Sam pressed on, thinking the ultimate in artistic autoeroticism would eventually emerge. He left no scene behind and everything uncensored. He vowed he'd never make any of it public, so that gave him liberty to visit every virtual brothel and dungeon imaginable to explore their most aberrant extremes.

But it was a journey into disappointment. The erotic fire Prometheus had given him quickly burned out because, as he discovered, the thrill was in the process, not the product. As his bound and nipple-pinched Mona warned, trying to use his own smut for arousal put his cock to sleep. Every time.

Didn't I warn you, twit?

And there was a mosquito in the dark that would not give him peace. He uneasily eyed his growing stack of artwork. It was tainted and he knew why: it was porn and therefore wrong. He knew it was wrong because of all the endless debates he had with himself to make it right.

"Pornography damages women," he'd heard women say. "It objectifies, dehumanizes, debases, and victimizes us. It inflames the entitlement of male privilege to the point where sexual abuse is tolerated, even admired and exported for entertainment."

"But everybody obsesses on something," Sam wanted to reply. "Even you women. Think about your addiction to shopping and chocolate. Why single out sex? Think about that, ladies!"

"Because sex looks like us," insisted women. "It is us. It has a heart and a brain and a life. It's not a commodity you can simply go out and buy. Or steal."

"You can't take away my fun!" Sam continued to object. "It's my right to enjoy my cock! And if porn helps, then so be it!"

"But at our expense? How'd you feel if everywhere you looked there were photographs of naked men? Naked men in magazines, in the movies, and on television? Men getting tied up, kicked in the groin, pegged up the ass, and tortured to death? How safe would you feel on the streets? And suppose there were creeps who actually did all these things, and not just to the fucking perverts who fantasize about it. Think about that, guys!"

Ahem. In a weekly TV magazine, Sam once counted eleven promotional ads for crime dramas that showed beautiful, half-naked dead women posing seductively on the floor in their last mortal acts. The point of these socially responsible programs was to demonstrate that crime didn't pay, no matter how appealing they could make it look.

But something wasn't right here. Sam knew that women were people just like himself, and they were not placed on earth merely as sex toys for his indulgence. He knew everything they said about pornography was true. And he knew he was fighting both those facts tooth and nail. Why? What about this had him by the throat and wouldn't let go? This wasn't just his penis calling all the shots.

On a whim, he leafed through his History of Art textbook from school, a massive tome whose previous contribution to his life had been to block cockroaches from coming up through an air vent on the floor. Not sure what he was looking for, he focused on paintings of nude women. The majority of nude males were consigned to Greek statuary and Michaelangelo murals.

Sam was intrigued by the section on odalisque paintings, a genre depicting pleasantly zaftig nude women, the epitome of the feminine form in that day, reclining unabashedly on lush divans surrounded by ornate, exotic trappings. Some were alone, others were attended by female slaves or a eunuch or two.

This was a minor rage in early nineteenth-century European art, when painting naked, white, Christian women was taboo. Whereas painting naked, non-Christian women, such as concubines in a Turkish harem, despite their being just as white, would be less offensive to the general public. Being inoffensive was not the point of odalisque art; it was a way to slip soft-core porn under the pre-Victorian radar. Or was it art? Sam wondered if those artists had mired themselves in the same conflicted drama as his own.

He turned to the chapter on Renaissance art. The centerpiece, of course, was *Mona Lisa*. As a rule, printed reproductions can't come close to the impact of the original work, but with Mona it didn't matter. Sam immediately fell into that smile, a smile that could lead to anything.

"What are you suggesting rather than showing, my dear?" he said aloud.

"What do you think?" the real Mona replied. "That I'm inviting you over for a game of badminton? My smile means anything you'd like, and we both know what you like. Does that make me porn? Should I show you some tit as well so you'd get the picture?"

"Jeez, of course not. You're great artwork. The greatest."

"But it seems I can turn on groins as well as minds, as you recently attested."

"Don't say that! That's absurd."

"Really? What about that lonely little man in his garret who, like you, thinks my smile was meant only for him. And that gets him so juiced he grabs his pecker and pumps. Isn't that what pornography is supposed to do? That's probably happened to a number of lonely little men in the past five hundred years. Why do you think they keep me behind glass?"

"Well, um..."

"And what about that illustration of Prometheus in your encyclopedia? Remember what that did to you as a child? Did the publishers find a way to sneak some homoerotic bondage porn past the censors? And is that any different from hanging paintings of naked harem girls in public art museums? It kind of confuses the issue, doesn't it?"

Right. Sam placed the drawing of his sex-machine-ravaged victim on the book next to *Mona Lisa*. The differences between the two pieces couldn't be more startling and obvious, but now there might be similarities as well. Not in the rendering, of course, but in the intention of the artist, the sensibilities of the viewer, the mores of the times, and what was currently trendy in the art world. How should those considerations be ranked in terms of aesthetic worth and social relevance? And was it even necessary to rank them at all? More troubled than ever, Sam closed the book.

After a particularly heinous mass shooting, Sam watched a video of a gun owner destroying his AR-15 assault rifle, the same rifle the army issued to its soldiers explicitly to kill people. "Now this gun will never kill anyone," said its owner, proudly holding up the pieces. Sam was impressed by the man's integrity and resolve, as were many others appalled by the murders. Seventeen souls had paid the price for someone else's Second Amendment rights.

Sam wondered about his First Amendment rights. He didn't want any part of porn world, yet he kept finding himself inexorably contributing to it. Would his drawings become like assault bullets with unlimited range, power, and duration? Would they send an impressionable pubescent boy spinning off into deviance like himself? Or pull the last hinge pin from the already unhinged and contribute to the gruesome death of another woman?

He looked at his machine victim, now with remorse. How many hinge pins did he have when he had drawn her? He could not rescue her—the deed had been done. But he could save her innocent sisters. In a fit of rage that had been festering for weeks, Sam destroyed the entire folder, fifty drawings—fifty sex rifles—lest they damage anyone else.

What insipid drama! What narcissism! What an impetuous and stupid thing to do. Are you going to burn all the encyclopedias and art history books as well? Do you really think you've accomplished anything with that vain, feeble gesture?

Yes! I've done a good thing, a decent thing.

Pah! You think you've cured yourself by disposing of the symptoms.

No! I've stopped adding more filth to an already filthy culture.

But your filth remains. You'll be at it again. Remember, twit, art cannot be ignored.

9

VIRIDIAN

SAM INDEED WENT AT IT AGAIN. He began two distinctly different portfolios of artwork, albeit with trepidation. One he filled with crystalline mountains, cosmic starscapes, sylvan faeries, and the like, which fell into the vaguely defined genre known as "visionary art" that was now in vogue. He called it his "above-the-waist artwork." His erotic art portfolio—below-the-waist, naturally—grew at a much faster pace, and this time he vowed to keep it.

But now the "below" art witnessed a change. Sam was still uneasy about drawing sex rifles pointed at women. His debate about the definition of porn had been inconclusive and confusing and was likely to remain that way. He resolved the issue by simply declaring it unresolvable. He also changed the genders of his victims to male, which seemed less criminal and more socially acceptable but was still a spineless strategy. That worked when he was fourteen, although what "worked" meant was debatable. But at least his drawings would no longer shame and scold him.

He'd also lost interest in extruding custom porn, knowing it led nowhere, but now painted simply to see what was roaming around his libido. In essence, he gave the goblins and pixies the run of the store. He tried to see his art now as mirrors, and despite not entirely understanding what they reflected, the more he viewed them as such, the less disturbing they were.

Soon both portfolios had grown too full and were too good to just sit in his studio and rot in the dark. It was *carpe diem* time again: time for a gallery show. Sam culled the best of his above-the-waist art and chose three relatively tame pieces from below. Now where to pitch them? He immediately rejected the prominent, well-established galleries before they could get a chance to reject him, as he had neither the name, recognizable style, nor the talent to attract the big buyers. The lesser-known galleries were also out, as they needed well-known names, styles, and talents to bolster their reputations.

Sam had noticed several storefront galleries run as pastimes by people looking more to hobnob among the aesthetes than to make reputations and money. Although more accessible to new artists, these places came and went with the seasons and were notorious for folding before paying their artists. Sam finally found a likely and respectable venue in the Galerie Outré, a gallery that specialized in showing the recently emerging genre called "outsider art." Its philosophy seemed to be that gems often lay hidden in the manure, and who cared about reputations?

"Outsider art," Sam learned, was the term applied to artists not part of the mainstream art world, but who were self-taught, idiosyncratic, and followed the beat of their own brushes. Galerie Outré was one of several businesses occupying a renovated warehouse as part of the city's urban renaissance program. The building also housed small bookstores, trendy boutiques, espresso cafés, furniture galleries, and artists' lofts. Bohemia never looked artier.

Sam attended an afternoon opening of one of Galerie's exhibitions to see what lurked on the outside. After a very disjointed conversation with the featured painter, Sam concluded that outsider artists needn't be part of the real world either. He thought the man's work was awful, populated with crude, cartoonish figures, hurriedly rendered and without any thought given to perspective, form, or complimentary colors. But the paintings were awful in an oddly endearing way and thus worthy of a place on the wall. Success in the art world, Sam sourly concluded, was meant for really good artists and really bad ones. The rest needed day jobs.

Sam spotted a late-thirties, well-dressed, and important-looking woman he presumed was the gallery's owner. He approached her.

"I'm Clara," she said, holding out her hand to shake his. "I'm the curator here at Galerie."

Sam introduced himself. "I'm looking for a place to show some of my paintings and, uh—"

"And you want to show them here?"

"Well, yes I do, thank you."

"Super! Why did you choose Galerie Outré?"

Sam couldn't say he was desperate. "Um, my art isn't a good fit for most galleries, and it's, well, controversial." He liked that word, controversial, as it disguised so many shortcomings and problems with plausible respectability.

"I understand," Clara said. "Then let's set a date for your show, shall we?"

Sam startled, thinking he'd missed something. "Don't you... wouldn't you like to see my paintings first before you—"

"Oh, that's not necessary," she said. "Life's all about risk-taking, right? You're taking a risk just by coming here, and so should I. Our philosophy is that everyone needs a place to shine, and especially outsider artists, as that's such a lonely, hard row to hoe."

"Well, that's great, actually. But as the curator, aren't you supposed to, uh, curate?"

"I am curating." She smiled. "I keep out the big names. They have lots of other places to peddle their wares. They try to get in here because we don't take commission."

"You don't take commission? But how do you stay in business?"

"It's a tax write-off," Clara said with a look that discouraged further questions about it. "How about four weeks from tonight?"

"That works." Sam was elated to have a show, but the honor felt hollow and unearned.

"Oh, yes," she added, "and you'll be showing with another artist. I hope you don't mind sharing the spotlight. She's actually here. I want you to meet her."

Clara walked him over to a stunningly attractive young woman with long, flaming orange hair wearing a red leather miniskirt, a black tank top, high black leather boots, and a small gold ring in her nose. Sam was astonished that he hadn't noticed her earlier.

"Viridian, this is Sam," Clara said. "I just signed him on to show with you."

Viridian took Sam's hand. "Hey," was all she said, but something in her smile caused something inside him to twitch. He saw the top half of a crow tattoo peeking above her low neckline that he swore winked at him. Under her tight-fitting top there appeared to be small bumps on either side of her nipples, indicating barbell piercings. *Oh my.* Sam could feel a hook being set.

"Great," Clara said. "I'll leave you two to get acquainted and work things out."

Sam collected himself. "So, Viridian, how long have you been an artist?"

"Oh, about twenty minutes," she said.

Sam blinked.

"Hmm, no, a mile and a half," she smiled. "No, five lifetimes, including this one."

Sam just stood staring, unsure how to respond. Viridian laughed.

"Actually, I started drawing when I was five," she said. "We lived in this ratty apartment in Cleveland. Have you ever been there? God, what a pit. Did you know the Cuyahoga River once caught on fire? All the chemicals and crap they pour into it. Although the lake can be beautiful. When you can see it, that is, through all the smog and the rain and shit." She paused. "Um, what was your question?"

"About your art," said Sam, now wishing he hadn't asked.

"Ah, my art. I'd like to show it you. Is right now okay? I also want you to see my crow."

Her crow? Sam almost fell over.

"Let's go back to my place," she said, "I only live a few blocks away."

Viridian gave him that smile again. He'd seen a similar smile before, perhaps in a painting by that Italian Renaissance dude? It had worked then and it was working now.

"Well," she prodded, "do you want to just stand there and veg out? Let's go."

They walked to an apartment building that had surely been constructed one hundred years prior and probably should have been demolished almost immediately. Sam followed her to her ground floor unit, watching her firm, leather-coated butt sway with every step. Viridian unlocked the door and let him in. He was aghast. Her apartment looked like the demolition had already begun. Piles of clothes, litter, cardboard boxes, thrift store furniture (and random assorted pieces of it), books, magazines, and putrefying takeout food containers covered just about every square foot of the floor.

"Sorry about the mess," she said. "I haven't been home in a while. Meet Elvis."

In the corner of the room in a large cage was a crow—a real one, not the crow he'd expected to see. Sam felt like an idiot seduced by an idiot's presumption. Next to Elvis perched a blue jay. Their eyes were glassy and their feathers splayed in scruffy disarray, as if they'd been kidnapped and tortured by a sadistic ornithophile. Bird shit speckled every surface of the small apartment, which smelled like one would expect a birdcage to smell. The instant the birds saw Sam they started shrieking, the racket ricocheting around the room. *This is what hell must sound like,* he thought.

"That's Priscilla, the jay," Viridian shouted. "I found them as chicks. Please don't tell anyone about this. Keeping wild birds is illegal."

"What about your neighbors hearing them?" he yelled over the din.

"Fuck the neighbors," she laughed.

She smiled at Sam, as if planning how to get him into the cage next. It wasn't her earlier bewitching smile, but now more of a predatory grin. The crazed birds, their frenetic screaming, and the ubiquitous filth made Sam feel like he was on the set of dystopian horror movie. Its star moved about the room effortlessly, seeming to know exactly where to step to avoid the bird shit and clutter.

Sam watched Viridian glide through her chaotic, filthy, rubbish-strewn world as if she were born to it. Perhaps she was. She now seemed a touch feral, a little cracked, and potentially very dangerous. Those possibilities, combined with her supermodel looks and pinup body, were reeling him in like a moth to a welder's torch.

Before you get too spellbound, twit, do you see any mirrors in her little hovel?

Sam looked around the room. Indeed, there were no mirrors.

The two birds ceased their raucous screaming as abruptly as they'd started. Viridian hauled out a large, tattered portfolio and opened it on her shit-spattered drawing table. Sam was instantly stunned. Her artwork was populated with fantastic, impossible creatures, hybrids of terrestrial and alien origin, all pleasuring one another with outlandish genitals yet to evolve. The drawings were large, done in pencil and watercolor, meticulously detailed and flawlessly rendered. Each must have taken weeks to complete. Sam knew watercolor was an unforgiving medium to work with, making her drawings even more impressive. He almost drooled on one. He wished he had a tenth of the young Goth girl's talent.

He found a clean piece of cardboard, placed it on a shit-covered chair, and sat. Viridian squatted on the floor in front of him, not seeming to care on top of what. She leaned toward him, turning her chest into a valley with a crow on one side and the hill of a breast on the other.

Sam knew right then he had to have Viridian, whether she was human or not. He wanted her more than he'd ever wanted anyone or anything. The immediacy and intensity of his desire amazed him. That the girl could so effortlessly hijack his body and soul frightened him. And the reasons for it all eluded him. This wasn't simply lust because lust was just the hunger for a fuck. Lust couldn't account for the desperate need to be assured he'd get another one. Or worse, the paralyzing dread of not getting one at all.

"Well?" she said. "What do you think of my work?" She gave him just a hint of that predatory smile again.

A hint was all it took, and it became painfully obvious this was the onset of obsession—all-consuming, soul-devouring, crotch-bewitching obsession. Sam knew this and he didn't care. He knew he was headed into an epic catastrophe, and he didn't care. He'd sell his soul to be one of those creatures in her private sex zoo, and he didn't care. That's the vexing nature of obsession: knowing and still not caring. He felt like he'd just stepped into an empty elevator shaft in a tower of interminable height.

Sam tried to shake off his trance to answer her question. It wasn't fair that someone so young, beautiful, and sexy could also be so goddamned gifted, he thought but couldn't say.

"Your art is simply incredible," he said quietly through the maelstrom of the moment. "How, uh... why, uh... how do you get these, see these ideas? Wow. Oh, fucking wow."

The plummet down the shaft was definitely affecting his speech center.

This pleased Viridian immensely. A viewer struck dumb by a painting is the ultimate compliment for an artist. The high is free, immediate, and narcotic. Viridian didn't care either. She had to hear more and was delighted that Sam was clearly addicted to being her pusher.

"Please tell me why," she said. Her steady, attentive gaze suggested he'd better choose his words carefully.

The pressure was on. Not only did Sam have to revive his brain and vocal cords, but also impress Viridian with his intelligence and artistic sensibilities, earn her respect, and somehow find the right words that would give him access to her entire crow. And do all of this while hurtling down a black, abyssal borehole.

"I'm not sure I can adequately express it," he said, trying for a reprieve.

"Try," she insisted.

"You're extremely talented," Sam ventured.

"I already know that."

Sam felt like his brain was put on hold. Nothing coherent was going to emerge from it, let alone anything intelligent. There was only one way through.

"I'm…" he said slowly, indeed choosing his words carefully, "really humbled by your artwork and your unbelievable skill. And your incredibly outrageous imagination. I could never come close to doing what you've done. I guess I'm just really envious."

Viridian remained quiet for a moment. "Wow. Thank you for being so honest with me. That's a rare gift. I'm moved by it."

That Sam did not expect. His heart skyrocketed. Her words swaddled him like a warm, thick, lush blanket ensconcing them both.

"Gareth would never say something like that," she added.

"Who?"

"Gareth. My boyfriend."

The long hurdle down the shaft abruptly and rudely terminated.

"Your boyfriend?" he asked like he'd just heard the term. His face darkened visibly, which seemed to please her.

"Well, he thinks he is," she said.

"What do you think?" Sam dreaded the answer.

"I don't know. Anything can happen."

A flicker of light returned to Sam's eyes. Viridian noticed this as well. She peeled herself off the shit-speckled floor and stood. "Time to get back to work," she said. "Time for you to go."

As Sam made ready to leave, Viridian surprised him with a warm hug, holding him a bit longer than he expected and pressing her chest firmly into his. If he wasn't completely in her thrall by now, that nailed it. Girls with steady boyfriends didn't hug like that.

"I'd really like to see your artwork," she whispered into his ear. "Especially the pieces you *say* can't come close to mine."

"Well, they're just—"

"They're perfect." Viridian took his arm and escorted him to the door.

Sam was back in the blanket with Viridian, but it was a cold and disquieting comfort, with her taunting crow, questionable boyfriend, and God knew what else hidden in the darkness. She'd given him heaping doses of despair and euphoria in the same spoon, and he eagerly swallowed both without question. And he didn't care. Obsession gives no middle ground. Or respite. As he was leaving her hovel, he looked over at the two caged birds.

"Save us, please," their glazed eyes seemed to say. "Save yourself."

Their warning was wasted. Crows on breasts, nipple bumps, tank tops, intimate hugs, and ravening desire for this woman consumed the rest of his day. What consumed him that night was colored every shade of Viridian. Her bizarre artistic menagerie kept trotting through his mind, unbidden, unwelcome, and waving about their strange sexual appendages and reminding him he could never imagine such things, nor birth them onto canvas, nor grow them to pleasure Viridian.

The next day Sam visited her with his below-the-waist portfolio and a large plastic sheet. They waited until her captives had finished with their hellish shrieking; Viridian just smiled and shrugged during the ordeal. Sam spread the plastic on her befouled drawing table, carefully positioned the heavy portfolio in the center as if it were made of spun glass, and stepped back. Viridian lightly ran her fingers across the black leather cover, sending a frisson up Sam's spine. Instead of opening the portfolio, she lifted a corner of the plastic sheet.

"You certainly come prepared, don't you?" she said. It sounded like a reprimand.

"Well, I didn't want, uh, the birds, you know…"

Viridian ignored him and opened the book. The first page showed a nude woman bound to a post in the subterranean lair of a huge lion-dragon-hydra hybrid, which was contemplating which part of his captive to ravage first. It was Sam's equivalent species to what paced in Viridian's exotic zoo, albeit, he admitted, an inferior one. She studied it in silence. He waited for a comment and got more silence.

Without a word, Viridian leafed through the entire portfolio as if it were a catalogue of automotive parts. Even his drawings of nipple piercings, which he'd thought would surely arouse her interest, were skimmed over. He was crushed. *So, this is life in her birdcage.*

"I like your work," she finally said.

Damned with faint praise. "Please tell me why," Sam was able to ask.

"I'm not sure I can adequately express it," she smiled, deliberately echoing his words. Her smile was like a knee to his guts.

"Do you want to hear more?" she asked. "Do you need to hear more?"

Yes, damn it! "No."

"Good."

Viridian closed the portfolio and handed it to him. "May I keep the plastic sheet?"

Sam nodded; it was all he could do in his disappointment. It wasn't supposed to go this way—down another elevator shaft. It was supposed to go into her bed, Gareth or not, somehow. Viridian gave him a quick hug over the large book. No soft press of her breasts on his, only the hard edge of the portfolio jutting into his already sore belly.

"See you at our show," she said, opening the door for him.

Sam eyed the birds, now quiet and eyeing him back. *Fuck you. Fuck all three of you.*

Get you into her bed somehow? Exactly how does "somehow" work in your world, twit? Her art plucks your twanger and you think yours will pluck hers back?

Well—

Do you really believe she's stupid enough to fall for that game? She saw it from the start.

Anything can happen. She said that.

Anything did happen. It's just not the anything you were hoping for. You know, Viridian is my kind of gal. I couldn't have twitted you any better.

10

THE OUTSIDER

BEFORE THE EVENING OPENING AT GALERIE Outré, Sam struggled with attire appropriate to outsider society fashion. Black leather seemed to be the rage, but the only such items he owned were his belt, wallet, and a pair of shiny side-zippered boots that only geeks wore to fern bars. He put on black underwear in the faint hope of Viridian removing it, along with black jeans, a black shirt, and a black suit coat. He looked like a hitman in a Bugs Bunny cartoon. It would have to do. What would Viridian be wearing?

To his delight and torment, not much: a low-cut black leather vest with nothing but skin underneath, a miniskirt the same color as her hair (now burgundy), and her black leather spike-heeled boots that laced halfway up her thighs. Most of her crow tattoo was visible, as well as a tattoo of what looked like a squid with bat wings circling her navel. In addition to her nose and nipples, her navel was also pierced, and Sam assumed so were other items lower. Trying not to stare at her, he kept finding himself staring.

Her most curious adornment was a shiny steel collar around her neck secured with a small heart-shaped padlock. His heart jumped. It could be a typical Goth fashion accoutrement that meant nothing. Or in the s/m world that usually indicated she was somebody's sex slave. His heart jumped again, then went cold, knowing that somebody was not him.

Clara saw Sam and extracted herself from a conversation with an elderly gentleman.

"So, my newest outsider artist," she smiled, "your paintings are fantastic. It looks like my risk was worth it. Are you sure you haven't studied under someone?"

"Only the jerk standing in front of you."

"Some talented jerk. Don't go too far, there's some folks I want you to meet."

Clara disappeared into the crowd. The room was filling up with the oddest mélange Sam thought possible. There were Goths from Viridian's world, swathed in black and festooned with chains, metal belts and girdles, amulets, and silver crosses suggesting membership in a cult that worshipped total nihilism or worse. The women wore tight-fitting, chin-to-floor Victorian gowns that covered everything, or tatters of gowns covering little. The gender of the Goth was not always apparent, as both sexes wore masks of heavy black eyeliner, glossy black lipstick, and rings, labrets, and studs through everything pierceable. Sam found little of it appealing.

Mixed in were representatives from the leather community, indistinguishable from the Goths except for their larger piercings and heavier collars. The oddest of all were couples of all gender combinations exquisitely dressed as if returning from formal fundraising dinners with extra cash in their pockets and of the mind to dabble in the fringe art scene. Sam assumed they came from Clara's mailing list. Not a soul from his world attended, though none had been invited. His below-the-waist mailing list was empty and would stay that way.

Viridian rushed over to Sam and gave him another breast-smashing hug and smile.

"Your work is fabulous!" she gushed. "Just fabulous! Now come look at mine."

Fabulous? Damned with fatuous praise, he brooded.

She took his arm and walked him around her artwork. The drawings looked even more spectacular framed and behind nonglare glass. The girl didn't know housekeeping, but she excelled at presentation, both personal and artistic. A tall, bearded young man dressed in a coral tank top and black leather kilt met them. His muscular arms and calves were heavily tattooed, and his earlobes bore shiny black plugs the size of hockey pucks, which they might have been.

"Sam, this is Gareth," Viridian said. She let go of Sam's arm and took Gareth's.

"Garth?" Sam said.

"*Gar*-eth," the other man corrected, extending his huge hand, the back of which was covered with a thatch of black hair. Sam had no choice but to shake it.

"Gareth is my top," Viridian said. "My master. My owner." She smiled, fingered her silver collar, and examined Sam for his reaction.

Her owner. It was true. Sam's response was silence and the formation of a cold void in his chest where his Viridian-based aspirations had lived just a few seconds ago. She'd have to be wearing a blindfold not to see it.

"That's great," he said.

"That's bullshit," Viridian said under her breath.

"Your work is fabulous, just fabulous," said Gareth.

The pair left to meet other arrivals, Viridian greeting everyone with her breast-powered hug. Sam sourly watched her and her hairy master flit about the room. She ignored Sam the rest of the evening and would not meet his eyes. The woman was just one exasperation after another. It would be easier to stop his liver function than to extinguish this obsession and its relentless pain. Unconsciously, his hand went to his neck, as if feeling a collar locked around his own throat.

And the hysterical irony is you put it there.

Yeah, I guess I did. But how do I remove it?

With the key, dimwit, what else? Look for it later. Right now, it's showtime.

Sam nervously stood before his dozen paintings, vowing he'd talk like a coherent, stable, outsider artist, which, he wryly thought, might disqualify him as one. One painting was of a crystalline volcano illuminated from within by the orange glow of magma. Instead of spewing ash and cinders, a beacon of light from the crater pierced through the stratosphere to the stars. Another painting showed an iridescent full moon rising above a mountain lake, its reflection casting an intricate silver mandala on the water's surface. He was really proud of both.

Beside that painting was another moonrise, but this one was being contemplated by a naked man hanging from chains in a towering cathedral vault with a heavy weight attached to his nether parts. Including this one in the show was a risk and made him mortifyingly uneasy.

Clara brought over a well-dressed couple, the woman in a black leather jacket, designer jeans, and white heels, and the man in a perfectly tailored suit and purple silk tie. Sam thought he was either a successful law partner or a crime boss. In the presence of such class, Sam fidgeted in his blue jeans, thrift store jacket, and dirty Reeboks. *Well, outsider artists are entitled to look grubby, aren't we?* he consoled himself.

No, twit, only grubby fools are entitled to look grubby.

I don't need this right now.

I disagree, you most certainly do.

Apparently, Clara hadn't noticed this painting before. "Well, well, well," was all she said about it. Then, "Sam, this is Jacob and Janice Green. You know, the Green Grocery stores? I'll leave you three to discuss this… most interesting piece."

The Greens stepped closer to study the painting, ramping up Sam's anxiety. After a long, nerve-racking pause, Jacob spoke. "Here I see a man who's feeling completely vulnerable and disempowered. Perhaps he's caught in the confines of a traditional theology with no modern relevance. Am I right on with this?"

"You are right on." Sam would have said "right on" to anything halfway intelligent.

"This is a very powerful symbol," Jacob said, seeming pleased with himself.

Symbol? Sam could not believe his ears. His secret was still safe. *There's nothing symbolic about this painting at all, you stuffy dipstick. It's a wank fantasy.*

"Yes," Sam said to Jacob. "That's very insightful, Mr. Green."

Jacob nodded and moved on to another painting. Sam relaxed. *What hooey! A symbol of disempowerment!*

Janice remained behind and examined the painting more closely.

"Um, what's the weight attached to?" she discreetly asked.

"It's symbolic," Sam said.

"Ah, yes, I see that now," she said and nodded.

Sam noticed a thirtyish woman in a dowdy dress looking at another erotic painting. From her conservative appearance, he presumed she was either a librarian or a grade-school teacher, two professions that didn't exactly shower one with disposable income for art. Yet her intense interest in this piece made him curious.

The painting showed a nude woman chained between two columns with a huge, winged demon exploring her openings with long, bony fingers. Not exactly appropriate for a library or classroom. In fact, that was what made his erotic art problematic, as he was about to find out.

"Do you like this piece?" Sam asked her.

"No, I don't," she said. "It terrifies me."

"Yeah, I understand. Sex demons can be scary things."

"No, you don't understand. My attraction to it terrifies me."

He understood but chose not to voice it.

"I want to buy it," she said.

Sam was thrice stunned. He was about to sell a painting, an erotic painting at that, and to the most unlikely of buyers, who was afraid of it.

"I have two daughters," she said. "I don't know where I could hang this."

"How about on the back of a closet door where no one can see it?" he said, hoping to inject a little humor into this somber conversation.

"Actually, that's not a bad idea." She riffled through her purse for her checkbook.

He decided not to quibble.

At the end of the evening, Clara found Sam beside himself with elation. The Greens had bought two pieces, the volcano and, surprisingly, the cathedral and its symbols. That made three paintings sold, including the winged demon, and all at no commission. Clara noticed the red "sold" dot under the demon.

"Well, look at that," she said. "You never can tell. Congratulations, Sam, you did great."

None of Viridian's pieces had sold—not surprising, as none were for sale, adding another eccentricity to the woman's collection. She and her Conan the Barbarian owner had left early with a group of Goth friends, probably to an underground club to get fucked up on the latest designer drug. Sam was actually grateful for their absence.

A pair of heavily tattooed and eyebrow-, nose-, lip-, and cheek-pierced young women in skimpy black lace fetish wear approached him. One nervously asked if he needed any models. Her shyness was adorable, but her rail-thin body, thick mascara, and oozing, unhealed eyebrow piercings were not. The other girl was as rotund as her friend was lean, her enormous breasts barely contained in her bustier.

"Sure," said Sam to the women, keeping all options open. They gave him their phone numbers. The one in the bustier blew him a kiss as they melted back into the crowd. He knew he'd never call either, but a new possibility emerged in his Viridian-drenched, Viridian-addled brain. It would be the ultimate form of flattery for any woman, narcissist or not. How could she refuse?

"Sure," said Viridian a few days later. "I'd love to pose for you."

Hot damn. "Nude?" Sam ventured to mumble, fearing this might lead to a reprimand at best or at worst a Gareth-assisted extermination.

"No," she said. "No nudity."

"Yeah, I understand. Gareth probably wouldn't like that."

"No, *I* wouldn't like that."

Cold damn. "Sexy clothes, then?"

"Of course."

Twit, you truly are a masochist.

Artists asking women to pose for them had been commonplace since brushes and paint were invented. A woman posing nude presented an opportunity for the artist to observe and practice professionalism. And posing nude in the artist's residence severely tested those boundaries, especially if the artist's credentials had yet to be established, and even more so when his intentions were flimsily disguised. Sam knew this, and he knew that Viridian knew this, and he knew the waters here could be very dangerous. But, as obsession dictated, he didn't care.

Two days later, Viridian arrived at Sam's apartment with a bag of all-black clothing, or what could minimally pass as such. She wore an oversized man's white dress shirt, black stretch pants, and Gareth's silver collar. Sam actually found a relief to see the collar; it presented a clear boundary that shelved any debate about whether or not to advance. He both prayed it would stay on the shelf and hoped it wouldn't. She withdrew a lacy bodice from the bag.

"Oh, my, yes," Sam said.

Viridian changed clothes in the bedroom, leaving the door ajar. Whether intentional or not, this gave Sam another item to obsess about. He peeked, beheld her naked backside, and, sure enough, obsession burned him to a crisp. She emerged from the bedroom wearing the bodice, her deadly black leather spike-heeled boots, and a black miniskirt with a hem one micron below her crotch. Her crow was now ninety percent visible. She smiled at Sam as if he were a favored truffle sitting on her plate.

"There's a dressing mirror in the other bedroom if you need one," Sam said, half out of hospitality and half curious to hear what she'd say.

"I don't do mirrors," she said, leaving no room for further discussion on the topic.

That left Sam more curious than ever. Viridian drifted around his studio, looking at this and picking up that, as if shopping in one of her thrift stores. She lightly perched on his drafting stool, smiled, and leaned forward toward Sam's rapt face and unsteady camera. No doubt she'd done this before. Her collar glinted in the light; he'd omit it from the final artwork with pleasure.

After several minutes of photographing her in different positions, and several more minutes of recovering from it, Sam asked her if she would pretend she was in bondage and held his breath for the answer.

"Of course," she said.

Without hesitating, she stretched her arms high over her head, as if hanging from her wrists. Her left nipple popped above the bodice, piercing and all, and took the rest of the crow with it. Unconcerned, she let it sit there.

"Like this?" Her predatory smile returned.

Sam could barely nod. He took a dozen shots before remembering he should breathe.

"Mirrors lie to you," Viridian said, seemingly immune to the strain building in her arms.

"Isn't it just the opposite? Mirrors reflect back who you truly are, right?"

"Mirrors show exactly what I want to see and nothing more. Are yours any different?"

Sam had no answer to give the woman and didn't know where to find one. And besides, thinking clearly was not possible at the moment.

Viridian lowered her arms, smiled, and tucked her errant nipple back into its bodice cup. She placed her hands behind her back in virtual handcuffs and leaned forward into the camera, creating a shadowed valley between her breasts—a valley that beckoned to Sam through the view-finder, imploring him to lick its hillsides clean down to the bedrock. She stood up straight and the valley disappeared, her arms still locked behind her. It was obvious she had experience being handcuffed and enjoyed it. Sam knew his self-restraint was being murderously savaged and for the thousandth time didn't care.

After burning through two more rolls of film, Sam asked for a photograph of her nude back. Viridian thought about it. She freed herself from the handcuffs, turned her back to him, and unhooked and dropped the bodice to the floor. She folded her arms across her breasts, knowing well what this was doing to him. Sam, struggling to hold the camera steady, knew as well.

"You know, Gareth really is a slimy bastard," she said, apropos of nothing.

Startled by this revelation, Sam had no intention of changing the subject.

"How so?" he asked, his ears on high alert.

"We were supposed to have this date," she said, her words turning slightly acidic. "You know, going out to the lake. Gareth knows about this deserted beach. A really great place for doing a nude bondage photoshoot. We planned it weeks ago."

Sam wished to hell he hadn't heard that.

"So yesterday I asked him about it, and you know what he said?" She stared at Sam as if waiting for him to guess. "The motherfucker said he already did the shoot with Glynna."

"Who's Glynna?"

"His cunt of an ex!" she erupted.

Sam had yet to see Viridian really angry, and it was a shock. Just how stable was she? When one is irretrievably obsessed, evaluating one's idol's sanity isn't usually a consideration, and perhaps it should be. Yet he detected windows to her vulnerability, windows he just might be able to slip through—if he was very, very careful. Sam felt like he was tiptoeing around an irritated rattlesnake.

"So he's still seeing his ex?" he asked cautiously.

Viridian said nothing, now clearly possessed by her own travail. She scowled and roughly ran her fingers through her hair, unconcerned that she was still naked from the waist up. Ignoring her collar, propriety, and common sense, Sam openly stared at her breasts and nipple piercings. Viridian let him stare, which disconcerted more than excited him. He had to find that window.

"How long have you been Gareth's, uh, submissive?"

"I'm not Gareth's anything," she snapped.

"Well, what about that?" Sam pointed at her collar.

"What the fuck business is it of yours?"

A slap, hard and brutal. "I just thought—"

"Maybe you should stop thinking."

At that, she decided the modeling session was over, walked into the bedroom, closed the door, and dressed. Still smarting from her rebuke, Sam realized he was now genuinely afraid of this woman, and even more so of the fierce magic she wielded over him. Viridian emerged from the bedroom, dressed and still fuming. Sam asked her to sign a model release form, fully expecting to get the pen through his eye. Viridian scribbled something illegible on the paper, grabbed her clothing bag, and left without saying another word.

"What the fuck?" he said aloud and slouched on the stool that just a half hour earlier had kissed Viridian's firm, pert ass. The stool wasn't the only one. He looked at the release form and was unable to decipher her real name. He could not decipher the real woman either, or his unfathomable enslavement to her, or the depths of the folly and pain he was willing to endure, and especially his complete impotence at affecting any of it.

Decipher the real woman? Pah! You care nothing for the real woman. She knows that. That's why she's been dragging you through the dirt.

Yeah, you're right.

You don't care about her, you don't care about yourself. What do you care about?

Sam sighed, stood up, and looked at the stool. The seat didn't seem to care whose butt had been on it. His situation became bitterly clear: Viridian and her wine-colored hair and crow-covered breast and pierced nipples would forever remain beyond his grasp. Another hard-edged, Viridian-coated misery to swallow. What gave him a smidgen of comfort was knowing she was in a symmetrical fix with her *Gar*-eth. Sam approved of this poetic justice and wished upon her endless anguish. That was mean and petty, he knew, but it sent a wave of pleasure coursing throughout his body. *That* he cared about.

That's called hatred, twit.

It's better than obsession.

No, it's not. It's the same. You're still obsessing, but now on your hate instead of her crow and nipples. That's what keeps you in her cage and wearing her collar.

But hate feels so much better than... this.

Hate's a very intimate connection, when you think about it. Look how close it's made us.

I don't hate you. I just don't like you very much.

Really? You hate what I do to you. You hate what I am.

How can I? I don't know what you are.

You hate that too, don't you?

If Sam had known how a zombie was born, he would have been horrified to see how close he was to becoming one. Stewing in his cauldron of Viridian-flavored hatred, or obsession, or whatever it was called, had reduced his will to mush. He was still able to work, eat, and bathe himself, but that was about all. Even his sexual fantasies of domination had been bleached lifeless by his involuntary submission to her. He had nothing left, nor the strength or desire to find something—the perfect candidate for a zombie. All that was missing was pufferfish poison.

After weeks of walking around in limbo, he finally woke up to discover he did indeed have something of importance: five rolls of undeveloped film and a studio filled with art supplies. That was a dangerous combination for a scorned and angry artist. A cold, grim resolve spawned a new obsession, one he hoped would lead him back to himself and remove his virtual collar.

The following months witnessed an explosion of artwork dedicated to the punishment, torment, and complete obliteration of the arch-criminal Viridian. Sam painted her as a goddess, and he painted her as a whore. He dragged her through the worst of her fears and nightmares, and he knew them all. Painting her into oblivion, he hoped, would exorcise this troublesome and vexing woman from his life.

But it didn't work out that way. The more chains Sam put on her, the more enslaved he felt. The crueler her tortures, the greater became her defiance and strength. He lashed out with every weapon in his studio, and she mocked him. He threw her into a prison of complete abandonment and got shamed for his brutishness. Sam did not like at all where this was going. There was no way he could win, which only resurrected and inflamed his hatred for everyone in this sad drama as well as tightening his collar.

"Move over," he muttered to those poor captive birds.

But the most infuriating and ironic part of the joke was that despite the large quantity and impressive quality of his vengeance art, he could not exhibit any of it for fear of her response and certain reprisal. She now knew where he lived and undoubtedly knew how to mutilate.

OVER THE NEXT FEW MONTHS, SAM'S rage diminished in frequency and intensity, as did the grip of his enchantment by Viridian, or so he told himself. He also believed a new romance would provide distraction and possibly unlock his collar. He admitted this wasn't the best motivation for starting a relationship, but perhaps it wouldn't hurt to play around.

Sam decided to try the singles' bar avenue to sex and recreation, but first he needed the appropriate outfit. He bought a wrinkle-free, pastel blue, polyester leisure suit and a wide-collared paisley shirt. He already had side-zippered black boots, so now he was ready to rock. Only shaped sideburns, a neatly trimmed beard, and a gold-plated neck chain were missing to complete the swinging-singles cliché. The facial hair he couldn't grow, the chain he couldn't afford, but at least he qualified as a single.

From the entertainment section of the newspaper, he compiled a list of the hottest hunting spots, many of which were strung along the lakeshore. That permitted late-night barhopping with less risk of getting stopped for a DUI violation. On Saturday night, at one lounge complete with hanging ferns and cozy red leather booths, he approached a woman sitting alone at a table, on which sat a tall drink with a little umbrella in it. She was a little older than Sam, heavily made up to look semipretty, and wore a stylish, low-cut dress and a bank vault's worth of gold jewelry. Sam winced at the prospect of having to buy jewelry to solicit her favors.

"Hi," he said, trying to sound hip and casual. "I'm Sam. Are you with anyone?"

She looked him over. "No," she said. "I'm Carol."

"May I join you?"

"Why not?" she shrugged.

It wasn't the warmest of invitations, but at least she didn't say "fuck off, asshole." He sat down, and the figure-skating eel went into action. "Do you come here often?" Sam asked.

Carol sighed. "Often enough." She leaned forward, revealing as much breast as the garment was designed to allow, and watched Sam watch her.

"This is my first time in one of these places," Sam said, quickly shifting his focus higher.

"One of *these* places? Is that so?" She glanced at his wrinkle-free suit and minimart watch, and her eyes began to flit around the lounge.

"Yeah. Say, Carol, can I buy you a drink?"

She picked up her cocktail and sipped.

"Oh, yeah. Is that a piña colada?

His glance bounced from the swells of Carol's breasts to her dark, mascara-framed eyes, which were looking at everything else in the lounge but him. After finding nothing better to look at, she leaned back in her seat and turned her attention back to Sam. "No, it's a mai tai."

"Oh," he said. "You like mai tais?"

Carol sighed again. "I'm sorry, Sam, I guess I'm just not ready for a romance."

Lacking any sense of his romance potential, or any sense at all, Sam took the rejection personally. Carol had invited him to join her, hadn't she? She'd showed him some tit, hadn't she? Romance? All he wanted was to see a little more tit. If this were to be a rejection, then damn it, she'd pay for it.

"If you're not ready for a romance," Sam icily said, "then why did you go to a singles' bar and sit alone?"

Carol stared straight into his eyes and with an equal amount of ice said, "Fuck off."

Sam immediately headed for the door, amazed he could find it.

You really shine at "one of these places," don't you, twit?

Fuck off.

Watch your language, asshole.

But at another hot spot on another Saturday night, it was Sam sitting alone at the bar in his leisure suit. There were a number of attractive prospects sitting around the lounge, but none had looked his way. That was fine. He was happy just to submerge himself in his schooner of draft beer and sulk. A tall, good-looking man who appeared to be pushing forty, wearing a tan polyester leisure suit, light blue silk shirt, and gold chain around his neck, sat down two stools away from Sam and ordered a beer. The guy's auburn hair was perfect, as was his thick Van Dyke beard. Sam wished he could grow a great beard like that.

He turned to Sam and nodded. His eyes seemed sad and tired. "Frank," he said. "Architect with Graham and Poole. Mostly commercial. Boring shit. And you?"

"Sam," Sam said, trying to imitate Frank's spare style of speech. "Illustrator with, uh, myself. It's okay, I guess."

Frank sighed. "I've been at this shitty singles' bar scene four months now. It sucks. Nobody's honest. No chick wants to date a guy with a kid. You got kids?"

"No."

"I got Molly. She's five. She's a doll. She needs a mom, you know?"

Single parents were usually women. That made Sam curious, but he didn't want to pry.

Frank answered his unasked question. "She left me," he said, staring into his beer. "Still don't know why. Something about finding her own voice. What the hell is that shit?"

Sam had no answer for that. Frank swiveled on his stool to look at a woman sitting alone at a table. He forcibly hauled himself up to his feet. "Wish me luck."

"Luck," Sam said and watched him go, then to the last of his beer he said, "Yeah, it sucks all right," and made ready to leave.

Then three utterly gorgeous blondes dressed in blue SAS flight attendant uniforms and carrying their overnight bags entered the bar and one, two, three, perched on the stools next to Sam. Without hesitation, the one sitting closest gave Sam a perfect smile framed by the most perfect teeth he'd ever seen.

"Hiya. My name is Anna. What's yours?" Her Swedish accent electrified her words.

Sam's cool and composure, scant as they were, withered in the face of such sudden and intense female interest—even more unbelievable, a very hot blonde's interest. *This can't be real,* was his initial and only response. *This happens only in movies and fuck books, not to me.* Anna sat looking at him, still smiling and awaiting his name.

"I'm Sam. Samuel." He desperately needed a script with more than one line.

"Sam Samuel? Really? That's funny!" Anna laughed and touched his arm.

That made him start to go giddy. "You can call me Sam."

"Okay, Sam," she said. "What do you do?"

"Um, I work."

"You work? That's nice. What kind of work do you do?"

"I'm a… an artist. A painter." He swore he was going to make this as honest as possible.

"An artist?" Anna brightened. "How exciting! You must sell a lot of paintings then?" Again, she touched his arm.

"Oh, maybe a few." It was still true, sort of. He didn't know an arm could become erect. *Was all this delightful touching a Swedish thing or a horny-woman-on-the-make thing?*

Maybe it's a "let's-fuck-with-this-jerk's-head" thing.

Yeah, most likely.

Sam, you really are a twit.

"Tell me, Sam," Anna went on, "what kind of paintings do you paint?"

"Oh, well, just things." Sam dared not tell her the truth, but he had to say something. And he was determined to keep the eel out of this one. Anna swept back strands of her hair and turned her megawatt smile to full power. She leaned a little closer to him.

"Do you ever paint nudes?" She lowered her voice and breathed, "If you do, I'd really like to see them, Sam Samuel."

Sam fought back a swoon. But now he was backed into a corner. If he told Anna the truth, he'd have to deliver the truth. All of his painted nudes were chained up and screaming—surely not a genre she'd appreciate. But if he lied and said no, he would still be in a corner but with a perfectly hot blonde unbuttoning her flight uniform and still insisting to see his paintings. There was no truth or lie that would lead to a perfectly naked Anna.

Sam resolved his dilemma by not saying anything. Puzzled, Anna withdrew her arm, turned to her friends, and whispered to them—he couldn't imagine what, but he became anxious.

She probably said, "Do you believe the loser sitting next to me? He's short, homely, and dresses like an American geek thinking he's something special."

What? Now you can speak Swedish?

I don't have to. It's obvious.

The three women laughed. That did it. Sam abandoned his beer and hopped off the barstool. Anna quickly turned around, surprised and disappointed. "Sam? Are you going so soon?"

Sam headed for the door and didn't look back. He swore he'd never see the inside of a goddamned singles' bar again. He stood outside in the parking lot, staring into the black water of the lake and thinking how lovely the muck at the bottom would feel as a grave.

You sure fucked that one up, twit. Or should I say "American geek"?

You had no idea what she said.

And you do? Is that why you left in such a snit?

My God! Why are you always so horrible to me?

If I were nice, you'd be suspicious and not believe a word I said, just like that hot blonde. That's why she's so scary. You think she's seeing someone else, someone you're not.

Crap! That's not true. That's–

So true and you know it. And besides, you deserve it, don't you, little Sam?

I… well, yeah, I guess I do.

Of course you do. That's why you're standing out here alone. And one more bit of advice: lose that tacky suit already. It worked about as well as your hippie disguise, didn't it? Next time, wear a clown costume.

The following day, Sam stuffed his costume into a Salvation Army collection bin. He stared at the faded red plywood box as if it were a coffin containing a body. His eulogy was to give the bin his middle finger, and he walked away, grateful for the burial.

Sam finally admitted that Viridian's collar still held him captive, and no art exorcism, counter-spell, or singles' bar dalliance was going to remove it. The zombie was still alive and afoot and wasn't going away. One evening, for lack of knowing what else to do, he sifted through his Viridian portfolio, now thick with paintings. Anger still chafed at his guts, like he'd swallowed a colony of termites.

He needed answers but only saw paradox, stark and grim. He was attracted to women who abused him and bored by women who wanted him. The more beautiful they were, the more he feared and distrusted them. And the crazier they were, the more he desired them. And he felt powerless at every turn.

Have you forgotten about me, Sam?

I want a real woman, not some mean, abusive bitch inside my skull.

Is that all I am to you? I'm hurt. And besides, you don't want a real woman. You can't handle a real woman. All you want is a fantasy woman so you can be in control.

No, I just haven't met her yet.

Oh, yes you have. Admit it, all you want is me. I'll always be your perfect lover. I know everything about you, everything you like, and I give it to you exactly the way you like it, and whenever you want. Where can you possibly find a better queen than me?

Just wait and see.

11

JUDITH

SAM WAS QUITE FINISHED JUST THINKING of, fantasizing about, wanking over, and obsessing on the electrifying promises a dominatrix offered, or his dream version of one. Now he wanted the real thing. But he faced three hurdles. One was fear, and with good cause. He knew that the torture in his fantasies could be exaggerated far beyond reason, and asking for the same in a dungeon might come as a brutal shock. There was also the possibility of permanent injury and embarrassing disfigurement. Yet, at the other extreme, a session might prove to be shallow and disappointing, even boring, leaving him with healthy body parts but adrift in disillusionment.

Two, he had no idea how to find a dominatrix, or how to proceed if he actually did. Although the pornography he'd earlier consumed portrayed the dominatrix as hyperbole and caricature, Sam wanted a lady of the real world. Where would women like that live and work? Prisons? Brothels? Renovated medieval castles? Those were the common venues in fuck books and low-budget porn films, but not here. And dominatrices were not listed in the phone book—he'd actually looked.

And three, he could not approach anyone with his basket of debilitating, unresolved, and possibly irresolvable issues with s/m. He knew he needed help, and getting help meant getting some courage. Not the courage to charge a machine gun nest or hog-tie an alligator, but picking up a telephone and making himself vulnerable to a stranger seemed just as daunting—far worse than facing a fusillade of bullets or teeth.

Sam had always viewed therapy as the recourse for losers, people who were sick and weak and needed constant fuel for their dramas. In other words, he agonizingly had to admit, people like himself. The arrival of this contentious inner voice had always concerned him, and now his inability to un-Viridian himself was the clincher. He called up Annie, a good friend of many years, who seemed to have been in therapy of some sort her entire life. She was also one of the most intelligent, perceptive, and stable people he knew, which said something about doing head work. She'd no doubt have dozens of referrals.

No, just one. "Judith," Annie said without hesitation. "She'd be perfect for you."

"Why do you say that?"

"Because she's not your typical therapist."

"Well, why do you say that?" he repeated.

"Just call her." Annie gave him the number.

Now there was a decision to make: whether or not to call Judith, followed by the question of when. Fully aware this drama could last forever and growing darn tired of it, he dialed. Judith's answering machine picked up. The outgoing voice didn't say Doctor Judith or Counselor Judith, just Judith. That threw him a little off balance, but her machine didn't care and patiently awaited his message. *Okay. Not your typical therapist.*

"Uh, hello, Judith, this is my name, Sam, and I got your number from my friend, Annie, who gave me your number and—"

"Hello, Sam. This is Judith."

Sam startled, not sure if the voice was live or recorded.

"Thank you for calling me," said Judith. Live. "I know that must have taken courage."

"Uh, well, yeah."

"And please forgive me for screening your call. That may have felt impersonal, but it's necessary in my line of work. Now, how can I help you, Sam?"

Stupidly, he hadn't thought that far ahead. "Well, I'm really okay and I really don't need any help, but there's something I could use some help on, with, so I called you."

"That was absolutely the right thing to do. Can you tell me a little about what you don't need help with?"

"Well, it's like I'm confused, um, I'm troubled by my, you know, my sexuality."

"As most of us are," said Judith. "That's definitely something we can work on together. Do you feel comfortable scheduling an appointment with me?"

Absolutely not. "Sure, that would be okay, or I mean great, I guess."

"Wonderful! How about this Friday? At ten?"

"Sure."

"I'm looking forward to meeting you, Sam."

Sam looked at the date as if it were his scheduled execution.

Judith's practice was in a large 1930s bungalow that had been converted into workspaces for anyone who needed them. The house was in a quiet residential neighborhood—a welcome departure from the cold, institutional ambiance of a clinic. The sign on the front door read, in bold crayon, "Please Come In!" Sam did. Judith's office was on the ground floor. Across the hall was another therapist. The second floor housed a massage practitioner and a small yoga studio. He knocked on Judith's door; it opened before he could change his mind.

Sam immediately liked Judith. She greeted him with warm handshake and without a trace of the officiousness he'd expected to find in this business. She was around forty, with long brown hair gathered in a loose bun. She was dressed in a conservative pantsuit, and she wore the serene face of the Madonna. She also had the figure of a Raphael model, to his delight and approval. He looked around the small office. A wing chair, writing desk, and end table bearing a teakettle and a basket of herbal tea bags. Three large potted plants crowded the room's only window, vying with each other for the light. A cheery oriental rug occupied the center of the room.

There was no clichéd psychiatrist's couch, but there was a comfortable-looking sofa with handmade pillows piled at one end and a raggedy teddy bear at the other. Next to the sofa was a low table with a bottle of spring water, a rubber frog squeeze toy, and a box of tissues. The diploma on the wall attested to a master's degree in clinical psychology from Columbia. A shrink's classic inquisition chamber this was not.

Judith took the wing chair. Sam knew where he should sit and did. The ceiling creaked and groaned as the yoga students coaxed their bodies into their asanas. He wondered if they'd be able to hear him as well. He arranged and rearranged the pillows, trying to get comfortable. After realizing the pillows were not the problem, he leaned back into the sofa and sighed.

"Sam, when you're ready, tell me a little about why you're here." Judith's rich, even voice was like a mild sedative. "And please take your time, we have the whole hour."

Judith opened a small notebook, placed it on her lap, clicked her pen, and gave Sam a smile that could have cracked a stalactite. But the notebook spooked him.

"My notes will be for our work together and will remain private between us," she said.

Okay. Sam began talking, first about how difficult it was to be a freelance illustrator, and an artist, and a klutz in fern bars, and every other drama in his life but the real reason he was there. Judith suspected he was dancing around something important and calmly waited him out, taking an occasional note.

"We have ten minutes left," Judith said, put down the notebook and pen, and looked at him attentively, as if she was waiting for something and yet expecting nothing. "You mentioned you wanted to talk about your sexuality."

Ooo, I just can't wait for the show to begin.

You're having a real problem with this, aren't you?

I'm not the one with a problem here, duh.

"Ah, yes." Sam took several deep breaths to calm himself. They didn't work. "Yes, well, it's like, I'm really perverted. I like s/m, I mean, sado-masochism. It's been horrible trying to live with it. I just don't know what to do about it, and that's, like, why I'm here."

Not very articulate, and unconsciously sprinkled with Valley girl-speak, but it was true, it was out, and surprisingly he was still breathing. Judith just sat there, her face open and warm, nary a gasp or twitch, the first human being to ever know his secret.

"Go on," she said. "Please tell me about it."

Sam waited until his pulse rate returned to the low hundreds. He was in for a penny, so he may as well spend it all. It all came out in a rush, Valley girls be damned.

"Well, here goes. It's like, I like pain and bondage and like to think about tying women up and torturing them and then fantasize about being tortured myself and I'm so ashamed of it and it's, like, really fucked up my whole life all my life and I know I'm sick and crazy and I don't know how to cure myself and oh shit, oh dear Jesus, what do I do?"

Sam took a deep breath, sat back, and regarded his confession as verbal vomit spewed all over Judith's expensive rug. He'd intended to impress her with how well and together he was. Which, he knew, was not the reason one should be seeing a therapist. And besides, looking good was no longer possible when barf was strewn everywhere. He looked at the pillows, teddy bear, rubber frog, and tissue box. Now he knew their purpose and wanted none of it.

"That was very courageous," Judith said. "And nothing you said shocked or repulsed me in the least. And Sam, you are not sick. Looking for a cure only reinforces the mistaken belief that you are. Let's not do that. You're just alone with this. Try to see this as a journey into discovery, a way to know the different parts of your being, no matter how dark and frightening they may seem."

He just sat there, his mouth open. He'd been half expecting to be rudely ejected from her office, or the morality police being notified, or any number of equally humiliating and absurd disasters he was capable of cooking up, but not this.

"I'd like to work with you on this. Are you agreeable to that?" Judith said.

Sam closed his mouth and nodded.

"I want to give you an assignment for our next session," she said. "Look at it as kind of a fun bit of homework. I want you to write down your history with s/m. Tell me how, when, and why you became so attracted to it. What is it about s/m that excites you, not only in your body but also in your mind? And please don't censor anything. We have to work with what's in there."

Sam was instantly captivated by the task and smelled something important afoot. Judith thought for a moment, shrugged, and withdrew a worn paperback book from a desk drawer.

"This may help you feel more comfortable sharing yourself with me," she said, handing the book to Sam. "This is what I enjoy. Don't look at it now. When you get home."

Sam drove home at warp ten, dashed up the stairs, jumped on the sofa, and caressed *High School Hellions* like a lover, trying to imagine what secrets about Judith it was keeping. Several pages were dog-eared, and he went right to them. It seemed Judith liked to be spanked. *Not your typical therapist indeed.* A fantasy bubbled up, and he thought he'd better squash it immediately.

As Judith had predicted, her intimate revelation encouraged Sam to articulate his. Never had homework held such appeal. He'd last used his typewriter to write a cell physiology paper in college. Now he dusted off its carriage and separated its ink-sticky keys to tell of different experiments. That very evening, he chronicled his entire history with sadomasochism, from goblins and Miss Miller to Amber, omitting and censoring nothing, and continually fighting down the temptation to embellish.

The second part of the assignment was more challenging: why was he so drawn to s/m? Although he'd burned through huge chunks of brain matter trying to figure this out, he'd never written anything down. That would be the key. Insights flowed effortlessly, with Sam typing fast and furious, trying to catch them before they could evaporate into the ether.

"Screw all the typos," he said aloud, hammering away at the keys.

"Easy on me, boy," responded his aging Smith-Corona.

Once everything had been discharged onto paper and made accessible, Sam realized that his predilection was not a congenital defect, a mental disorder acquired in his parents' bedroom closet, or something he'd caught from a toilet seat. S/m, with its emphasis on dominance, submission, and punishment, perfectly reflected his relationship with his mother. Were her reprimands and scolding the only form of love he could believe? Was pain the only way he could feel anything? That might explain why he fantasized about torturing women as payback. But how had that gotten eroticized and turned back on himself? And what made pain so arousing?

Well, that's why I'm seeing Judith.

No twit, that's why you're seeing me. Or am I just a dark part of your being?

What? Now you have all the answers?

I am the answer, dimwit! Haven't you figured that out yet? Sheesh!

Their next session began with Sam returning *Hellions* to Judith. She replaced the book in her desk drawer without comment. Sam had run through a dozen things he wanted to say about it, all of them ill-advised.

"Thank you, Judith," was what came out. "It really helped."

"You're welcome. I believe you have something else to give to me."

Judith spent twenty minutes reading Sam's homework while he anxiously watched and manhandled the rubber frog. He had to smile when he realized he'd picked it up. Judith's face was unreadable, although at one point she slightly raised one of her eyebrows. Over what, he would have killed to know. Judith occasionally jotted down notes in her book. After an eternity, she gathered the typewritten sheets together.

"May I keep these for a while?" Judith asked. "They'll remain private, of course."

Sam's belly froze. It dawned on him that his most intimate secrets, all the sordid details of his sex life, were now in the hands of someone who was essentially a stranger. Oh, what she could do to him! Notify the vice squad and the newspapers. Blackmail. Diagnose him as the ultimate case-history boy for her PhD thesis. She'd become famous. He'd be institutionalized. Paranoia had never seen such excess.

"Or if you're feeling uncomfortable with that, you can have them back," she said.

"You can keep them," Sam said, grateful that Judith couldn't see the horror show that had just paraded through his head. Or could she?

Judith smiled as if she had. She lifted up one sheet to examine another.

"It appears a common thread in your life and sexuality," she began, "involves the dynamics of dominance and submission. As children we have no choice. We're born into that kind of relationship. With some boys and girls, as in your situation, this can become eroticized and birth an attraction to sadomasochism. If you're trapped in a submissive relationship by a powerful authority figure, perhaps learning to enjoy submission, even to the point of sexual release, becomes the only way to survive it. Does that make sense to you?"

Sam looked at the frog in his fist and nodded. "Oh, yeah."

"Can you think of anyone in your life who might fit that role?"

"Oh, yeah."

"I WAS ALMOST SIXTEEN," SAM SAID at the beginning of their third session. He was lying on the sofa with the frog perched on his chest. He wondered how many hands had been on the thing. Dirty green with bulging orange eyes, it was a more comfortable diversion than clutching a pillow or a teddy bear, and he was glad it was there.

"You were almost sixteen," prompted Judith.

"Oh, yeah. One morning my mom said she wanted to have an important talk with me. I was sure it was about my wank… masturbating. I just couldn't leave myself alone, you know. Mom had to know about it. Locking myself in the bathroom for half an hour at a time, and washing my sticky pajamas and everything. But she never said anything."

"Until that morning?"

"Oh, no. It was much worse. 'Sam,' she said, 'now that you're almost sixteen and an adult, you can understand adult things.' That gave me a kind of a thrill, actually. Like this was going to be a special privilege. Maybe driving lessons. There was this motorcycle I was—"

"Sam, I know this is difficult for you, but please stay on track."

"Okay. She said, oh God, then she said that Dad had completely failed her as a husband and now she wanted me to be the man of the house."

"Were those her words?"

"Yeah, pretty much. I heard them but didn't exactly know what they meant and really didn't want to know. Jesus, my father, my own father. I was too freaked to freak out."

"Describe the scene for me."

"We were sitting on the back porch steps. Mom sat really close to me and held my hand. That was really weird and uncomfortable. Part of me was there holding her hand because she was my mother and I had to hold her hand. The rest of me was frightened and, I don't know, somewhere else and trying to get away as fast as I could."

"What was the day like? Sunny? Overcast? What did your backyard look like?"

"Sunny. It was summer and getting warm. She liked to plant flowers instead of a garden. 'Gardens are too much damn work,' she said. I remember looking at the nasturtiums, with those big red and orange petals. You can eat them, you know, like in a salad. I always liked nasturtiums, but that morning I hated them.

"Why?"

"Because they were happy and safe just being flowers and didn't have to deal with what was happening to me."

"Describe how you were feeling then."

Sam stretched out the frog's legs. "Cold. Hollow. Like a pumpkin getting its guts scraped out with a spoon. I felt like my life was being sucked down a sewer forever. But here's the funny part. At the same I was excited, like this was some huge special honor. I was now an adult and doing important adult things, instead of playing with my friends, my nonadult clueless friends."

"What happened after that?"

"It was totally bizarre. I heard her say things about Dad, personal intimate things, things that happened on their damn honeymoon, for God's sake! Things that happened that very morning. Things Dad'd kill me for if he ever found out I knew. Things I really don't want to talk about."

"You don't have to. Go on."

"It was weeks before I could look Dad in the eye. It was like Mom and I were having this affair right under his nose. We'd go out on these, well, like they were dates. She liked to take me shopping for clothes and shoes. We'd have lunch together at fancy restaurants. There was a part of me trying my best to be her... friend, or something, I don't know. And there was part of me that was crazy and howling to get away. Thank God my friends never saw any of this."

Sam swallowed hard. He felt his chest tighten.

"Continue when you're ready," Judith said.

"Yeah. We'd take long walks together holding hands. She'd tell me these really personal stories about her life, about her parents, about some guy she was in love with and should have married instead of Dad. Mostly it was about the awful, insensitive things Dad had done to her for eighteen years."

"Things she said she knew you'd never do?" Judith asked.

Sam sat up. "Yeah. How'd you know that?"

Judith wrote a few notes, then put down her pen.

"If you could go back to that morning when you were almost sixteen, as an adult, as you are now, what would you say to your mother?"

He was silent for a minute, staring into the frog's wide eyes. "I'd kick her goddamned teeth in." He reached for the box of tissues.

Judith sat patiently while Sam wiped his eyes and nose.

"Sam, what happened to you," she began, "happens to a number of children at that age, boys as well as girls. It's called incest, emotional incest, and it's extremely damaging."

"But isn't incest about fathers, you know, doing it with their daughters?"

"That's one kind of incest. What you experienced is another. Your mother turned you into her surrogate spouse for her own needs. And you couldn't protect yourself any more than a little girl could fend off her two-hundred-pound father. The consequences are just as severe and profound, no matter what gender you are. This is not small and nothing to be ashamed of. Don't underestimate or disregard how crippling incest can be."

"I was incested," Sam said to the frog, feeling a curious kind of relief spread throughout his body and begin to untie knots he'd lived with for so long he didn't know were there. Then he thought about Amber and her stepfather, and a knot retied itself.

"Incest can doom any emotional relationship," Judith continued. "Whenever a woman opens her heart, you feel just as disempowered as you felt on that morning. You're denied meeting your own needs, or even knowing you have them, because you're too busy attending to hers. That means you can never be fully present with a woman; she doesn't really know who you are. And neither do you. There are no boundaries. You didn't learn where your mother ended and you began. That's the dreadful curse of incest."

Incest. Wow. I was incested.

Careful, twit. You're treating this like an excuse.

Give me a break, will you? I was incested, for God's sake!

Sam rolled this new, illuminating, liberating verb around in his brain. Then he darkened. He vividly remembered that incident but had always regarded it as just another grievance in a long line of many about his mother, and he'd considered it to be no big deal. Until now.

"The goddamned bitch," he said through his teeth.

"Sam, it's okay to feel your anger," Judith said, "but please don't think in terms of fault or blame. Your mother was just trying to get her own needs met, inappropriate as it was. She was doing her best to get by in a loveless marriage."

That goddamned bitch! I'll feel my fucking anger, all right.

He squeezed the frog so hard its rubber eyes bulged out. Was it now afraid of him? He silently apologized to it and set it down on the table. He didn't know what to do with his hands. He sat back and stared straight ahead into space. After a minute he calmed down.

"What do I do now?" he said. "I feel like there's this… this enraged monster inside me that wants to… I don't know, do something I'll regret."

"That's completely understandable. You've just awakened to a serious violation of your boundaries. Several violations, in fact, and it appears it's been going on for some time. That would make anyone furious."

"So, like, how do you get boundaries? You order a boundary kit as advertised on TV?"

Judith laughed. "Only if you get free steak knives. No, most children acquire boundaries naturally—they come as we differentiate ourselves from others and especially our parents. But some, like you, are not so fortunate. Your early boundaries were disregarded, as you've just learned.

Now you must learn to make them from scratch. There's nothing you can do about the past trespasses. Just forgive yourself for not realizing it happened or being able to protect yourself—you were only a child, remember? Then just resolve not to let it happen in the future."

Sam was still lost, which Judith could see in his expression.

"The first step is to simply acknowledge that you do have boundaries," she said, "although you initially may not know where they are. Then you must recognize when they're being violated. That's the difficult part. Even more bloody difficult is protecting them, and knowing how. Doing all this takes vigilance and practice—a lot of practice. That's something we can work on."

Sam thought about this. "It would really be helpful, you know, to have some kind of, what, boundary alarm? Something that goes off when there's been a break-in? I know that sounds a little silly but—"

"Not silly at all," Judith said. "You do have one, actually. It's called your body. It has a number of alarms, but you have to listen to them. Like a knot in your stomach or a flash of anger. A tightening in your chest. Your body is telling you to look out, there's something out there trying to get in. Do you know what I'm talking about?"

"Yeah, I think I do." Sam picked up the frog and asked it, "Anger, huh?" The frog nodded.

"Like I said, this takes practice," she said. "It does get easier over time."

Judith tore a sheet of paper from her notebook and wrote on it. "There are many resources and support groups for female survivors of sexual incest, but unfortunately there's not much available for men. Here, this is a start."

She handed him the paper, on which she had written the names of two articles. "You've done some incredible work today, Sam, powerful work. Be especially kind to yourself this week."

"Yeah."

"Think about boundaries, and about *using* your anger, instead of *it* using *you*. Okay?"

"Yeah."

Sam fumed all the way home. *Yeah, I'll think about it, for sure. The goddamned bitch.* As he drove, he looked back through his life as if it were a muddy floor needing to be hosed down. *I'm sorry, Amber, for thinking you were a crazy slut and rejecting you. I was incested. I'm sorry, Viridian, for being such an obsessive and duplicitous letch. I was incested. I apologize for pissing on your patrol car, Officer Hardy. You see, I was shit-faced drunk, and I was incested.*

Sam liked where this could go. He was sure Judith would not.

A few days later, after the flight of his epiphany had landed, Sam saw something he did not like in the least. Being incested, whether it was emotional or physical, whether it was debilitating or not, was not a manly thing. Men should be tougher than that. He could not go out drinking with his crew and blubber on about how inappropriate his mother had been with him.

But you have no problem blubbering to a woman, though. Right?

Well, yeah.

I like it when you're stuck on manly. It keeps you saying such entertaining things.

Sam found the two articles in the library and dutifully read them. They were little help, basically repeating what Judith had already said about incest and admonishing men to accept their trauma as real and valid. He was at a wall. Knowing he'd suffered from incest was fine, but now what to do about it? Strangle his mother? Sue his father for his dereliction of duty? There were no clear answers that jumped out at him, and paying Judith gobs of money so he could just lie there, maul her frog, and covertly eye her breasts gave him little hope.

He admitted all this to Judith at the beginning of their next session—but omitting the breast-ogling part. She probably knew it anyway.

"There is no single pill or magic insight that can change this," she said. "Behaviors are learned, and the more you practice them, the more ingrained they become. It's like you've been programmed without your knowledge or consent. Instead of trying to stop a negative behavior, which can ironically strengthen it, begin a new, positive behavior and practice that. As you become more aware of the old negative patterns, you can catch yourself and go in another direction. After a while that behavior loses its power and frequency. They say the brain literally grows different neural pathways to accommodate this."

That gave Sam pause to think. "So, when a woman wants something from me, or says she wants me, that's why I feel so disempowered? I feel I have no choice but to attend to her?"

"Exactly. Now, when you find you're being accommodating and uncon-sciously obedient, when you get yourself roped into caretaking, don't try to stop it. Instead, see it for what it is and simply decide to do something else. It will get easier over time."

"Practice again?"

"You can't get away from it."

That gave Sam more pauses. After one of them, he decided to take a risk. "But what about being, um, like, *consciously* obedient?"

Now Judith paused. "Like to a dominatrix?"

"Yeah. But how can something like submission, which can be so toxic and damaging, as you say, become so erotic when a dominatrix demands it?"

"No one really has a definitive answer for that," Judith said. "Sex has both a physical and psychological component, and a sexual experience can connect the two to form some unusual associations and behaviors. Perhaps it's those neural pathways again, growing and linking up in odd ways. That's how fetishes and phobias are acquired. Unlikely objects, people, and certain activities become eroticized to defy all sense and reason."

Again, Sam thought about Amber and her specific sexual desires. And his own. He then reached a conclusion he wished he hadn't. "Then a dominatrix could somehow be an eroticized version of my mother?"

"Basically, yes."

"Gawd!"

"It's not hard to understand," Judith explained. "Your mother is the first and most powerful relationship in your life. She's completely dominant over you. She has to be. And for many people, that becomes the template for future relationships with women." She picked up Sam's assignment. "Do you now understand why the dominatrix shows up so often here?"

He nodded. All this made sense, but it still didn't sit right. The dominatrix in his fantasies looked like many people, beginning with Miss Miller, but his *mother? No, no, no!*

"It may not be her intention," Judith continued, "but a dominatrix can unknowingly recreate events from your childhood. She's acting out the dynamics of submission and dominance to extremes. So, in a sense, she *is* taking on the role of your mother. That can be a powerful learning experience. What you do with that is up to you, but don't expect her to help you with it. That's not her job. Do you see that?"

"I think so." But Sam's attention was elsewhere, trying desperately to exorcise his mother from the persona of his perfect nighttime tormentor.

*But she **is** your perfect tormentor, little Sam. So am I. What's the problem?*

What's the problem?! I can't have my own goddamned mother turning me on! Jesus!

She's not, twit. I am!

But I don't know what the difference is! There must be a difference. There just has to be!

Then make one.

What? How?

The same way you make everything. You're doing it this very second.

Sam had to jump out of this hellish track and right now. He picked up the frog and began squeezing its huge eyes. Judith noticed that, and he quickly put it down. He shoved his mother to his mind's back burner and, in its place, thought about submission and dominance as a learning experience. He was becoming intrigued by the idea.

"So, Judith… can a dominatrix also be a therapist?"

"Ah, we're getting a little off track here."

"Well, it's an important track to me."

"I know, Sam, I know."

"So can she?"

Judith looked at Sam for a moment, thinking hard. "Yes. Of a kind," she said cautiously. "But know they're not certified. And not all are stable. Or know what the hell they're doing. They can also do you great harm. Sam, you have *got* to be careful!"

Judith's sudden flash of concern both disquieted and touched him. And he was now getting very curious about how she knew so much about the subject. "But what should I be careful of? Or should I say *whom?*"

Judith reached into her desk drawer and pulled out a file folder. She leafed through it, withdrew a sheet of paper, and carefully folded it in half as if beginning an origami sculpture.

"Your interests are not all that uncommon," she said, folding the paper again. "There are healthy ways to approach this, and ways that are less so. You may not be aware of it, but there's an entire community of people out there, common, ordinary people like yourself, who practice sadomasochism rationally and responsibly. At least they try to. They call themselves 'kinky.'"

Sam lit up like a flare. "Really? What? Where? Who?" He felt like an exploding kernel of popcorn bouncing around the office. "You mean I'm not sick and perverted? I'm not a fucked-up paraphilic nut case? I'm just *kinky*? That's all?"

Judith nodded. "Well, someone can certainly be kinky *and* mentally unstable, but I don't think that applies to you."

"My God." Sam sat back on the sofa, feeling euphoric and reborn, like any wanderer who'd been lost in the darkness and now come into the light. He caressed the frog like it was his own heart. Judith handed Sam the paper. He held it carefully, fearing it might disintegrate.

"These are some resources you might find helpful. There's an s/m educational and support group, and some books and articles about it. Oh, and there's one book, a classic s/m novel to keep you in the spirit of things, so to speak."

Jesus, what sort of therapist is she? "Jeez. What can I say? Thank you. Now we're really off track, aren't we?"

"Let's just say we're on a different track."

Sam felt a question balloon within him, bulging out his brain like the eyes of the frog. Judith seemed to know what it was but sat back and said nothing.

"If I were to be very careful," he said, "how might I find someone to be careful with? Do you know what I mean?"

"I do." Judith thought for a long moment, then wrote on another sheet of paper and gave it to Sam. It was a telephone number.

"This is Carmine. She's a dominatrix here in town. She's a professional and charges for her services. You might want to… talk to her."

Sam's heart shot up into his throat, and he struggled to breathe around it.

Judith leaned forward in her chair toward him. "You may tell Carmine I gave you her number," she said soberly. "She knows me. But you *must* keep this confidential. It may be construed as pandering, and I could lose my license."

Sam, already humbled by the trust Judith had shown him, swore on every sacred icon in the pantheon that he'd keep mum. He had another question, an even more dangerous one.

"Um, well, Judith, how do you know about all this stuff? I mean—"

"Good luck with Carmine," Judith said.

12

CARMINE

SAM SLIPPED CARMINE'S PHONE NUMBER INTO a desk drawer and hid it under a writing pad. He checked on it so often—to make sure it hadn't self-destructed or been stolen—he now likely qualified as having a certified and previously undocumented obsessive-compulsive disorder. Just seven little digits had become enormous in significance—either a gateway into a palace of unimaginable delights, or a hair-trigger sex bomb waiting to send his deviant ass screaming into the face of oblivion.

After several days of waffling, Sam picked up the telephone and forced his finger to dial. Another finger hovered over the disconnect button, ready to send the abort signal to the bomb.

"Hello, this is Carmine."

Sam waited, expecting a recorded message.

"Hello?" Carmine said again.

Oh God. It wasn't a machine. It was her. A real, live dominatrix in the flesh and blood, and she was waiting for him to speak.

"Uh, oh, wow," Sam was barely able to squeak out. "I'm, like, calling for Carmine."

"This is Carmine. Who's calling, please?"

Sam sputtered out his name. Carmine laughed; she knew exactly what was happening.

"Thank you for calling me, Sam. That was very brave of you, yes?"

"Um, yes."

"I can imagine. Tell me, how did you get my number?"

"Well, my therapist—"

"Judith?"

"Oh. Yeah. You know her?"

"Intimately. Now, how can I help you, babe?"

Babe? That sent his rehearsed speech and brain into gridlock.

"I'm, well, I've always been into s/m and wanting to be, like, a...
thing... to a dominatrix." He couldn't say the word.

"A thing meaning a slave?"

"Ah, yeah, a submissive slave, right?"

"Absolutely. You're doing just fine, babe. Go on." Carmine's ear seemed
to gently draw forth his words, like silken fingers pulling on his tongue.
Sam melted into those fingers.

"And I've always thought about it and I've never been to one, and—"

"Ahh, so you're a newbie?" Carmine interrupted. "I just love newbies.
They're so cute and scrumptious. Especially when they're scared."

"I'm a newbie?" Sam had never heard the word.

"Not for long, babe," Carmine laughed.

Her bright and easy laughter eased his jitters. "I have to confess," he
said, "I thought a dominatrix was supposed to be, you know, cold, hard,
and bitchy."

"Cold, hard, and bitchy comes later. Count on it. For now, let's just
be human, okay?"

"Okay!"

"Good. The first step is for us to get together socially, maybe over
coffee, and become better acquainted. After all, we *are* going to become
very intimate with each other."

The topic of sex usually didn't arise between Sam and any woman he
was seeing until their fifteenth conversation, or so it seemed, and then only
maybe. Hearing it guaranteed after only two minutes made him lightheaded.

"Sam, are you still there?"

"Yeah."

"Super! It's easy to lose someone at this point. How about next Monday
morning, maybe around eleven? I work at home, so please keep this
address private, okay, babe?"

"Jeez, of course."

Carmine gave him her address.

"I'm so looking forward to meeting you, my little newbie," she cooed
and hung up.

Sam just sat there gripping the receiver. He noticed that his finger was still frozen above the disconnect button. He looked at the address. *Oh mercy, she lives just two blocks away.*

So, horny boy, now you can get a real woman, a mean, abusive bitch, but on the outside your skull, right?

Um, well, yes.

Have fun. Just remember where you live and who lives with you.

The following five days were the longest five days in the history of time. At one minute to eleven, Sam parked in front of her house, as walking might give her a clue that he lived close by. He was still apprehensive about his first safari into sex jungle and feared this predator would eat him alive. But not today. This was a social call, right? He was safe, he kept reassuring himself.

Carmine lived in a modest and ordinary-looking two-story house on a small lot. Sam had passed by it several times while walking in the neighborhood, never suspecting the unimaginable world it harbored. A man of about thirty was raking leaves in the front yard. He smiled and nodded to Sam. Was he a yard worker? A boyfriend? One of her slaves? Another newbie? Sam didn't like mysteries like this, especially now. Sam nodded back, collected himself, and walked up the porch steps. He wondered if the guy knew the score.

Sam rang the doorbell, held his breath, and prepared to wade into the jungle. Nothing happened. He rang again. Nothing happened again. He prayed that Carmine wasn't home and prayed she was. The yard man stopped raking and watched Sam with undisguised amusement. *Yeah, the motherfucker knows.*

The door to that world swung open. Carmine looked nothing like a jungle predator. She was slightly overweight, pleasingly pretty, and wearing blue shorts and an oversized white T-shirt. Her light red hair was short and disheveled, her face was slightly sleep-bloated, and the wrinkles around her blue eyes said she was in her forties. She was holding a cup of steaming coffee.

"Hi, babe," she said. "Sorry, I just woke up. C'mon in for some coffee. I'm not human until my first cup."

Sam was seriously flummoxed. *Dominatrices sleep? They're addicted to coffee? They look like shit in the morning? Is this the right address?* His fantasy dominatrix lay shattered on the front porch. He followed the real one inside.

Then reality got even stranger. The living room was an explosion of clutter. Sam picked his way through and over stacks of books, magazines, computer printouts, piles of dirty laundry, and audio cassettes strewn around the floor begging to be crunched. The kitchen was in even worse shape. Carmine noted the disgust on Sam's face.

"Sorry about all this," she said. "Rat's hoping I'll beat his ass for this mess."

"Rat? The guy out in the yard?"

"Yeah. He wants me to stand over him all day long with a whip, like I have nothing better to do. He pulls shit like this all the time. He's a whiner. He's on his way out."

Goodness, am I on my way in? Sam regarded the shambles. It would be easier to scrape the house to the ground and rebuild rather than clean it. And could he do it without whining? Carmine's breasts swayed under her T-shirt as she moved about the kitchen. She caught his eyes on them. "Pretty, aren't they?"

Sam reddened. "Um, yeah."

Carmine laughed and handed him a cup of coffee. "Here you are, my little newbie."

The coffee was instant and the cup bore traces of its previous beverage. Carmine led him upstairs. The second floor was a large single room and was as clean as the floor below was cluttered and filthy. A bare mattress lay in the center of the room with four large eyebolts screwed into the floor at its corners. A leather-padded bondage horse stood off to one side; a vertical X-shaped wooden rack leaned against the opposite wall.

Several more eyebolts were screwed into overhead rafters with chains hanging from two of them. A door to an adjacent room was closed and secured with a large, heavy padlock. An assortment of whips, floggers, and paddles hung from wall pegs. Next to the mattress was a low table holding two candle stubs, a dozen wooden clothespins, an alligator clip, a bottle of rubbing alcohol, and a small pocketknife—evidence of someone's near demise at the hands of Carmine.

"You're not breathing, babe," she said.

Carmine unlocked and opened a large wooden chest at the far end of the room.

"My toys," she said. "Go ahead and look through them."

Carmine sat cross-legged on the floor very close to Sam and watched him.

At first, he was reluctant to touch anything, as if scorpions were hiding among the items. He saw far more dangerous items: a leather bondage harness, black lace lingerie, smaller whips, a coil of chain, restraint cuffs, blindfolds, an assortment of clamps and clips, and an evil-looking black leather hood that laced up the back. Sam had to keep forcing himself to breathe.

Carmine toyed with his hair and ear as he perused the chest. Sam knew he was wandering deep into shark-infested waters, but oh those shark fingers in his ear felt so nice. She reached into the chest and withdrew a small black box. Inside was a smaller black box with attached electrode leads. Sam had no idea what it was or how it was used but was very sure he wanted no part of it.

Carmine noticed his reaction. She picked up the two wires.

"Stick out your tongue, babe."

"Huh? No. No way."

She pinched his ear and held it. He froze. "When I give you an order," she snapped, "you better damn well obey it!"

It was a jolt. Warm, affable Carmine had instantly morphed into cold, hard, and bitchy. What had he expected from a dominatrix? Tea and cookies?

Surprise! Welcome to domination, twit.

Carmine finally released his ear. It hurt. "Now. Stick. Out. Your. Fucking. Tongue," she said with metal in her voice, holding a wire in each hand.

Sam obeyed and got a second jolt on the tip of his tongue, which sent him jumping off the floor and Carmine into a fit of laughter.

"Oh, we are going to have so much fun, my little newbie!"

Now Sam wasn't so sure they would. Her sudden switch to hard and bitchy rattled him. He could feel himself sliding into a trap he might not be able to escape. Carmine pulled him back down on the floor. She opened a drawer in the chest that held an assortment of rubber dildos and anal plugs of various sizes and colors. He stopped breathing again, but now out of fear. She picked up the largest, a thick, black rubber monstrosity that was over a foot long.

"This one's called 'The Rhinoceros,'" she grinned, then rubbed its grotesque, bulbous head on Sam's cheek. He thought about where it had probably been last.

"Sometimes I like to leave it in for an hour or two as punishment," she said, nodding to the bondage horse. "Do you like being punished, babe?"

Sam's horrified face gave his answer.

Carmine laughed, put away the dildo, and pulled Sam over to the mattress. She pushed him down on his back, lay down beside him, and continued her affectionate touching.

"Tell me about yourself," she said. "Tell me about your kink. What you like, what you *really* like, and what you don't like. I'll need to know everything."

Carmine's menacing smile prompted him to be judicious about what he revealed, especially after that electric shock and seeing her frightening arsenal featuring The Rhinoceros. But he'd gone this far, and running for the door would certainly be rude. And risky. And would she let him? There was no road but straight ahead.

Surprisingly, he was able to reveal the intimate details of his sexuality easily and without embarrassment, no doubt abetted by Carmine, who slowly and methodically unbuttoned his shirt as he talked. She showed no sign of distaste or judgement over his confession, but rather the opposite, smiling as if she were hearing about aberrations she particularly enjoyed. Sam assumed she did.

"Ah, so you're a masochist, are you, my little newbie bottom?" she cooed.

"Bottom?"

"Yeah, bottom," she said, now down to his last button. "As in, I'm the top. Oh, yes, indeedy, I do love a good masochist." She spread his shirt and started toying with his navel.

Sam's brain was fast losing focus at her touch. Her fingers went lower. "Mmm, oh yes, I have a pretty good idea of what you need."

"What I need?" Sam stared at her, eyes wide, brain suddenly back on the job. "Like what?"

"Like you'll find out when you're tied up and there's not a damn thing you can do about it," she said and laughed.

Sam swallowed hard. He imagined an ax murderer might laugh the same way before striking. Carmine traced her fingers along the inseam of his pants up to his crotch. "The next step is to set a playdate."

Sam noted that payment had not yet been discussed. "Uh, how much—"

"Let's not worry about that, babe." She started massaging him through the fabric.

Not only was this becoming a little scary, but increasingly arousing as well. He was getting close to coming, and with surprising speed.

That unnerved him even more. *No. Not here. Not now. Not until I can understand this.*

You mean not until you can control this? Good luck with that, newbie.

Sam looked at his watch. "I think I need to go now. Y'know, get back to my life and all."

"Aw," Carmine pouted.

She released her grip, reached across his chest, roughly grabbed his wrist, unbuckled his watch, and tossed it away. Sam let her, not knowing what else to do or if he could even do it. Still firmly holding down his wrist, Carmine procured a set of heavy police handcuffs, seemingly out of nowhere, and snapped one cuff on his wrist. She rolled him over, locked both wrists behind his back, and pulled him up and onto his knees. Sam was too startled to resist and too astonished to panic. Was she that strong, or was he that enervated?

Carmine opened his shirt and toyed with his nipples. "I like seeing you this way, baby," she whispered into his ear. "You're so open, so vulnerable, and so helpless."

She sucked his earlobe and bit it, then pinched both nipples, hard. Sam screeched and leaped off the mattress. Carmine lunged after him and pinned him to the wall with her body. She twisted his nipples again and kissed him, flicking his tongue with hers.

"This is just a taste of things to come," she said softly into his ear.

All Sam could taste was fear. He was handcuffed. At her mercy. Totally. Time to panic.

"Please, please, please let me go. Please!"

"Are you begging me, baby?"

"Yes! Yes! Please! I'm begging you!"

Carmine stood back and regarded his sheet-white face and ragged breathing.

"All right, baby, it's all right. It's okay." She buttoned his shirt, pushed him against a wall, and gave him another kiss, deep and tongue-soaked. She unlocked and removed the cuffs.

Without saying another word to her, Sam was so out the door it wasn't funny. Rat was still raking the yard. He looked at Sam's frantic flight, smiled, and waved. Sam didn't wave back.

Back in his apartment he collapsed on the bed. *I'm safe, I'm safe, I'm safe,* he reminded himself a dozen more times. Fantasy handcuffs were one thing; real ones were another. The disillusionment stunned him. He thought himself undeservedly lucky to have escaped and in one piece, and he swore he was done forever with his sick dominatrix fixation. All it had cost him was a minimart watch. *I'm safe, I'm safe.*

But that night after his hand crept south, his oath disintegrated with the memory of Carmine's tongue, her shark fingers and handcuffs. She had raised the bar into the stratosphere for erotic theater, and there it would remain. The main actor was no longer an assemblage of sexy photographs and steamy stories, but a real woman with a real dungeon only one phone call and two blocks away. That fettered Sam in a grip that no handcuff could match.

> **So, how did you like your real woman, twit? Did she scare you?**
> *Oh God, yes.*
> **That's her job. Did she turn you on?**
> *Um, yeah.*
> **That's also her job. Isn't it funny how those two are connected?**
> *It's not funny!*
> **It was! I had a great time! I liked seeing you confused, baby. You're so open, so vulnerable, and so helpless. What did you think of her Rhinoceros, by the way?**
> *That thing could have broken my asshole!*
> **Would Judith have recommended someone who'd break your asshole?**
> *I don't know. I don't know if even she knows.*
> **Maybe Judith thinks you're better off with a broken asshole. Maybe Carmine and Judith are secretly in cahoots to break as many men's assholes as they can.**
> *You think so?*
> **Twit, you truly are a twit. Didn't you like being handcuffed?**
> *Absolutely not. I hated it.*
> **Then why do you keep thinking about it?**

It was true. In his mind, the handcuffs were still locked on; he didn't have the key, and there was only one person who did. Despite that asphyxiating, panicked moment of genuine captivity, Sam knew he needed to be handcuffed again to prove how much he indeed hated it. Eroticism has a way of contorting logic and sinking good sense. He knew this and kept reminding himself of it frequently, but he was simply unwilling to be sensible. And that seemed to make sense.

After enduring a two-day marathon of anxious perseverating, Sam dialed Carmine's number. After pressing the telephone bomb's abort button nine times in a row, he let the call go through.

"Carmine?"

She recognized his voice. "Hey, it's my little newbie!"

"Yeah. I'm, well, I was wondering if we could, you know…"

"Play?"

"Um, yeah."

"Of course we can. That's really great, babe," Carmine said. "How about now?"

"Now? But, okay, but—"

"Great! I'll be right over."

"But, but—"

"What's your address?"

Sam gave her his address.

"Hey! That's only two blocks away! Super! Give me fifteen minutes, babe."

She hung up before Sam could sputter out another "but." The bomb's fuse had been lit, and this time there was no abort button. Sam tidied up the place and took a quick shower. Less than a minute later, the bell rang and, still in his bathrobe, he answered the door.

Carmine looked like sex on a stick, dressed in a sheer black blouse with a lacy black bra visible underneath, a red leather miniskirt, and high heels. A thin black leather choker with a small fabric rose in front circled her neck. She was overly made up and looked every inch a hooker. Sam didn't care. He stared at the choker; it was the sexiest thing he'd ever seen.

"Can I come in, dear," she said, "or shall we do this on the porch?"

Carmine slipped through the door and then into Sam's robe and grasped his testicles, right there in the kitchen, for God's sake. This he'd been expecting, but in the first fifteen seconds? She pulled him closer and kissed him lightly on the lips; he had no choice but to kiss her back. She released his balls, took his hands, slipped them under her blouse, and placed them on her breasts. He finally came out of his trance and knew what to do next. Carmine firmly held his face and gave him all the tongue she had. Handcuffs or not, Sam had not a smidgen of control.

"Let us do our job," said the rose on her choker.

"Where's the bedroom, babe?" she whispered into his ear after nibbling on it.

So much for foreplay. Sam nodded to the door and Carmine towed him in.

Sam's robe came off and his electricity went on. Carmine immediately went to work. She looked through her bag, withdrew several lengths of rope, and pushed Sam down on his bed. She quickly and expertly tied his limbs to the four corners of the bed, stripped off her clothes, and lay on top of him. She'd left on her choker.

The knots were triple-tied; escape would be impossible. Sam again felt the panic bloom in his chest. But soon his chest became more interested in other sensations as Carmine kissed, bit, stroked, teased, and pinched every square inch of him. Then she sat up.

"Don't you go anywhere, babe," she laughed. She reached into her bag, rummaged around, and pulled out his wristwatch. "I believe you forgot this."

Carmine buckled the watchband around his genitals and sat back to watch the effect, which was to induce an erection, whether he wanted one or not. He did.

"What time is it, babe?"

Sam strained to see the dial and couldn't.

"Is it time for you to go?" she asked. "Or time for you to come, hmm?" She let loose another round of laughter.

Sam couldn't speak. He wouldn't have known what to say anyway. Carmine found a condom in her bag and quickly rolled it onto him. She sat astride him, humped for a minute, and before he could come, hopped off him and fellated him to climax. He swore the woman had three tongues and knew how to use them.

Carmine looked at his watch, still in place. "Not bad," she said to herself.

She unbuckled the watchband and, leaving Sam restrained, went into the bathroom to wash up. After making a quick phone call, she returned. Still naked, she sat between his legs and stroked his thighs and deflating penis. The unbelievable sex had distracted his fear, but he was still bound, and again anxiety creased his face.

Carmine untied one of his hands. He started to relax until he realized he couldn't reach the other knots and was still a captive. She sat beside him, amused by his distress. "Touch my breasts, dear boy. Touch my nipples."

He did. The intimacy slightly calmed him down. Carmine parted her thighs.

"Put your finger inside me."

He did.

"Now taste your finger."

Sam hesitated, then obeyed. The taste was surprisingly pleasant, salty and sweet and smelling like a banana.

"Oh, do I have plans for you, babe," she said and gave him her executioner's laugh.

"What plans?"

"You'll see. Maybe some punishment. Maybe some pegging."

"Pegging?"

"With my Rhinoceros, of course," she said with a ravenous smile on her lips.

"That would be wonderful," Sam lied, more concerned about her smile than that monstrous rubber beast.

"You're such a sweetie, my little ex-newbie."

Carmine quickly dressed, gave Sam another deep french kiss, and untied the rest of him. Then she was out the door just like that. Sam sat up in bed, dazed and astonished. He'd never climaxed so quickly with a woman. He wanted Carmine to come back and tell him what to do. He wanted her to tie him up and keep him forever. And he never wanted to see her again and didn't have a clue as to why.

You sure are a hard boy to please. A beautiful woman, an expert in sex and domination, is lusting to cream you in her dungeon, and for free. What more could you want?

I want my life back.

You only think you do. And you're asking an enslaver for freedom? Sheesh!

She has no respect for boundaries!

Yes, she does. She stops at customs every time she goes to Canada.

That's not funny! My boundaries! She just does whatever she wants.

That's what she's supposed to do. That's why you called her! And you have no respect for your boundaries. That's just a groovy word you learned from Judith, and you have no idea what it means. And by the way, does your asshole still work?

Uh, yeah.

Fabulous! At least there's one part of you that knows what it's doing.

It was Carmine who called Sam a week later to make another play date, this time in her upstairs dungeon to administer some "ahem, punishment," she said with a touch of menace. Sam could see that scary grin of hers over the phone. He had known this was coming and dreaded it. It was now boundary time. He frantically rummaged through his brain, trying on this excuse and that alibi and found nothing except that which should have been his first choice all along.

"I'm sorry, Carmine," he said, "I'm really scared of all this, and I'm just not ready to go any further."

"That's okay, baby," she said, "I understand. I guess all this can be a little overwhelming at times. So can I. Thanks for being honest with me."

"Yeah. I'm sorry."

"Don't be sorry. It's okay, it really is."

"I'm sorry."

"You've done something new and scary, Sam. You've been very brave. You're now resisting confronting your fears. We can work on this together, you know."

"I'm sorry."

"Please stop with the apologizing! I said it was okay. Just call me when you're ready, babe."

Sam slumped back in the chair, enormously relieved. Carmine was letting him have his boundary.

Well, you may be an ex-newbie but you're still a twit. You finally got your dream come true—a real woman to abuse you. Was it worth it?

I guess so.

You guess so? It sounds like you're still confused.

Yeah. I just don't know what I want anymore.

At least you know that. But don't complain. You got your watch back.

13

Mistress Morgaine

SAM FINALLY LOOKED AT THE LIST of s/m resources Judith had given him. It was still hiding in his desk drawer, growing larger and more ominous like a long overdue bill. Since his two conflicted trysts with Carmine, he was reluctant to investigate the world of kink any further. But the list chewed through his brain like hungry termites, giving him no peace. Still, it was a door, and the only one around, so he opened it.

All the books Sam had previously read about s/m were unabashed smut and didn't pretend otherwise. But these on the list didn't seem like porn, and he bought all three. The first viewed s/m through a social anthropological window, as one would study the incomprehensible rituals of a primitive tribal culture, although Sam suspected the author was masking his own interest in the subject. Another book explicitly documented gay s/m activities that made his most bizarre and risky experiments seem lame. He had no idea male genitals could endure such treatment and still function. Maybe they weren't supposed to; the author didn't say.

The third book further exacerbated his agitation. Written for women, it encouraged them to find and express their dominant natures and showed ways to exercise that power over men. It was essentially a manual for how to become a dominatrix. Sam quickly discovered this was not typical shallow porn, where he usually found such material, but seemed practical and grounded, such as learning how to be a welder.

He devoured the book like it was a box of confections until he got to the particulars of male submission. Some of the activities struck him as beyond offensive and looked like they'd been stolen straight from *The Chateau of Cruel Bondage*. He groaned. Nowhere could he find a sane and sensible entry point into this exotic world that so continually haunted his days and nights.

So, the reality of male submission now turns you off? Not what you expected, eh?

Jeez, what guy in his right mind would want to grovel on the floor and lick dirty boots and drink someone's piss? Ack!

A lot of men have that kind of mind. Or they're highly motivated to get one. You're perfectly capable of doing that too, as we both know.

Not a chance!

We'll see about that. Lust can work miracles, you know.

Judith's list also included information about an s/m educational and advocacy organization on the West Coast that held meetings, gave workshops and demonstrations, and hosted live s/m dungeon parties. Sam considered immediately moving out there and to hell with the trouble and expense. He promptly joined the group and began receiving their bimonthly newsletters. He couldn't believe it: an entire subculture devoted to practicing in the light what he did alone and furtively in the dark. His exile was over.

The newsletter was a virtual kinky buffet. It offered articles about various s/m techniques and how to inflict them on others safely and effectively. Each issue featured s/m and bondage fiction, usually a poem or story—essentially the author's jack- or jill-off fantasy. Most were poorly written and crudely illustrated, but their points were effectively made. There were also personal ads, the majority being from men aching to grovel and thirsty for piss, searching for dominatrices with whips and full bladders. Most titillating was the calendar of kinky events, with something perverse, pleasurable, or both seemingly happening every other day.

Unfortunately, this ongoing orgy was three thousand miles away and called out to Sam incessantly. He was becoming frantic to jump in, or into anything that might be closer at hand. He thought about calling Carmine again, but her overpowering dominance intruded too far into his personal life and he was thin on boundaries. He was reluctant to ask Judith for another referral, and besides, she was a therapist, not the Yellow Pages of Kink. He could return to pornography—not much of an option as it had proven to be shallow, repetitive, and boring. What remained was nothing, and this kind of nothing was becoming unbearable.

He called Judith, not for another phone number, but again for that terrifying word: help.

A day later, he was sitting on her sofa trying to get comfortable. Something wasn't right.

"Did you see Carmine?" Judith asked.

"Um, yeah."

"How did your session go?"

"How'd you know we had a session?"

"Because that's what she does. And your face is red."

That made his face redder.

Judith leaned toward him. "Sam, know that she and I are both professionals and practice confidentiality. Nothing said here will leave this office."

"That's… good." He looked around the office. "Um, where's the frog?"

"I gave it to a client. Sometimes it's better therapy than me!" she laughed. She put down her notebook. "No notes today. Just tell me what you're comfortable sharing."

He needed to hold something. He eyed the teddy bear and immediately rejected it. He sighed, folded his hands, and told Judith everything about his two visits with Carmine—everything—and in graphic detail. There was simply no other way to recount it. He wondered if he was breaking a confidence, but Carmine said nothing about swearing him to secrecy. Judith listened attentively to his chronicle. He couldn't tell if he saw the slightest of smiles on her face or if was imagining it.

"The ambivalence you're feeling about being handcuffed," Judith said after he'd finished, "is perfectly understandable. What does fantasy captivity give to you?"

Sam had to think on that. "This sounds nuts, but I feel safe and as if I'm being taken care of."

"No responsibilities either?"

"Yes. Yeah! So why is that so erotic?"

"It's a vacation from your job," Judith said. "A vacation from attending to a woman's needs. You can finally relax and enjoy yourself. Taking the initiative and responsibility for the entire sexual encounter, as men have been conditioned to do, can turn anyone off."

"But then I freaked out when the real Carmine handcuffed me."

"Of course. In the fantasy, you're always in control. But in the real world, you're not. Because of my referral, you were fairly confident that Carmine was okay, and she wasn't going to truly harm you, right?"

"Yeah."

"But your body didn't know that, and bodies have unmistakable ways of telling you how they feel, like we talked about. Especially when a boundary is being crossed, as dominatrices are supposed to do. Were you also afraid when she tied you down on the bed?"

"Yeah. Even more so because it was in my own place. But then why did I come so quickly?"

"Fear and arousal are neighbors, so to speak. The brain and genitals are both hardwired into the endocrine system. You've heard of the 'fight or flight' response, haven't you?"

He nodded.

"I'm not an endocrinologist," Judith said, "So I can't give you the particulars. But when you're frightened, there's a massive adrenaline dump into your bloodstream. That gives you the energy to either run or confront the threat. It's not surprising that the gonads get goosed as well. There've been documented cases of people getting uncontrollably randy after surviving life-threatening experiences, and that's probably why. Not that I'd recommend it."

"This is confusing. Then it seems like my fantasies... my desires... are wanting to put me in some kind of danger just for a thrill. That's really kind of sick and crazy, isn't it?"

"Think about people who go skydiving and rock climbing. Even that new crazy thing base jumping. Pretty intense for a thrill, wouldn't you say? Stand back and you'll see those activities are far more dangerous than a pair of Carmine's handcuffs. In fact, to some people the danger can become addictive. So we have to be careful when we throw around the terms 'sick' and 'crazy.'"

Sam frowned. "Then how do I live with this..."

"Paradox?"

"Yeah, paradox."

"Well, you can do therapy for years trying to deconstruct your conflicts, and there are therapists who'll do that with you. But the associations you've made with pain and pleasure could still persist and plague you. Simply understanding something by itself may not make it go away. I prefer a more pragmatic approach, as you've seen. What's sick and crazy, in my view, is continually doing something that you know doesn't work."

Sam sat quiet, thinking. "Do you have another frog?"

Judith laughed. "No, but I have something else. Do you know what a koan is?"

"Cone?"

"*Ko*-an. It's a type of Buddhist meditation exercise that's designed to reveal the limitations and inadequacies of the mind. It's done by contemplating an unsolvable riddle—a paradox. You've heard the age-old philosophical question, 'What is the sound of one hand clapping?'"

"Yeah?"

"So what *is* the sound of one hand clapping?"

"I, well, that's… impossible to answer. There can't be any sound."

Judith pulled a slim volume down from her shelf. "But when practicing a koan, the question must be asked, and asked in a certain way. And it is possible to answer it, but not how you might think." She gave him the book. "Why don't you give it a try?"

Koan. It made total nonsense to Sam, but it was worth a go. Back home he carefully read through the book. According to its guidelines, he was to focus on two incompatible or opposing principles with a clear and open mind and at the same time not expect an answer. Then an answer comes, but not from a direction or in a form one presumes, just as Judith had said. *Hmm.*

Sam didn't have a clue what all that meant. He sat cross-legged on a large pillow on the floor, the recommended meditative position. He closed his eyes and concentrated on watching his breathing. He wasn't sure he was doing it right, but he could feel himself begin to relax.

Next was clearing his mind. That was more challenging, because if you're trying to think away your thoughts you're still thinking. So he visualized a tiny janitor in his head sweeping away his thoughts into the trash heap. But that didn't clear a thing as now his mind was filled with tiny janitors with push brooms.

Then he tried contemplating a koan riddle. He'd already seen that the idea of one hand clapping didn't get him anywhere, so instead he held decency in one hand and depravity in the other—clear opposites and the essence of his problem. But how did one contemplate concepts? After a few minutes of attempted contemplation, nothing happened, which was what was supposed to happen, but he was waiting for something else.

Sam kept at it and kept getting more nothing. Then he tried something less cerebral and more corporeal: the opposition of pain and pleasure. He knew both places intimately and they teemed with paradox and visuals—the perfect koan fodder. He imagined fantasies of erotic torture, hoping that would do the trick. It did. He started to get an erection. The book didn't say anything about this. His knees began to hurt. *What crap.*

Then, from somewhere buried deep in his neural network, a memory emerged unbidden from when he was three. It was of Mrs. White, the mother of his best and only friend, Tommy, also three. The Whites had lived next door to Sam's family in a dingy apartment building in Chicago. Sam smiled, remembering that he and Tommy together were a far greater hell than the sum of their parts.

One afternoon, they filled up Tommy's bathtub and played boats with their shoes. Shoes made terrible boats because they immediately sank, which proved true with every shoe in the White household. When Mrs. White discovered the ruination, she grabbed both of Sam's wrists with one hand, hauled him off the floor, and spanked him hard while he kicked and cried. She pinched his butt and sent him home, shocked and bawling. From the screams behind him, Sam knew her fury had been turned on her own child.

He remembered crying for an hour. His mother was bewildered, thinking he was hurt, but she could find no sign of injury, and he refused to explain. Afterward, he feared and avoided Mrs. White, but at the same time was inexplicably attracted to her. Sometimes he wished she would spank him again, and of course he didn't know why.

Now, as an adult, he did, and there was no mystery as to why this particular memory had arisen. *Was this the koan's doing?*

Well, look at this. Are you still looking for your Mrs. White?

I guess so.

Do you believe she's only a neural pathway?

I don't know. And I don't know how to know.

Yes, you do, although I'm reluctant to recommend it.

Sam knew what it was. It meant seeing another dominatrix. This time not an amiable newbie-creamer like Carmine, but a genuine, fire-breathing, merciless predator. A she-monster from the uncharted Stygian depths of the erotic underworld. Carmine had given him a taste of domination, and despite the handcuff fiasco, he still wanted more, and he knew he always would. There would be no debate about this decision.

Maybe you should—
I said no debate!

THE ONLY PLACE WHERE SAM COULD find a dominatrix was in a contact publication sold at his favorite porn shop. His last raid had been well over a year ago, and this time made him just as anxious as his first. Ignoring the sex toys and magazines, Sam quickly found the booklet and bought it sight unseen. He weaseled out of the store slicker than snot, clutching the instrument of his ecstasy (or doom). At home, he cautiously opened the prize, thinking about Pandora all the way, as if caution would have made any difference.

The booklet looked like it had been printed in someone's basement and designed by people who couldn't design, written by people who couldn't write, and marketed for people who couldn't care less about that. Sam went straight to its heart—the personal ads. The ads were divided into two sections: men seeking women and the reverse. At that time, anyone in between those poles was out of luck; the country was still locked in the alternative sexuality dark ages.

Most of the ads were from men offering themselves for stud service and boasting of their main assets as having frightening proportions. The few ads from women were dubious sounding at best. "Looking for a stud who can give me miles of his meat" was one come-on Sam found as sexy as a bowl of vomit. He wished those folks well in finding one another.

The s/m section was just as disheartening, primarily ads from men seeking dominatrices, which made him just another sheep in a vast flock bleating for a beating. Their ads were as tawdry as their desires, a typical one reading, "Worthless slave seeks to worship You Mistress to lick your boot heels and punish the bad boy," or "Married man wants to use as your toilet." Apparently, the magazine did not offer editing services.

The few ads from professional dominatrices jumped off the pages like spiders. The most venomous showed a buxom brunette, her face hidden behind a black eye mask. She was also dressed in black: bodice, panties, and thigh-high leather boots. In the background, a naked man, his identity also protected by a leather hood, was stretched on a vertical rack with a large, unidentifiable object hanging from his testicles. Her name was Mistress Morgaine. She dangled a pair of handcuffs before the reader, inviting him to be next.

Oh yes, that would be me.

Oh no, you'd better run while you still can.

No debate! No debate! No debate!

Sam just had to contact Mistress Morgaine. After all, what could she possibly do to him through the mail? He decided his letter should be handwritten rather than typed; it would be a more intimate introduction to a very intimate adventure and might impress her. Impressing the Mistress became his new raison d'être.

He wasn't versed in proper slave etiquette for correspondence, so his words were on the obsequious side, with careful attention paid to proper capitalization (or lack thereof). He'd heard that capitalization was critical when approaching a dominatrix. The Dominatrix, or Domme for short, and all things Female must have initial capital letters. This included any reference to Her and especially Her pronouns. Anything to do with males, slaves, and submissives was in lower case, naturally: I/i, She/he, My/me, U/us, O/our, and Y/you. Sam thought all this was a bit silly, but it was intrinsic to the scene, and he'd better obey the rules. *Obey.* That word was acquiring a new and sinister feel.

As her ad instructed, Sam wrote down his desires, experiences, and fantasies, and got a boner doing it. *Whoa.* These things might actually happen to him. He ripped up the letter. The second draft was more grounded in the real world, but his penmanship got sloppy and he threw it out. Near the end of the third draft, he made a grammatical error. The fourth draft had a typo in the middle. The fifth had a spelling error in the fucking first sentence.

Midway through the sixth draft, it occurred to him that perhaps these miscues were trying to tell him something. He stopped to think about it and decided to make a list of the positives and the negatives. The negatives piled up quickly:

1. An abusive bitch would boss me around—the very thing I hate the most.
2. My genitals could be irreparably damaged or removed altogether.
3. I could get a nasty disease from her gear.
4. My asshole could get broken, perhaps permanently.
5. I'd have to mutate into a fawning sex pervert, and I might not be able to mutate back.
6. I could get arrested by the vice cops and thrown into a jail cell with genuine sex criminals hungry for an asshole to break.

7. I could suffer severe emotional trauma.
8. I could be killed in a sensational and gruesome dungeon accident.
9. My bank account really can't afford this.
10. And the most terrifying: I'd like being a slave so much I'll never return to my normal life.

Then he looked at the positive side:
1. This issue has plagued me since puberty, sabotaged all my romances, destroyed my sense of goodness and grace, and steeped me in crippling shame, and I have to find out, once and for all, if this is what I want.

Maybe you should look at the real reason, twit.
2. I'm obsessed and horny.

Sam decided to forego the contrived intimacy of a longhand letter and typed the seventh draft. Miraculously, it contained no typos:

```
Dear Mistress Morgaine,

i saw Your very exciting ad in Lewd and Lucky
Magazine and i would like to apply to be Your
devoted submissive and slave. i have been a true
masochist all my life and i beg You to train me to
serve You and accept Your dominance and i agree to
receive Your punishment as You see fit.

Yours in submission, slave sam
```

Seeing his name in lower case spooked him, as if he were seeing it on his tombstone. He licked the envelope shut and got a paper cut on his tongue. How perfect. He stood before a mailbox and stared at it. The thing was cold, merciless, and devoid of all remorse or humanity, squatting there like a fat blue gnome, and swallowing dreams and destinies down its big toad-like mouth without a care or kind words. The mailbox was silent, as most are.

Sam crept closer to the gnome, opened the flap, laid the letter on its tongue, and hesitated. He looked at the letter, the door to his future, his offering about to begin its fateful journey into Mistress Morgaine's mailbox and hopefully her heart. The encounter struck him as quite strange, an act of displaced sex. The gnome was now part of the game, like a bouncer at a brothel door. The letter was still in his hand; it was not too late to save himself.

The gnome could no longer remain quiet. "Are you sure you want to do this, citizen?"

"Yeah, I have to."

"I'm sure you do. Now feed me and move along."

Sam, you're talking to a fucking mailbox.

I talk to you, don't I?

Sam tilted the flap and watched the letter and his life slide down the gnome's gullet.

"Now it's too late!" jeered the gnome. "Too late! Too late!"

Sam checked his own mailbox several times a day, his heart tingly with expectation during the trip downstairs, and leaden with disappointment on the steps back up. He knew this kind of venture excelled as a drama magnet and wondered if it was the beginning of his torment at the hands of the cruel Mistress Morgaine.

Within a week, the cruel Mistress responded. The heavily perfumed envelope contained several pages. The first was a note written in Mistress Morgaine's own terrible hand:

```
Thank you slave sam for your respectful letter
and the offer of your submission as My slave. My
instructions are as follows. To qualify for My
slave you must completely accept and embrace My
philosophy and My rules. you will completely and
honestly fill out My questionnaire. you will sign
My liability release form. you will mail these to
Me without hesitation. I will soon have you on your
knees and crying and begging Me for more.

Yours in Dominance, Mistress Morgaine
```

The note was signed with a blood-red lipstick kiss. Sam kissed it—real lipstick, from Mistress Morgaine's very lips to his. Like a hallucinatory drug, the remote kiss infused every cell in his body, filling him with her sex magic. Without knowing what was happening, Sam now found himself in her thrall. And worrying that maybe it was too late.

The second page proclaimed her manifesto:

Mistress Morgaine,
Goddess of Domination

Do you love Dominant Women and wish to serve Us with all of your body and soul? Then come kneel before Me. I am a supremely sadistic Dominatrix who will give you very good reason to. In My dungeon you will get not what you want but what you sincerely deserve. I am not the ordinary, boring, and weak Woman which you quickly tire of, but a Woman who is beautiful, exotic, strict, and sincerely cruel. I am Divine Narcissism taken to its most extreme. I am this because that is who I am and what My slaves expect from Me although My slaves have no right to expect anything at all.

As your Dominatrix I will create a magic theater of pain, pleasure, and paradox. I receive My training and ordination from the very powerful and secret Gynotopian Society where all Women rule all men with an iron whip. No earthly Woman can assume this authority although many try to. In Gynotopia We Women have this iron authority and wield it without any mercy. In Gynotopia and on Earth the slave will know this is Our world and Our rules and We can do whatever We want to you and We will.

Well, he wasn't seeing the woman for her literary skills. But her reference to pain and paradox made him take notice. Perhaps she knew all about koans, particularly his. This feeble premise stamped Sam's passport for a trip to Gynotopia. The feebleness concerned him.

On page three were the rules for the Dungeon of Goddess Domination:

The Rules of Mistress Morgaine's Goddess Temple Worship

1. Mistress is never wrong.
2. Mistress is always right.
3. Mistress has absolute ownership and authority over Her slave's sex life.
4. Her slave exists only to attend to Her needs.
5. Her slave must worship the ground She walks on except when She's walking on him.
6. Her slave must instantly and immediately obey Her orders without hesitation.
7. Her slave must always anticipate Her needs and attend to them instantly.
8. Her slave is not entitled to have needs, and Mistress can rightly ignore them.
9. Mistress is entitled to express conflicting, vague, or ambiguous commands.
10. Mistress may change Her needs and commands at any time and without a warning.
11. Any hesitation or reluctance of Her slave to follow Her commands or attending to Her needs will result in severe punishment. That might mean he is being ignored.
12. Any incompetent, unsatisfactory, unacceptable, or resentful behavior of Her slave in the performing of Her commands will result in severe punishment.
13. Mistress may severely punish Her slave at any time for any reason or for no reason at all.
14. Mistress is entitled to change any of Her rules any time, and for any reason or for no reason at all, and without a warning.
15. If Mistress determines that punishment does not result in satisfactory obedience or if Her slave shows the slightest act of disrespecting behavior and defiance then:

16. Mistress is entitled to eject Her slave from
    Her dungeon and into the lonely and cold void of
    Mistresslessness. Her ex-slave will be ejected
    naked if She so desires it.
17. These Rules of slave Ownership and slave Conduct
    are to be rigorously followed and obeyed, for
    better or worse, in leather and in pain, until
    Death or something equally freaky do U/us part.

His lipstick-induced high abruptly crashed. Just who the fuck did this cunt think she was? Mistresslessness? Cute. Being ejected into the street naked? Not cute. Sam conceded these preposterous porn-novel rules were all part of the game, and to proceed meant swallowing every one of them. Somehow.

The next page listed the s/m activities she practiced, and he was to check those he'd consent to. The list was longer than a Chinese restaurant menu and with many dishes he'd not heard of. He read through them with growing feverishness. Overnight bondage? Playing with another woman? Chastity training? Electro-stimulation? Hell, it wouldn't hurt to check yes to every box, whatever they were. Actually, it would turn out to hurt quite a bit.

The last page was a consent form that released her from liability no matter how badly he, the consenter, was demolished. It also included the amount of her tribute—more than half his monthly income. Little did she know he was obsessed enough to pay double that, or desperate enough to pay anything. The note admonished the applicant to respond honestly and immediately, include his telephone number, and he'd better be on his knees when he did it.

Sam thought she was kidding about the knees. He didn't know Mistress Morgaine had no sense of humor. He also didn't know he was about to stumble into the largest and best-equipped dungeon of the most experienced, most gorgeous, and most ruthless professional dominatrix in six states. Her perfumed envelope would stink up his mailbox for months.

Sam filled out the questionnaire and signed the consent form, deliberately not on his knees. He slipped these into an envelope, along with his hard-earned tribute in cash, and licked the envelope flap like it was Mistress Morgaine's sincerely sadistic labia. No paper cut this time, but he almost gagged on the taste of the glue. He hoped she would taste better.

Again, he stood in front of a mailbox.

"Are you sure?" the gnome said. "*Really* sure?"

"Yes. I'm positive. I've worked it all through."

"Whatever. Feed me."

Sam stared at the envelope. It was another dominatrix bomb with a time-delay fuse. He'd light it now and die later in Mistress Morgaine's dungeon. It was the beginning of a slow-motion suicide. The autopsy report would indicate the victim had died minus his testicles.

"Hey!" shouted the gnome, "I haven't got all day, I have a public to serve!"

"I'm afraid," Sam said.

"Then be brave and be quick about it!"

"But how?"

"How, you ask? You invent courage on the spot when you need it," the gnome said. "Like right now. You do something bold and then agree to deal with whatever happens. I see it all the time. Now feed me or move along, citizen."

Sam watched the letter slide down the gnome's gullet, taking his future with it.

"Ha, ha! Too late! Too late!" would ring in Sam's head for days.

And for those days, he lived in absolute dread of his own telephone. Understandable, as there might be a ravenous, slave-eating Gynotopian shark on the other end determined to devour his precious bits. He bought an answering machine to screen his calls, as if that would actually protect him. That evening he went out for dinner and returned to hear a message:

"Good evening, slave. You know who this is. I will soon have you begging and screaming. Return my call immediately."

Sam listened to the recording seven times—twice to write down her phone number as he had trouble gripping the pen. Four times listening to her low and silky voice wrap itself around his throat and genitals. And once again to make sure he heard everything right. With only four sentences she had him shaking like a plate of jello. *My God, what could she do with more? And in person?* "Return my call immediately," she'd said. No, she'd commanded it. To this point Mistress Morgaine had been a safe and tantalizing game. Now it had become deadly serious.

Sam immediately and without hesitation called her back without thinking. Thinking, he rightly knew, would scuttle the entire venture. And he'd sure better obey her first order. And without thinking, he got down on his knees. That surprised him. To his utter relief, her answering machine responded. Then to his absolute terror, Mistress Morgaine picked up, and the tall, busty fantasy in black leather was suddenly very real and very much in his face.

"This is Mistress Morgaine. Who is this?" Her voice was sultry and her mood impatient, appropriate for a haughty Goddess from Gynotopia.

"This is Sam, uh, I mean slave sam," he mumbled. *How to sound slavish?* "And I'm calling you back, Mistress… um, is calling you Mistress okay?" He grimaced at his buffoonery.

Astonishingly, Mistress Morgaine remained on the line.

"I'm not yet your Mistress, and being my slave remains to be seen. Is that clear?"

"Yes, Mistress, I mean, I'm sorry, I don't know what I mean."

"Your apology is accepted," breathed the lovely and dangerous Mistress. "What you're doing is very brave. I like brave boys."

The compliment spread throughout Sam's body like ravaging army ants.

"I also liked what you checked in the questionnaire," she said. "Some things I liked very much. Now, my pet, what are your expectations of me?"

"I, uh… expectations?"

"You don't understand the question?"

"No."

"I'm not surprised," she said, "most men don't. Well, that's not important. What's really important are *my* expectations, and I have many of them. As my slave, it will be your job to fulfill them, immediately, instantly, and without hesitation. Do you understand?"

"Yes."

"I'm not sure you do, but you will. I'll soon have you screaming and begging for more."

Screaming and begging for more. That seemed to be the standard dominatrix tagline, and not a very original one. But what did he expect? They set a date for a session in five days.

"Bring your best manners, my soon-to-be slave," she said. "I will tolerate nothing less."

Slave. Sam tried the word on. It didn't excite him like he'd thought it would. It sounded alien. It made him feel fragmented and disoriented, like he had the body of a man but with Gynotopian genitals transplanted on, and the mind of someone he didn't know—or would even want to.

Are you sure you really want to do this, citizen twit?

Yes. I'm being brave. Mistress even said so.

Good. Do you know why Mistress likes brave boys so much?

No. Why?

It's more exciting for her when she turns them into quivering cowards.

14

MISTRESS MONSTER

SAM WONDERED IF THERE WAS A Uniform Code of Female Domination that stipulated a mandatory waiting period before an s/m session, the purpose being to make the client torture himself ditzy for days with obsession, anticipation, and fear. With Carmine and now Morgaine, five days seemed to be the standard. Any less and the man's suffering would be incomplete; any more and he might die in an explosion of semen. Sam had no choice but to go ditzy. He also couldn't leave himself alone. He might not have his genitals much longer, so why not enjoy them while he still could? Then he feared he wouldn't have enough of them left for Mistress Morgaine's sincerely cruel attentions.

Five days of relentless mental s/m later, the evening finally arrived. Sam parked in front of her house twenty minutes early and waited, assuming the lack of punctuality would result in very bad things happening to him. He studied her house; like Carmine's, it was an ordinary-looking post-war, one-story bungalow giving no indication of being Gynotopian property and housing one of its revered goddesses. Seventeen minutes to go. Sam discovered he could freeze the hands on his watch by just staring at them.

But the hands finally thawed and, as instructed, Sam nervously stood at her back door, the threshold of Mistress Morgaine's chateau of cruel bondage. A hand-lettered sign on the door read *slave Entrance*—not your ordinary bungalow welcome mat. A black cat crouched on a window ledge and watched every move Sam made through slitted eyes. He reached to pet it. "Touch me and die," its hiss warned. The ill-tempered thing must belong to the Mistress.

There was the doorbell. It wasn't too late. He could still turn around and escape. He watched his finger press the bell. For one long minute nothing happened. *Maybe she's not home. Maybe she forgot and I'll survive.* He again reached for the bell and *oh holy shit* the door swung open. There stood the Dominatrix Mistress Morgaine, wearing a tight-fitting black leather dress and stiletto-heeled shoes that made her a foot taller than he. Her face was hidden in the shadows.

"Don't ever look at my eyes, slave!" she immediately snapped.

Sam instantly dropped his gaze, stunned by this sharp, unexpected greeting. There was no doubt who was in charge here. "Too late, too late," he could hear the gnome and cat sing. Mistress Morgaine stepped back and beckoned Sam to enter the hell world of Gynotopia. If Carmine's play space was a sex convenience store, this dungeon was a supermall. One entire wall of the large, dimly-lit basement room displayed chains, coils of rope, leather restraints, whips, floggers, and other mysterious and dangerous-looking implements made of wood, metal, and rubber whose uses Sam did not want to imagine, and yet he wanted it all.

There were several elaborate bondage constructions: the wooden vertical bondage rack Sam had seen in her ad; a large, sturdy chair festooned with leather straps with its legs spread wide; and a leather-padded bench with wrought-iron manacles bolted to its corners. The centerpiece was a large, sturdy, Medieval-looking wooden rack complete with a winch that could easily dislocate joints, no doubt snatched from the Inquisition Museum of Curiosities.

In one corner of the room was a cubical cage made of heavy steel bars that could have restrained a gorilla. The door was locked with a large padlock, and a steel hook hung from the cage's center bar. Sam had seen similar hooks in a butcher shop. At the far wall was an ornately carved, high-backed, large wooden chair, painted black and upholstered in red velvet cushions. Mounted above the chair on the wall was the corpse of a crow with its wings spread wide and nailed to a board. It spoke of dark magic—sinister Gynotopian magic—and seriously spooked him. "Abandon all hope, ye who enter here," the bird's lifeless, glassy black eyes seemed to say.

With a flourish, Mistress Morgaine swept onto her throne holding her scepter, a thin, wicked-looking black cane. It took Sam enormous effort not to see who this creature was.

"Strip, slave," she hissed like her cat. "I want to examine my property."

It took Sam a few seconds to realize that meant him. He knelt to undo his shoelaces.

"Nice and slow. Do a nice striptease for Mistress."

Sam complied. Soon he was naked and feeling about as sexy as a cow pie.

"Kneel."

Sam knelt. She rose from her throne and deftly tied his hands behind his back with a length of rope. He tested the bond. It held. Now it was absolutely, positively, and officially too late. Mistress Morgaine grabbed his hair and pulled back his head.

"Are you trying to escape, slave?"

"N-no, Mistress."

"Do you know what I do to my slaves who try to escape?"

"N-no, Mistress."

"I castrate them."

If Sam could have shit, he would have.

Mistress Morgaine laughed. "I will not castrate you unless you beg me for it, worm."

Beg to be castrated? Unthinkable. Not possible.

You think so, twit?

"You may keep your balls," she said, "for the time being."

Sam's relief was barely palpable through his terror. Mistress Morgaine took his belt and looped it tightly around his neck.

"Next time I'll get you a proper collar," she said.

Next time? Oh, I think not. Please let me survive this time, Sam decided after only four minutes in her thrall.

Mistress Morgaine roughly grabbed his genitals and stuffed them into a leather restraint, leaving the head of his fear-shriveled penis exposed.

"Look at the poor little worm," she said. "It's afraid."

To emphasize the worm's condition, she whapped it with the cane. Sam screamed.

"I like to hear my slaves scream," she said. "You will be screaming a lot for Mistress."

Sam truly had no idea what to do or say next. Mistress Morgaine the hot booklet fantasy and Mistress Morgaine the terrifying reality lived on opposite arms of the Milky Way. And her odd referral to herself in the third person struck him as bizarre, adding an otherworldly and palpably deranged cast to this horror show. His only road was to follow her orders the best he could and pray for deliverance from this monster.

Mistress Monster attached a leash to the genital restraint and stretched it taut. "Pay attention, slave. These are my rules," she said, leaning forward into his ashen face. Sam reactively started to look up.

"I said to keep your eyes down!" she shouted and slapped his face. "That's the first order I give you and you fucking disobey it?"

The slap was another unexpected and brutal reminder of his predicament. It jolted him to the bone. He'd asked for mistreatment, and this was it. What he'd naïvely expected would be a fun game had turned into a living nightmare. He genuinely feared what may come.

"Do you think you're free to disobey me?" she said. "Didn't you read my list of rules?

"No, Mistress. I mean, yes—"

"Did you say yes? Are fucking with me?" She slapped him again.

Sam's voice froze, mainly because his brain didn't know what to give it.
Oh my God! What the hell is going on here?

She's fucking with your head, twit. And your head is too fucked up to know that.

What do I do?

There's nothing you can do. What I'm doing is taking notes.

"Answer me, slave! I'm talking to you!"

"I'm sorry, Mistress. I will not obey—disobey you. I'm sorry." He braced himself for another slap.

Mercifully it didn't come. Mistress Morgaine eased the tension on the leash but still held it firm. "Know this, worm," she said contemptuously, still in his face, "I am a lesbian and I have absolutely no use for men. Men are utterly pathetic. Their little worms are just as pathetic. Both are completely worthless!"

She laid the tip of the cane on the tip of his cock. "Do you know what a worm is?"

Sam was still in shock from the slaps and couldn't speak. He nodded weakly. She raised the cane and made ready to strike. He tried to move back but the leash held him firm.

"I could slash your worm bloody," she said, and gave it a sharp crack. Sam screamed. *"Jesus!"*

"My name is not Jesus!" she shouted and again slapped his face. "Of all people!" She struck the worm again, harder.

"Please, no more!" Sam barely felt the sting on his cheek for the pain in his worm.

"And my name is not *please!*" *Crack!*

"*Gaah!* Please, *please,* Mistress!"

"That's better, worm. Now you listen carefully: if Mistress is ever too cruel to you, just say the word 'mercy' and I will release you. Do you understand?"

Thank God. "Yes, Mistress."

"And also know this, worm: if I ever hear the word 'mercy' escape from your lips, I will throw you out of my dungeon and you are never to return. Do you understand *this,* worm?"

"Yes, Mistress." *I'll sure as hell be doing that anyway,* he just decided.

"Are you a pathetic, worthless little worm with a pathetic, useless little worm?"

"Yes, Mistress."

"Now, shall I castrate the little worm?"

"No, please no, Mistress."

"Good answer, slave," she said tapping his skull. "It means you're still here, even if the little worm is not."

Sam looked down and saw what she meant. The alleged worm looked like a small, fleshy concertina desperately trying to crawl into his belly to escape the attentions of this thoroughly frightening woman. Two blood blisters had bloomed on its head.

"There are more rules. Learn them well. You will always address me as Mistress Morgaine, or Mistress, or Goddess, or Ma'am. You will not speak without first asking permission to do so."

"But if I can't speak then how can I—"

"Do not speak!" *Crack!*

The worm could retreat no further, and what remained behind sprouted another blister. Sam was completely at sea, or on another planet. Alien sharks eyed his balls, waiting for the order to attack. Mistress Morgaine grabbed his balls, pulled them upward, and gave them a light tap with her cane that sent him into blinding agony.

"You will obey every command without hesitation, or you will be hung up and Mistress will beat you." A couple more taps on the balls told him where that would be.

Mistress Morgaine waited until Sam stopped screaming and tried to catch his breath. He'd never suffered such excruciating pain, and just from light taps. He couldn't imagine surviving anything harsher, which certainly might happen. He feared his testicles would never fully recover. Then it dawned on him that she might know even worse abuses.

"Your balls are tougher than you think, slave," she said. "Shall we find out?"

The shock on his face was his answer. She rested the cane on his balls.

"There are more rules," she said. "You are never to touch any part of Mistress, or you will be hung up and severely beaten. You are not to come without permission or Mistress will severely beat you even worse. Do you understand all this, worm? Now do you know what a beating means?"

"Y-yes," he whispered, understanding nothing but fear for himself and his genitals.

Mistress Morgaine released them and gave him a few more minutes to recover.

"You listen to me carefully, worm," she scowled. "This is not a game I play. This is real, very real. This is my life. It's who I am. I do not fuck around. This is not a fucking game. Don't ever think it is. If you fuck with me or play games with me, I will destroy you."

"Y-yes, Mistress."

She let that sink in, then continued her lecture. "Also know that I'm a female supremacist. I am a true goddess, and I'm superior to men in every way. Men are utterly pathetic and worthless. Men should accept the natural supremacy of women and beg us for the privilege of groveling at our feet and being beaten."

Her arrogance was so astonishing that a laugh almost burst out of Sam.

Mistress, sensing Sam's skepticism, grabbed the belt around his throat, forced his face to floor, stepped on his neck, and venomously hissed into his ear, "I told you, I do not fucking play games!" She cracked him sharply on his ass. "This is real! You got that, you fucking worm?"

"Y-yes, Mistress."

Mistress stepped away and let Sam have his head back. "Kneel up," she said.

He struggled to his knees—difficult without the use of his hands. He dared not struggle in his bonds lest he watch his testicles bounce along the floor. He tried to remain upright, balancing on the edge of hysteria as well. *This bitch is totally crazy and I am so going to die* caromed inside his skull.

Sam's involuntary trembling greatly pleased Mistress Morgaine. She lounged back on her throne, crossed her impossibly long legs, and sharply dug the toe of her shoe into his balls. He hovered around his body, too terrified to stay in it, and saw in sharp relief the shocking picture the two of them presented: the leather-clad dominatrix with her trembling naked captive kneeling before her. Brave boy indeed. Sam had seen similar pictures in sleazy porn magazines, which he'd found pathetic and utterly repulsive. And now look, here he was, in the same magazine.

Isn't life funny, twit?

Sam didn't feel like laughing. He tried to sidetrack his terror by studying the minutiae around him. He focused on the diamond pattern of her sheer black stockings, following the design down her long legs to the points of her shiny black stiletto-heeled shoe that menacingly bounced his balls. He saw his face reflected in the sheen of her shoe leather; it was the face of an opossum lying dead on the highway. Was he looking at his future?

Mistress Morgaine rose from her throne and unzipped and shed her leather dress, revealing the outfit he'd seen in her ad: black leather bustier and minuscule black panties. Her enormous breasts overflowed the cups of the bustier. She was exquisitely proportioned, the epitome of voluptuousness. Sam stared at the mounds of her breasts, fighting the compelling urge to look higher. His worm was oblivious to it all.

"My other slaves would now be rock hard," Mistress said, tapping the worm's battered and bloody head with her cane. "Don't you find Mistress sexy and exciting?"

"Oh yes, Mistress."

"Then why are you not rock hard?"

"I, I don't know, Mistress."

"Is the little worm frightened?"

"Yes, Mistress."

"I haven't even begun to scare it," she laughed.

She untied Sam's wrists, locked a leather cuff onto each, and attached them to an overhead bar that hung from a cable running to a winch. She strapped a bar to his ankles, spreading his feet wide apart, and hoisted him off his heels. She roughly tied on a blindfold.

"Stick out your tongue, worm," Mistress Morgaine ordered.

Sam did and felt an erect nipple run across it. She removed the blindfold.

"Look at my breasts, worm."

Her breasts were now fully exposed above the bustier. She cupped them under his nose, squeezed and rolled her nipples, moaning softly as if pleasuring herself.

"Get a good look, little worm," she said. "Enjoy looking at my beautiful breasts because a look is all you'll ever get. You will never touch their silky softness."

No matter, as stark terror had disabled his lust for breasts, perhaps permanently, he feared. Mistress returned them to their bustier home, and that was the end of the evening's pleasantries. Then she went to work on him, and she was not kind. She winched him higher on his tiptoes, then whipped, beat, slapped, pinched, kicked, punched, scratched, and scolded him for almost an hour. Midway through the demolition, she snapped a leather device around his balls.

"Do you know what this is, worm? Do you know what it's for?"

"No, Mistress."

"You're about to find out."

Its purpose became immediately and horribly clear when she hung a heavy weight from it. The pain quickly escalated, approaching unbearable. Sam panicked, fearing that irreversible damage to his testicles was now in progress. She added another weight. He screamed and begged to have it removed.

"Are you calling out for mercy?" she taunted. "Do you remember what that means?"

Sam seriously thought about it. "My balls," he gasped, "I don't want—"

Mistress Morgaine briskly slapped his face. "Did I give you permission to speak?"

"N-no, Mistress."

"You worthless piece of shit! I give you a rule and then you ignore it?"

"No, Mistress."

"No?" She slapped him again, harder. He was so deep into shock he barely felt it.

"Yes, Mistress."

"Well, which is it? Yes or no? And don't you dare fuck with me!"

"I… I don't know, Mistress." It finally dawned on him that he was screwed no matter what he said, and that was part of the game. "Mercy" hovered before of him, daring him to speak it.

"You're afraid I'll damage you?" she said and lightly touched his reddened cheek.

"Y-yes, Mistress." He was shocked by her concern and wondered if he'd seen the worst.

Not a chance. "Your balls are worthless!" she screamed and slapped him again. "Your balls are what's fucking up the planet. Your goddamned balls are the cause of everything wrong in the world. You'd be much better off without your balls, you pathetic worm. I'd be doing you a huge favor by cutting them off."

She walked over to the winch. "But first let's make you completely helpless." She hoisted him completely off the floor. The growing strain in his distended arms seemed to be happening to someone else. Mistress Monster withdrew a large hunting knife from a side cabinet and held its edge against his distended scrotum.

"Now, shall I cut off your balls, worm?"

Sam was too petrified to answer. The sharks were upon him. As if a veil had suddenly lifted, Sam saw himself as a newspaper headline. It could happen right here, right now. Women were being abducted, mutilated, and murdered every day, so why not him? It would be the well-deserved price of his degeneracy. Even if he lived, it would be as a eunuch, a fitting fate for a sex degenerate.

Could he sue the cunt? No, that would be too kind. Yes, he would sneak into her house, tie her up, and torture her to death. No, not to death—she should live on, mutilated and miserable. As revenge for his loss, he'd cut off her nipples with her own knife and say, "You'll never have these again for your pleasure, you goddamned whore!" Then he'd attack the silky softness of her massive breasts with the knife and a soldering iron. But did he have a soldering iron? Where was it? Did he lend it to somebody?

Sam had heard that just prior to a violent accident, the mind mysteriously slowed down time, as if to give the victim a moment, a reprieve, to reflect on life and perhaps repent. Sam feared he'd just had his moment. *Oh God! Oh God help me!*

God is not allowed in here, twit. She's the goddess in this place. Weren't you listening?

Oh God oh God oh God.

Oh, chill out! You've got a safe word, don't you? Weren't you listening to that either?

Don't get me in trouble!

Twit! You're already in trouble! There's a knife at your balls and you haven't figured that out yet? Sheesh! Now let's see how much trouble we can get you into.

No! No! No!

Try this on her: I piss on your silky soft tits, you skanky, arrogant cunt!

"No! Please!"

Sam got another hard slap to his face.

"No, please what?" Mistress Morgaine shouted.

"No, please, Mistress!"

Mistress Morgaine was clearly amused by Sam's naked terror. She finally lowered him back onto his feet and returned the knife unbloodied to the cabinet. He was still too frozen in panic to feel relief. After a few minutes of ragged breathing, he calmed down. He tried to relieve the pain in his outstretched arms and couldn't. He would keep his balls and took his only comfort there.

But not for long. She added another weight to the ball stretcher. Sam shrieked, now more out of fear for the delicate tissue than the escalating pain.

"You should enjoy this while you can, my pet," laughed Mistress Morgain. "My castrated slaves can't." She set the weights to swinging, increasing their strain.

Sam looked at his reflection in the huge wall mirror before him, taking in the details of his predicament. He did not understand what he was seeing; he did not know himself. He could see Mistress Monster's back in the mirror: her long legs, her stunning figure, her smooth, firm ass. Her long black hair glistened like the river Styx. He wanted to destroy every inch of it.

Mistress Morgaine finally released Sam from his torments. He immediately collapsed to the floor. She slunk back into her leather dress, leaving the front unzipped, and ordered him to stand. He struggled to his feet and just stared at the mounds of her breasts above the bustier cups. Breasts that terrified far more than aroused him. *That* was a first.

Mistress stared back, impatient and irritated. "Don't just stand there," she snapped. "Zip me up, worm. You should have anticipated this duty. Are you truly that stupid and fucking worthless that I have to tell you everything?"

The scolding stung Sam worse than any of her slaps, whips, or weights. He did as she bade, too furious to enjoy sliding the zipper along her body and breasts. Something important had just happened, something from his past, something familiar and evocative. Sam knew he should pay attention to it, but he sensed Mistress Morgaine was not in the mood to process.

Instead, she tossed him a condom.

"Put this on, get down on your knees, and masturbate in front of me," she said.

Sam unrolled the condom over the blistered, limp fish of his penis. Wanking had always been a private affair, and violating his modesty was apparently Mistress Monster's next infernal abuse. *Will there ever be an end to this?* But the worm was dead beyond all hope of revival.

Thoroughly disgusted, Mistress Morgaine towed it and Sam back to her throne. She made him kneel before her, leaned back into the plush chair, and lightly poked his balls with her scepter. Sam now knew what *lightly* could do. He glanced at the dead crow above her. It seemed to be watching him in mute sorrow. *Will I end up like that?*

"Your performance tonight was absolutely abysmal, slave worm," she said at last. "Mistress is extremely disappointed in you."

The reprimand was a swift club to his guts. The woman would just not cut him a break. He couldn't imagine what he could have done better. Scream louder? Grovel lower?

"But Mistress will allow you to return for another training session."

Another training session? Not a fucking chance, you fucking bitch.

"Yes, Mistress," Sam was barely able to croak. "Thank you."

She held the toe of her shoe under his chin and he kissed it.

"Very good, my pet," she said. "You're learning. There's hope for you yet. Now, keep the belt around your neck, get dressed, and go home. When you get home, strip naked, keep your collar on, call me, and masturbate for me."

"Yes, Mistress."

Sam was elated. *I'll be free. I'll live. My balls are safe!*

He escaped home. He was free, but not quite. As she instructed, he stripped, and, still wearing the belt collar, hopped on the bed with the telephone. The worm was flaccid, raw, and too painful to touch. He delicately grasped it and dialed. Her machine answered.

"Mistress Morgaine," he mumbled into the phone, "this is Sam, your pathetic worthless worm slave. I am your devoted, humble, and worthless servant and—"

Incredibly, on the first stroke, a geyser of semen erupted from his penis, splattering it everywhere—on his chest, face, and appropriately into the mouthpiece of the telephone. Although he wasn't even sure she was listening, he gushed about her beauty and dominance and every other cliché he thought she was expecting to hear. He did not say he wanted to tear her fucking tits off or that he'd just had the most instantaneous and intense orgasm of his life.

He hung up the dripping phone. It was finally over. He was still in shock and due for another. A minute later, after only two strokes this time, his cock erupted again, providing the second most intense orgasm of his life, a feat he'd thought not possible of the human testicles.

Just what the hell did she do to me?

Sam assessed the wreckage in the bathroom mirror. His back, shoulders, chest, and butt were covered with marks and bruises from the beatings. The head and shaft of his penis were swollen and speckled with blood blisters. There were foot-long bloody streaks along his sides and back where she'd raked him with her fingernails. His buttocks were laced with long, purple welts from her cane. His testicles ached nonstop.

He took a long shower. He needed to wash Mistress Monster from his life, the bruises and welts, the lint from her carpet, his dried jism, the memory of the entire evening, everything. The shower didn't work. He took a second shower. That didn't work either. He felt polluted, irreversibly damaged, and forever fallen from grace. He feared he'd never be whole again.

But given a choice, Sam did not want a single neuron of her memory purged. In fact, he thought about screaming in her dungeon that night and for many nights to follow. There, in his own bed and safe from her predation, she became even more monstrous and vicious, the scene always ending with the complete destruction of his genitals. To his astonishment, even the idea of castration began to grow on him, and he lamented it could only be done once. He could not begin to fathom this inexplicable union of terror and sex, only that it worked and worked very well. It seemed she was a sorceress as well as a monster.

What did you expect, twit? You got what you asked for. A genuine, firebreathing bitch outside your skull. She was exactly what you want a woman to be: uncompromising, abusive, and indisputably dominant.

No! She was horrible! She truly is a monster!

And she gave you the two hottest orgasms of your life. Even I couldn't have done that.

I just don't know what to do now.

Yes, you do.

The gnome had said he should deal with it. Like the antihero in some twisted parable, Sam knew he must pay the price for his lust and blind devotion to it. Mistress Morgaine was the Minotaur in the labyrinth, the siren on the rocks, the avenging goddess made mortal, the dark sorceress who would destroy any fool who dared challenge her supremacy. Maybe she was right. Maybe some women did possess a mysterious feminine power, a sexual magic giving them absolute tyranny over men. His two geysers confirmed that. And now he was the latest in a long line of worms condemned to live with the terrible knowledge of that power and its spell-binding eroticism. Does dealing with it mean becoming the eternal fool in a no-win story?

How's dealing with it going, twit?

I hate her. I want her. I want to kill her. And I want to give her my balls. This is insane! How do I live with this?

What makes you think you can?

I want answers, not your smart-ass shit!

And what makes you think I have any? Do you want to magically think all this away? Poof! Do you want me to do it?

What about those unbelievable orgasms? How do you explain that?

Oh, that one's easy. It's the secret power women have over men.

What!?

You gave her all your power and now you want it back? Dominatrices don't have a return policy, fool! She knows your balls far better than you ever will, and can make them do anything she wants, as you just found out. She knows this because that's her job and she's very good at it. What did you think you were walking into?

I had no idea.

Of course you didn't. Being a dominatrix doesn't make her stupid or oblige her to become your stupid fantasy of one. How are your poor balls feeling now?

Sore. Empty. Angry.

Angry? They're elated! Do you want to know why they pumped out so much so quickly? Mistress Morgaine knows. She held a knife to their throat and then gave them back their lives. Wouldn't that make you want to celebrate?

15

THE LADIES OF LIGHT

THE DAMAGE SAM SUFFERED IN MISTRESS Morgaine's dungeon, both on his body and in his mind, left him feeling like that opossum roadkill he'd seen in her shoe: flattened, battered, and not sure which side of the highway was safe. He hadn't become the sniveling degenerate he'd feared, but he wasn't quite back to himself either. He felt like that zombie again: unfocused, insubstantial, staggering around in a daze, addicted to and haunted by the unrelenting memory of her dungeon and its bewitching and perplexing eroticism.

Welcome to post-traumatic slave world, twit. Are you enjoying your visit?

It's a living hell. I'm fucked.

Fucked is such an interesting word, isn't it? It means both one's delight and one's doom. And can you always tell the difference?

Of course, I can!

Indeed, you can. Oh look! There's Sam hanging from the rafters, bruised, bleeding, scared shitless, and pretending he's not being abused. Get the picture yet?

Yeah, I guess I don't.

You're not going to find what you need there, Sam. Ever.

Again, Sam found himself slouched on Judith's sofa, now playing with a Gumby. The toy wasn't helping. Not even the frog could help him now, he decided. Maybe Judith couldn't either. He wondered if her education included doing post-mortems on s/m sessions, as that's all it seemed he was bringing her.

Judith sat in her wing chair, quietly thinking about what Sam had just told her. "How are your testicles doing?" she asked.

Sam was so far beyond embarrassment that modesty became irrelevant. "Epididymitis. I'll be on meds for two weeks. They say it'll be months before they're completely healed, and I'm not supposed to... come until then. Talk about being punished! It took three hundred dollars to find that out. Add that to cost of the session, and now include this—"

Sam caught himself. "Jeez, I'm sorry, Judith."

"It's all right. It sounds like you're also paying emotionally."

"Yeah, I sure am. I swear I'll never allow myself to be abused again."

Judith wrote in her notebook. That didn't bother him anymore. "Well, that's certainly a worthy objective," she said, "but will you recognize abuse when you see it? Abuse can be subtle and sneaky. People get abused all the time but don't figure it out until later, and later is usually too late. Some never figure it out."

"Yeah, well, this I figured out, and good."

"Indeed. You've had an extremely unique experience, one that few people will ever know. Mistress Morgaine gave you a gift, actually. She showed you abuse in ways impossible to ignore. You've done well to survive. You had the courage to explore, and now it's time to reap its benefits."

"Benefits?!" Sam spurted. The Gumby sprang out of his hands. "How can any good possibly come out of this? Not only am I totally mangled, but I'm also still being mangled by this damn paradox mind-fuck of mine. I get off on being abused! Look how hard it made me come! Jeez! How do you explain that?"

"Remember what I said about an adrenaline dump?"

"Yeah. I suppose. But how do I fix that? How do I get my life back? Another koan session?"

How about a session with me, worm? I'll fix that all right!

Sam hadn't told Judith about the other voice. That would open a barrel of worms. And he feared what she might say about it. Or do.

Wise move, twit.

"Let's try something else," Judith said. "First, I want you to honor yourself for being courageous enough to take the risk you did. That was huge, if you think about it. Enfold yourself in compassion and give yourself credit for being an explorer."

"That's kind of a stretch, don't you think?"

"Well, it's true, isn't it?"

"I suppose."

"Then I'd like you to do something even stretchier. I want you to thank Mistress Morgaine. Thank her with all your heart and soul. Thank her for for giving that experience to you."

Sam was incredulous. "Thank her? You can *not* be serious. After what she did to me?"

"I'm completely serious. You must accept that she's stronger, smarter, and more powerful than you, and there'll always be women like that. Accept that's what attracts you, for whatever reason, and stop pretending it doesn't. Accept that you can't become a victim and win. Does any of that make sense to you?"

He nodded and picked the Gumby from the floor.

"Good. You must accept all of this," Judith said. "And then thank her. Deeply and sincerely. That's where you'll find your freedom."

Accept all that? Sam sat back, a bit stunned. Another mountain to climb. Just not possible. Sam looked at the Gumby in his hands. There was something about its wide eyes and dufus smile that pissed him off.

"Yeah, okay, I'll give it a try," he said, not at all certain he would.

"There's another reason you need to do this, Sam."

"What's that?"

"To release your anger. Or at least begin to."

He looked up at Judith, unsure what to say.

"No one can be abused like you've been and not be angry. You're still angry at your mother, with good reason. You're utterly furious with Morgaine, with better reason. Even Carmine has a way of getting under your skin. You're angry at all women, including me."

Sam set Gumby on the table, face down. "I'm not angry at you, Judith. You've done nothing bad to me."

"I'm a woman, Sam. That's enough. I think it's time to think about why. Any ideas?"

Sam looked at Judith, sitting there calm and steady, and not a hint of judgement or reproval. Yet he could feel a monster within him needing to erupt in her face and seek... what? Revenge? Power? She was right. Why was he so fucking furious at women?

"Well, there's that boundary thing we talked about," he said.

Judith nodded.

That's just a silly word you learned from her, remember?

Sam ignored that.

"And because women have something I want—"

"Like sex and approval?"

Well, that sure went straight to the heart of it. "Yeah. It pisses me off that I want it, and that I can't stop from wanting it. It pisses me off that I've got to jump through all their goddamned hoops to get it, and then I still don't get it! What pisses me off even more is being such a needy, weak, little weenie always chasing after them. I'm utterly furious at myself for being so dependent on them! God, I'm such a wimp!"

Sam simmered for a while. He picked up the Gumby. It still irked him, and he set it down. He picked up the box of tissues, pulled one out, looked at it, then set it down as well.

"Sam, you've put yourself in a no-win situation," Judith said. "Not only are you not getting what you want, but by wanting it, you're giving away all your power. Added to that, you feel powerless to prevent it. And knowing all this and not being able to change anything makes it even worse."

"Yeah. And so I want to explode."

"Uh-huh."

"But how can I force myself *not* to want sex, knowing that I'm setting myself up to lose? That doesn't seem possible. Yeah, you're right. I'm screwed no matter what I do."

"Give yourself another option," Judith said. "Sexual desire is a natural and normal feeling. It's an essential part of being human. What makes it so insufferable is how you pressure yourself to act on it. Just because you're horny, that doesn't entitle you to anything. Try letting go of that agenda and see how you feel. Try to accept those feelings and your passion for simply what they are, rather than as an imperative to be blindly obeyed. Cherish them as one of the miracles of simply being alive."

Sam looked at Judith but didn't see her. He saw something else he couldn't quite name.

"By *you* deciding what to do with your desire," she continued, "by looking at other options, you may find something has shifted with your power issue. Can you see how that might work?"

He knew what it was, but it still had no name. *Decision* came the closest. "I do. I sure do."

"And another thing. You might find that women start showing up differently in your life. Not as a threat but something else. You might even begin to see who they are and resent them a little less."

Sam picked up the tissue.

"Go home and think about all this," Judith said. "Acknowledge your incredible courage for taking the risks you have. Especially coming here. Be good to yourself. And then thank Morgaine with all your heart."

Sam *decided* to consider it—that made the task seem less preposterous and threatening. Admittedly, he was reluctant to give up his nights screaming in the Mistress Morgaine's fantasy dungeon, yet he mourned all the days he'd lost to anguish and despair as a zombie, trying to escape his seemingly inescapable enthrallment. Weary and at wit's end, he made another decision—not to consider, but actually *take* Judith's advice, as strange as it seemed. He would thank Mistress Morgaine as sincerely as possible. Not to her face, as she didn't have one, but to her memory, still vibrant, toxic, and erotically radioactive.

He cleared a space in his living room, stripped (as that seemed appropriate for the occasion), sat down on his pillow, and breathed slowly for a few minutes. He tried to think about nothing and saw that it was, as usual, futile. He summoned Morgaine's visage, a much easier task: long, perfect legs topped by enormous breasts, topped by a faceless void.

Then he tried playing koan. It wasn't difficult to visualize the opposites: a blood-blistered penis and silky soft breasts; bruised balls and a semen-drenched telephone. But those scenes ignited both his lust and anger, threatening to obliterate any koan senseless enough to show up. He couldn't dampen either response, so he surrendered them, feeling as hot and furious as he needed to be.

After his emotional maelstrom finally burned itself out, Sam surprisingly found himself in the center of that calm of nothingness he'd been struggling to attain. There were no explanations, no judgements, no expectations, just pure nothing. Inexplicably, in the next instant, a burst of white light enveloped him, so sudden and startling that for a panicked moment he thought the The Bomb had been dropped.

Perhaps it had. What surprised him even more was that everything about that horrible evening now felt absolutely perfect—the scolding, the insults, the beatings, the brutality, and the pain. It all was as it was supposed to be. Then he thanked Morgaine, the woman inside the dominatrix suit, from deep within his heart, and unbelievably felt a surge of love for her.

Well, that *was a shocker.*

To you and me both.

Even more shocking, the meditation worked. Although no epiphanies emerged, Sam felt calmer and less disoriented. It was a small taste of empowerment, and it was just what he needed.

And it was a good time to get it, because a few days later his answering machine presented him with this: "Hello, my pet slave. I believe you're due for your next training session. Call me at once without hesitation. And bring me the collar from your dog."

Sam was baffled. *Dog? What dog? Am I the dog?*

Then it hit him—she was confusing him with another one of her worm slaves. *What the hell?* She'd been the singular, obsessive, and devotional focus of his life for almost two weeks, and she didn't know who the fuck he was. That stung as much as those taps on his balls—almost.

"Don't even think about going back, you fool," his balls screamed. "No matter how much you think you love her." For once, he listened. *What to do?* Not return the call? No, she'd certainly keep after him as the runaway slave who'd be duly castrated if caught. But how could he stand up to this overpowering tyrant? His aching, aggrieved testicles insisted he find a way.

Clutching this tenuous resolve, he called and, as expected, got her answering machine. *Would she be listening?* "This is… Sam," he breathed out. No slave sam. No worm. Not now, not ever. "I'm sorry but I—"

"Oh, you're thinking about running away, are you, slave?" Indeed, she had been screening the call.

"I can't do this. You're just, this is all just too—"

"Do you remember what I do to insolent, disobedient, runaway slaves?"

Sam knew but held fast to his mission. He could feel the acid in her voice and worried it might drip through the phone line. He had no idea how to proceed.

"You'd better think about this," Morgaine said. "You'll never, *ever,* find a Mistress of my quality and dominance anywhere. My dungeon has no equal, and I have no equal. Are you absolutely sure you want to give that up?"

"I'm sorry but I—"

She hung up on him. Her willingness to do so both surprised and hurt him. But it was done. He was off the hook. *Thank God.*

No, thank Mistress Morgaine. Again. Haven't you learned anything here, twit?

I don't know what I've learned.

Really? You haven't learned you don't like a knife at your nuts?

Yeah, that I've learned.
Really? Then why do keep wanking about it?

AFTER HIS TESTICLES HAD FULLY HEALED; the trauma of that nightmarish evening had subsided to a vague, almost imperceptible ache; and Mistress Morgaine had been consigned to fantasy, where she thrived as erotically and frighteningly as ever, Sam declared the incident officially dealt with so he could move on.

And he knew where to go. He'd finally accepted that seductive, dangerous women were his bane, so naturally, their opposite, women of light and love, were the answer. The symmetry of that logic felt solid, tidy, and made to order. Life, however, is fluid, seldom tidy, and always has its own plans. But that chilling dictate from the Mistress's manifesto would not remain silent—the one warning that he'd quickly tire of ordinary women. It abraded Sam and his organs, vital and otherwise, to think she may be right.

Sam cast about for his ladies of light. He didn't precisely know what a lady of light was, only what she wasn't. But he knew their symptoms. The depressed, moody women of his past disastrous forays into romance were still around and just as depressed as ever, but now they were walking the road to physical, emotional, and spiritual wellness. It seemed to be working superbly well for them, so he thought he'd better follow behind. He was certain these women knew something he didn't, which, he sourly admitted, he'd always believed anyway, but that didn't mean it wasn't still true.

Please run that by me again, twit.
Um, I don't think I can.
Of course, you can't. It's garbage. Good luck on your newest doomed voyage.

The Mind Flower was a small bookshop on the edge of the university's campus, operated by the followers of an East Indian guru. From the books in the window display, Sam inferred the shop's focus was the attainment of spiritual enlightenment by purchasing books on how to attain spiritual enlightenment, and there seemed to be no end to the various pathways. Wary of being assimilated into some cult, he'd never gone in.

But now seemed like the right time. Curiously, he felt just as nervous entering this shop as he had on his first porn excursion years ago. The store's enlightened staff, he presumed, would sense his diseased aura as easily as they could smell a skunk, and he'd be thrown out before he was two feet through the door.

Instead, he received a loving, compassionate smile from the young woman behind the sales counter, which threw him further. She was dressed in a brightly colored Indian sari, a saffron choli top, and sandals. Her nose was pierced and the center of her forehead bore a red bindi. She would have blended into any market in Delhi except for her rotund figure, strawberry-blonde hair, and freckles.

"How can we help you today?" she sweetly and serenely asked.

Help. That word became the hook. Then and there, Sam decided he needed all the help he could get, or at least buy, and this was just the place to find it.

"Oh, I'm just browsing," he said.

"Wonderful. Take your time," she said, her eyes never leaving him.

He wandered among the immaculately ordered shelves of books, magazines, meditation gongs, vajras, and other Eastern esoterica, all gently perfumed by bowls of smoldering incense. He became self-conscious under the woman's loving scrutiny as he browsed. *Browse.* What a shallow and coarse term for such a high-minded intention as selecting a path to transcendence. He wished he'd said something more... evolved.

How about "I'm opening my heart chakra to find the next step on my spiritual quest"? That would have frosted her cupcake.

That makes me want to puke.

Well, it's true, isn't it? Just change "spiritual" to "foolish."

Sam bought two books: one was the journal of a young spiritual quester who found his bliss by dragging himself from one end of Nepal to the other. The other was a compilation of Eastern mysticism, quantum physics, and Meso-American mythology distilled into a unified theology that would raise the planet's vibrational frequency and heal it. Sam suspected he'd never open either book but would add them to his growing pile of should-reads. If he couldn't attain nirvana, perhaps his bookshelf might.

The Anglo-Indian princess seemed pleased with his choice of books. He noticed a large bulletin board next to the front door that displayed the business cards of various spiritual, new-age, and alternative healing practitioners. Photographs on the cards indicated most of the entrepreneurs were women, and pretty ones at that. *Oh yes, this is the path for me.*

You bet. A buffet of every type of distraction possible.

What distraction? These are all valid, uh, you know, spiritual things.

Oh? Women are now "spiritual things?" Is that any different from being sex objects? It's the same old song, twit, just different words.

There was also a bright orange flyer tacked to the board—hard to miss as it covered up a dozen business cards. Sam skimmed it until the words *tantric yoga* and *sex* caught his eye. He knew what sex was.

"What's tantric yoga?" he asked the young woman. Her smile vanished. *Curious.*

"There's books about it over there." She pointed to a bookcase and turned away.

Her surprising reaction got him even more interested in tantric yoga. There was a talk about it that very evening. He was there.

The presenters were a young married couple who apparently were still in nuptial bliss thanks to their practice. Tantra, they said, is a pathway to enlightenment that uses sex, done consciously, as the vehicle. Meditating on one's chakras, the body's energy centers, was central to the practice. Sam had heard about chakras and how important they were for spiritual growth. But they remained mysterious, esoteric, and just beyond his ability to feel them, or intuit them, or whatever the hell you did with chakras. He worried he had been born without them. He also wasn't clear about the difference between sex and conscious sex, but he assumed there had to be one, and that's why he was there.

Across the room, sitting calmly on a purple pillow, was a dark-haired woman of around forty in lavender shorts and an oversized, unbuttoned white shirt covering a low-necked, snug black tank top. Her long hair was gathered into a bun somehow held together with a couple of chopsticks. She looked like a sexy female Buddha. Sam's meditative focus shifted from his supposed third eye chakra to one much lower. He caught her eye and she smiled back at him.

Her name was Mauve, he learned on their way to a juice bar after the presentation. Mauve was wearing a black leather jacket, although the night temperatures didn't require it. They sat down in a booth and Mauve removed the chopsticks from her bun, sending her hair cascading down her shoulders. She shrugged out of the jacket and then her shirt. *Black tank tops will be the death of me*, Sam thought.

"I like your jacket," he said, thinking it might mean what black leather usually meant.

Not this time. "Thank you," Mauve said. "It's my animal skin, my protection. When I'm wearing it, I feel more powerful and closer to my wild nature, my natural woman. You know, the goddess within me."

"Goddess?" *Goddess again.* That simultaneously intrigued, repelled, and spooked him.

"Yeah. The sacred feminine principle. Men have their God and we have our goddesses. You know, Kali, Freya, Hecate, Quan Yin. They talked about that tonight, right?"

"Right." Sam struggled to recall what had been said and prayed Mauve wouldn't quiz him. Already the charade was beginning.

"Most men run for the hills when they hear the word *goddess*," she said. "They feel nervous, threatened, like she's coming after their balls or something. But I sense that you're different. There's a certain energy around you. I think you understand who the goddess is and what she's really about, and you've made your peace with her."

How Mauve had intuited all that, and so quickly, puzzled him, but he wasn't about to protest or question it. He vividly remembered his last encounter with a goddess who definitely had been after his balls. Would she be Mauve's goddess, too? Still, the compliment warmed him.

Ahh, the power of positive feminine regard. It's like a drug to you, isn't it?

And what's wrong with that?

Twit! Everything's wrong with that if you're an addict.

"Yeah, I've seen an aspect of the goddess," Sam said. "Indeed, she is very... powerful."

"So mote it be," Mauve said, smiling. "Not many men are willing to admit that."

Another nice fix. Doesn't that feel great?

Go away, damn it!

Not a chance! I wouldn't miss what's coming next for anything!

What's coming next?

What do you think? Why are you here with her? To be lectured about goddesses?

Mauve sipped her chai. "What did you think of the presentation?" she asked.

"Well, I'm not sure I know what sexual energy is. I mean, sex is sex, right?"

"Not really. Sexual energy is not the same as sex. It energizes sex, but it's more about awareness and feeling the energy moving through your body. The sensation in your genitals is your focus. But instead of having an orgasm, you move that energy through your chakras and open them up. That's where true transformation happens. That's what tantra is supposed to do. Does that make sense?"

Sam wholeheartedly approved of conversations about sex with a woman, as that might lead to actual sex later, but that usually happened after several dates. With Mauve it happened after only five minutes and with startling candor. That in itself should have been a cause for celebration, but he had no idea what the fuck she was talking about.

"Uh, I guess it doesn't," he said. "This is all very new to me."

Mauve regarded him for a moment, thinking. "I know I'm being forward, but you seem like a man I can be forward with."

"Well, thank you."

"You're safe. I felt that right away."

"Thank you again." But *safe* nettled him. It didn't feel like a compliment; it had another meaning he couldn't quite get and suspected he wouldn't like. But what the hell.

"Forward away, Mauve."

"Would you be open to exploring tantra with me?"

Sam had zero experience with any solicitation from any woman of any kind, let alone such a direct one and from such an attractive woman. His response was to open his mouth.

"It wouldn't be about sex," Mauve said. "At least not at first. But how about trying some exercises and just see where it goes? Do you feel okay with that?"

"But we barely know each other." Sam was still in disbelief. A beautiful woman was offering herself, and why was he demurring? Something didn't feel quite right here.

"Can we say we ever truly know one another?" she said. "My parents were together for fifty years and still didn't know each other. But I know my intuition, and it says to proceed with this man." Mauve gave him a luminous, lady-of-light smile.

Sam put caution aside and lit up as well. "Agreed."

"Good! Let's go back to my place," she said.

Mauve lived in a large, third-floor studio apartment. At first Sam thought he'd walked into a greenhouse; potted plants formed a solid green bank along the south-facing wall. The room was clean and orderly but spartan. The only furnishings were large pillows arranged around a faded oriental carpet and a restored solid oak desk neatly stacked with textbooks and notebooks. The room's centerpiece was a sturdy massage table, which he immediately thought could be used in other ways. *Bad Sam. Bad boy.*

Mauve turned on the desk lamp and closed the curtains. He examined the books on her desk. Some were in Chinese.

"I'm in acupuncture school," she said. "Only one more year to go. Have you ever had a treatment?"

"I haven't. Isn't that done with needles? Doesn't it hurt?"

"You can hardly feel them, they're so small."

Gee, that's no fun, Bad Sam wanted to say and was sure glad he didn't. Mauve spread a sheet on the massage table then removed her shoes. And right there, as he stood and watched, she took off her shirt, wriggled out of her tank top and bra, and lay face down on the table.

Tantra. Oh yes.

"Let's start by you giving me a back rub," she said. "Are you comfortable with that?"

"Um, if you're comfortable with that."

"Well, I'm half naked in front of you, aren't I?"

Mauve rested her face on her arms and closed her eyes. Her breasts plumped to either side underneath her. Sam was no masseur, but one doesn't need much training for a back rub. He began on her neck and shoulders, then gently kneaded the smaller muscles along her spine. Mauve smiled and began the human equivalent of purring.

Sam lightly ran his fingertips along the sides of her breasts. More purring. *All right, then.* He gently worked the soft flesh with his thumb and fingers. Mauve seemed to be in tantric bliss. He hooked a finger under the waistband of her shorts and slowly pulled. The purring stopped.

"Not tonight," Mauve gently said. "It's not time."

"Sure, I understand." In that moment Sam felt the balance of power tip away from him, and he knew it would be damned hard to tip it back.

Mauve sat up and stretched, unabashed by her state of undress. She smiled dreamily, put her shirt back on, but didn't button it. Goddess or not, Sam was liking this natural woman.

"Now it's your turn," she said.

He instantly froze. Many of Morgaine's welts and scratches were still visible.

"Uh, I haven't had a shower in two days," he said.

"No problem. You can use mine."

Sam remained immobile. *I'm dead.*

You so are.

"Is there a problem?" Mauve asked.

"I'm not, well, I guess, I'm just not ready for this." *Lame, oh so lame.*

"You're not ready for this? Two minutes ago you were all over my tits and now you're telling me you're not ready? What's going on?"

Sam sighed. Mauve folded her arms across her chest and stared at him.

"Well, you'll have to know eventually," he said and started to unbutton his shirt.

"Good," she said flatly. "Honesty is good."

Sam removed his shirt.

"Holy shit," Mauve said. "What happened to you?"

He told her.

Mauve listened without expression. She remained silent, thinking. Sam just stood there, exposed like a criminal locked into a pillory in the town square and awaiting the worst.

"We can work on this, you know," she at last said.

"Work on what?"

"Sam! This is not healthy. You know that. Look at you!"

Sam put his shirt back on. He couldn't look at Mauve. The lady of light indeed. He felt like an ant shriveling to a crisp in the circle of white spiritual light under her magnifying glass. He'd never felt more ashamed and diseased.

"Say something," she urged.

"It's who I am. I'm sorry."

"You're sorry for who you are? That's even worse than your... your sickness. Jesus, what the hell was I thinking?"

"I think I'd better go."

Mauve nodded.

Jesus, what the hell was I thinking?

You weren't thinking at all, twit! What did you think was going to happen? Could you really see Mauve dressed in black leather with a whip or fawning at your feet in handcuffs?

I thought she could help me.

Oh, so now you're back to being sick again. Then why didn't you accept her offer?

Maybe I should have.

Indeed. Not all handcuffs are made of steel, you nice, safe man.

16

THE SAFE WOLF

SAM WAITED UNTIL HIS BODY LOOKED like a normal, healthy male body again, at least on the outside, and he decided it should stay that way. The liberating light he'd seen in Judith's office had disappeared in the harsh glare of Mauve's luminescent chakras, and he didn't know how to turn it back on. The darkness of Morgaine's dungeon still illuminated his nights, but going back there was out of the question. What to do now? Where to go?

Back to the Mind Flower, back to the fountain of help. The bodhisattva maiden was behind the sales counter.

"How was your trip into tantra?" she asked.

Sam's glum face was his answer. Her smile brightened. The woman certainly didn't hide her biases. "What's next on your journey?" she asked.

Sam startled. "How do you know there's something next?"

"There's always something next."

Smart girl. I may hire her and take some time off.

Sam perused the bookshelves for the next something. He remembered once seeing a book titled, *You're Okay Just the Way You Are.* But one could always be more okay, and buying this book would do it. Was there ever such a book with the premise of "You're a piece of shit, so quit pretending you're not and just learn to live with it"? At least it would be honest. But not in this bookstore.

He returned to the bulletin board and examined it more closely. It appeared to be divided into sections. One displayed the cards of various types of therapies, some of which smelled a bit dubious. Dream therapy. Primal emotions therapy. Aroma therapy. Past life regression therapy. Try anything off the road of normality and call it a therapy, no license, training, or integrity required. Sam suspected there were nuggets of wisdom and healing buried in these practices, but sifting through the rubble seemed too laborious and not worth the money.

Another section advertised more grounded alternative healing practices. He knew that naturopathy and homeopathy had been around for ages and now in the 90s had edged into mainstream acceptance. In addition, there was Rolfing, reflexology, acupressure, acupuncture, Ayurvedic medicine, moxibustion, reiki, and so on. The more Sam considered all the many possibilities for healing, the sicker he felt. Perhaps that was their point.

There were also notices advertising ongoing support groups. Most were legitimate and worthwhile. Alcoholics Anonymous. Drug recovery groups. Survivors of domestic violence. Survivors of incest. He paused to think about that one. A sex addiction group caught Sam's eye and he guiltily passed it over. It seemed if there was any vice, affliction, or abuse, there was a group to deal with it.

One card jumped out at him. A weekly discussion group about New Age relationships. Sam had seen what misery old age relationships had brought him, and he became interested. "New Age," as he'd learned over time, was the term applied to a loose assemblage of philosophies and beliefs about living in harmony with oneself, with others, and the earth. Fundamental to New Age thought was raising one's consciousness and practicing love and compassion. Enough people doing that, it was believed, would usher in an era of global peace and love. In simpler words, the New Age. Its paradigm was just as simple: if it feels right, it is.

New Age activities could look like many things, from mindfully eating a tofu and kale salad to taking an astral journey to Pleiades Level Nine, but generally it entailed folks meditating, chanting, smiling, and hugging each other, whether they wanted to or not. Given rigid Old Age morality, repressive religions, dogmatic thinking, and parochial politics, anything New Age had to be better. Sam was on board.

At the first meeting of this group, Sam discovered another benefit to the New Age: there were far more women walking this path than men, and they were keeping an eye open for guys who'd evolved beyond their dicks. Indeed, one New Age tenet declared that testicles, or more specifically testosterone, were the pariah of the planet, and it was incumbent on men to manage them properly. Mistress Monster had given Sam an enraged lecture about this, which had been echoed in less strident but just as resolute conversations with other women. Testosterone had caused him enough problems, and he despaired at being given another.

Sam took his seat on one of the large pillows arranged in a circle around the meeting room and appraised the scene. He was one of four men among twenty women, a favorable ratio, and everyone was looking around at everyone else, no doubt with New Age relationship on their minds. He thought, if you were to take away the pillows, substitute mai tais for herbal tea, and add a few hanging ferns, you'd essentially have a single's lounge. Or close enough.

A dark-skinned, raven-haired beauty walked into the room and looked around for a vacant pillow. There was one next to Sam and she headed right for it. He couldn't look away from her. Her eyes were the brightest blue he'd ever seen. She was wearing a low-cut peasant blouse and a loose skirt. She gave Sam a quick, warm smile and set down her bag. She bent over to look through it, giving him a clear view down her open neckline. He looked away but too late. Her firm, brown breasts had already hijacked his brain and arrested his breathing. She settled into the pillow, closed her radiant eyes, and calmly sat, oblivious to the turmoil sitting next to her.

Sam thought he ought to do likewise. He closed his eyes and calmed his breathing. He tried to visualize the pure white light of consciousness, but it kept changing into the peasant blouse beside him. He sensed some movement and looked. Indeed, she'd leaned close to him.

"I'm Lynn," she said, her blue eyes glittering.

"Sam," Sam could barely whisper.

Lynn said nothing more, closed her eyes, and returned to her reverie. His reverie was now toast. The pure white light never stood a chance.

The facilitator of the group entered the room. She wore no nametag indicating such, but everyone seemed to know who she was. A heavyset crone in her late sixties with a streak of purple in her gray hair, she was dressed in a brightly colored muumuu accented with a necklace of seashells and beads. With some effort and wincing, she sat down on a pillow and settled herself. She closed her eyes, folded her hands across her lap, took a deep breath, and appeared to meditate. Others in the room took the cue and did the same. For Sam, serenity was simply not possible at the moment.

"My name is Heart Feather," she began after a few minutes of silence. "I want to thank all of you for coming tonight to talk about being in relationship, especially the men. It's a shame so few of you are here, and I know that took courage."

Sam didn't appreciate hearing his gender being chastised. He also noted that Heart Feather had dropped the article when she'd said *in relationship*. He suspected that was important in some way, and he probably wouldn't like that either.

Heart Feather continued. "Changing the current paradigm of relationship indeed takes courage and commitment from both genders. It's time we evolved beyond our old ways and patterns. That's the heart of the New Age movement, to challenge and reform. In this group we're going to visualize what relationship looks like, what it feels like, and how we can open ourselves to new possibilities for relationship and ways to make it flourish."

She stopped to look around the circle, nodding and smiling at each individual. *Courage*, she'd said about the men. Sam didn't feel particularly brave at the moment, just mildly irked. Not the best way to proceed, he knew, but he couldn't douse the ember smoldering in his gut.

"Let's go around the circle," Heart Feather said. "Introduce yourself and say a few words about what brought you here."

Sam was confident he could say his name without any trouble, but what would come after that concerned him. Thank God he was near the end of the queue.

After a few of them spoke, it became clear to Sam that the women here were highly intelligent, keenly intuitive, and frighteningly perceptive. He knew he could never be half as aware or as articulate. Then it hit him. Women knew the emotional landscape far better than he ever would. That meant *relationship* would always be on their turf. That pissed him off. But if he wanted to have a relationship, or *relationship*, he'd have to accept that. That pissed him off even more. Therefore, women had to be wiser, smarter, and essentially perfect to justify his unconditional surrender to their authority.

Is that why I'm so angry at them?

You tell me. And we are wiser and smarter than you, so suck it up. Are you angry at basketball players because they're taller than you?

No. Yes. Damn right I am!

Sam masked his anger well—he'd become good at that as he'd had enough opportunities to practice over the years. He looked at the other men in the circle who seemed to be interested in this New Age show and tell. Now he understood why there weren't more men here: most were just intuitive and perceptive enough to know a trap when they saw one.

Do you know why you don't trust us, twit? It's because you're not trustworthy yourself.

What? I'm totally honest, or at least I'm trying to be.

Pah! Look how angry you are at women, and then see how nice you are to them.

So?

You assume they do the same thing to you.

It was Lynn's turn to speak.

"My name is Lynn," she said. "I'm here tonight seeking healing, with the goddess's help."

Oh my God, another goddess freak. Something inside Sam deflated.

"I feel like I'm possessed by a darkness in my soul," Lynn continued. "A darkness in my sexuality that has prevented me from knowing the gift of relationship."

Oh, really? Sam started to reinflate.

"There's violence within me," she said. "Sexual violence and pain that I've turned inward on myself. I don't know why it's there, but it shouldn't be. Relationship and sex should be about joy and pleasure, not pain and self-abuse. I came tonight to learn how relationship can show me a healthier path."

Sam just stared at her. *I don't believe this.*

Believe what? You've found your kinky soulmate? She's trying to heal her dysfunction, and all you can think about is reinforcing it. What a guy!

"What a courageous admission," said Heart Feather. "Indeed, violence has no place in the world, or in our beds, our bodies, or our beings. Violence is the result of an imbalance caused by the domination of the masculine, the patriarch. If we were to cultivate and express the nurturing feminine within us, we'd see much less violence and more peace. Thank you for sharing that with us, Lynn."

Heart Feather looked straight at Sam. "Would you agree with that?"

Sam stared back at her. He was still reeling from Lynn's confession, in essence his own. Heart Feather's jabs at masculinity surprised him and stuck in his throat. He went from irked to truly peeved, and his anger soon turned into an acidic pit in his stomach, where he felt something dark and savage start to incubate. His face grew hard.

Watch it, twit. You're outnumbered and outgunned here.

I have to say something.

How about kiss my patriarchal ass, you self-absorbed, flaky, misandrist bitch?

Nowhere near good enough.

Lynn turned her magical blue eyes toward him. He took a deep breath.

"No, I wouldn't," he said to Heart Feather. "I think reducing a complex issue like violence into such simplistic terms can obscure its real causes and is a just another way to avoid taking personal responsibility."

Heart Feather regarded Sam for a moment. "Thank you for sharing that. And what would you say taking personal responsibility looks like?"

Sam regarded her back, that thing in his stomach kicking to get out.

Careful, Sam.

Fuck careful.

Sam had run out of words and steam. "I don't know," he sighed. He could feel Lynn's gaze still on him. He couldn't look at her.

"Then perhaps you'll find out tonight," Heart Feather said. She looked at the woman sitting on Sam's left. "And what brought you here tonight, dear?"

Sam added humiliation to his already roiling stew. At least he didn't have to ad lib any reasons for attending this inquisition. He tuned out of the group to sulk. He didn't care why people were there, or about visualizing the difference between relationship and *a* relationship, or anything else this bitch might have to say. He visualized kicking his own stupid ass for even being there. The only item of interest was sitting on a pillow to his right, seemingly engrossed by the discussion. He glanced at Lynn. She smiled and winked. He had to say something, anything to keep her engaged and interested.

So the two of you can embark on a journey of sexual violence and mutual enabling?

Maybe. What do you care?

Jeez, you are really off the deep end tonight. That kind of turns me on, actually.

Sam noticed movement in the room. Apparently, Heart Feather had announced a fifteen-minute break. Lynn stretched her long, brown arms and turned to him.

"That was sure something you said to her," she said. "And I completely agree with you. Blaming the masculine is just a cop-out. It's a way of trashing men and not looking like a sexist."

Sam just swam around in those brilliant blue eyes.

"Here," said Lynn. "Give me your hand."

If she'd asked for his pancreas, he would have complied. Lynn took his palm and lightly traced the lines with her fingertip. He felt a swoon approach at her touch.

"Ah, your heartline is strong," she said.

"Are you reading my palm?"

Lynn closed her eyes. "Yes. I have an intuitive gift for this. Hmm…"

"Hmm what?"

"I'm getting a strong vibe. Yes. It seems we've been lovers in a past lifetime. Maybe several lifetimes."

The swoon hit Sam broadside and swept him into the clouds.

"But being lovers is not on our path in this life," she said with her eyes still closed, which meant she couldn't see his face turn ashen when he hit the ground. *What the fuck?*

Lynn opened her eyes and looked into his, still holding his hand. "No, we have different paths to take in this lifetime. I know you understand because we've done this before. I knew that right away. That's why I can feel safe sharing this with you."

She squeezed his hand, released it, and smiled.

Safe. The fury in his stomach needed to erupt but he wouldn't let it. He just nodded. Be nice.

What the fuck? She reels me in then cuts me out? What the fuck?!

What did you think was going to happen?

But she smiled at me! Three times!

And that means she wants to boink you? Would you rather she flip you the finger?

But lovers in a past life? I could strangle the bitch!

That would certainly help with her violence issues. She pulled out the rug before you could step on it, didn't she? It was a kindness. She knew what you wanted. At least have the balls to thank her for that.

"Thank you, Lynn."

She gave him a brief hug and stood up. "Got to find the loo," she said.

Sam watched her walk across the room. Heart Feather was animatedly talking to a small group of women. The other three men in the room sat by themselves, isolated and mute. Sam, the safe, rejected man, sat on his rage. It was his problem, not Lynn's. But rage wouldn't buy that. Rage put Lynn and Heart Feather and every other woman in that room and on the entire planet square in its sights. Judith was so right about that.

Sam thought he'd better leave and as quickly as possible. He stood and walked out of the building, leaving his past life girlfriend with a mystery when she returned. She felt safe with him. *Safe.* Safe was no reward. Safe smacked of emasculation. With an unexpected jolt, *safe man* surged into his brain like acid reflux. Fury exploded outward from his guts, expanding like a star going nova. He prayed it would incinerate every goddamned trace of safeness. *And take my goddamned feminine half with it!*

Whoa, Sam!

You! Are you my goddamned feminine half?

Only half? Twit, you insult me. And besides, I don't believe in New Age sewage. Past life lovers. Pah! And calm the fuck down, will you?

Sam stood outside the building and tried to catch his breath. His anger did what all anger does when denied proper expression: it precipitated into depression. It seemed that everything he'd learned on Judith's sofa about understanding and managing his anger was proving to be useless, and that depressed him even further. His boundaries were violated. Rage denied. Nothing had changed. Nothing was left but despair.

Feeling numb to the bone, he stared at the streetlight overhead. Moths swarmed around the glowing bulb, frantically seeking a union that could never be. He felt like weeping for the poor bastards. The fluttering wings became hypnotic and soothing, and thankfully so, because it edged his blood pressure away from danger.

Well, your track record with the ladies of light sure has been stellar lately.

All I want is a damn girlfriend? How hard can that be?

No, you want a savior, not a girlfriend. It doesn't matter if she's swinging a whip or a fairy wand, you'll still throw yourself at her feet and want her to manage your life. The only difference is where they hurt you—one hurts the outside, the other trashes you inside. And then you'll love her for doing it and hate her for the same reason. What girlfriend on earth would want that horrid job?

Isn't there anyone in between? Maybe I just haven't met her yet.

You crack me up, Sam. There's no "in between" with something like this. Do you know why this keeps happening to you?

I'm a twit?

Worse. You're a safe twit.

A soft male. That's what the magazine article called him, a soft male. Sam assumed *soft* meant lowering one's defenses, opening the heart, freely expressing emotions, and being kind, supportive, and nurturing—admirable qualities all. But soft also attacks the heart of masculinity, as any man with a penis knows. The indictment stung mightily. Being safe was bad enough, and adding *soft* to that was beyond intolerable.

But he felt compelled to finish the article. It accused men, particularly those attracted to New Age thought, of going overboard in developing their feminine side, as if human behavior could be so handily parsed and remedied. Softness in men, according to the author, had emerged in response to the criticism, some of it warranted, that women were hurling at men about the oppressive and toxic dominion of the patriarch.

This was not the first time Sam had heard this, including Mistress Morgaine's scathing discourse on the subject with him as a literally captive audience. Although the article's language was more polite, its essence was not that different. Sam thought it was grossly unfair that men had to shoulder the blame for all the world's problems, but then again, it was men who were running the show. There had to be something in defense of his gender, but he could find nothing. No wonder goddesses were popping up everywhere.

Even before his encounters with Heart Feather and Mistress Morgaine, Sam was well-acquainted with the feminine side and its virtues—he'd heard it often enough. To his mind, it was basically everything he was not and should be. He had been determined to evolve himself a feminine half, or find it, or get in touch with it, or whatever one does to resuscitate a missing half, assuming one exists. Because that's what the ladies of light were urging him to do.

"But that's not what women want!" screamed the magazine.

Then what the hell is? Sam screamed back. Once he finally understood the game, the women changed the damn rules.

Or wiggle their fingers differently inside you?

I'm not fourteen anymore!

No, you're not. But I still do it to you all the time. All of us do.

Sam looked at the women around him; they were doing something most curious and unsettling. They were seeking their strength, their empowerment, their inner wolf-warriors, by gathering in circles, passing around talking sticks, sharing, chanting, drumming, and dancing around bonfires, which they thought liberated them from their formerly oppressed and depressed lives, like pupae morphing into butterflies.

Now he looked at the men. They were gathering in circles around football games on TV, passing around smoking joints, sharing deer- and pussy-hunting stories, drinking beer, swearing, farting, and dancing like the dude in the end zone who'd just scored a touchdown. This was incorrect, the women and now Sam concluded. But what was correct? Again, look at the women.

So Sam and two hundred other male wolf-warrior aspirants met every Saturday morning at a community center, where they sat in an enormous circle, passed around a talking stick, shared, drummed, chanted, danced, and grunted *a'ho* after someone spoke, no matter what was said. *A'ho* was Native American for "I agree with your words, my brother." There was no appropriate English equivalent other than *amen*, which smacked of politically incorrect religious dogma.

It was quite a ride. Two hundred men drumming all at once and as loudly as possible stupified the senses. But Sam was now in a brotherhood of men defining themselves as men separate from women, which meant they were ironically dependent on women from whom to separate and searching for that which they didn't remember losing.

Sam was perplexed. What were they looking for? Wild manhood? Wolf-scout merit badge? To be soft and still get hard? No one seemed to know, precisely. All he was finding were words and stories, impressive ones to be sure, but he couldn't connect them to anything real and substantial. It was like having an electrical plug in a world without outlets. After spending a month of Saturdays sitting in a circle with his wolf brethren, Sam felt he was going nowhere. The drumming started to hurt his hands and ears, he heard too much whining amid the sharing, and he felt like a shameless usurper and damn fool trying to play Native American.

"This is a difficult time to be a man," admonished a fellow wolf-warrior.

"A'ho," Sam mumbled back.

But if it looked like a door and quacked like a door... Sam drummed, shared, danced, and a'ho-grunted with all his heart until one morning a female worker at the community center walked through the meeting room on her way to another. Immediately the room became silent. Then the grumbling and muttering started, and the stricken girl couldn't walk out fast enough. Two hundred wolf warriors sure showed her their strength and power. *A'ho!* Then the warriors were asked to pair up and work on their father wounds and witness each other's pain.

Sam was in pain all right, but not over what his father had or hadn't done. He left the men's circle early and angry. Disgusted by all the Native wannabes, angry at himself for biting on another empty hook, furious that he was still safe and soft, and enraged because women were becoming better wolf-warriors than he would ever be.

We're just so horrible, aren't we? We shit all over your masculinity, and all of your drumming and chanting isn't getting it clean, right?

Yeah.

And because one small woman could instantly turn a room full of two hundred strong, powerful wolf-warriors into petulant little boys?

Yeah.

Now who are you really mad at? Your soft, safe self who can't stand up to take a piss unless some goddess approves?

Um, yeah.

Sheesh! No wonder you're furious! Don't blame us women, twit. We can't give you back what we never took. And remember it was your decision to give it to us.

The problem, Sam rightly knew, was that he didn't remember making that decision. That was just how his life always seemed to be, and knowing this made his predicament seem worse. He didn't precisely know how this had happened, or when, but his mother was certainly the culprit. He also suspected that every woman he'd ever known was involved. Someone had to pay for this, but who? He was running out of places to look.

There was one place left—a weekly men's support group held at a local church. He'd earlier seen the notice at the Mind Flower and tucked it in the back of his memory. This church was tangentially religious in the traditional sense and progressive almost to the point of heresy. It was run by a woman minister who believed that whatever elevated the spirit was holy, no matter what it looked, sounded, or smelled like. It was home to whatever group needed one, including various twelve-step support groups and the group that would be Sam's next exploration.

At the meeting, Sam was one of a dozen men sitting in a circle on hard, metal chairs—no cushy pillows allowed here. Not two minutes into the discussion, Sam realized what he'd walked into: a men's backlash group. Some men, perceiving their gender was being continually chastised and denigrated by women and the feminist movement, felt they needed to fight back, and sitting among their fellow victims helped. They were angry men, men like himself, Sam had to admit uneasily.

The angriest man of all chaired the meeting. He was around forty, already balding, and bordered on obesity. He began by introducing himself and reciting his recent history of abuse at the hands of a woman. He said he was in the middle of a child custody battle with "the meanest, most despicable, ball-busting bitch ever to walk the earth," railing as if he'd rehearsed the line. Sam assumed the guy was losing the battle.

"Women have it easy," the man hissed. "They're just like their damn cunts. All their shit is neatly and conveniently hidden away, and they make damn sure to keep it that way. While our shit is sticking out, like our dicks, where everyone can see it, so it's us they blame for everything that's wrong in the world. God, what crap! What fucking femi-nazi cunts!"

He was actually spitting as he spoke. His face became so red with rage that Sam feared the man was about to incur a stroke. He continued the spraying tirade, "All this feminist crap about being oppressed and disempowered by the patriarchy is just that—crap! It's all bullshit." He held up a book; Sam couldn't make out the title but had noticed a pile of them on a desk in the corner of the room.

"It's all right in here," the man said. "Read it for yourself. The bullshit that feminists are pulling on us—on everyone! They fuck with the numbers and statistics to make it look like they're getting screwed, and we're always the bad guys. They say we have all the power when that's not true at all. Jesus!"

Sam became uneasy. He could feel this zealot's vitriolic words trying to bore their way into his guts, looking to reignite that ember. He worried they might succeed. This was starting to feel more like a Wehrmacht rally than a support group.

But the red-faced man was not done; now he was venomously targeting "soft males." Sam squirmed in his seat hearing the phrase.

"These guys are called sneaky fucks," the guy foamed. "They're sleazy wimps who buy into all this emotionally sensitive soft male crap to worm their way into a woman's pants. What a cheap goddamned racket. There's a special room in hell waiting for these nutless little eunuchs!"

That wouldn't be you, would it, sneaky little twit?

God no! This guy is crazy. He's totally lost it. I want no part of this!

Crazy like you, maybe? Pah. I've seen how you operate. I've seen that game. And I know what you think about when you're in one of your tantrums about women.

That's nothing like this!

Are you so sure? Get a good look at this circus, twit. See where you're headed.

Sam wanted to get up and bolt for the door, but fear of the andro-nazi Brownshirts kept him in his chair. Besides, he wouldn't know where to run, but it sure as hell wasn't here.

17

HELTER SKELTER

THE FINAL PAINTING OF THE VIRIDIAN series rested on Sam's easel. In it, she wore a black lace bodice and leaned against a massive stone wall with her arms behind her. Her eyes were closed, as if floating in of one her quirky reveries. A large iguana was chained to the wall by an iron collar, straining to touch her. She remained just beyond its reach. Such power gave her such joy.

Iguanas were not known for being emotionally expressive creatures, but Sam saw deep despair in its eyes. The more he looked at the painting, the more agitated he became, but he could not look away—it was a new kind of masochism he'd just invented for himself. He stared at the iguana's collar and a fresh surge of bile coursed through him. It was his pattern all right. Viridian had all his power because it was his decision to give it to her. Because he wanted something from her. The trouble being he didn't remember deciding or what exactly he wanted.

On a whim, he hauled out the entire Viridian series and arranged the paintings and drawings around the room—over two dozen of them, to his surprise. He'd never before seen them as a group, and he didn't like what he saw: abuse, victimization, and rage at both the model and the artist. It was a paean to foolishness and obsession. He wanted to burn them. Better yet, tie Viridian to the stake and burn her on the pyre of her own effigies. *How fitting that would be!* But it still would not give him satisfaction. Or unlock his collar.

If you eat one cookie you might as well have the whole bag. Sam disgorged the contents of his entire below-the-waist portfolio and leafed through it. He was startled to see so many reptiles in the artwork: living, extinct, and mythical. Pythons, boas, vipers, hydras, dinosaurs, turtles, lizards, and, of course, dragons. Occasionally a large feline prowled through the scene. But why so many reptiles? Why not giraffes and gerbils? Every time a painting called for a powerful player, a reptile got the part.

Why not? Think about reptiles and what they do so well. They've even named part of the brain after them. My favorite part, actually.

Reptiles are just a symbol for my cock, that's all.

Are you serious? Dude, you've seen an enormous amount of artwork. You've studied psychology. You know your little drama inside and out, having wallowed in every last puddle of it. And "a symbol for my cock" is the best your twit brain can come up with?

All art is symbolic. What else can it be?

It can be anything you want. You use it for mental masturbation. Now it's a fortress. You're hiding behind your symbols because you can't deal with what they symbolize. Have your precious symbols unlocked Viridian's collar yet?

Sam looked around the room. Two-dozen Viridians glared at him through the bars of their painted prisons. His collar began to constrict.

"Why are you doing this to me?" cried one Viridian. She was tied to a chair watching a newly hatched clutch of alligators tear ragged strips of flesh from her body.

"Because I hate you," he said, facing an onslaught of remorse.

"Why? Because I wouldn't have you?" she said. "Because I wouldn't animate all your degenerate fantasies about me, and now I must do so on canvas and suffer for all time?"

"Yes. You must suffer for all time. Horribly."

"I hate you too," said another Viridian, chained to a stone wall and bleeding from her breast. "I hate mirrors and I hate you. We all do."

"But why?" Sam protested. "I gave you everything you wanted. I did everything to please you. How can you possibly hate me for that?"

Viridian ignored the boa constrictor slithering up her thigh as she hung from chains. "Because we don't want mirrors!" she cried. "We wanted you, the real you, not our reflection!"

This he understood. He wouldn't want a mirror either. Would he find Viridian so enthralling if she did everything he wanted? That Viridian saddened him. She bored him.

"Look at me!" Viridian screamed. "Feel the space between us, feel that vast empty chasm that cannot be bridged. You despicable creep. You made that chasm. You love that chasm far more than what it separates, don't you?"

That one knocked him flat. He'd had quite enough. He remanded the Viridians back to solitary confinement in their closet prison. There they would sit and suffer until what—he wanted more abuse? Wanted them burned? Died?

Art cannot be ignored, remember, Sam?

He had an idea. Since he couldn't slog, squirm, think, or koan his way out of his Viridian-colored house of mirrors, he might as well put them to good use. The paintings had served their purpose, or as much as he would allow, so why not turn them loose on the rest of the world? Art can't be ignored, and if he couldn't ignore her, neither should anyone else.

Sam drew up his plans and immediately ran into a problem. Besides being lethally seductive, Viridian was also volatile, unpredictable, and very dangerous. He frequently likened her to a human scorpion. What would she think about seeing herself displayed and abused in full public view? What would she do? The solution, albeit a cowardly one, was simple but laborious: have the show in another city, and there was one just three hours' drive away.

And there Sam found the perfect venue: a small gallery that focused on sexuality, specifically alternative and fringe. He didn't expect to make a fortune from the show, since the more alternative and fringy people were, the less money they had, it seemed. He expected something else, although he was loath to speak it. He knew well if you expected something, you'd either not get it or you'd get its confounding opposite. Therefore, if he didn't expect success, then it would happen—which was the same thing as expecting it, and the cycle would continue ad nauseum. Sam frequently liked to tie his brain into knots like this. Now he understood why its tissue was called convolutions.

Sam drove the three hours and found the Mondo Carne Gallery in a very fashionable section of the city. There he met Herb and Pauline, the owners. Herb was an affable man in his forties with a warm, open face and a body that could have played offensive tackle. Pauline, his wife, was as small as Herb was huge, and Sam wondered how they worked that out in bed. Pauline was pert and perky with stylish short blond hair; a wide, luminescent smile; eyeglasses with thin metal rims; minimal makeup;

and no chest to speak of, although her low-cut black dress showed most of it. She struck Sam as a librarian who might moonlight as a porn star.

"We made a killing in real estate," Pauline told Sam, "and opened this place on a lark. It's been a real adventure."

Herb smiled, nodded, and stood with his hands in his pockets.

"You wouldn't believe some of the really great people we've met along the way," she continued. Herb cocked his eyebrows as if he knew something and kept smiling.

"I can imagine," Sam said. He looked around the gallery. Their current show was a series of black and white photographs that documented unusual body modifications. He didn't know the human tongue could be split in two like a snake's, but there it was on the wall. The most unusual of all was a photo of a pierced uvula. Sam couldn't look at it without gagging.

"How long have you been doing erotic art?" Pauline asked him.

She touched his arm as she spoke. He liked that. He was tempted to respond with "twenty minutes" á la Viridian, but his better sense jumped in the way. "Oh, about ten years, but I didn't do much until recently."

Sam had brought an envelope of photographs of his work and handed it to the couple.

"Oh, wow, amazing. Oh, wow," Pauline kept repeating as she looked through the prints. Herb's eyebrows again raised and stayed there. Pauline pulled a jeweler's loupe from a desk drawer and closely examined one print.

"What's that weight attached to?" she asked. "His balls?"

Sam guessed she'd seen a few. "Well, actually, it's symbolic."

"It sure doesn't look symbolic to me," she said in a low voice.

A tall, statuesque brunette entered the gallery.

"Indeed," Herb said. "Excuse me folks, but Katy's here. Good meeting you, Sam. Really looking forward to your show."

Herb embraced Katy, kissed her on the lips, and the pair walked out the door. Startled, Sam turned to Pauline, not sure what to expect, but he was met with a broad smile. "That's Katy, Herb's partner."

"His partner?"

"He has several," Pauline said without a trace of reticence. "So do I. We're swingers, have been for over five years. You might as well know. Does that shock or surprise you?"

"Uh, no."

"I didn't think it would, dear. Not with the kind of art you do."

Dear? Sam wondered whether Pauline was the sex he'd get by not expecting sex, which made him expect he'd have sex with Pauline, which meant he would not have sex with Pauline, so it was back to not expecting sex so he could have sex. He unknotted his brain and shoved it back to doing business. They agreed to have the show in four weeks, giving Sam time to have it framed. Pauline wrote down her phone number on a slip of paper and poked it down his front pants pocket, causing him to jump.

"This is classified," she said and kissed his cheek.

Sam made the long drive home thinking more about sexual expectations than art shows.

This show would have no magical mountains or shimmering moons; just scenes of Viridian's torment with a few male victims thrown in to prove he was an equal opportunity abuser and not a complete misogynist. *It's all symbolic*, he kept reminding himself and uneasily thinking about sex rifles. He took the two dozen pieces to a framing shop, wondering whether the store had a policy regarding the content of the artwork. The saleswoman took in the paintings without comment, which apparently was its policy. He thought he'd better get used to this.

Pauline had asked him to write a press release and artist's statement that she'd give to the newspapers and send out to her mailing list. Newspapers? Publicity? Sam hadn't expected this and wasn't sure he wanted it. But he couldn't imagine Viridian being on anyone's mailing list or even reading a newspaper, so he figured he was safe.

He came up with, "The artist is an explorer journeying into the dark reaches of the erotic underworld to take snapshots of its habitués caught in acts forbidden in the above world. The pictures he brings back reveal an inner landscape where art and eroticism have carved a terrain of ineffable complexity, mystery, and beauty. The artwork contains messages, some disturbing, that bypass the artist's censors—messages that say art, sex, and spirit are just convenient words that we mistake for the less-convenient realities behind them."

Wow, thought Sam. *Impressive, deep, and rife with controversy and intrigue. Who could resist taking a look?*

Wow. Impressive indeed. If only you believed it, especially the last sentence.

Jeez! Why can't you leave me alone? I've found some courage. I'm out there. I'm finally embracing my art instead of despising it.

And what will that give you? A place in the Who's Who of Deviant
Outsiders?

What's wrong with that? I'm entitled to have some perks, damn it!

**You're entitled to nothing. And when does entitlement ever
get satisfied? Be careful, twit. Vanity can be the most subtle and
sneaky of sins. And the most expensive.**

Sam mailed the press release to Herb and Pauline, feeling he'd just
set powerful forces in motion that could not be recalled. He knew that
waffling, wimping out, and second-guessing himself would invite a living
nightmare. On the other hand, Pauline's number still sat on his desk,
essentially a gift coupon for sex à la mode. If he didn't expect it. Which
he very much did. After several days of another kind of waffling and
wimping, Sam called her.

"I can't thank you enough for that press release, Sam," Pauline gushed.
"It was fabulous. Mysterious. Seductive. That should really bring them
out of the woodwork!"

"Like termites?"

"Yeah. Like termites with money. When are you coming down, dear?"

Dear, again. "Well, I'm thinking of hanging the show the day of
the opening."

"No sooner?"

"Uh, well, I suppose I could," he waffled.

"Then you will. Come the night before, okay?"

"Okay. Is there a motel nearby?"

"A motel? Are you serious?" Pauline asked.

"No, not really." *Ah, yes, a waffle with Pauline syrup.*

"Fabulous! You'll stay here. It's settled then." She hung up.

Sam's hunger grew, with Pauline's "settled" being the appetizer. He
considered the prospect definitely arousing. She was attractive in a plain,
country-girl kind of way, thin as a laser beam and with a chest so flat he
wondered if she'd had a double mastectomy. Yet her porn star attitude
and ease with her body outsexed everything else. He also wondered
whether she liked goblins and where she stood on the Moebius Strip of
sexual expectations? But he was mostly irritated with himself for yielding
to these distractions instead of thinking about surviving the infamy sure
to come.

Surviving the infamy? Just who the hell do you think you are?

Am I doing the right thing?

I look forward to the day when you stop asking me twit questions like that.

Answer me, damn it!

As you wish. Nothing you do is the right thing. You should have learned that by now. Right is when you learn from it. Wrong is when you don't. There, are you happy?

No.

Too bad. And by the way, Herb has a black belt in Aikido.

Now how on earth do you know that?

I saw it hanging on the wall. You would have too, but you found Pauline's chest, or lack of one, far more interesting.

Aikido. Great.

Pauline was ecstatic over the paintings. "And fabulous job on the frames," she said, although Sam had had nothing to do with it. Pauline was gifted with a designer's eye and knew exactly what should be hung where and how to arrange the lighting. Sam was impressed. As she worked he wondered what Pauline looked like naked. She caught his wondering and smiled.

"Thinking about having sex with me?" she asked.

Jesus, the woman doesn't mess around. "Um, well, maybe."

Pauline laughed. "You're so sweet. Well, I must admit I've thought about that too, hon. But mixing personal and business? No. Too icky."

What? Sam had been positive the woman had had "fuck me, Sam" written all over her spare body, and now it's *no* and *too icky*? But his disillusionment had to wait because at that moment Herb walked into the gallery with Viridian on his arm.

"Hello, Sam," she said, her words plunging the room temperature toward absolute zero. "It's been a while, hasn't it?"

"Do you two know each other?" Herb asked.

"Apparently not," said Viridian, staring hard at Sam.

Sam stood with his mouth hanging open, feeling like he was encased in ice.

Viridian released Herb's arm and slowly walked around the gallery, looking at what Sam had done to her. Everything was out, raw, bold, and unapologetic: Viridian hanging from chains, Viridian in bondage, Viridian bleeding, and, most audacious of all, Viridian naked. Unlike her earlier desultory appraisal of his portfolio, here she studied each painting meticulously, saying nothing, revealing nothing. Sam carefully scrutinized her for the faintest clue of how his future might unfold, if indeed he had one.

Viridian stopped in front of herself kissing a human skull and examined the painting more closely. She finally spoke. "Did you use a real skull here?"

Sam nodded. "Yeah."

"Interesting. Those are not easy to find. I see you took some liberties with me."

"Uh, yeah."

There was nothing else to say. Sam ran through the possibilities. How would it happen? A boot to the groin? His arms dislocated? Both eyes gouged out? *But wait, maybe Herb and his black belt would protect me. But wait again, Herb and Viridian are probably lovers. I'm dead.*

Pauline clearly now realized why Viridian looked so much like the model in the paintings; Herb was still a step behind. Pauline, full of chutzpah, touched Viridian's arm and chirped, "You must be so thrilled, dear, to see yourself in such fabulous artwork."

Viridian just looked at Pauline, who immediately withdrew her arm—a bad sign. Viridian walked over to the still semipetrified Sam, gave him one of her breast-mashing embraces, and whispered into his ear, "I'm so honored by this. I really am."

Sam had been prepared for anything but that. His metabolism revived. His guts, twisted like the rubber band on model airplane's propeller, resumed their normal shape. His sphincter relaxed from its thousand-pounds-per-square-inch crunch.

"Uh... I... um, well," Sam could only croak through the constricted tubule of his throat.

Viridian smiled. "Did you really think you could hide this from me forever?" She waited for that to work its way through his head. "We should do another show together sometime."

Viridian encircled Herb's empty arm and the pair left the gallery. Pauline seemed to be just as stunned as Sam.

"Small world, isn't it?" she said.

I'm still alive, thought Sam.

That night, Pauline gave Sam their guest room. She said she had a date, pecked his cheek good night, and left. She didn't come home until morning. Through the wall Sam could hear Herb and Viridian going after one another almost all night. Herb was quiet. Viridian was not and emitted sporadic cries and yelps—probably her nipple piercings being twisted. The noise didn't bother him nearly as much as knowing what was causing it. The combination of that, his still-lingering obsession, and his relentless imagination concocted a new torture for the books. But he finally got his fondest wish: spending a night with Viridian—sort of.

The show's opening was as exhilarating as his previous night was awful. The gallery had a large and eclectic patronage that looked like an amalgam of a bar mitzvah, a vampire funeral, and a bikers' convention. Herb and Pauline bought four paintings before the opening, which now bore red "sold" dots. The way things worked in a show, or so the artist hoped, was that one red dot would attract another by telling people this stuff was good so they'd better jump on it.

Another draw was that Sam wasn't local. An artist who hailed from afar carried an inflated reputation, as if the distance from the gallery were directly proportional to the weight of the name. And if buyers weren't certain whether the art was good, important, or garbage, they looked for clues, such as the artist's biography, history of past shows, published reviews, and the current number of red dots. Never mind whether the review was in *The National Review of the Arts* or *Newsletter from the Chateau of Cruel Bondage*.

One gallery goer couldn't have cared less about the artist's credentials. A tall, attractive, and curvy young woman adorned with Goth jewelry and wearing a short, close-fitting, low-cut red leather dress approached Sam. Her short, jet-black hair was styled to perfection. A finely detailed oriental dragon tattoo circled her left breast. With the barest hint of a smile, she handed Sam her card: *Seraphina, Bondage Model.* Her objective seemed clear: to replace the enigmatic and haunting Viridian as his model.

Sam had seen photographs of the famous Seraphina in erotic art shows and s/m-oriented publications. Her specialty was Shibari, an unusual and daring form of sculptural art using intricate Japanese rope bondage and a woman, often nude, as the medium. Seraphina looked far sexier on glossy paper than standing before him in her abundant flesh.

"Interested?" she asked, having given Sam plenty of time to examine her wares.

It seemed Seraphina was a woman of few words. That one carried a dozen implications, few of which boded well for Sam as he noticed Viridian watching them with great interest. Viridian seemed permanently welded to Herb for the evening and had been regarding Sam with benign neglect, which was better than murderous intent, but now her attention was most welcome. Sam knew he was no Shibari master, or master of any kind, so a white lie to Seraphina seemed his best option.

"Well, you see," he began, appraising Seraphina's bust while looking into her eyes, "I'm still working with my current model, and she'd probably murder me if I looked elsewhere." He nodded toward Viridian, who smiled and nodded back. Seraphina quickly figured it out.

Most women did not like rejection in general, and sex-associated rejection even less, and Seraphina not at all. "Yeah, I'd probably murder you too," she said icily and walked away.

Sam wondered how she'd go about doing it and with what. Art was not supposed to be a dangerous profession, but now he suspected otherwise.

Then an even greater danger walked through the door. At his Galerie Outré show, Sam had noticed a particular man at the opening night gala. He was about forty and of slight build, with short hair—not bad looking, and his attire suggested he had a good job, probably as a computer geek. He'd asked Sam about a painting, and Sam had responded with the same disengaged speech he gave all browsers unless he suspected the browser might be a buyer. Sam had thanked the guy for his interest and turned away, a clear, polite signal that the conversation was terminated.

But the guy hadn't understood. He'd followed Sam around, still asking questions—odd, personal questions having nothing to do with art. Questions that a wily detective might use to trick a suspect into a confession: "Do you ever dream about Hitler? Is your father still alive? What's your blood type?"

Sam had wondered if he was indeed being investigated. And by whom? Sam had told him he needed to talk to other people, assuming the guy could take a hint. But like many other socially clueless people, he couldn't, and Sam had worried about the man's mental condition. *Goodness, I have a stalker. How cute.*

Now, it seemed that same geek had traveled three hours to continue his stalking. Upon seeing him, Sam instantly froze. *How the hell did he find out?* The guy spotted Sam and zeroed in like a heat-seeking missile. Sam was now genuinely concerned. He turned from the man and walked away, expecting a hatchet in the back at any moment. Being stalked suddenly stopped being cute.

Geek followed behind and startled Sam with, "Have you ever read *Helter Skelter?*"

Sam's alarms instantly sounded. "About the Charles Manson murders? No. Why?"

"I read it once a year, on the day it happened," said the geek. "Did you know that Sharon Tate was eight months pregnant when they stabbed her to death? Two for the price of one, right? She was so beautiful and now she's so dead."

The guy gave Sam a rictus grin and turned to view the paintings. Sam no longer wondered about the guy's sanity. Everything in his life abruptly disappeared and was replaced by cold dread. Pauline, ever the social creature, was flitting from couple to couple, no doubt looking to turn them into buyers or potential romps. She spotted Sam's distress and hustled over.

"What's wrong, hon?"

"You see that guy over there?" Sam nodded at the geek. "I think I've got a stalker."

"A stalker? Really?"

Sam's face said, "I am not fucking joking."

"Well, that's the price of fame, hon. Relax, I'll take care of him."

His attempts to relax drove him deeper into anxiety.

A minute later Pauline returned, her face just as pale. "Who *is* that creep?"

"I told you, my personal stalker. You know, the price of fame. Why? What happened?"

"What happened? He asked me if I was a prostitute! I almost slapped him. 'Whatever gave you that idea?' I asked him. You know what he said? He said he could smell a prostitute a mile away. I told him to go straight to hell. Then he asked me for the phone numbers of other prostitutes I might know. Do you believe the nerve of that guy? Jeez! I'm getting ready to call the cops!"

Herb walked over, surprisingly sans Viridian, and Pauline quickly recounted the incident. Herb looked at the man and flushed red.

"Be careful, Herb," said Pauline. "Don't get us in trouble."

Sam spotted the geek with his nose an inch from a painting of Viridian's tush.

Trouble. This show seems to attract it.

Herb confronted the man. Sam couldn't make out what was being said, but he knew talking sense to the guy was futile. Then Herb took the man by the arm and not too gently escorted him out the door. On the way out, geek turned, his eyes dark and fierce, and stared hard at Sam. *Helter skelter.*

Pauline took Sam's lifeless arm. "It's okay, honey, these things happen."

"Has this ever happened before?"

"Well, no, but don't worry about it."

Worry now became Sam's new profession. Should he inform the police? What could they do? Incarcerate the man for being geeky? For idolizing mass murderers? For a crime he hadn't committed but was about to? Were art, fame, and Seraphina in bondage worth his life?

Well, are they?

Of course not. But why all those strange questions? What does he want from me?

Think about what he said to Pauline. He sensed her promiscuity, either from her flirting or maybe the smell of an active vagina. Prostitute was his only available conclusion, right?

Yeah, I suppose.

Now, what does he sense in you? He doesn't have to examine your behavior or sniff your crotch. Who you are is plastered all over the wall. He sees the sexual violence in your art and smelled your own attraction to it. Helter skelter, right?

Great.

That's one price of vanity. I warned you.

There's more?

More than what you can afford. Didn't expect this, did you?

The show ran for six weeks. Sam sold two more paintings. Added to Herb and Pauline's purchases, that covered all his framing expenses. For most shows that's a screaming success. Both the mainstream and outsider art scene ignored the event, much to Sam's great relief and sullen disappointment. The best news was that he'd survived his stalker and Viridian. No rapes, murders, or other atrocities had been attributed to his sex rifles, and six of his children had found homes. His earlier fears had been groundless, never mind that he'd acquired a new one.

18

PLANET S/M

THE MODEL AND SOON-TO-BE VICTIM WAS a young woman, slightly zaftig, with long, bright-red-dyed hair, and freckles. She sat in a director's chair, naked from the waist up with her wrists tied to the chair's arms. Standing beside her on the stage was Meredith, the founder of Planet S/M and the evening's presenter. The topic of the meeting was erotic torture. Meredith held up a three-foot line of wooden clothespins strung together. Sam, along with the rest of the audience, sat rapt, eager to see what would happen next.

"This is called a zipper," said Meredith, dangling the contraption in front of the wide-eyed and just as eager girl. "It's a scary little toy, isn't it, dear?"

The redhead enthusiastically nodded.

"The zipper has a well-deserved and fearsome reputation based on several principles," Meredith turned and said to the room. "One, a clothespin snapped onto the skin hurts. Two, many clothespins hurt more than just a few. Three, some body parts are more sensitive than others. Four, as everyone here knows well, clothespins hurt even worse when they're taken off. And five, worse is multiplied by a thousand when they're suddenly yanked off. Once applied, it sort of looks kind of like a zipper, hence the name."

Meredith went to work, and in a few minutes the zipper ran across both of the girl's freckled breasts.

"The longer it's left on," Meredith smiled, "the louder the scream."

It would turn out to be true. For twenty minutes Meredith talked about other places one could put nasty items on men and women, leaving her plaything to suffer. The redhead broke several eardrums in the room when Meredith gleefully unzipped her.

Sam had not expected such a scream. He was seeing and hearing many things these days that he had not expected, and being in that room was one of them. The traumas of his conflicted flings with Carmine and Mistress Morgaine had since faded, but the lure of the dominatrix still sparkled, and he knew it always would. He was determined to find another one, but this time with better discernment, more reasonable expectations, and less idiocy. To facilitate his next domme hunt, Sam now had two resources that had previously been unavailable: access to the kinky subculture through Planet S/M and a computer.

Pauline and Herb had told Sam about Planet S/M, an educational organization dedicated to supporting that practice. It was similar to the group he'd found on Judith's list except, to his joy, this one was in town. Planet S/M held monthly meetings that discussed everything kinky, from the psychological and political issues inherent in that lifestyle to hands-on demonstrations, such as this evening's zipper presentation. The stated mission of the Planet was to present s/m as a healthy option for expressing one's sexuality as well as rehabilitating its sordid reputation.

Sam found all of this utterly liberating. He was now among sympathetic, like-minded people who not only understood his predilection but also celebrated it. As he watched the redhead breathe into her pain and try to calm down, he marveled at his remarkable situation. He'd been to many workshops before, ranging from how to repair a lamp to Eastern meditation techniques, but never how to zipper up a breast. Who'd have thought?

He remembered attending his first meeting. It had been held in a large classroom of an old high school no longer used as such. *How education has changed,* he'd wryly noted. He arrived early, took a seat in the back, and tried to become invisible. He watched people enter. Many were in couples, both same and opposite sex, their relationships advertised by collars and attitudes. Everyone here seemed to belong here, animatedly greeting and chatting with each other if it were a college reunion.

About half were in street clothes like himself, but the other half were clad cap to boot in black leather adorned with chains, studs, and spikes. Sam thought about all the cows that had died to clothe this crowd. But then, these were people's street clothes as well, and he wondered what sort of soul would be brave (or deranged) enough to be out in public so attired. He certainly wasn't, and he imagined he was surrounded by tattooed and body-pierced aliens who'd been hiding among earthlings, waiting for events like this to emerge.

Tonight, Sam was feeling far more comfortable. He found himself easily talking with people regardless of their sexuality and wardrobe. They were not aliens—just ordinary folks with ordinary jobs and ordinary lives who simply did extraordinary things to one another. He saw that the leather world was not comprised of sex fiends, degenerates, and amoral creeps, despite some people acting the part. But he suspected not everyone in the room was completely trustworthy either, as was true for all rooms everywhere, no matter what their purposes or compositions.

Sam attended every meeting. The first thing he learned was that the scene was officially called BDSM, a convenient acronym that encompassed all the categories of kinky activity. BD stood for bondage and discipline, DS for dominance and submission, and SM, naturally, was sadism and masochism. Using the correct language in any context had always irked him, whether it was political, social, and now sexual, and he refused to use the term, much to the indignation of proper BDSMers. Despite this community's tolerance of all things and people deviant, they could be just as intolerant of all things and people who were not. Folks will be folks.

Sam heard about another acronym, an important one and the de facto law in the kinky world: SS&C, standing for Safe, Sane, and Consensual. At first, he thought this was just a slick slogan for BDSM club members, but he learned otherwise at the next Planet S/M meeting. There was no presenter that evening, just a roundtable discussion about the phrase, moderated by Meredith. Sam sat in the back of the room, his usual perch, and the safest, sanest one he thought possible.

Until Carmine walked in, as he should have expected. She saw him, immediately brightened, and sat next to him. Although Sam had parted with her amicably, it had taken everything he had, and he worried he might not have enough strength to do it again. And would he want to? He nervously watched her to see what she'd do next.

"Hey, baby," Carmine said and smiled. She lightly kissed his cheek and then watched him to see what he'd do next.

Which was nothing. When Sam realized that Carmine wasn't going to handcuff him and eat him alive, he relaxed and couldn't help but give her a broad smile. She squeezed his hand, let it go, and turned to the podium. Sam struggled to keep his attention on the meeting.

Meredith started the discussion. "The phrase 'safe, sane, and consensual' came out of the gay BDSM scene in New York City in the early 1980s. As more and more kinky people were coming out of their closets, they realized there was a need to create a rational and responsible face to a somewhat scary and shady-looking practice. SS and C not only covered all the bases, but also served as a reminder to the players to play right. Safety and sanity, and common sense for that matter, are qualities we humans have yet to perfect. We have to start somewhere, and an s/m dungeon is a good place as any, and where it's needed most. Right?"

Everyone in the room agreed.

Meredith continued. "One problem with safe, sane, and consensual is the terms are not absolute or clearly defined, as most of us know or will painfully learn. For example, what does 'safe' mean? Anyone?"

A question thrown to an audience was usually met with silence because no one wanted to speak first and risk looking like a fool. Not so with Black Dragon, a tall, swarthy man known as an experienced and much-feared dominant. Many people in the kinky scene adopted aliases to protect their identities or enhance their reputations. Black Dragon sounded a bit pretentious, but who'd be afraid of a dominant named Pink Hamster? If Alpha Male was an office in the BDSM community, Black Dragon would be a perennial candidate for it. No one would dare say "fool" to his face, except perhaps some smart-ass femme bottom who wanted to be slowly and painfully exterminated.

"To me, the definition of safety is fluid and arbitrary," Black Dragon said. "I've had one bottom whine about safety when I laid a welt on her butt with a cane. Another thought a half-dozen needles through her nipples was perfectly acceptable. And I've never done anything to anyone I haven't tried on myself. I think safety is not as much about what you do, but how you do it and how you treat it afterward."

"Then you're a qualified medical practitioner?" Carmine spoke up. "Are you prepared to handle any emergency that might come up?"

The look on Dragon's face suggested that he and Carmine had tangled before. "No, of course not. But I do have a brain and experience. We all know how to apply band-aids. I don't do anything without first thinking about what could happen and how to deal with it. And if it seems over the top, I won't do it. No matter how much she begs for it." He laughed at his wit.

Carmine didn't. "That's very admirable. I hope everyone here is as competent as you."

"By its very nature, BDSM is dangerous," interjected Meredith, hoping to defuse the tiff. "All players know that, and if they don't, they shouldn't be playing. Accidents will happen, and the best we can do is use our experience and common sense beforehand to prevent them."

"Common sense?" said a man in front. "That's rich. Horny will trump common sense every time. Remember that guy in LA a couple of years ago?"

No one in the room seemed to, or at least didn't want to be reminded.

But the man pressed on. "Yeah, you all know what I'm talking about. The dumb fuck wanted to see how much weight his balls could take. An eyebolt in the ceiling ripped out and he was suddenly lying on the floor looking up at them. What do you tell the doctor, eh?"

"Or how about Lilly?" added a woman. "In the hospital with third-degree burns on her ass because her brain-dead top didn't think to have a fire extinguisher handy when doing fire play."

Another woman spoke up. "And that chick who almost bled to death after—"

"Whoa, people!" interrupted Meredith. "We've all heard gruesome stories. Let's not turn this into a gross-out fest. I think we all know what's safe and what isn't. If it's questionable, don't do it. That's an easy enough rule to remember. Now let's move on to 'sane,' the second pillar. If safety is hard to nail down, sanity is even trickier. Most people might think, and with good reason, that all BDSM players are insane because look at what they do, for God's sake."

Meredith waited for the laughter to subside. "Who wants to begin?"

Carmine stood up. "That's not so funny when you really think about it. No one in this room can define sane with absolute certainty, but we all know crazy when we see it. I believe we move along a sanity continuum that constantly changes, even throughout the day. We're sane doing our jobs, less so in the dungeon. Sane with some people, flipped out with others."

"Are you speaking from experience, Carmine?" Black Dragon asked.

"Where else?" she shot back. She turned to the room. "Look, defining sanity is not the real issue here. Let the shrinks jerk off over that. What's most important is protecting ourselves. We all know that BDSM attracts a wide range of personalities, and some hover at the edge of mental illness and instability. Just look around the room, right?"

Everyone laughed except Black Dragon.

Carmine continued. "We don't have any vetting procedures to screen out dangerous people. And we don't have experienced vetters who are authorized to do so. And even if we did, people lie anyway to get what they want. The real, certifiable nut cases reveal themselves only after the fact, so all we have is our good sense and gut feelings."

"That's not very precise," Black Dragon said. "Or accurate."

Carmine let loose with one of her cackles. "So, Dragon, do you run a detailed evaluation on every pretty little thing who wants to taste your whip? Or can you imagine *her* subjecting *you* to a battery of tests before she accepts your handcuffs? Really now."

"That's what negotiation is for, Carmine. You should know that."

"Negotiating is useless when you're hungry, horny, and stupid. You should know that."

"Now, people, let's be nice," said Meredith.

Carmine leaned over to Sam and whispered, "The man invented the word *asshole*."

Her comments on sanity struck home with Sam because he questioned his own daily, considering his vexing inner inhabitants. But the possibility of moving along a continuum, toward and away from sanity according to circumstances, eased his mind. He'd always thought sanity was an absolute and any slight deviation was cause for alarm. Now perhaps not.

Perhaps, you think? It sounds like you don't really know.

It's better than giving up and rubbing snot into my hair.

Today it is. And just what point on this continuum is sane enough to judge sanity, hmm? You know damn well what I'm talking about.

He looked at Carmine obliquely; her focus was still on Black Dragon as if she was planning something. The woman seemed as wise as she was wicked, an intimidating mix, and her continuum was definitely broader and more adventurous than his. Was she sane when she'd handcuffed him? Was he sane when he'd called her a week later to play? And what about his eagerness to submit to Mistress Morgaine, a complete stranger? That did not demonstrate a sound mind, only a possessed cock. Sam decided that, in this scene, *sane* had nothing to do with mental health; it just meant reasonable and responsible, which anyone could convincingly fake, as he well knew.

"'Consensual' is the last pillar in our slogan," said Meredith. "I want to say something about this. Consent is hugely important because it separates violence from abuse. What could be simpler or more concrete than consent? Either you agree to it or not, right? But it's often not that simple and straightforward. There's the issue of *informed* consent. When you're negotiating with a top before you play, do you really understand what's about to happen to you? Do you know the price you may have to pay?

"And how many people sign a document without first carefully reading it, or even reading it at all? We assume the other party is trustworthy because that's what we want to believe. That's what happens when better sense gets clouded by the crotch. It's too easy to sign or say anything and pray you get lucky. We've all been there. Consent is not just saying yes or no. It requires clear thinking and vigilance. These are issues we'd do well to consider before we do say yes."

Sam squirmed in his seat. He remembered naïvely signing Mistress Morgaine's consent form without question. He had known he was giving up all his rights, but he hadn't known what that really meant, and, worse, he hadn't cared. Indeed, horniness trumped safety, sanity, and everything else that stood in the way. His way was to pray he'd get lucky, and with her he didn't.

I disagree. You were very lucky.

You call epididymitis lucky?

You still have your balls, don't you? I call that undeserved good luck.

"The heart of all safe, sane, and consensual play is the safe word," Meredith continued. "We all know what that is. Players can dream up whatever words they want to use and what they mean, but the rule is inviolate: respect the bottom's safe word. And keep in mind that tops need to have safe words, too. Not only with their bottoms, but with themselves as well. That requires a clear, attentive mind and sometimes enormous willpower. We're human, too, you know. Any comments about safe words?"

Black Dragon started to speak, but Sam tuned out of the discussion—he'd had enough to think about. Again, he thought about Mistress Morgaine. Her memory was as persistent as it was seductive. The woman was utterly ruthless and bordered on malevolent, but, he had to admit, she still played by the rules. She had given him *mercy* as a safe word, and even though using it meant expulsion from her dungeon, he'd still had its protection. If, of course, that had occurred to him. Thank the stars she was not in the room, although he could not be completely sure of that.

But his first dominatrix was. He could sense Carmine getting fidgety, as if ready to spring, hopefully at Black Dragon and not him. He worried about what she'd say to him when the meeting was over. He didn't know whether to again accept her handcuffs and lose his freedom, or run away and lose his heart's dream. Mostly he feared that decision would not be his.

It wasn't. When the meeting adjourned, Carmine kissed Sam's ear, then bit it. "Great seeing you again, babe," she whispered. She stood and zeroed in on Black Dragon.

And that was it. Sam was, all at the same time, immensely relieved, disappointed by unexpectedly having his hopes dashed, and feeling bloody foolish for even perseverating about the drama. He thought it best to leave before Carmine decided to return for more than just his ear. Suddenly her loud, distinctive laugh echoed around the room. She, Black Dragon, and Meredith were animatedly engaged in conversation. The man did not look too happy, and Sam did not envy his predicament.

In subsequent Planet S/M meetings, Sam learned about bondage techniques, electrical toys, the fine points of negotiation, emotional pitfalls during play, types of floggers and whips, play piercings, breast bondage, caning, electrical toys, show and tell for adults, and much more. He was continually astounded by how casually and unashamedly people revealed what they did to themselves and each other. Like the zippered girl, many of the demonstrations included live models. Full nudity was prohibited, but there was enough skin to make things interesting.

At the beginning of each meeting, he would invariably scan the crowd, hoping to spot a single woman with an affliction compatible with his. But he had no way to descry that and would probably not know how to proceed if he did. Planet S/M policy stated that soliciting play partners at meetings was neither appropriate nor condoned, but it always inappropriately remained on Sam's mind, and probably everyone else's too, he assumed.

What he did find at Planet meetings, and disarmingly so, was having verbal intercourse with young, attractive female submissives—always those of others, of course. Submissive women of all ages, colors, and morphologies abounded. They wore chain or leather collars to indicate their statuses and were as perky and affable as they came, as their Masters or Mistresses were always nearby. The girls loved getting attention and loved even more disabusing someone's lewd intentions.

When a collared, pretty slave girl caught Sam's gaze on her, she'd give him a coy smile, which he knew meant, "Look all you want to, sir, but don't touch, and you certainly can't have." After every piece of eye candy, he wondered whether the resulting indigestion was worth it; before each bite he decided it was.

The other vital resource for finding a dominatrix was the computer. Instead of skulking around porn shops, Sam could now relax in front of the screen, naked if he wished, and peruse the directories of professional dominatrices. These gals had immediately jumped on the Internet, as it greatly increased their market and allowed them to display their business with enticing detail. Their websites disclosed everything: their dungeons, equipment, bondage furniture, activities they practiced, rules, fees, and photographs featuring their bound and naked clients enjoying themselves. Online fantasy sessions could reach the moon.

Sam used their websites as pornography as well, imagining the pleasures and torments of life under Mistress Extrema Brutella Sadistica La Strict's spiked boot heels. The women no doubt encouraged this virtual frottage as it generated interest and business. With a few remarkable exceptions, most of their websites read pretty much the same, as if there were a downloadable dominatrix boilerplate.

To those who could not afford sessions, lived too far away, had spouses who would frown on such behavior, were reluctant to meet dominatrices in person, were ambivalent about their desires, or just scared shitless, a few professional dominatrices offered domination by mail. Sam was a bit puzzled as to how this was done, but he assumed it was a safe risk and set out to try it. He found one dominant woman in Canada who specialized in this. Her photograph (it may or may not have been her) showed an attractive vixen with dark bedroom eyes and shiny, oiled-up breasts in a lacy black bra who promised strict domination beyond one's wildest dreams.

I can dream pretty wild, Sam thought and grew increasingly curious about how she could top that. As instructed, he mailed her a money order—adjusted to Canadian currency—as well as a brief list of his submissive desires and a signed note stating he was of legal age, and waited. A long month later, he received a packet containing color photographs of her oily breasts, two audio cassette tapes, and offers to purchase other items that would extend her intimacy, such as more photographs of her chest, her soiled underwear, and additional cassettes.

Sam decided he could do without the underwear. He stripped, propped up her photographs on a pillow, turned on the cassette player, and made ready to obey it. He was then treated to a lame five-minute monologue in a contrived, almost silly drone, describing how he'd be forced to lick her boots and be whipped senseless in the dungeon of her palatial country estate. It was like being dominated by a form letter with his name inserted in the blanks. The second tape contained generic masturbation instructions that didn't even bother to include his name and was as erotic as reading an appliance manual. *Well, that sucked.*

Buying sex products online could be risky because there was no guarantee of reputability, and the vendors would then have your credit card number. Sam suspected many of these ads were scams, placed not by gorgeous dominatrices but by a consortium of crooks living in another hemisphere. One could purchase photographs, dirty underwear (he still could not fathom the appeal), jack-off fantasies (as if he needed more), and the latest, hottest sex toys and masturbation aids. One ad promised wanking could be made more glorious with the Turbo-Auto-Masturbator, which came "complete with many exciting attachments for only $499 that would surely give the submissive sex slave the glory of submissive ejaculating glory." Much was lost in the translation.

Online kinky dating services were also disappointing. The ads placed by pro dommes were generally trustworthy because that was how they got clients. Surprisingly, there were ads from women who desired sex slaves to "satisfy their insatiable lust" with no mention of money. This sounded too good to be true because it invariably was, especially to the poor fool who actually believed that a beautiful, horny, dominant woman would be dying to have free, hot, kinky sex with any homely, overweight stranger with bad breath, psoriasis, and behavioral disorders.

Instead, what the fool got was an opportunity to purchase a slave-training kit: an array of expensive sex toys sold by the lady's personal distributor. Many of these alleged dominant and hypersexed women were insidiously inventive in setting up the sting. An ad casting the hook, "Come into my s/m dungeon of this crule Dominant mistress i am that and I teach you ecstasy of submissive and sex slavery" offered only "crule" frustration, examples of atrocious grammar and spelling, and a chance to piss away money and wank to another shallow fantasy.

Sam also discovered the world of female sex slaves pleading for a dominant master through online dating sites. It struck him as odd that these young women were all agonizingly cute, perfectly proportioned, and willing to travel anywhere to submit to anyone's outrageous, sadistic sexual desires. Out of curiosity, Sam responded to several ads, and received replies right away with descriptions of the advertisers' interests and intentions. Two of the responses had identical wording. Sam presumed what he could expect from these girls desperate for domination were nude photographs, soiled panties, and coupons for the latest masturbation devices.

The computer also accelerated the pornography industry to light speed. Sam had read that over three-fourths of all online activity was porn browsing, and from his own surfing he didn't doubt it. Every type of s/m porn came out of the closet and spread its wares on the sticky table, and the possibilities for kink multiplied like fruit flies in a compost pail. Some online porn relied on the browser's fantasies to hijack his common sense. With a little staging, some s/m activities could be made to look authentic, but they might have been dangerous in the real world, where the real penises and vulvas lived.

On the computer, Sam saw that if something atrocious and painful could be done to a woman, it would be, and to women who were willing, if the price was right. Even more bizarre, the woman need not be real. Computer-generated imaging made anything possible, and for the Internet goblins, there were no limits to their creativity and indecency. The worst and most worrisome scene showed a tightly trussed naked woman skewered by a long metal pole through her vagina and out her mouth. She was being turned over a pit of glowing coals, as if she were a rotisserie feast for the hungry browsers. Of course, the scene had been fabricated, but Sam had to look closely to see it. How could anyone find this erotic? He didn't want to know.

Although barbecued girls existed only as pixels, Sam found some websites that showed authentic s/m practices that were almost as extreme, such as men and women being suspended by their balls and breasts, respectively, or having those same parts skewered with needles and nails. One man had two large needles attached to electrode wires thrust clear through his balls. From his frantic howling in the video, Sam was certain the play was not being faked. How could testicles survive such treatment?

Maybe they couldn't. Sam found very little credible information about the medical consequences of extreme s/m play, and when he did, there were plenty of opinions about it. Many players edged past that with permanent body modifications, such as tattoos and piercings. Braver souls ventured into ear lobe plugs, more inventive and larger piercings, extensive cuttings, and sub-dermal implants. Boldest of all were those who underwent branding and ritual scarification as done in many tribal cultures. It seemed that the beauty of the human body could always be improved.

Some hard-core players took these practices a step (or three) further with procedures that defied sense and sanity. One man had over time split his penis down the middle, for what reason Sam couldn't imagine. Another had rerouted his urinary canal—apparently dissatisfied with the existing plumbing arrangement. And a woman had managed to elongate her labia—somehow—so they could actually be tied into a loose knot.

Most disturbing and incomprehensible was the practice of *nullo*, the abbreviation for genital nullification, the removal of the penis and testicles. The threat of penectomy and castration were often used as fear games in edgeplay, but Sam saw several photographs (and wished he hadn't) attesting to the real thing. One über-masochist claimed to have sliced open his scrotum, held one of his testicles in his hand, replaced it, then sewed himself back up, with no ill effects, he said. *No ill effects?* There were no photographs, so Sam assumed—and hoped—this was just the idiot's fantasy. He shuddered thinking about the other über-idiots who might think differently and try it themselves. Sam could not see the bizarre ingenuity of s/m ever being corralled.

Sam had finally arrived at the geomantic center of kinky indulgence, yet he felt no nearer to resolving his ambivalence about s/m than when he'd set off on his long, exhaustive odyssey. He'd tried pornography, professional domination, and online dalliances. He'd been educated, tortured, disillusioned, emotionally ravaged, and nearly destroyed, and for what?

Do you still think desire is a place? A dominatrix or a sex slave who'll give you what you want whenever you want it?

What else could it be?

That's a very good question. Ask it the next time you surf the sleazy side expecting to find your bliss. Ask it of yourself, not some search engine. And when you end up finding nothing, which you will, ask me.

19

THE DUNGEON PARTY

THE DISTANCE BETWEEN SAM'S FANTASY VISION of s/m and its reality was steadily dwindling. And somewhere in that space he noticed he'd stepped over a line. He wasn't sure where it was, or when it happened, but he now found himself looking at s/m as a place of possibility and adventure, rather than a swamp of decadence, degeneracy, and withering shame. An outsider viewing a dungeon party might think otherwise.

Pauline and Herb invited Sam to one. The swingers' club they belonged to also lent their facility to the leather community for these quarterly events. Herb was the kinkier of the two; Pauline said she just dabbled in BDSM. She made it clear to Sam she wouldn't dabble with him, but he was welcome to accompany them to a party. He knew the six-hour round-trip would be grueling, but for an honest-to-goodness real dungeon party he'd endure a six-day drive.

The rules of etiquette for guests were brief and simple, as Pauline explained. "You can observe all you want, but don't touch anything unless you're invited to," she said. "The rules for the players are more complicated, but you don't have to worry about that. Dungeon masters patrol all the play spaces to enforce the rules and stop any questionable or dangerous play."

"Dungeon masters?" Sam asked. "I had no idea this was so well organized and regulated."

"It has to be," Herb said. "Look at what you're working with, what you're trying to control—sex, violence, pain, and more sex. Those are extremely explosive ingredients just by themselves. Mix them together with a hundred horny people and watch out!"

An attractive young woman wearing a leather collar, lipstick, and a thong greeted the trio at the door where they had to sign in. Another nymph wearing even less took their coats and gave them each a chit. Sam was startled by how relaxed these ninety-nine-percent-naked women were while attending to strangers. The coat-check girl caught his stare and smiled back. Sam decided that, so far, he liked dungeon parties a whole bunch.

They entered the main dungeon room, which was the size of a gymnasium. Sam's first impression was that he'd stumbled onto the soundstage of a Hieronymus Bosch painting being adapted into a movie directed by and starring Caligula. One third of the cast was naked, another third was halfway there, and the last third, covered head to foot in black leather, was either watching the first two-thirds or chaining them up to something for impending demolition.

Cozy booths lined the length of one wall with leather-clad and zero-clad people in them, chatting and schmoozing as if they were at a church social. Several pool tables were scattered around the room. On one, a woman wearing nothing but makeup and black thong panties was tied to its four corners. Several men and women stood around the table, feasting on the sight. One man lightly tapped the soles of her feet with a cue stick, setting her to squirming.

Bondage furniture was everywhere: leather-padded benches, wooden horses, Saint Andrew's crosses, stretching racks, and a large, freestanding, wooden A-frame that could restrain two victims at the mercy of several floggers. Many of the room's columns were already in use as whipping posts. A hefty blonde woman was tied to one, limply hanging from her wrists in post-beating bliss, her buttocks striped red by a cane. An adjacent post restrained another blonde, her butt being caned by a bearded, heavyset man wearing the standard biker uniform: black boots, black leather vest, and dirt-encrusted jeans that had once been blue, suggesting that his wardrobe was not just a party costume.

Katy met Pauline, Herb, and Sam. She was wearing a full-length, see-through, fishnet bodysuit that Sam thought had been painted on. She kissed Herb, took his arm, and led him to a vacant booth. Pauline waved at someone she knew. She squeezed Sam's hand, kissed his cheek, said "See ya later, honey," and disappeared into the melee of the movie set.

Sam wandered around the room already in mild shock, his eyes and brain overloaded by seeing his dearest fantasies come to life, naked, writhing, and screaming barely two feet away. Most of the victims were women, some were overweight and some severely under, some were positively gorgeous, and all gave Sam a continuously nagging semierection that he could not address.

Sex was permitted only in small rooms designed for that purpose for singles, couples, and any other combination. Each compartment was furnished with a single bed, a table stacked with clean linen, and a large observation window. Half of the rooms were already occupied. Sam had never before seen two people fucking in the flesh. They looked and sounded exactly like what he'd seen in porn films, except those actors had not looked back at him and smiled.

Another room housed four large hot tubs, each containing a human bouillabaisse. Sam considered jumping in, clothes and all. He found the restroom. Curiously, there was no gender designation on the door. Naked and semi-naked men and women were coming and going, men using the urinals, women the stalls. Well, if convention and propriety were banished from the building, modesty should logically follow.

Sam discovered that violation of modesty could also be used as torment. As he stood at a urinal, a short, muscular, mustached, and eyebrow-pierced man in a leather vest was taking a keen interest in watching Sam hold it and wring it. Sam unhappily knew there was no muscle that could accelerate urination, so he had to endure. The mustached man knew this as well and enjoyed Sam's embarrassment. As Sam scurried out the door, the man gave him a wink. Sam did not want to think of what the guy was into.

On the other hand, Sam was very intrigued by what the guy might be into. No one knew how to hurt a man better than another man, and where to do it. The primary targets, naturally, were the testicles. For such delicate and sensitive items, the balls could endure some surprisingly rough treatment, being stretched by heavy weights being a favorite. Sam had attended a Planet S/M meeting about male genital torture presented by a well-known gay master, who was notorious for his sadism and heavy play and who introduced the room to a very scary device called the Elasticator.

The Elasticator was invented to castrate farm animals. Its ability to scare the living shit out of male masochists was a fortuitous discovery.

Resembling a complicated pair of pliers, it applied a thick rubber band around the base of the scrotum. The band cut off the blood supply to the testicles, causing them to die, wither away, and in a few days drop off. It was a dangerous—therefore extremely exciting—s/m toy, assuming the band could be removed, and in time, and the bander knew how. Sam vowed never to go near one.

He saw a directional sign reading *Blood Sports Room.* Curious, he followed it. Coming from the room were two women, naked from the waist up, who looked barely old enough to have driver's licenses. Each had a dozen disposable syringe needles pierced through the skin of her breasts. The needles in one breast were laced to the needles in the other, drawing them together and creating an interesting and probably painful pattern. The girls gaily chatted with each other, eager to display their decorations and grit to the rest of the party.

The floor of the blood room was covered with heavy plastic sheeting. The room held three massage tables that were also draped in plastic. It was far from being a surgical suite, but at least some attempt had been made toward sanitation and safety. On one table another breast lacing was in progress, performed by an older man with a heavy beard and half-moon glasses perched on the end of his nose. He might have been an artisan jeweler repairing a watch, except this watch yelped and wriggled as he inserted each needle.

A group of people crowded around the second table, where a butch lesbian was sewing together the outer labia of her girl. The butch was not using thin surgical sutures but heavy red thread and a large needle. The woman's vulva had started to resemble the seams on a bloody baseball. She was not tied down and struggled mightily to keep her groin immobile while the stitching was in progress. Sam had heard intense screaming coming from the room, and this apparently was the source.

On a third table sat a naked young man who did not look well. Two women gently held him steady. Rivulets of blood ran from a large, intricate design that had been incised into his chest. The sight made Sam queasy. Another ear-splitting scream came from the sewing table and Sam hurried out.

He passed by the sex rooms. In one he saw Pauline sitting astride her current lover, humping away. She'd not had a double mastectomy, as he'd earlier wondered. Her breasts were barely noticeable mounds crowned with large, erect nipples. She even joked about it.

"When I was made up in heaven," she'd earlier said to Sam, "I missed going through the tit line and went through the cunt line twice. It was so worth it!"

Pauline saw Sam staring through the window and, totally unfazed by his voyeurism, smiled and blew him a kiss. Sam waved back and wandered away, totally fazed. He'd once planned to be underneath Pauline himself, and seeing it happening with another man stung.

He wandered past the hot tubs and back into the main playroom, stumbling around like a zombie and with all the cognitive skills of one. Every post and piece of bondage furniture was in use; every story, photograph, and fantasy in his libido's archives surrounded him. The shows were free, the pain and screams were genuine, and naked girl flesh was everywhere. But one could only absorb so much. Sam hoped his brain was filing all this away for later consumption, if brains worked that way.

In one corner of the main room, Herb's dark-haired Katy hung from her wrists on a whipping post, gently swaying in a trance. She'd either lost her fishnet suit or it had rubbed off. Her back and butt were laced with red welts. Herb was sweating and breathing hard, his face as red as Katy's ass. He motioned Sam over and handed him the flogger.

"I'm beat," Herb gasped between breaths. "Take over for me, will you?"

"*He's* beat?" laughed Katy. "That's sooo funny!" She smiled at Sam through half-closed eyes and awaited his attention.

Sam had never been on this end of the whip before and hesitated; he was stepping onto a high wire without a net. But he had to do something. He lightly swished the flogger's leather tails across Katy's butt.

Herb leaned over to him. "Katy's an unbelievable pain slut. She wore me out and she'll do the same to you. Give her all you have, my friend."

Despite Herb's confidence, Sam balanced unsteadily on the wire. He gave Katy a mild slap on the butt with the flogger. No reaction. Another whack. Nothing from Katy. Then a much harder whack and got the slightest jump and the softest of yelps. Sam looked over at Herb, who just smiled and shrugged. Sam had no idea what to do next.

Then Pauline joined the threesome, naked, beaded with sweat, and beaming like she'd just won the Oscar for Best Orgasm.

"You've never flogged someone before, have you?" Pauline said to Sam.

"Um, well…"

Pauline took the flogger from his unsteady grip. "Here. Here's how it's done."

Pauline gave Katy several mild strokes across the shoulders, then several less mild. Katy closed her eyes and rocked in time with the beating. Pauline applied a dozen sharp whacks on each butt cheek, each blow harder than the previous. Katy was now moaning, her breathing becoming ragged and rapid.

Then Pauline started beating Katy's back and butt with a colossal fury that seemed incongruous for a woman so diminutive. After about a dozen wicked strikes, Pauline dropped the flogger and massaged Katy's butt. She reached around and fingered Katy's nipples and pinched them hard. Katy stifled a cry. Several minutes after the fact, Sam discovered he had an erection.

Winded herself, Pauline handed the flogger back to Sam.

"Here you go, hon," she said. "Make sure not to wrap the thongs around her sides, and keep away from the kidneys."

"Where are the kidneys?"

"Down low. Just stay on her upper back and butt and you'll be okay."

Sam let Katy catch her breath. He stood off to one side so he could strike both buttocks at the same time. He tested the heft and weight of the flogger. He was waiting, for what he wasn't quite sure.

"Go ahead, hon," Pauline said.

Sam swung and hit Katy with all the force of a hummingbird fart. A half-fart powered the next blow. Katy, eyes closed, waited to feel something. She couldn't see Sam's reticence, only feel it. Sam swung again, but midway through the arc he felt all the strength drain from his arm like a toilet being flushed. The thongs barely flapped on Katy's skin.

"Sam?" Pauline said.

Sam? What are you waiting for?

I don't want to hurt her.

Of course you do. You jack off about hurting her. Katy wants you to hurt her. She jills off about being hurt. What is the problem here? C'mon, I want to see some action.

I'm afraid.

Afraid of what? You're the one holding the whip.

You know what it is.

You've been afraid like this before. Remember how you played it?

He couldn't forget it. He focused on Katy's crimson butt, still slowly rocking from Pauline's beating. The chaos and babble of the dungeon party faded into white noise. Sam felt himself fall inward and backward in time to that frightening evening with Amber. It didn't matter that it was Katy and not Amber before him, he felt the dissociation again begin. It was too late. Sam knew there was only one way he could go: out on the high wire.

Goblin Sam snatched the flogger from Sam's tenuous grip, took careful aim at Katy's butt, reared back, and brought it down with everything he had. The loud crack echoed around the huge room. Katy shrieked and jumped. Pauline's eyes popped out like hardboiled eggs. Herb suppressed a laugh. People stopped whatever they were doing to look around for the source of the scream.

Sam dropped the flogger and rushed over to Katy, her mouth agape in shock and her body ringing from the strike.

"Oh my God, Katy. I'm sorry. I'm sorry. I'm so sorry!" he cried.

Sam wanted to touch and comfort her but didn't know where to put his hands, which were shaking now more than his victim. Katy looked at Sam with surprise and confusion.

Pauline stepped between them and pushed Sam away. She grabbed Katy's hair, pulled her head back, and sharply spoke into her ear. "Did you like that, bitch? Do you want another?"

Katy took a deep breath, closed her eyes, and nodded. Herb picked up the flogger, had a few soft words with her, rubbed and massaged her butt cheeks, and then resumed flogging her with light strokes on her back. Pauline led Sam to a vacant booth. After a minute, he remembered who and where he was.

"I screwed up, didn't I?" he said, still shaking.

"Yeah, you sure did," said Pauline. She leaned closer and, in measured words, said, "Never, *ever* apologize to your bottom."

"What?!"

"That undermines if not totally destroys your dominance. It breaks the spell. It leaves her in limbo and not knowing who's in control. That can be a very scary and confusing place, especially when she's already off the planet like that."

Sam looked over at Herb and Katy, dancing with each other in flogger time.

"Wow. Jeez. Wow. God, I didn't know. I'm sorry."

Pauline sat back in the booth. "It's okay, honey," she said. "For someone who's a sub, being dominant is not easy. It's an acquired skill and mistakes will be made. Herb's a born dominant. It's his second nature. And he still makes mistakes. It's not in your nature, and that's perfectly okay."

"Did I hit her too hard?"

"Well, you sure surprised me, but 'too hard' is not in Katy's vocabulary."

"I just didn't know." Sam sat and thought for a moment.

"Sam? You look like you want to say something."

So you're finally going to tell someone?

Yeah. I have to.

Why? I'm the only one who needs to know.

Because I have to. I just said that, didn't I?

He sighed. "Yeah, I do. Something happened just before I hit Katy. At first, I could barely move my arm, like someone was holding it back. But everyone was watching and I had to do something. Then I went into a kind of trance. I know this will sound like I'm crazy, but there's this creature, this presence inside me. I call it my goblin. I've seen him before and I know where he comes from. He's like my Mr. Hyde. He terrifies me. I'm afraid once I let him out, he'll do something really terrible. What's worse, he might not want to go back inside."

Hearing himself speak the words for the first time let him feel just how truly frightened he was, and always had been. He felt just as naked as Pauline.

"But he did go back in," she said. "And you came back."

"Yeah, this time, but what about the next? I don't like hurting people, especially women. But at the same time, I'm so angry at them and I do want to hurt them, and you saw what happened when I was given the chance. I got stuck. I got stuck between what I think is right and wrong. I couldn't hurt Katy, but this goblin sure as hell could."

"Yeah," said Pauline, "you, or this goblin of yours, did hurt Katy. You hurt her but you didn't harm her. Do you understand the difference?"

"I guess not."

"There's a fine line between violence and abuse. Most people here know that line, but not everyone knows where it is. Katy likes to be hurt; she enjoys pain. You saw that. And I think you do too. But I don't think either of you like to be abused, right?"

Again, Sam thought about Morgaine. "Yeah, right."

"What makes it confusing," Pauline said, "is that what looks like abuse may not be. You'll see violent acts here, but it's not abusive violence. The difference is consent, and it's up to the consenter to keep that straight.

Unfortunately, not all do, or are capable of it. Some don't even want to. Maybe you'll have to experience this yourself to know."

Sam thought about this.

"Watch Katy and Herb play," she said. "Watch them carefully and you'll see what I mean. Katy knows that line and can take care of herself. Herb also knows. That's why they can play so hard together."

"I guess my goblin doesn't know where that line is."

"I think it does, and it chose abuse." Pauline took his hands. "That's why you're so troubled by this. Sam, you're a good man and a kind man. It's not like good, kind people to hurt one another. That goes against our very nature. But here in this building, we can do it. We can hurt each other but still stay away from abuse. Or at least try to. It looks a little crazy, but is it?"

Sam looked at his hands. They finally became still and Pauline released them. "It's crazy if we lie to ourselves about it."

"Crazy and dangerous," said Pauline. "Because s/m play can be so intense, even the smallest lie or even a half-truth can have brutal consequences. And not just to the body, you know. Sometimes you have to screw up once or twice to understand that."

"But what should I do, now that I screwed up and crossed that line with Katy?"

"It's okay because you crossed right back, and now you know. That's what mistakes are for. Katy knows all this is new to you. She also knows we'll look out for her. That allowed her to feel safe with you. She'll be all right. Well, maybe except for her ass!"

Sam tried to let this sink in. *Safe. That damn word again.*

Now do you know why you hit Katy so hard?

Yeah. To destroy my safety. And hers.

You want to be dangerous, don't you?

Yeah. Really dangerous.

Will that make you a whole man? Is that your missing piece?

Maybe. I don't know, damn it!

Well, you'd better find out before you hurt someone, especially yourself.

Herb and Katy, who now wore a heavy robe, approached the booth. Herb draped a blanket over Pauline and whispered to her. Katy bent down and surprised Sam with a warm hug.

"Are you all right, my dear?" Katy said.

Somewhat stunned and very relieved, Sam said, "Yeah. Are you?"

"Never better," Katy smiled. "Now, whenever I sit down, I'll think of you."

Pauline stood up and wrapped herself in the blanket.

"Come with us," she said to Sam. "This is something you have got to see."

Sam noticed most of the people were already leaving the main play-room. He followed his companions through a door he'd not noticed before. This led to another large room, a half-size basketball court with a high ceiling. In the near corner of the room Sam was startled to see Carmine, looking utterly gorgeous in her makeup and skimpy fetish wear. She'd bent a naked man over a bondage horse and was shackling his wrists and ankles to its legs. On a table beside the horse was an array of dildos, including The Rhinoceros. The man was in for the pegging of his life, and he looked like he couldn't wait. Sam was able to slip by the couple unseen.

The main event was at the other end of the room. An overhead winch normally used to lift the basketball backboard out of the way now sus-pended a naked woman about four feet off the floor. She hung from ropes tied around her wrists and thighs, and her legs were spread wide and tied to eyebolts in the floor.

Sam was utterly spellbound. He'd seen similar scenes in pornography, but not in the flesh just ten feet away. The woman was attractive enough to star in any video, porn or not. The crowd gathered along the walls to watch. Pauline pulled Sam to the side, where they sat on the floor next to Herb and Katy. Pauline cocooned herself in the blanket and held Sam's hand.

The other star of the show was Black Dragon, strolling around like he owned the place. Sam thought it very fortunate that he and Carmine were at opposite ends of the room, and he hoped it would stay that way. Black Dragon had brought two large duffel bags. One contained an assortment of mountaineering ropes, neatly tied in bundles, along with nylon straps, pulleys, clips, carabiners, and other devices useful for hanging women from the ceilings of basketball courts. He rummaged through the other bag and withdrew a single-tail whip.

The whip, four feet long and ending in a single leather thong, was a beloved implement of tops who know how to use it and, of course, of those brave souls on whom it was used. Those who'd mastered the single-tail car-ried them coiled on their belts and strode about like Wyatt Earp proudly sporting his Colt. And the single-tail was just about as dangerous. The tip moved so fast that it broke the sound barrier, causing its signature loud crack. Cowboys and drovers used the single-tail to startle draft animals into motion rather than tear open their hides.

But not here. After flexing and limbering up the whip, Black Dragon went to work. A few practice strokes acquired the range of the target. With a single-tail, a practice stroke stung just as ferociously as a real one. The target looked absolutely fear-stricken, and well she should have been. Despite his posturing and bravado, Black Dragon did know how to use the whip. The first strike left a three-inch welt on the woman's shoulder, and she screamed at full volume. The second strike raised a mirror-image welt on her other shoulder, causing an equally loud scream. Symmetry, it seemed, was critical to the man's performance.

Soon the woman's back and buttocks were crossed with welts, some open and bleeding. Black Dragon allowed his victim a minute's respite between each lash to recover, but now his kindness was at an end. He walked around to her front side, found his range, and laid a stripe across her right breast. She shrieked and kicked the air. He struck her left breast, then the right, and back and forth between the two without a break. Black Dragon's skill and accuracy were clearly evident as both nipples remained untouched and pink.

The scene enthralled the room. Sam had heard the couple was famous for extreme and intense play, and this was just another one of its capers at the limits of reason. But he was unexpectedly struck ashen and struggled to quell his stomach. Pauline leaned over to him.

"Are you all right, honey?"

"Uh, no."

"Do you want to leave?"

"No, I'll be okay," he said, though not at all sure. *How can this possibly not be abuse?*

The woman's howling and thrashing became so frenzied it attracted the attention of a dungeon master. The man, who was dressed all in black except for a white armband as his badge and carrying a walkie-talkie as his weapon, approached the couple. Black Dragon ceased the beating and looked like he was ready to turn the whip on the intruder. The woman hung from her ropes and sobbed uncontrollably.

Without any warning, Sam came face to face with a paradox. The act of flaying bound nudes lived at the heart of his hottest fantasies, yet seeing it actually happen had caused the opposite reaction: shock, revulsion, and alarm. A stark truth emerged: brutalizing a woman, or anyone, ran against every fiber in his being, as well as every rule of civilization, decency, and humanity. But in this room, it was celebrated. Something was very wrong here, yet he knew he'd later find arousal in the memory. Something was very wrong indeed.

What's the problem, dear boy? Are we having an attack of conscience? Have we decided to reform?

I'm thinking about it. This can't be right.

But your cock thinks otherwise. Just look around the room. Everyone loved watching it. Everyone but you.

I wasn't expecting to feel this way.

Of course not. Haven't you learned anything about expectations? You're still steeped in doubt about this new life of yours and think you'll find yourself here.

Why not? This is where I belong. I've found myself at last.

Pah! All you've found is another dead end. You haven't figured that out, but your stomach sure has.

Black Dragon and the dungeon master exchanged a few words and then, surprisingly, hugged each other. The girl was lowered into Black Dragon's arms. He steadied and untied her, and they embraced, she still sobbing and heaving. Remarkably, despite her tear-streaked face and her body laced with purple welts, she managed to smile at her lover.

Black Dragon wrapped his woman in a blanket, helped her to the floor, and laid her head in his lap. He stroked her hair and soothed her face as if they'd just had gentle, loving sex. Sam just gaped at the couple, unable to comprehend what he was seeing. The show was over. People filed out of the room to continue with more private entertainment, leaving the huge space to Carmine and her squealing peggee, both of whom had been oblivious to all else.

Pauline took Sam's arm and walked him back to their booth. Herb and Katy took a detour to the hot tubs. Still in mild shock, Sam had the distinctly uneasy sensation of being watched—not by anyone in the dungeon, but by something outside the building who was waiting for him to come out. It watched with great sadness. Sam's stomach still flirted with nausea.

Well, now that you've seen all these naked women be tortured to your cock's content, do you feel strong and powerful? Do you feel like you've come home, Master Sam?

No. I feel more lost than ever.

I'm not surprised. Look at yourself. Look at your costume.

He did. In his black shirt, black jeans, and black leather boots too small for his aching feet, he was sweating like a pig. And then he looked at his accoutrements: a borrowed riding crop, keys on a long chain, and a dime store folding knife clipped to his belt like he was some kind of commando wannabe looking for a comic book battle. He looked ridiculous because he *was* ridiculous.

But how can others here dress this way and look so good while I feel like an imposter?

Because you are an imposter. What do you think all this is? The real world? Why do you think people here call themselves players?

But what about Katy? And that poor girl who was whipped? That can't be faked.

Oh, their pain is real enough, but their act remains. Just like yours, except, unlike you, they know it's an act.

But it doesn't feel like one.

Indeed. Do you know who's outside watching you? You are, from the other side of your favorite chasm. And it doesn't like acts. You've gone down a road the rest of your body missed. That's why your belly aches. I'm watching you too, but unlike you I'm having a great time.

God, you're a hideous bitch!

Don't complain. That's just the way you like me.

I don't like you at all!

Then why am I here, hmm?

Pauline shed her blanket. Sam had long since overdosed on skin and regarded Pauline's nudity with weariness.

"That was a little too much to take," he finally said.

"Yeah, I know. Black Dragon and April squick a lot of people."

"Squick?"

Pauline laughed. "Yeah, squick. A combination of being squeamish and freaked. Needles squick me. So does cutting. Felching squicks Herb."

"Oh God, what's felching?"

"You really don't want to know."

"Yeah, well, I've been squicked but good, and I'm still trying to figure out why."

"You don't have to like everything that goes on here," said Pauline. "I certainly don't. We all have our squicks, and there's no law that says we shouldn't. The important thing is if you're feeling squicked, just look the other way and try not to judge."

"That's good advice," said Sam, reluctant to hear a word of it. "But Pauline, how can all that vicious whipping Black Dragon did to April not be harmful, as you say? You saw her. If she wasn't being abused, she sure as hell acted like it."

"You saw them afterward."

He slumped back in the booth and sighed.

"Remember, Sam, don't judge."

He nodded.

"It's late," Pauline said. "It's time for you to go home. You've had quite a night and you have a long drive ahead of you. I have more, um, business to take care of." She leaned across the table and kissed him on the lips. "'Till then, honey."

She wrapped herself in the blanket and left.

The party was still going strong. The biker dude was now naked and stretched between two columns. His former lady victims were taking turns beating him, one with a flogger, the other a cane. With each strike, his enormous belly shook like a washtub full of pink, hairy jello. The pegged fellow followed behind Carmine on a dog leash, walking very gingerly (he was still wearing The Rhinoceros).

Sam looked over at Black Dragon, April, and another couple sitting in a nearby booth. The two men were comparing photographs on their phones. April sat slumped in the corner of the booth, staring at nothing. Wrapped in her beige blanket, she looked like a fried girl burrito. Small bloodstains had soaked through the fabric.

Sam had seen enough. He gave his chit to the nearly naked coat-check girl whose tired smile said, "A smile is all you're getting from me, Clyde."

Yes, it was time to go home, wherever that was.

20

ONYX

SAM AWOKE THE NEXT MORNING WITH the vivid memory of the dungeon party still embedded in his mind. Like a bizarre, delirium-soaked dream, he couldn't shake off his lingering disorientation. He felt he'd been kidnapped from his comfortable life, thrown into the backcountry of the wild and fearsome crotch cannibals, and now he somehow had to find his way home.

Paradox kept reverberating in his mind. It was like looking through out-of-focus binoculars. He tried to bring the two blurry images together: fantasy s/m and real s/m. Dream screaming and real screaming. Hurting and harming. Black Dragon flaying April. April kissing Black Dragon. The images just wouldn't jive, and Sam feared they never would. Perhaps this couldn't be processed or understood. It just was. Like a koan.

Pauline called that evening to check up on him.

"I don't know who or what I am right now," he said. "Nothing makes sense."

"There's really no easy or reasonable way to absorb all this," she said. "You're like a fifth-grader suddenly shoved into grad school. Just let it be, and be easy on yourself. And by the way, Katy says hi and to tell you that she's fine and loves to sit down."

"Thanks. That was nice of her to say."

"Sure, hon. There's another party scheduled in a few months. Interested?"

"Ah, I'll have to think about this."

"Of course, you do. You've been through it and have a lot to process."

"Yeah."

Process? What did process really mean? He'd heard the word enough times in his New Age meanderings and still didn't understand it. Processing, he concluded, was essentially verbal masturbation, either with yourself or done mutually with another person who was equally processing-addicted. Processing meant talking about one's issues: emotional issues, relationship issues, issues with sex, issues with intimacy, issues about having too many issues (or not enough). There was never a lack of issues because issues have the unique ability to self-replicate. To Sam, issues were as integral to *relationship* as rubber was to a hockey puck.

And what did a processed issue feel like? How much talking was necessary? Did a bell on some meter somewhere ring when the processing was all done? Would your tongue cramp up? And after an issue was processed to a slow and painful death, why did it keep coming back, zombie-like, to plague you again?

Does your brain hurt after all this processing?

Yeah.

It should. Brains are not made for that kind of torture.

How can we ever understand anything unless we think about it?

Twit! You can misunderstand something just as easily as you can understand it. Your life is an excellent example of that. Your little processing game is like trying to dig a hole in water. There's no end to it.

But I need to make sense out of this!

Manufacturing sense would be more accurate. Then you can make up anything you want to get your processing fix. You're going to do it anyway.

So what do I do?

Stop torturing your brain with processing. Let it have a good time for a change. Have it think about Katy's boobs. Or better yet, mine.

SAM SAT AT A TABLE BY himself in a small café, sullen, horny as usual, and thinking about sex, or, rather, its unwanted absence. He was hoping he'd get lucky this afternoon and meet a lady as kinky as himself. The café,

The Rusty Griddle, was a good place to do it as it was a sort of social hub for the local leather community, although he now suspected that getting lucky in this bizarre world might not always turn out to be a good thing.

An absolutely gorgeous brunette entered the café. Tall and voluptuous, she could have walked off a magazine cover. She spotted Sam and immediately headed for his table. She was wearing a crimson silk blouse unbuttoned to reveal the tops of full breasts barely contained in a lacy black bra. Long, perfect legs extended from her black leather miniskirt and terminated in black leather spike-heeled boots. She sat across from him, leaned forward to reveal more bosom, and sent a wicked smile slithering into his gonads.

"You're Sam?" she asked. "The artist? The really fabulous erotic artist?"

"I am."

"I'm so thrilled to finally meet you. My name is Mistress Lucretia Lash. You may have heard of me. I'm a dominatrix here in town. I'm known for being extremely cruel, and I've always wanted an artist for my plaything and sex slave."

Lucretia withdrew a large, unlocked padlock from her purse and handed it to him.

"Go into the men's room," she said. "Lock this around your balls and bring me your underwear."

Sam blinked himself awake and stared at the vacant chair across the table. *Why the fuck do I do this to myself?* he muttered for the millionth time.

Because you know how much I love to see you suffer, my little plaything.

I'm so glad I could entertain you.

What's wrong, didn't you like my outfit? You bought it for me, you know.

In the real world, a leather lesbian couple walked into the café. One was obviously the top—hard-faced and butch in black leather biker's garb. The other woman was her femme bottom, small and sylph-like, and so unearthly-looking that Sam thought he was still in his fantasy. She was wearing a long black lace dress with the fingerless lace gloves currently popular with Goth women. Her head was shaved except for a single, jet-black French braid that ran almost to her waist. Every piercable part of her finely featured face bore small silver rings: ears, lips, nose, and eyebrows. She would have looked perfectly at home in a Pharaoh's tomb or on the Klingon homeworld. She pulled out the chair for her Mistress and then alit onto the other.

Sam forgot all about Lucretia and stared at the two women, transfixed. They looked toward him, smiled, and politely nodded. They began a conversation with each other in muted voices, occasionally looking his way, making him equal parts intrigued, anxious, and titillated. He could not turn away from the fascinating pair.

To his astonishment and concern, the femme stood up and delicately approached his table. She was a study in metal. A wide steel collar circled her thin, bird-like neck. A heavy chain was locked around her waist with a padlock. Smaller chains were locked around each wrist in addition to the half-dozen steel rings that served as bracelets. Even her ankles bore thick iron shackles. She sounded like Marley's ghost as she walked.

"My name is Onyx," she said politely. "And you are Sam? The fabulous erotic artist?"

The odd synchronicity of her and Lucretia's inquiries startled him but seemed in line with the even odder world he was visiting. Sam stared at the apparition before him and nodded.

"May I please join you?" she asked.

"Please do," he said. *Onyx. How appropriate*, he thought. Everything about her—her makeup, attire, and even her fingernails and toenails—was black. Even her irises were black, though he wasn't sure if they were real or contact lenses. Then Sam uneasily realized that everything about this Onyx said "vampire."

Along his journey into the leather underworld, Sam had learned that vampires were not just confined to film and young adult fiction. A small, virulent, and very secretive subset of the BDSM community played this game in all seriousness. Most were lesbians with a passion for blood. They observed a strict tradition of nebulous origins involving elaborate rituals and initiations passed down from vampire mother to her daughter. Some even had their cuspids filed into fangs by vampire-friendly dentists. Although these faux vampires couldn't perch on ceilings or live for centuries, they exhibited enough paranormalcy to give Sam the willies. And now one was within biting distance.

Onyx gracefully sat down and smiled at Sam as if he were a tidbit on a plate. He saw no fangs among her teeth. That was very good, and he relaxed about a tenth of a percent. He took a few moments to examine what patiently sat across the table. Her delicately arched eyebrows and heavy black eyeliner were not cosmetics as he'd first thought, but tattoos. And the intricate designs on her sheer dress were not part of the fabric but also black tattoos that covered almost every square inch of her arms, chest, and abdomen. Her breasts hung loose, and through the fabric Sam could see a large silver ring through each nipple.

Onyx calmly let Sam look all he wanted, amused by his nervous attentions. He glanced at the butch, who sat watching the pair and grinning like the Cheshire cat.

"Thank you for allowing me to sit at your table," said Onyx as softly and formally as if addressing royalty.

"My pleasure," he said, although "My utter terror" might have been a more truthful response. He stared at her collar; he could see no clasp.

"It's been welded on," said Onyx, seeming to know his question. "It can't be removed."

"My God. Didn't that hurt?"

"Oh my, yes, but not as much as my brandings."

She pulled down the right shoulder of her dress to show a series of strike marks burned into her upper arm. Sam looked over at the butch, who, still smiling, nodded at him. He thought he'd seen every possible species that inhabited the s/m world, but nothing quite like this. "Jesus," he muttered.

"My name is Onyx," she said sharply. "Jesus was a dead white man on a wooden cross." She then caught herself. "Oh my, I am really sorry I said that. I really am. Did that offend you?"

Onyx had jumped from cynic to sincere in less than a microsecond. "No, not at all," he said. Petrified, yes; offended, no. *Who is this creature?*

When Onyx bared her shoulder, Sam saw, beneath a cloud of tattooed bats on her collarbone, a red, crudely drawn outline of a crow on the top of her breast. Another crow. That bird seemed to be the totem creature of all women weird, Gothic, and beyond.

"That crow's not a tattoo, is it?" he asked.

"Oh no. It was done with a razor blade." Her unnerving smile implied there was a chilling story behind this that Sam wasn't sure he wanted to hear. "Mistress and I saw your show at Galerie Outré last year. Your artwork is absolutely fabulous. I really, really mean it."

"Thank you."

"No, thank *you* for sharing with us the gifts of your visions. You are a fabulous artist, just fabulous."

Sam regarded Onyx. She certainly knew all the right things to say, but he wished she knew a few more adjectives. Yet beneath her fearsome and alien visage, which she wore with such casual poise, was emerging a woman of unexpected warmth and kindness. Sam's wariness receded, replaced by curiosity and an even more curious kind of sexual attraction. Here was someone who apparently lived with her razor blades and edges as if they were teddy bears.

The waitress set down a tray with a pot of tea in a cozy and two cups.

"I'm sorry," Sam said to her, "but I ordered coffee."

"Courtesy and compliments of Mistress," Onyx said. "It's green tea. It's much healthier for you than coffee. It has antioxidants."

Green tea? What did Onyx want from him besides a pint of blood—deoxidized blood?

Onyx resumed her formal demeanor. "Mistress and I have a business proposal for you. We would like to commission you to paint a full-body portrait of me. Naked, if you will. If this is agreeable to you, what would you charge for such a painting?"

Sam was awash with relief knowing that his blood was now safe. He also felt like he'd just boarded a roller coaster. The rises and dips were comprised of the fear of vampires, the appeal of seeing Onyx naked, the absolute revulsion of doing artwork on commission, the desire for money, the fear of Mistress being dissatisfied with the portrait and twisting off his head, more desire for money, fear of seeing his blood oozing out, and the appeal of more naked Onyx.

The ride would not end there. *Don't say yes to something you'll regret*, Sam could hear a familiar voice say. His last commission had been two years ago—an illustration for a magazine cover. The artwork had been dragged through four agonizing revisions by three art- and tact-challenged editors who viewed freelance artists as overrated, overpriced, conceited whores who deserved such abuse. *Never again*, vowed Sam afterward. But then, none of those editors had been Onyx naked.

"Well, I'm really not a portrait artist," Sam mumbled, stepping very carefully and not sure how the sentence would end. "And commissioned work can be very difficult because of the expectations and—"

"Mistress and I will gladly accept whatever you do. We would be honored to own one of your fabulous paintings. We truly would."

The roller coaster began to level off. Sam examined Onyx's body a little more closely. She sat upright to make the display more prominent.

Replicating the tattoos was going to be a bitch, and he was sure he'd not seen half of them. Onyx poured the tea through a strainer into the two cups with precision, ceremony, and grace, as if she had been born to the task.

"How important is the accurate representation of your, uh, body art?" he asked.

"Just as close as you can get," Onyx said, looking at Sam while pouring perfectly. "We're not anal about detail. What would be your fee?"

Sam was thinking. Setting prices on his artwork was never straightforward or easy. Charging a flat rate by the hour was impossible, as some pieces bloomed in under twenty minutes while others demanded days of tedious work, not to mention correcting an endless cascade of mistakes. Usually, he would just grab a number out of thin air and that was that, except he'd double it if the buyer was a magazine editor. Judging by Onyx and the woman known as Mistress, Sam decided he'd give them the benefit of thrift store prices.

As if sensing his quandary, Mistress approached the table. Onyx immediately stood and offered her chair. The butch sat down; at close range she appeared much larger and could have passed as a linebacker with boobs. She extended her hand to Sam.

"Liz," was all she said.

"Mistress," said Onyx, now kneeling on the floor beside Mistress Liz. "Sam is interested in our proposal, and I think he's not sure how to price it. Is that right?"

"Right," said Sam, grateful for and a bit unsettled by Onyx's perceptive abilities. Or was it mind reading? He'd heard somewhere vampires could do this.

"Understood," said Liz.

"Would you accept eight hundred?" Onyx suggested.

Sam sat back, stunned. He had been thinking less than half that. Lesbians and money simply did not go together. Mistress and slave looked at each other. Liz nodded.

"Eight-fifty," Onyx said.

"Eight will be fine, just fine," Sam said, not wanting to appear greedy or supercilious.

Onyx yipped and clapped her hands.

Liz shook Sam's hand again. "Done," she said. "She's all yours."

"Um, she's all mine?" Sam was not sure he heard right. He didn't want to misinterpret anything, especially with such a potentially dangerous anything as Onyx. "What does 'she's all mine' mean, exactly?"

"You can put me in any pose or predicament you want," Onyx explained.

"Surprise me," Liz added.

"I'm not sure if I understand what you're saying," Sam said, his mind racing into a future modeling session involving Onyx and kinky things. "I can put her in, uh…"

"Bondage," supplied Liz.

Onyx smiled and nodded.

Sam sat there like a ventriloquist's dummy, minus the ventriloquist.

"I'll be there," Liz said, "to make sure she behaves and doesn't hurt you."

Onyx grinned at Sam like a cobra hypnotizing her prey before striking. "I'm completely harmless," she said. "I'm as safe as they come."

Liz sat back and howled. Onyx kept gazing at Sam. This combination of beauty and menace both seduced and terrified him. What could he do to Onyx that hadn't been already been done to the extreme? And what could she do to him?

"Okay," he said.

"Yes!" Onyx shouted. Liz said nothing and again disappeared into her Cheshire cat grin. Sam would never accuse Liz of being overly talkative. They set a date for the modeling session.

"One last question," he warily added. "Are you two, uh, you know?" He gestured to the cutting on Onyx's breast.

"Vampires?" Onyx asked with a glitter in her deep, black eyes. "What if we were?" She laughed, stood up, and leaned forward toward Sam's silent, paling face, and said with a smile, "Don't worry, dear boy. You're safe with us." The smile implied safety didn't apply here and never would. "Vampires are just posers. We eat vampires for breakfast."

Sam could believe it. Liz just winked at him. But again, they hadn't said they weren't.

On the appointed day of the photoshoot, Sam was still unclear about what he wanted, both artistically and otherwise. He was still nagged by a persistent suspicion of their true agenda, which might include his exsanguination. Both of these women looked like and could easily qualify as enforcers in a postapocalyptic dystopia where exsanguinating people was routine and vampires ruled.

The doorbell chimed. Sam admitted the pair into his apartment—Liz in the standard black leather biker uniform and Onyx wrapped in a floor-length black velvet robe. Her small feet were bare, and she wore a headpiece of crow feathers arranged to form a crown. Onyx, Queen of the Bat People and Notorious Vampire Eater. Intermingled with the feathers were silver fabric snakes and a few small skulls of real ones. The visage would have sent all three mythological, snake-haired gorgon sisters fleeing for their lives.

Onyx shed her robe and handed it to Sam. She was naked beneath the veneer of head-to-toe tattoos. The crow had been recently recut and had lightly scabbed over. This made Sam a bit squeamish, and he prayed he wouldn't puke on her highness.

"Some girl, eh?" Liz said.

"Urk," croaked Sam.

Onyx, completely comfortable wearing only her crown, picked around his studio and examined sketches, books, art supplies, and the minutiae of his life and profession. He followed her every move, trying to discern the details of her tattoos, and trying less successfully to see the body beneath them.

Liz walked into the kitchen. "Got any green tea?"

Sam, in his one concession to hospitality, had purchased a box of green tea from a specialty tea shop. He'd no idea there were so many varieties of green teas and for so many purposes. Tea was fucking tea, he'd always assumed. He'd asked the saleswoman to pick out a green tea. As a gift, he'd added. She'd shrugged and chosen a box of Lung Ching. "It's from China," she'd said, seeing that Sam was clueless. "Your friend will like it."

"I have some Lung Ching from China," Sam said, trying to sound like an esteemed tea consultant to the Ching dynasty emperor.

"Fabulous choice," Onyx said, "let me serve it."

"Please do," said Sam, not knowing what to do with tea, green or otherwise. He marveled at the sight of this naked, tattooed, pierced, bird-snake-bat woman puttering about his kitchen and poking through the cabinets. *Fabulous.*

He sat on the floor with Liz at a low table in the living room, both of them saying nothing, just smiling at each other and listening to Onyx's soft, domestic tea-making noises in the kitchen. He ran through some possible icebreakers. *Is Liz short for something? How long have you been a lesbian? How much blood do you drink at one feeding? How many words do you actually know? Maybe it's just better if I didn't say anything.*

Liz's inscrutable smile said, "fabulous decision."

Onyx entered from the kitchen bearing a tray Sam hadn't known he had. On it she'd arranged three juice glasses as teacups, a pot as a teakettle, and a strainer. Sam was impressed. The woman could probably make lasagna from a can of beans. Onyx poured the tea with the same ceremonial grace she'd shown at the café and then obediently knelt at Liz's feet. The tea smelled like brewed compost and, he assumed, would surely taste like it.

Sam studied Onyx's tattoos more closely. Her body looked like a cross between an M.C. Escher lithograph and a caffeine addict's doodle pad. Most of the patterns were comprised of a murder of crows, a dance of cranes, a swarm of wasps, and a something of winged serpents, with arcane symbols, runes, comets, pentacles, and more bats filling the spaces in between.

Tattoos even crept down her shaved pubic mound, and he saw rings through her labia. Onyx smiled and parted her thighs to afford a better view. There was a ring through the clitoral hood as well. Sam was about to ask if that hurt, but he knew the answer. Liz carefully watched Sam carefully scrutinizing Onyx's canvas. Her portrait would be hell to paint.

Onyx, ever the attentive slave, sensed Sam's need and turned her body to present more designs. Curiously, her upper back and buttocks were devoid of tattoos but speckled with scars; most were white and healed, some were still red and raw. She felt Sam's question.

"Mistress has a special flogger," Onyx said. "The thongs have carpet tacks embedded in the end. She can actually flay out little chunks of flesh." She saw Sam's face pale and smiled.

"What!? You have *got* to be kidding." Sam prayed this couldn't possibly be true.

"We never kid," Liz said. Onyx rolled back her eyes, mimicking rapture.

"Holy shit." Sam felt a massive squick approaching.

"I'm a very heavy bottom," said Onyx, her black eyes sparkling. "No one can break me. Not even Mistress." Onyx slyly looked at Liz.

Liz grabbed Onyx by her braid, pulled her head back, and held it. "Rue the day I do, bitch," said Liz. Onyx laughed. Liz kissed Onyx on the lips and released her. Sam could only sit and stare at the loving couple.

"Leather dykes play much harder than men, you know," Onyx said with obvious pride and pleasure and rubbing her neck. "Even the leather boys. That's because we women know pain intimately and can deal with it. Do you think a man can survive two days of labor and then childbirth, for goddess's sake? Not likely. And the blood? Blood freaks men out. We bleed once a month, so blood is nothing to us."

That's an odd thing for a vampire to say, thought Sam. *So maybe they're not vampires; maybe they're something worse. Carpet tacks, Jesus!* The squick arrived and spread throughout his body like a spilled jar of sulfuric acid.

"Leather dykes get shit from all sides," Onyx said. "We're outcasts from everything. As lesbians we have to keep ourselves hidden from the ignorant bullies and Neanderthals of the white-bread world. And being kinky alienates us from the so-called enlightened vanilla dykes. They accuse us of reinforcing the victimization and oppression of women. 'That's the ultimate of politically and socially incorrect,' they say. They don't understand it. They refuse to understand it. They see us as diseased and traitorous. The cunts! Shit! Shit!"

Onyx's rage clearly was long in the making—and well-founded as well. Sam remembered his own days as a Neanderthal and the sexist slings he'd cast without thought. Had he offhandedly besmirched Onyx or one of her kindred back then? Or worse, was it with covert malice? And far worse, was he still at it? He was glad the two couldn't see his past crimes—or could they, with Onyx's ability to psychically snoop? He vowed to make his caveman days officially over.

Just like that, huh?

I have to start somewhere.

Then start by never saying another word. That'll guarantee it.

After Onyx calmed a bit, she continued. "The history of us, the first leather women, is really sad. Our community was small, and we had to keep it secretive and tight. We even had special signals to one another. Times were really that weird. We established a strict code of conduct and a set of rules regarding our s/m play. We stood by it. We still do."

"It's called Old Guard Leather," contributed Liz.

"Yeah," Onyx said. "The liberated leather dykes of today don't have a clue what that means, or what we did for them. But that's the way of the world. What really pisses me off, on top of taking all this shit from everyone, especially men, is having to educate them as well."

"Amen," Liz said.

"Present company excepted, of course," Onyx quickly added. She touched Sam's arm. "You're one of the few brave men we know. You've walked your own hard road and you've seen ours. We see it in your art. We respect you. We wouldn't be here otherwise."

Sam's caveman winced. He felt like he'd just been dissected without anesthesia and then sewn back together, just for laughs.

Onyx stood up and stretched. "C'mon," she said, "it's showtime."

Sam had cleared a space in his studio, although he wasn't sure how to use it. Onyx took to the center of the room, her face open and expectant and hands clasped behind her back. Her feet were wider apart than what seemed comfortable, and she thrust out her bosom. She stood quietly as if waiting to speak her lines in a school play.

"That's called the 'present' position," Liz explained, seeing Sam appraise the pose. "A slave must always assume it before her Mistress. Onyx knows well not to fuck with me about it."

"Carpet tacks," Onyx said.

"Indeed," Liz said in her special, economical way. She sat on a drafting stool that squeaked and groaned with the load. It was accustomed to the delicate touch of Viridian's ass, not that of a linebacker.

Sam walked around Onyx and examined every angle, both through his eyes and his camera's viewfinder. Onyx closed her eyes and her breathing became shallow. She quivered imperceptibly as if she could feel his attention slide along the curves and valleys of her body. Sam imagined the same thing and kept sliding his eyes. After a few minutes he had a rough idea of what he wanted to do. Onyx remained rapt in her stance, motionless except for occasional frissons that skittered across the mural of her body.

"Permission to get wet, ma'am," Onyx said.

"Denied," said Liz.

"But ma'am—"

"I said denied."

Wow, thought Sam. *She gets turned on having her back shredded into hamburger and just by standing there?*

"It's the way you're looking at me," Onyx said through her reverie, again seeming to peer into his mind. "I can feel it."

Sam startled. Onyx's telepathic memos were becoming more than just coincidence and now edged into a worrisome privacy invasion. What else would she find hidden in his closet? Since he could do nothing to keep the door closed, he continued to survey, enjoying his newfound eye power. The camera's shutter happily clicked away in agreement.

"Would you please put your hands behind your back?" Sam asked Onyx.

"Don't ask her," Liz said. "Tell her. And you don't have to be polite. It's actually better if you're not."

Curious, Sam thought. *Okay.* "Put your hands behind your back," he said as sternly as he could, thinking this was how orders should sound. Onyx instantly complied. *All right then.* He took several shots.

"Now, lie down on the sofa."

Onyx did.

Wow. I think I like this. "Spread your legs."

Onyx did.

I definitely do like this.

Sam took some close-up shots of her vulva. Even her labia were covered in ink.

"Move your hips up." *Click, click.* "Higher." *Click, click.*

Onyx not only responded to his directives but also began to anticipate them, giving him angles he wouldn't have considered. Sam was not sure what he'd do with a dozen pictures of a tattooed vulva, but now he had them.

"Now pull your rings apart," Sam said. *Click, click.* "A little wider." *Click.*

"You can do better than that," said Liz.

Onyx complied, pulled wider, and gasped. She definitely was off-planet. Fluid began to seep from her crevice. Like eye power, word power was becoming a narcotic to Sam, his mind oozing just as heavily as Onyx's vagina.

"Ma'am, please?" Onyx cried.

"It looks like you're disobeying me anyway," Liz said. "Okay. But no touching!"

"Maaaaaaam!"

"Shut up, bitch."

"Time for a break," Sam said, more out of needing one for himself. Onyx sat up from the floor where she'd slid. There was a wet spot on the sofa. She inhaled deeply and let it out. Her eyes seemed shinier than before, as if illuminated from within. He was dumbfounded; he'd done nothing to the woman.

"Oh, nothing?" Onyx smiled.

Liz lifted Onyx off the floor like she was a pillow, laid her on the sofa, and vigorously rubbed the limp girl's arms. Liz asked Sam for a blanket.

He found one and changed rolls of film. He could hear soft whispers between the two from the other room.

When he returned, Onyx was sitting on the sofa looking perky and rested. Liz resumed her perch on the anxious stool. "Good job," she said to Sam. From her, that spoke volumes. Onyx shed the blanket, assumed the *present* position, closed her eyes, and stood motionless.

"Do you have any rope?" Liz asked.

Sam did, having found a bundle of tie-down rope in the trunk of his car. It was stiff and scratchy and a little dirty from use.

"Sisal?" Liz asked. "No hemp or nylon?"

"I'm not really, uh, experienced at this sort of thing. Sorry." Sam suddenly felt his soaring fling with dominance die like a snowflake in a furnace.

"No problem. Go ahead, she's had worse," Liz said.

But there was a problem. Given the extraordinary extent and detail of Onyx's tattoos, the rope and ink would compete against each other. Sam hadn't considered this until now. Onyx just looked at him with those liquid, feral eyes, hungry for whatever he could dish out.

Unexpectedly, Sam saw something bright flitter across Onyx's body, then it was gone. He couldn't retrieve it but knew it was still out there. He had an idea. An overhead beam ran across the studio, with a small screw eye set in the center. The screw had formerly supported a light fixture, but it would work.

"Wrists in front," Sam told Onyx. She instantly obeyed, eyes shining, which gave Sam a whole-body tingle. *A sex slave. Oh yes, I want one. This one.*

Sam bound her wrists together with several coils of rope and threaded the loose end through the eye screw. He pulled the rope taut, drawing her arms upward, and tied the loose end to a doorknob. *It's a studio, not a dungeon,* he reminded himself.

"Don't pull on this too hard," he told her. "This is a photoshoot, not a session."

Onyx nodded. Liz watched closely. The poor stool creaked and threatened to splinter. Anticipation filled the room like a bug bomb had gone off.

Sam slowly circled Onyx, scanning her outstretched body, not entirely sure what he was looking for. He studied her through squinted eyes. *There! There it is!* A pattern briefly emerged in the clutter of tattoos. The camera's shutter, now set to automatic, clattered like a machine gun. Onyx closed her eyes and dipped her knees, straining both her wrists as well as the eye screw. It held, miraculously.

Satisfied that he'd finally captured a rare, elusive creature in his camera after a long and laborious hunt, Sam breathed deeply and relaxed. Seemingly spellbound, Liz rose from the stool, to its immense relief. Who knew where Onyx was?

"Look," Sam said to Liz. "Look at this." He pointed to the tattoos on Onyx's right thigh. "Do you see how the crows spiral up?"

"Yeah."

Sam pointed to the other thigh. "Now look at the cranes, spiraling up in the opposite direction." He followed the design upward with his finger. Onyx shivered at his touch.

"Yeah?" said Liz.

Sam continued tracing the designs, more engaged in describing the arc than what his fingers were actually touching. But Onyx was very much aware of it; she closed her eyes and leaned into his touch.

"See how the two spirals cross each other here, where one turns into wasps and the other into these snake things?" Sam drew his finger across Onyx's belly. "And here." With both hands he traveled between her breasts, across her shoulders, and up her arms. "And here."

Onyx's shivering increased.

"Do you see it? Do you see the pattern?"

Liz squinted at the human canvas hanging from the screw eye.

"It's a double helix," Sam said. "It's the DNA molecule."

"Fuck me," Liz said.

"Were the tattoos designed this way?" he asked. "It's ingenious."

"No, they weren't. Fuck me."

"Permission, ma'am?" whined Onyx. "Pleeeease?"

"Denied," Liz said. "Well, fuck me."

"There's your painting," said Sam, in total awe of, and eternal debt to, whatever kink-friendly muse had dropped by his studio to haul his floundering ass out of the fire.

Onyx let slip a cry, went limp, and hung from the screw eye. Sam just stood there, astonished by both the woman's phenomenal eroticism and the screw's stamina.

"Did she... ?" Sam asked.

"Looks like it," Liz said.

"But how?"

"Sometimes she's all clit. And she's in one big shit-pile of trouble."

Liz and Sam untied Onyx and lowered her arms slowly to ease the strain in the sinews. Liz wrapped her up in the robe and laid her on the sofa. Sam wanted to reveal his discovery to Onyx, but she was maybe only two percent there with them.

"She'll be like this for a while," Liz said. "I'd better get her home."

Liz gave Sam a big bear hug then took his hand. "Thank you. Thank you," was all she said.

Sam cleaned up the dishes. He considered dumping the rest of the tea into the compost but decided he'd better hold on to it, just in case—the case being the very sexy sex slave Onyx, who would hopefully be heading his way again soon.

Do you mean the lesbian sex slave Onyx?

Yeah, that one. Shit.

Do you really want one? Could you handle one?

Maybe.

Maybe is nowhere near good enough, twit! Do you think owning a person is a snap? Look at those two. Onyx can't piss without permission. Would you be able to know what she needs and then give it to her?

Well, I could learn.

No, you couldn't. You either have it or you don't, and you don't. I should know. And you sure as hell wouldn't be able to fool Onyx like you try to fool everyone else. Her prescience is a little scary, isn't it?

Yeah, my God.

She'd always be one step ahead of you, and then who'd be topping whom?

Sam had a brief vision of Onyx, the tattooed vampire dominatrix. His breathing stopped.

Be very careful with that, twit. Carpet tacks, remember? Jeez! That even squicks me.

Sam burned through the painting as if he were running the four-hundred-meter sprint against the world's best, with Onyx as the gold, silver, and bronze medals. It turned out fabulously. The helix was subtly suggested; if the viewer knew what to look for, it jumped out like a monkey. He called the pair to conclude their business over tea at the café. They would be floored, he hoped.

And they were. Sam must have heard "fabulous" fifty times from Onyx, and, as expected, once from Liz. His ego expanded to fill the available space. Liz pressed eight crisp one-hundred-dollar bills into his hand. Sam forced himself to sip his green antioxidant, thinking and waiting for the right moment. The Amazing Psychic Onyx created one for him.

"Did you like topping me?" she asked. "You know, ordering me around?"

"Uh, yeah. Yeah, I did. A lot."

"But it doesn't come naturally to you, does it?"

"No, not really. It shows, huh?"

"It does," she smiled. "But that's because you're a bottom. And that's okay."

"Being dominant has to come naturally and easily," Liz said. "Especially with a strong submissive like Onyx. If you're not equal to that strength and you're not on your game twenty-four seven, she'll chew you up into little pieces. She's like holding the tiger by the tail. Onyx is a fuck of a lot of work, but she's worth it."

What did I tell you, hmm?

Liz grasped Onyx's hand, and Onyx turned into a black puddle on her chair.

"Men just can't understand a woman the way another woman can," said the newly loquacious Liz. "There are subtleties and nuances that go right over your head. Women know where women live, and what we feel, and why. Women are wired differently than men, and we know where the wires go and what they do. Topping a woman is more than beating the shit out of her. You have to beat her into a very special place and then bring her back."

"We can speak to each other without speaking," Onyx added. Sam believed it.

"Right," Liz said.

"Sam, you're basically a submissive, like I am," Onyx said. "We actually discussed what you might need and whether or not we could give it to you. We've never played with a man, but you're the closest we've come. You may take that as a supreme compliment."

"I will." He didn't like the way "submissive" sounded, especially when applied to him. But two vampire dykes topping him? One a vicious butch and the other fatally femme made him woozy in the knees and horny in the head.

"But why would two lesbians even consider intimacy with a man?" he asked.

"Because s/m transcends gender," Onyx said. "It's about power and empowerment and total surrender to the goddess, blissful surrender. That's where it's at. It's not about sex. Sex is just the gravy on the meat. Sex can even be a distraction, a sideshow making you miss the main event."

"So what is the main event?" he asked.

"You never know until you get there," Liz smiled, "and recognize it."

"Well," Sam began, treading carefully so as not to fall into petulance, "you have to be in the show to begin with."

Onyx and Liz eyed one another. Sam imagined great slabs of communication flowing between them through their psychic hotline. Something here just didn't make sense. *Onyx is a strong submissive?* he thought. *Chewing her top to pieces? Liz has to match that strength? Aren't submissives are supposed to be... submissive?*

At length, Liz nodded to Onyx. Their confab was apparently over.

"If you can let go of the sex," Onyx said to Sam, "would you consider being topped by a lesbian?"

Sam perked up.

"Not by us," she continued, "or me. We have someone in mind who'd be perfect for you. She's just beginning her practice as a pro domme, and she needs clients."

"A beginner?" Sam wanted an experienced veteran, someone who was expert at cleaning his clock in places he didn't know were dirty. But a beginner?

"We're all beginners," said Onyx, still tuned in to Sam's frequency. "Even Mistress and I. And everyone has to start somewhere. Are you interested?"

Sam was, and he knew he was, but he had to pretend to think about it.

Do you really want to do this, twit?

You bet. Why not?

Why not? Haven't you learned a thing about these so-called dommes? They're not real. They don't know you. They don't know what you like. I do. If you want to obey someone, then obey me. You've been doing it all along anyway.

"Sam?" Onyx asked.

"Okay. Yes."

You damn fool!

"Woot! Woot!" Onyx shouted. "Here's her number. Her name is, um, well, she'll tell you her name. We've already told her about you."

"What? Why?" Sam was as startled as he was thrilled.

"We had a… feeling," Onyx said with her half-human, half-alien smile.

"Right," Liz agreed, Liz-like.

Sam held the scrap of paper as if it were his ticket to heaven.

Or hell, Sam. Or hell.

21

LADY INDIGO

JEEZ! JUST WHAT IS YOUR PROBLEM with this?

You are always the problem, twit. You still don't know who I am, do you?

You're one of my multiple personalities?

Crap like that is why I call you a twit. But come to think of it, that's not a bad guess.

Are you my mother?

Your mother?! Ick!

Well, you sure act like her.

That's because you act like her little boy.

And you're mean and awful like she is.

Of course I am. She showed me how. She showed me a lot of things, especially how to keep you in line. You like being kept in line, don't you? It's what you want. It's what you need. She knew it and I know it. It's love to you, isn't it?

I don't know what you're talking about.

Pah! You know exactly what I'm talking about. That's why I'm here. To love you, little Sammy. To love you just the way you want it. I can do things your mother can't. Or any other of your dominatrix wannabes. Especially this newest one.

We'll see about that.

We certainly will. Enjoy your trip to hell.

Sam kept the ticket Onyx had given him in a desk drawer with his safety deposit box key, his birth certificate, and his social security card. He didn't know why it belonged there, it just did. But it would do nothing unless he used it to make a telephone call.

It began in the oddest way ever. "My name is Sam," he said after she answered. "I was given your number by Onyx and Liz, and I don't know who I'm supposed to be talking to."

After a brief pause, he heard a bright laugh, then, "You may call me Lady Indigo."

"Lady Indigo. Yes, ma'am."

"Whoa. You're jumping the gun there. Despite what Onyx might have told you, I am not quite yet your 'ma'am.'"

"I'm sorry, ma'am, I mean Lady. Lady Indigo."

"Good!" she said. "You've already learned something. That's why slave training is called training. Keep this in mind: if I decide to take you on, I don't expect you to perform perfectly. In fact, I'll discourage it. I require authenticity, not some slave act. Do you understand?"

"Yes."

"I'm not sure you do, but you will. You can count on it!" she laughed again. "Onyx told me a little about you, but I want to hear it with your own words."

Sam was surprised by her relaxed, amiable demeanor and candor. He heard none of the contrived clichés parroted by Mistress Morgaine and Carmine, nor could he detect a trace of the attitude that some dominant women enjoyed throwing around. He was also immensely relieved he could drop the slave act he was no good at anyway. But that left him without a way to proceed, other than to just start talking.

"Okay," he began. "Yes, well, ever since I was, I mean in puberty, I've been, um, turned on by, you know…" He had no idea why he'd suddenly become tongue-tied.

"Let's try this another way," she said. "What do you fantasize about when you masturbate?"

My God, the woman gets right to it. But his tongue went deeper into bondage.

Lady Indigo seemed to understand his reticence. "If we're going to work together," she said, "I'll need your complete honesty, your absolute bottom-line honesty. Don't try to impress me like you're probably thinking you have to. I must know everything down to the last nubbin. S/m is a very dangerous business, and wrong or incomplete or false information could lead to serious damage. And not just to your body."

Deception was now unthinkable, and even if he was a world-class fabricator, Sam was certain the woman could spot it in a second. "Okay. I fantasize about being a slave. Being tied up and tortured."

"That's better. By a woman?"

"Yes."

"Is that why you called me? To add me to your fantasy album?"

That nailed Sam to the wall.

"Answer honestly," she said.

Sam wondered if her day job was as a prosecuting attorney. *Honesty,* she said. Nothing else was going to work with this woman. But telling the truth meant you first had to find it.

Lady Indigo jumped into the lengthening silence. "Sam, if you're thinking about writing a good-looking resume for me, don't even try. Slavery is a position where you can't possibly look good. *Comprende?*"

His tongue suddenly freed itself. "Okay. Yeah, there is that fantasy stuff about being a… slave, but there's more. I'm trying to understand why."

"And you think I'm going to tell you?"

"No. Maybe. I don't know." This conversation just would not go his way at all. But then, it wasn't supposed to. "But I believe I'll find out with you."

Now it was her turn to stop and think. "I believe you will."

This Lady Indigo was beginning to impress him. If she was a mere beginner, she certainly didn't talk or act like one.

"Okay. I'm going to give you a writing assignment," she said. "This will be your first task. You are to answer these questions. Are you ready to write this down?"

For once he was. "Yes, m… Lady."

"One," she said, "what are your intentions?"

"Intentions?"

"What you hope to achieve with me. You've just told me about one and there's sure to be others. And know that I'm a lesbian, so sex is absolutely out of the question. I'm not a prostitute, and this is not a game I play."

Her words had a hard edge, as was appropriate for a dominatrix. Sex wasn't high on Sam's agenda, but getting the door slammed in his face still smarted.

"Okay," he said.

"Two, what sorts of things do you like? Write down a list. And again, you'd better be truthful because they may actually happen to you."

Sam prayed they would.

"And don't pray for them either, you little slut," she laughed.

"Okay." *Jeez, are all leather dykes mind readers?*

"Good. Three. What are your hard limits? Those are the activities you'll absolutely not consent to. It's essential that you're clear on that. Then list your soft limits. Those are things you've never done but would like to try."

In his mind Sam joyfully and immediately began to compile his list.

Again, Lady Indigo jumped ahead of him. "Sam, are you paying attention?"

"Yes, ma'am. Oh, shit, I mean Lady."

"Ma'am is now acceptable."

Sam's heart lit up.

"Four, make two more lists, what kinds of things you'd like as rewards and what you'd like as punishments."

He thought of the old joke: what do you do to punish a masochist? Answer: nothing. "I'm not sure of the difference." He laughed.

"You will be. Five, write down your history with s/m and what previous experiences you've had, and with whom. You don't have to name names. That should be easy enough. Also describe your spiritual path."

"My spiritual path?"

"Spiritual path. We all have one but most of us aren't aware of it. Are you?"

"I don't know. I'm not sure."

"Well, this will be an opportunity for you to find out, won't it?" She laughed.

Sam didn't laugh back. Something about this adventure had just turned prickly.

"Now, here's the fun part," she added. "Write out a sexual fantasy. It doesn't have to relate to the real world. And keep in mind it's not a script that will come to life. You can be sure of that. It's just so I can get a sense of who you are and what you want."

"Just one fantasy?"

Lady Indigo laughed. "You are a greedy little boy, aren't you? And keep it under one page. If you can."

Lady Indigo also referred Sam to a magazine article about shamanism and advised him to read it carefully. She gave him her home address, a surprisingly trusting act, and told him to mail her his assignment when completed. Sam resolved to start immediately.

The following day Sam returned to the Mind Flower bookstore, thinking it the only place in town that might have this particular magazine. The freckled young woman was still there and remembered him. She'd lost her bright red sari for faded blue jeans decorated with designer-torn holes and a fluorescent green T-shirt bearing John Lennon's psychedelic gaze. Sam kept staring at the T-shirt, and not because of what it covered.

"What's on your path today?" she asked, smiling as always.

Sam shook off his trance. "Today? I'm looking for an article in the magazine *The Eastern West*," having no idea why it was called that. "Do you carry it?"

"We sure do," she said brightly. "We even have back issues. What's the article called?"

Sam hesitated, not sure why. "'Shamanism and the Left-Hand Path,'" he said.

That startled her out of her smile. "I think we have that," she said warily, now regarding Sam with reservation.

She opened a cabinet containing piles of magazine back issues and pointed to a stack, seemingly reluctant to touch it. "Look through there."

As if it were meant to be, Sam found the article right away. He brought the magazine to the sales counter.

"So, the left-hand path, is it? Are you going to be hanging from any *hooks*?" she asked and gave him the receipt.

She was left-handed, but Sam thought best not to point that out. "I don't know. Maybe. Do you recommend it?"

She turned away without answering.

Sam read the article, and its relevance to s/m jumped out immediately. It was about the transformative power of surviving a physical ordeal—an essential step on the path to becoming a shaman. Hanging from hooks was one way; there were others, thankfully. The article read:

```
There are no classes that teach you how to pass
through an ordeal; you must learn as you go. That's
where true transformation and growth really happen.
A shaman can point the way and even walk with you
for part of it, but ultimately the journey is yours
alone. You are pushed into territories unexplored.
```

You're forced to discover what you're made of, what
you're capable of, and what you're terrified of.

Sam had no intention of becoming a medicine man wannabe, but he
smelled something important lurking in the fog. Apprehension yielded to
curiosity; curiosity beckoned to courage. He could not possibly walk away
from this. What was this Lady Indigo up to? Could she really be that wise
and savvy, this woman half his age? Or was he projecting onto her some
goddess persona to fit his needs?

**You do that with women anyway. You make them your tormen-
tor or your redeemer. You'll still end up resenting her for being
smarter than you, right?**

Yeah, I suppose so.

Then why are you doing this?

I want a dominatrix, damn it!

I already know that. Why?

I'm not sure anymore.

Fabulous! Add that to your list of so-called conscious intentions.

The first draft of his assignment was mostly bullshit, with Sam dishing
out what he thought Lady Indigo wanted to eat, and, thank God, he
caught it. The second draft was better bullshit, but it would have to do.
He mailed the intimate envelope and waited. And waited. Paranoia once
again ruled his mind. The letter carrier turned the package over to the
feds for investigation. A neighbor stole it from her mailbox and is planning
blackmail. Lady Indigo gave it to the tabloids for a handsome sum... .

She finally called.

"Well?" Sam asked, hoping for the best and anticipating the worst.
"What did you think?"

"I liked what you wrote."

"Um, well, can you elaborate?"

"I could but I won't."

That startled him, annoyingly so. "Why not?"

"Because the material is for my benefit, not yours."

Sam rankled.

**You wanted domination, twit, and now you're getting it. Get
used to it.**

"I suggest we meet socially before we play," Lady Indigo said, sensing
his darkening mood. "And since you haven't asked, my fee is fifty for a

couple of hours or so. I'm just beginning my practice, so I don't feel right charging more. Is that agreeable?"

Fifty? "Jeez, yes." Sam couldn't believe it; Morgaine charged three times that, and for only one hour. Lady Indigo was upending everything Sam knew or expected of a dominatrix.

"Ah, and there's one more thing," she continued. "I'm doing this in partnership with another woman. Do you have a problem with that?"

"Well," Sam said, feeling a rug underneath him being tugged, "I thought it would just be you and me."

"That's just how it is," she said.

Expectations will kick your ass every time.

"Why don't you come over and meet us? We'll talk and maybe soak in the hot tub and see how the chemistry goes."

Sitting in a hot tub with two naked dominatrices? "That sounds, uh, really great."

"And before you get any hot ideas, buckaroo," she added, "remember that we're both dykes and happy to stay that way."

"Agreed." *Damn.*

On the appointed evening, Lady Indigo answered the door clad not in standard leather fetish clothes, but in a baggy sweatshirt and cargo pants. She was around thirty, pleasantly attractive, taller than he, a little curvy, and the swells under her sweatshirt suggested her breasts were large and unconfined by a bra. Sam couldn't tell if her long, wild tresses were burgundy or black. Whether she was a lesbian or not, he would have loved to see her naked. Eventually he would, but not on this evening and definitely not to his liking.

"The hot tub's broken, sorry," Lady Indigo said and invited him in.

How can you possibly break a hot tub? There went the second expectation, kicked in the ass.

Lady Indigo introduced her colleague, Jenny, who also was dressed in sweats, lounging on a thrift-store sofa. Unlike the voluptuous Lady Indigo, Jenny looked every bit the stereotypical butch dyke: thin and wiry, with buzz-cut hair, six ring piercings in one ear, and stony gray eyes. Their living room looked like a rummage sale.

"We just moved in," Lady Indigo said, clearing a pile of laundry from a threadbare wing chair. Sam sat and noticed a leather riding crop on the fireplace mantel. He didn't see any horses.

The three sat, drinking Diet Pepsis, and talked. Or, rather, Lady Indigo talked. She was clearly intelligent and well read, and from her highly opinionated views, Sam suspected she didn't regard ignorant and uninformed fools kindly. That made him uneasy. What made him uneasier still was that these two women knew all the intimate details of his sex life, and he knew absolutely nothing about theirs, other than their orientation.

That puts you at the ultimate disadvantage, doesn't it?

Yeah. There's more and more about this I'm not liking.

Domination is being forced to do what you don't like, twit. When will that sink in?

Realizing there was nothing he could do about the ultimate disadvantage except walk out the door, Sam relaxed into conversation as normal folks did—until they got down to a business that normal folks usually didn't. Lady Indigo leafed through her calendar.

"Oh my, looky here at this," she said, smiling. "How about setting our play date for a week from this Friday?"

Sam thought for a second. "Isn't that Good Friday?"

"It sure is!" Lady Indigo let loose with a cackle. That worried him.

Sam was as much a Christian as he was a walrus and couldn't imagine a more perfect way to thumb his nose at conventional religion. Then a curious and startling synchronicity struck him: Good Friday was a trial of pain and a test of faith leading to transformation, just as the article on shamanism presaged. That was nothing to thumb noses at in the least.

Despite his atheism, this particular event actually lay close to Sam's heart and heritage. Although his family was not religious, Christian icons and holidays were everywhere, and it was impossible not to know their stories. His first and most influential encounter with Jesus occurred as a child when he came across an illustration of the Crucifixion in his newfound font of wonder, the family encyclopedia—the same place he'd found his other martyred hero, Prometheus.

The detailed lithograph showed Jesus of Nazareth, nearly naked, nailed to a cross, and hanging in unimaginable torment. Or was it rapture? To Sam there seemed to be no difference. He'd inexplicably envied Jesus's ordeal: the man's job was finished; there were no more travail or obligations—nothing left to do in life but just hang there and die. Looking back on this, Sam wondered how horrible his life could have been at age six that he would crave such a fate.

Now walking to his own Golgotha, Sam could appreciate the immense potential for change that a crucifixion offered. If you were naked and suffering in full view of the whole town, the only sanctuary to be found was in heaven or in one's mind, and you were highly motivated to get to one of those places as quickly as possible. The alignment of the two Fridays became curiously compelling. Who could be more loving and, simultaneously, crueler: God or a dominatrix?

Lady Indigo told Sam to start a journal and write in it every day, in ink, no matter how silly or mundane the subject matter. He frowned at the task. Journal was another name for a diary, which he always considered to be a vapid indulgence for moony twelve-year-old girls, depressed drama queens, and the height of narcissism for anyone else. Not a thing for real men. But real men didn't let women boss around and beat them either, so a journal it would be.

"Your journal is very important," Lady Indigo said. "And know that I will always have access to it. You're to write about what you're feeling and why. Anything you want us to try, write it down. Anything that doesn't work for you, write it down. Anything you have to say to me, no matter how it might make me feel, *write it down*. And be honest about it. You must be completely honest with me at all times. S/m is dangerous! Communication is essential. There is now no excuse for miscommunication."

"I understand," Sam agreed, though he had no idea what this might entail.

"Good," she said. "And I'll know if you rip out any pages, so don't censor it or try to deceive me. The journal is not for my benefit—it's for yours. You'll see."

"Okay."

"Then we'll see you on Good Friday!" She let loose with another cackle.

Sam's initial journal entries were droll, contrived monologues about the tribulations and observations of his day. They embarrassed him and rightly so. The pages couldn't be torn out, so he was stuck with this testament to self-absorption and idiocy. The following entry was a lame apology for the first two, and again there was no delete button.

He gave up trying to impress Lady Indigo with intelligence and wit, his usual strategy for finagling his way into a woman's favor and bed. Besides, she was clearly not the usual woman, and he suspected thoroughly finagle-proof. And a bed was nowhere in the picture. Something unusual was afoot. No sex and no schemes to get it. What was left? Just who was this woman? Releasing his usual sex-centered agenda made him bolder.

His journal entries now became less self-conscious and more honest, and so he began a unique friendship with this manly little book.

Just as it did every year, Good Friday finally arrived, and Sam parked his car at Lady Indigo's house fifteen minutes ahead of schedule. "Do *not* be late," Lady Indigo had warned him, implying there'd be hell to pay if he was. He waited in his car, thinking about heaven and hell and where he might end up tonight.

At the appointed time, he knocked on the back door as instructed. No response. He knocked again. Nothing. *Do all dominatrices do this just to be a pain? Of course they do, they're dominatrices and causing misery is their thing. Maybe they forgot. Maybe they're flaky. Women get flaky. Kinky dyke women probably even more so.*

So your Neanderthal days are over, are they?

Damn!

Despite having so little to get riled about, he did nonetheless.

One minute and several irritated knocks later, Lady Indigo finally opened the door, if indeed it was Lady Indigo. The frumpy lesbian in sweat clothes had morphed into a woman who was absolutely stunning in exotic makeup and a slinky, low-cut black lace gown. Through the sheer cloth, he could see the flash of gold rings through her nipples and labia. Lady Indigo let Sam absorb the vision, knowing quite well what it was doing to him. Sam gladly forgot his snit at the sight of her.

He entered their basement dungeon. Jenny was standing there, clad in black biker leathers, holding a set of handcuffs and a wooden paddle and looking like the leader of an all-dyke hit squad in eager search of its next victim. Their game was transparent: the good domme-bad domme scene. *I got this*, Sam thought, completely oblivious as to who really had whom.

The basement was furnished with medieval-looking artifacts appropriate for an evening of inquisition and torment: large mirrors in ornate frames; dark, heavy drapery; candles burning in wrought-iron escutcheons; and censers of smoldering incense. A lush, dark-hued oriental rug lay in the room's center. On it was a low table with a black diaphanous veil covering objects that Sam suspected were hazardous to his health. He would be right.

A sturdy wooden bondage rack leaned against one wall. Oil lamps flickered on either side, giving the ominous device the appearance of a sacrificial altar. A cross would have been too cute. Everything about the room said, "You have now left your home planet and welcome to the garden of deadly delights."

Her tardiness at the door was not mentioned; Sam would soon learn that Lady Indigo lived unapologetically in her own time zone.

"Kneel," she said.

Sam startled at the crisp command. It had begun. How had he expected it to begin?

"Give me your journal." He handed over the book. "Now strip."

Sam stood and obeyed, too flustered to be embarrassed.

"On your knees," she ordered.

Her string of terse commands continued to throw him, but still the game beckoned. He quickly dropped to his knees. She circled his neck with a length of heavy chain and inserted a padlock but did not close the shackle. She leaned close and looked steadily into his eyes.

"Listen to this," Lady Indigo said, "And listen carefully." In the silence Sam heard the shackle click shut. A small electric arc jumped from one side of his brain to the other. "Think about what just happened."

Sam heard the click but didn't quite understand her point. His brain was fixated on the gold labia rings just a foot from his face. Lady Indigo didn't seem to mind. She sat down on a large, wooden throne-like chair. Jenny moved behind him, out of sight.

"Bend over on your hands and knees," Lady Indigo said.

Sam complied, absorbed by, of all things, the color of her toenails, an iridescent purple.

"Kiss my feet, slave."

Slave. The word did not excite him as he'd expected. It felt like being forced to wear shoes that were too tight, and tough shit if they hurt. He lightly kissed the tops of both her feet. It was the first time he'd actually touched her—never mind where—and then *slave* started to sound a little better.

"Now pay careful attention," she said. "These are my rules. You will obey them or else."

"Else" was quickly demonstrated by a hard crack on his butt from Jenny's paddle.

Sam suppressed a cry. "Yes, ma'am."

"You are to address me as Lady, Lady Indigo, or Mistress. Ma'am is no longer allowed. It makes me feel old. You will address my sweet accomplice Jenny the same way."

"Call her Lady Indigo?" Sam said with a grin.

Another crack of the paddle told him his humor was not appreciated.

"You will do whatever we tell you and immediately," Lady Indigo said, glaring at him. "You may not speak without asking permission to do so. You may not touch either of us, although we may touch you wherever we want and with whatever we want, is that clear?"

"Yes, Lady." Sam bristled at the harsh lecture, then reminded himself that although she was not Mistress Monster, she was still a dominatrix, and this was what they did.

"And no more fucking jokes."

"Yes, ma'am."

Whack! went Jennie's paddle.

"*Ow!* Yes, *Lady*."

"Now, this is very important." Lady Indigo leaned forward. "Your safe word is *crimson*. You do know what a safe word is, don't you?"

"Yes, Lady."

"Do you know how to use it?"

Sam knew, or he thought he did, but now he wasn't sure. "I think so."

"You think so? You'd better know so. If at any time you need the play to stop, just say 'crimson' and we'll talk. Sounds pretty simple, doesn't it?"

Sam nodded. She leaned close to his face.

"Well, it's not! And you will certainly find that out. You must be your own guardian! You must be fully aware of what you can take and what you can't, and you must be responsible for yourself. That responsibility is huge. Don't ever place that on me. Do you understand?"

"Yes, Lady."

"I don't think you do, but you will. You'd better. S/m is a very dangerous business!"

Lady Indigo firmly grasped his collar and looked deeply into his eyes. Then she did something unexpected. "I'm going to give you your slave name. This is important. You are now 'Magic.' It means clarity of intention and focus, and you should never, ever forget that!"

Jenny's paddle reinforced the warning with a sharp crack. That one *really* hurt, and he tried not to cry out.

"Focus!" Lady Indigo shouted. "What is your intention, Magic?"

Whack! shouted the paddle.

"Stop that!" yelled Sam without thinking.

Lady Indigo grabbed his hair and pulled his head back.

"What did you say?" she hissed into his face. "We give the orders here, not you! Haven't you heard a single fucking word I said?"

Jenny whacked him again. He gritted his teeth. The two amiable dykes from the sofa two weeks ago were now gone, replaced by that hit squad. The game was turning sour.

"Focus! What is your name?" Lady Indigo barked.

Whack!

"Jesus!" Sam cried.

"That's not your name!"

Whack! Whack!

"Magic," he mumbled through his pain-induced stupor. *At least it wasn't worm.*

"Good. What does that mean?"

"Intention and focus," Sam said, parroting what he'd just heard.

"And what does *that* mean?"

Silence.

Lady Indigo laughed and massaged his stinging, reddening butt.

"You will get to know Magic," she said. "You will become Magic. Now, focus!"

No paddle this time. Sam waited for his anger to subside, and the two women abided him.

"I don't know what you mean by focus," he finally said. "I just don't."

"You will," Lady Indigo said more civilly. "Now, kneel up."

Sam did, grateful his butt was temporarily out of danger.

"You will remain on your knees like this unless we tell you otherwise," Lady Indigo said. "Keep your hands behind your back and your eyes down. That is your slave position. Clear?"

"Yes, Lady."

Jenny gave Lady Indigo the handcuffs. They were robust and heavy—the genuine police article, not a cheap toy found in a sex shop. Lady Indigo locked his wrists behind him and sat back to observe their effect. The first and last time he'd been handcuffed, he'd instantly panicked and begged Carmine for release. But this was different. Here he felt... safer.

Then he thought about those two clicks, the collar's padlock, and now the handcuffs, and the power and significance those small, inno-cent sounds wielded. He tested the handcuffs; their security was beyond question and would remain so until Lady Indigo removed them. *If she* decided to remove them, and when. Fear entered the room and safety began to evaporate.

Lady Indigo sensed his anxiety. "Focus," she said softly.

Sam tried to focus, but focus on what? Fear? That would make him freak out even more. He saw a blue mailbox jeering at him. This had been his decision. He could have said no, and now it was too late, too late. More panic burbled in his throat.

"Talk to me, Magic," she urged.

"I'm scared."

"Good. You'd be a damn fool if you weren't scared. I'd kick your ass out of here if you weren't scared. I have no use for macho assholes or nutcases. Remember your name. Never forget your name or what it means. And remember you have a safe word."

"Yes, ma'am."

"And don't just 'yes ma'am' me. You can't get off the hook so easily with me. Do you understand?"

More silence. "No, ma'am. I'm sorry, I just don't."

"Good. That's more honest. And I'm not *ma'am*. I just told you that, remember?"

"Yes, ma'am, er, Lady Mistress Indigo."

"You're fucking hopeless," she said and turned to Jenny. "Should we beat his hopeless ass?" Jenny grinned. Lady Indigo grasped the handcuff's chain. "Where's the key?"

"I don't have it," said Jenny. "I gave it to you."

"No, you didn't. I don't have it either."

"What?" Sam screeched, again feeling the magma of panic rising in his throat.

The women burst into laughter. "Don't worry," Lady Indigo said to him. "We'll either find it or we won't."

The magma inched higher. "But, but what if you don't?" he cried.

"Then you'll have a real problem, won't you?"

Before he could contemplate that, she bent down and lightly pinched both his nipples. He jumped. She pinched harder, watching him carefully. He winced. Then harder. He took it. Then as hard as she could, her teeth set and eyes blazing. Sam just stared back, equally as fierce.

"Well, then," she said, finally releasing him, "I'll squeeze your safe word out of you yet. You can count on it."

A second more and she would have, thought Sam, breathing again, his chest on fire.

Jenny whisked the veil off the table, revealing an array of whips, floggers, canes, riding crops, and even kitchen utensils.

"Bring me three of your choice," said Lady Indigo.

"What? How can I?" All he could think about was the lost handcuff key.

"How can I, what?" she echoed.

"How can I, Lady... Indigo Mistress?" he stammered. His brain and tongue, having been stomped on by two infuriated nipples, couldn't link up.

"That's better," she said. "Even if you still can't get my name right. Fetch them with your teeth, of course. And stay on your knees, slave."

Slave. Now that word felt like a tick auguring deep into his hide, to a place he'd never find. Sam crept up to the table and scanned the implements, having no experience with any of them. He was horrified to see a garlic press in the pile. One by one he retrieved three of the smallest and most benign-looking whips. Jenny howled at one choice. Apparently in whip world, smaller didn't necessarily mean kinder. The missing handcuff key thankfully appeared and he was freed, but not for long. They affixed him to the bondage rack with leather cuffs, his backside exposed.

Lady Indigo dimmed the lights, switched on the boom box, and then rounded to Sam with one of his chosen floggers. In time with the music, she started whipping his shoulders and butt, first with light strokes, then building in strength and frequency. He'd heard about the rapturous endorphin ride a flogger provided, and for the first time he was on the train. The pain melted into whip-laced pleasure, like receiving a vigorous massage rather than enduring a punishment.

Indeed, Lady Indigo displayed not a trace of the malice Mistress Monster had and seemed to enjoy her sadism for its own sake. To his surprise, Sam's back and butt didn't resist the pain of the beating but welcomed it. Lady Indigo sensed this as well and happily complied. Each lash became like a caress between them. He was struck, literally, by the wonder of the act. No thinking was required, only receiving. Stimulus and response. Rarely does life present its workings with such stark simplicity.

What a strange place to feel such intimacy. What a strange place to find such asylum. Was this Pauline's hurting but not harming?

Between blows, Lady Indigo occasionally paused to soothe and massage Sam's burning flesh. She pressed her body into his backside, grinding her breasts and hips. *Damn dyke*, Sam thought but dared not say.

"Focus, Magic," the lady whispered into his ear as a lover would.

Then it was Jenny's turn with her little whip. His intuition about her laugh had been correct: smaller was indeed nastier. At length Sam was released, albeit reluctantly, and made to kneel in his slave position and watch Lady Indigo and Jenny go at each other with a heavy flogger. Between rounds they stopped to kiss and fondle each other's breasts and groins through their clothes. Onyx had said leather dykes played harder than any other species of s/m fanatic, and now he believed it.

The evening concluded with Sam's much anticipated crucifixion scene. He was again affixed to the rack, this time front side out with his arms outstretched and blindfolded. He felt clothespins snap onto his nipples and thighs. The women spattered his chest with hot candle wax, and then switched to ice water, which curiously felt the same. They turned up the music and left him to enjoy his ordeal.

But it wasn't much of one. Sam wanted more. His cock had been disappointingly neglected and just dangled there with nothing to do. He concentrated on the clothespins biting into his nipples and thighs, but the pain was fading. *Damn!* He strained against the leather wrist cuffs and almost slipped out of them. *What the hell?* Focus wasn't doing its job either, whatever the fuck that was supposed to be. Disappointment was polluting his precious fantasy scene, turning it into a sullen sulk, and he couldn't seem to stop it.

Shit! What an unbelievable asshole I am! Pissing all this away.

Twit! That's because you're still stuck in fantasyland. What were you expecting?

But, well, she's supposed to be a dominatrix and–

Look around. Where are you?

In a dungeon, of course. Jeez!

No, you're not. You're in the basement of some dominatrix wannabe's lame idea of a dungeon. Got the difference?

It's... what I want; it's why I came here.

Then why are you pouting? And you are getting exactly what you want—a slave wannabe's lame idea of an s/m scene.

No! I'm not giving this up.

Have it your way.

Okay. *Focus.* Lady Indigo had been screaming that into his face all evening, so why not give it a try? He took in the room—the hypnotic flickering of the candles, the lush, ornate furnishings, the enchanting drumbeat of the music, and the illusion of being bound and captured. So what if he really wasn't. So what if this was just a basement—it had to be somewhere. But it certainly was a unique space and tonight it was all meant for him. *Let that be enough. Focus.*

Sam closed his eyes and stood fast in his mock bondage. Better than nine-inch nails through his flesh, he admitted. He focused on the drumbeat pounding through his body. Soon it turned into a trance and spirited him away, plunging him down to the planet's molten core and then flinging him upward into the cool expanse of the firmament. *What did Jesus think about on that excruciating afternoon?* In the beginning was the word, and the word was focus.

His two tormenters finally returned.

"How long?" Sam asked, truthfully not knowing if it had been one hour or three.

"Thirty minutes," Lady Indigo said, smiling.

She and Jenny plucked off the hardened wax droplets from his chest and thighs. Then they freed him, neither seeming particularly impressed that he had "risen," as he'd lamely joked. Easter was two days away. What happened two thousand years ago was not funny and neither was this, he realized. He had much to think over.

"Kneel," said Lady Indigo. She bent forward, grasped the collar's lock, and again stared into Sam's eyes, now glassy and distant. The shackle clicked open and again the electric arc jolted Sam out of his trance. Lady Indigo smiled.

"Welcome back," she said.

The two women watched Sam dress and helped him wobble up the stairs to recover in the living room. Most unlike herself, Lady Indigo said very little. This allowed his brain a welcome respite. When she was satisfied that he was able to drive, she said the session was over and he could go home.

Sam apprehensively asked if another would be possible.

"Oh yes," Lady Indigo replied without hesitation.

Oh joy. She returned his journal.

"Be sure to write in this every day," she said. "We'll talk soon."

She gave Sam a long and sensual embrace, followed by a surprisingly warm, soft hug from hard-bodied Jenny. Sam drove home, light and euphoric, on an ass still sore and stinging. The marks, welts, and aches would persist for a week, delightful souvenirs of that magical evening.

So, domination has become delightful and magical? Boy, are you ever in for a surprise.

How do you know so much about it already?

You've given me decades of practice, of course.

22

THE CONTRACT

IT WAS BRILLIANT. SAM NOW HAD a perverted persona named Magic. He'd send Magic, not himself, into Lady Indigo's dungeon as the fawning weenie groveling at her feet. It would be his game, with him still in control. That would make a splendid entry in his journal, but he thought he'd better change fawning weenie to submissive and omit the part about games and control. Which wouldn't leave much, but he felt that would surely please her.

"That would surely fool me, do you mean? Is that what you really want to do?"

What? Lady Indigo?

Sam stopped writing and listened. "Lady Indigo?" Nothing.

Now *that* was strange. It was clearly her voice and not his inner one, but whose? It seemed that *strange* was now the new normal in his life and he shrugged it off. He looked at what he'd written in the journal and cringed. He *was* trying to fool her. He couldn't rip out the page because then she'd know. But he couldn't leave it in to broadcast his semifraudulent and sneaky intentions. Maybe he should write a retraction. Yes, an apology full of regret and self-recrimination. That would show her how honest he was.

Showing her anything will show how fraudulent and sneaky you truly are. You're off to a great start, slave Magic.

Lady Indigo?

No, it's me, twit. Who else would it be?

What just happened? I just heard Lady Indigo say something to me. This is starting to freak me out.

Gee, it must be getting a little crowded in there. What with you, me, that groveling weenie Magic, and now Lady Indigo joining the party.

That's not funny. Help me out here.

Why should I?

Because I'm asking you, damn it!

Okay, since you so politely asked. One, Lady Indigo is in charge here and not you, duh. That's why you're paying her. Two, you will never fuck her and you'd best accept that right now. And three, I strongly advise not to wank about her either.

Um, I already have.

I know. Stop it. It's making me jealous, and you do not want to do that.

But what about that voice I heard? Was that real?

Is mine?

I don't know.

Then think about it. And why don't you ask Lady Indigo if she has access to your head. I'd be quite interested to hear her answer.

Three weeks passed and Lady Indigo still hadn't called. That made him uneasy, then worried, and then angry. Sam took the initiative and dialed her number, unsure whether to complain, rage, or grovel.

Lady Indigo, as was her irritating right, said nothing about the hiatus. "Instead of doing a single session," she said, "I propose we do a contract."

"A contract?" This surprised and delighted him and his well-deserved pout evaporated. Then he thought about Mistress Monster's list of rules, reeking with her outrageous, sexist Gynotopian decrees. His stomach sank.

"Do you have a problem with that?" Lady Indigo asked.

"Well," he said glumly, "I kind of already did that. It's everything I hate about this scene. All the groveling and scolding and insults and being called the scum of the earth and a pathetic, worthless little worm. I'm sorry, but yeah, I do have a problem with that."

Lady Indigo laughed. "That sounds like Mistress Morgaine. Is she the one you wrote about in your assignment?"

"Yeah. Do you know her?"

"Everybody knows about Morgaine. You're lucky to have survived. Or have you?"

"You know, I'm not sure."

"I get it," she said. "No, our contract will be much different. A contract is very common in the leather community. It lets you know what you're getting into. It can be as loose or specific as we want. It will specify the number of sessions and their duration. It establishes boundaries and determines what activities will occur and what won't. It defines expectations and sets out rules of behavior for both of us."

"Both of us?" This was new.

"Of course. It's actually a detailed form of negotiation."

"Negotiation?" Sam said. "I thought submission was, well…"

"One-sided? I get to do whatever I want, and if you don't like it, tough shit?"

"Um… yeah."

Lady Indigo laughed. "Ha! That's every bottom's pet wet dream. In the real world, things work a little differently. Players who have their heads screwed on straight will first negotiate before they play. They'll agree about what they're willing to do and not. Limits are defined. Safe words are agreed upon, and so forth. It also gives each person a chance to check out the other. Bottoms don't want crazy-ass tops, and tops are just as much at risk in other ways."

"But what happens when you're tied up and the top decides to disregard the negotiations?"

"Then you're fucked."

"Great."

She laughed again. "S/m is dangerous business," she said. "I've told you that a zillion times. It's not one hundred percent safe, but negotiation reduces the risks. You've got your gut feeling as well. And if it turns out a top can't be trusted, word gets out, and then *they're* fucked."

Sam thought about this. "But what good will that do when you're already, um…"

"Dead?" Lady Indigo said with a touch of theatrical menace. "Look. We've already played, and you survived that, right? And we did negotiate first. That was your writing assignment, as you recall. Don't worry. You're perfectly safe with me and you know that." She broke into a Simon Legree cackle, suggesting otherwise.

"Thanks. That really helps."

"Sometimes I just crack myself up," she said. "Ah, me. Now, the contract just takes negotiation one step further. It's is not a legally binding document, but rather it's a focus and a reminder of our commitment to one another. *And* to our impeccability. And to having a right good time, too. Interested?"

Sam knew he was and kicking the tires would be pointless. "Where do I sign?"

"Not so fast, cowboy. As my slave, you'll be strictly held to a list of rules and conditions. Some of them Morgaine would approve of, so you'd better keep your eyes open and your fly zipped."

He laughed. "Yeah, I want to do this. I really do."

"Excellent! I'm thinking about a seven-session contract. How does that sound?"

Seven sessions in Lady Indigo's dungeon? He became lightheaded.

"Uh, that sounds… it works. Yes."

"Good. I'll send it to you. I want you carefully read it and think about it just as carefully. And think with your brain. Do you understand what I mean by that?"

"I do."

"Make sure of it. Call me when you're ready to commit."

Two days later, Sam received the document in the mail. He eagerly read through it, having no idea such a thing could exist let alone be enacted. The first set of provisions looked like they were taken from the charter of *The Chateau of Cruel Bondage*. He would agree to a seven-session contract, with one session every week or two, each lasting no less than eight hours and no longer than twenty-four. As her slave, he would agree to respect and honor the Lady Indigo, obey all her commands without hesitation or complaint, and willingly and competently perform all the tasks she assigned, as the contract read. *Well, that's what a slave is and does.*

Sam again thought about Morgaine's rules. Some were similar to Lady Indigo's but had been presented in much harsher terms, with a few absurdities thrown in for bad measure. Live and learn, he often reminded himself, but had he? He knew that s/m slavery was essentially a blank check on his time, body, and energy, and despite the excitement brewing within him, he also suspected he'd eventually be faced with the fine print. He worried about what it might say and presumed he wouldn't like it.

The contract also gave him two safe words: *yellow* meant "this is too much" or "time out," and *crimson* meant "stop everything at once and let's talk." *That seems reasonable.* Any health issues or physical limitations would be respected, provided he first informed Lady Indigo. *Good, more reasonable.* He would agree to clear and honest communication, as s/m was dangerous. *Of course it is, but how many damn times do I need to hear it?*

The next clause addressed sex, or its absence: he would have no intimate or sexual contact with Lady Indigo. This he already knew and accepted, but seeing it in print still burned. Then things got interesting. Lady Indigo, however, could give "slave magic" (notably uncapitalized) to others for that purpose, providing that both parties consented. Sam's imagination joyfully ran amok.

You agreed to think with your brain, remember?

Why do you care?

Because your imagination should be dedicated to me, that's why.

Sam read on. He was not allowed to participate in any s/m activity outside the contract without Lady Indigo's permission. *No problem; she's the only game in town.* Lady Indigo would administer punishments or rewards in accordance with his performance. *Yes!* He would be subjected to ordeals of bondage and torment as determined by his desires and Lady Indigo's creativity and sadism. *Yes, yes, yes!*

He would serve as a maid, butler, errand boy, handyman, decoration, furniture, pet, or any other object that served Lady Indigo's need and whim. *Whatever.* In exchange for all this, he would pay her fifty dollars a session and also provide her with housework and domestic service. *Only fifty? That can't be right.* He circled the clause to ask about it later.

Any breach of trust, irresponsible behavior, defiance, or neglect of responsibilities and duties and would result in the termination of the contract and expulsion from her dungeon. Sam vowed to be the most perfect slave ever but worried whether expulsion included being clothed. He was also to assume responsibility for his own emotional caretaking, and any processing or support would be at Lady Indigo's discretion. *Well, that's what Judith is for and besides, she should be used to it by now.*

Interesting things then turned into gnarly ones. The next clause read, "I understand this contract will initiate a spiritual journey and Lady Indigo will act as a guide and facilitator. I will consider Her at all times as the living embodiment of the Goddess and treat Her with the honor and respect due that position."

Sam's zeal hit a nail and instantly deflated. This was supposed to be s/m, not some kind of flaky spiritual quest. He'd had enough of those. He'd also had more than enough of the "Goddess" and all her bitchy, man-eating acolytes like Morgaine. But he knew the Goddess was eventually going to show up in a female domination scene, and he'd just have to swallow it. Everything comes with a price, he had to concede.

The next provision further deflated and perplexed him as well: "I VOW TO BE IMPECCABLE AS THE KEEPER AND GUARDIAN OF MY SACRED BEING AND ALWAYS BE RESPONSIBLE FOR THAT TASK."

It was an oath and obviously a very important one, as the upper case indicated, but what the hell did it mean? He had to look up the word impeccable: "behavior in accordance with the highest standards of propriety." Fine, but who would define propriety, and in relation to what? Lady Indigo, of course, and that made her and her goddess even more powerful, controlling, and irritating. Sam didn't like where this adventure was headed. And how could he swear to an oath he didn't understand?

The last clause finally delivered the goodies: "In return for observing, complying with, and executing the above clauses and provisions, I will be shown the possibilities of submission, slavery, and mundane and magical s/m."

But the goodies had a catch—why was he not surprised? Mundane and magical s/m? What was the difference? Another mystery. This clause was as vague as the previous were specific. But that did leave plenty of wiggle room for fun possibilities, and perhaps that was the point. It was a no-brainer. He would throw caution to the wind and sign.

So, twit, throwing caution to the wind is your idea of guarding your sacred being?

Well, maybe not.

Do you know what your, ahem, sacred being is? Do you even have one?

I must have one. It's... it's—

Maybe it's me, numbnuts. Haven't you learned that by now? And I'm perfectly capable of guarding myself. What you need to guard against is your cock taking the wheel.

A few days later, Lady Indigo called Sam to talk about the contract. They read through the articles together to discuss his questions. He'd had several.

"The contract says each session will cost fifty dollars," he began apprehensively. "Are you sure? I mean that seems really low. Jeez, with Morgaine I paid—"

"Do you want to pay more?"

"Um, well, no, but—"

"I'm a student," she said. "I'm learning too. That figure seems right to me, and that's why it's there. And besides, I'll be working your ass off in compensation. So don't complain about it, okay? Next question?"

"Yeah. The contract talks about submission and slavery. What's the difference?"

"None in my book," Lady Indigo said. "I use the words interchangeably. But a lot of people in the leather community don't, and they'll nit-pick and hair-split the nuances until doomsday. Being kinky qualifies you to be a fucking authority on the subject, didn't you know? And besides, a contract has to cover your ass every which way possible, right?"

Sam laughed. "Yeah, I suppose it has to. Okay, well, this business about sex and being given away to others. What sort of others do you, ahem, have in mind?"

"I thought that might perk up your pecker. Nothing is guaranteed. I'm working on it, so cool your jets. And before you get too hot and sweaty, keep in mind that this clause, and the entire contract for that matter, are not about meeting your sexual needs."

Sam realized he had been holding out for that, as thickheaded and chimeric as that was, and he'd better find a way to pour cold water on his jets.

"Um, this no-intimate-contact rule," he said. "Well, you broke that repeatedly in our first session, as I very much recall. Now isn't that a breach of contract?"

"No, that's not a breach of contract, or of conduct," said Lady Indigo. "I can do anything I want to you and with you, remember? The reverse is not true."

"But that's not fair."

"Fair? I don't believe that word appears anywhere in the contract, does it now?"

"Uh…"

"Fairness does not apply here and never will. Only honesty and impeccability will count. In fact, *un*fairness will be a major player in my dungeon. Do you understand why?"

"Well… no."

"Do you even know what impeccability means?" she asked.

"Sure I do. It's behavior in accordance with the highest standards of propriety."

"That's what you read in some dictionary. In mine, impeccability is an unswerving commitment to your being. It's how a warrior stands. It's keeping your balance in the face of unpredictable and uncontrollable circumstances. You're creating stability and protection out of absolutely nothing. Do you understand how this can be?"

"I'm not sure."

"Well, you're going to be severely tested on impeccability. Are you ready for that?"

"Yes," Sam confirmed.

Lady Indigo laughed. "Yes, you say? No one is ever truly ready; they only think they are. You'll be ready sure enough when the day comes, slave Magic!" and she let out one of her nerve-scorching cackles.

Sam couldn't seem to get a grip on all this. How could the woman be so intelligent and reasonable one minute and a screeching lunatic the next?

They agreed to have their sessions on Saturdays and set a date for the first one. Lady Indigo reminded him to keep up his journal entries, gave him a list of personal items to bring, and again urged him to focus, focus, focus. *I'm not a goddamned camera, camera, camera*, he steamed.

"I have one last question," Sam said. "Do you believe in mental telepathy?"

Lady Indigo paused. "Why do you ask?"

"Well, a few days ago, I heard you say something to me. Inside my head."

"What did I say?"

Although they were on the phone, Sam felt like her face was a millimeter from his and staring at him full power. Something very odd was at work here.

"You said that I shouldn't try to fool you in my journal," he said.

"I've already told you that *outside* of your head. That's very good. That means those words are alive within you. It means I'm getting through. Were you going to try to fool me?"

"Um… well… maybe. Yes."

"And those words stopped you?"

"Yes. And other words. Are you angry I tried that?"

"No, of course not," she said. "I expected you to. I also expect you to continue trying to fool me. Fooling yourself and other people is something we all do. We do it to get by in the world. It's a very difficult habit to break, and we're going to break it together. There are other, much better ways to get by. You'll see that. What will make me angry, really angry, is if you're not willing to try to break that habit."

"I'll give it my best."

"I'm sure you will. And there's one more thing you should know about s/m."

"It's dangerous?"

"More than you know," Lady Indigo said. "Do you remember the contract mentioned magical s/m? Do you know what that means?"

"I'm not sure. No, I don't."

"Not many people do. S/m can have enormous transformative potential. That's why I told you to read that article. That's why I gave you your name. The true definition of magic is to change something. That's what ordeals are for. Transformation is seldom a gentle experience. It can take you to places you don't normally go, or even want to go, and some very strange things can happen there. Like visions and voices. Do you understand any of this?"

"Yes, I think I do."

"Good. Then it seems our contract has already begun, Magic. See you in a week."

Lady Indigo hung up, and Sam just stared at the tiny holes in the telephone's earpiece, amazed at what had just come out of them. *God, what has my dick led me into?*

Right where you want to go, God might say to your dick.

Did you hear what she said about her words being inside my head?

Of course I heard.

Then why didn't you hear them?

Because she wasn't talking to me, moron! She doesn't even know I'm there and you'd better keep it that way. Maybe you need to start paying attention to the words rather than where they come from. Except for mine, of course.

Change happened very quickly in Lady Indigo World. She called Sam with some news.

"Jenny's moved out," she said. "And I've moved into an apartment. Here's the address."

Sam took note and then asked, "What happened?" not expecting an answer.

"Do you really expect me to answer that?"

"I guess not. So it'll just be you and me then?" *Yes! Now we can really rock!*

288

"Nope. I've taken in a new roommate. Her name is Danielle. She's also a lesbian, and she's occasionally kinky. Know that she'll be around, and she's cool with what we'll be doing."

"Well, I'm not cool with it," Sam said.

"Tough. If you want to proceed, you'll learn to be."

Sam thought about this new twist in a new way. "Will she, like, be part of our play then?"

"I'll pretend I didn't hear that."

Damn. Another ass kick. "Okay."

Lady Indigo told Sam to purchase a leather cock ring, one that could be locked, and said where to get it. Sam had previously visited sex shops, but only to buy pornography. The displays of sex toys, mostly dildos and anal plugs, had struck him as tawdry and uninteresting if not outright repulsive. But this newly opened store catered to the BDSM and fetish crowd. It was located in the industrial section of the city, and after countless wrong turns, he finally found it.

Nervous as a lamb walking into a boutique abattoir, he entered the store. Unlike the porn shops he'd patronized, this place was clean, brightly lit, and smelled like a tannery instead of a bus station men's room. He purposefully walked among the aisles to give the appearance of a man on a mission instead of an indolent porn junkie with smarmy business on his mind.

A half dozen customers were in the store, all men and all seeming far more comfortable than he. Most were perusing the magazines and videos. A large, hairy brute was adjusting a heavy leather and chain body harness on his "boy" (or boi, as Sam had learned was the conventional spelling in the gay BDSM scene, to distinguish it from pedophilia); neither seemed embarrassed, only excited. The sales clerk behind the counter was an attractive, fortyish woman wearing a loose-fitting, low-cut dress. Sam saw tattoos on just about every square inch of visible skin, suggesting that, beneath her dress, she was covered in a full-body tattoo suit. She ignored Sam as if he were just another one of the toads looking for a thrill, and then he realized she wouldn't be wrong.

One section of the store displayed every sex toy imaginable for men, women, and those in between. Sam found the counter with s/m devices for men. There were several dozen items made of leather or steel or both. All were designed for the restraint and discomfort of a guy's package, and none were cheap. The tattooed lady approached Sam and asked if he needed help. There was no road ahead but the truth.

"My Mistress ordered me to buy a cock ring," Sam said casually, as if he was asking for the shoe department. "One that can be locked." His lack of embarrassment surprised him.

Upon hearing this, the lady brightened and became his best friend. She opened the case and gave him a quick run-through of the products.

"This is my favorite," she said, pulling one item from the shelf, a leather strip that held seven steel rings of decreasing diameter. "It's called the Seven Gates of Hell. Here, hold out your thumb and pretend it's your cock."

Sam flushed red and did as he was told.

"The rings constrict the cock," she said and slipped the rings down his thumb. She circled its base with her thumb and fingers and squeezed, turning his thumb into an unexpected erogenous zone. "The rings make getting an erection oh so painful."

The price tag was fifty-five dollars. That would make Sam's bank account oh so painful. The woman held onto his thumb a little longer than necessary before releasing it. Sam pointed to a leather cylinder about two inches long that was held together with a row of snaps.

"A ball stretcher," she said, grinning. "And they come even longer."

Sam gasped and she winked. One contraption puzzled him: a tangle of thin leather straps decorated with metal studs and snaps. The woman withdrew it and expertly snapped it together into two loops.

"This is very nasty," she said. "It separates and constricts the balls until they turn purple. It hurts like the dickens, or so I've heard."

Sam thought to ask for a demonstration but thought better of it.

"Who's your Mistress?" the tattooed lady asked, surprising Sam and looking at him like he'd better answer and do it quickly.

He hesitated. "Uh, just someone," he replied. The lady kept staring at him.

"Um, Lady Indigo," he said and knew why he could never be trusted with state secrets.

"Mmm, don't know her. Is she new in town?"

"I, uh, don't really know."

His eyes darted to the large red chrysanthemum tattoo blooming across her left breast and then quickly looked away. Sam knew it was not polite to stare at a woman's breasts, but it was difficult not to when there were pictures all over them. She didn't seem to mind. In fact, she pulled down her neckline to display more. He saw a web on the top half of her areola where a spider no doubt lay in wait on her nipple for some lucky fly.

"Wow. That's really beautiful," Sam said. Then something dangerous crossed his thumb-swollen mind. "Are you a dome? I mean, a domme?"

"Yes, I am," she said. "But I only top women. Sorry, dear. Would you like to become a woman? That can be arranged, you know." Another wink turned Sam's blush to crimson. "Not today, huh?" She laughed. "Well, your Mistress is a lucky lady, sweetie pie."

Sam chose a simple leather cock ring that fastened with a small luggage lock.

"Fabulous choice," she said. "It's a good newbie ring. But how about this one?" She held up a heavy steel manacle with a padlock the size of a grapefruit. Sam paled. "No? Well, it will be here when Mistress needs it." Another mischievous laugh.

Sam paid for the ring in cash.

"See you again, sweetie pie," she said.

Sam would think about her all day. And night.

23

THE CAR WASH

THE NIGHT BEFORE THE FIRST SESSION of the contract, Sam had dream of a jet plane crashing. He was both watching the jet struggle to lift from the runway and while onboard at the same time. The heavy jet could not gain altitude and crashed to the earth in a massive fireball. He could see the faces of the terrified passengers through the windows, as well as the back of the seat in front of him, which would be the agent of his death. Would he panic with everyone else on board or calmly sit to meet the face of God?

The dream unsettled him, especially on the dawn of this new and risky venture. Was this a premonition? Would he die of a heart attack or stroke in Lady Indigo's dungeon? Or perhaps the dream was a metaphor for another type of change. He liked this option, but the frightening alternative lingered, making him uneasy, like knowing a large spider was hiding somewhere in a dark room.

Sam arrived on Lady Indigo's doorstep at precisely ten in the morning. As instructed, he brought personal items, a sleeping bag, his journal, and his *almost* never-been-used cock ring (he had no self-restraint). He knocked. No response. He knocked again and waited. *Here we go again.* He waited a few more minutes then knocked again, his excitement turning to shit. After five minutes, he was ready to detonate and God help the bitch. Then the bitch appeared at the door in a bathrobe, looking like she'd been dragged through the sewers of Gotham—twice.

"I was out late last night," Lady Indigo said, with no smile, no apology, no nothing.

What the hell happened to you? he wondered, wishing he could have been there to see it. He entered her new apartment and glanced around. He saw nothing dungeon-like about it and frowned. Lady Indigo pointed to a large walk-in closet at the end of the hallway.

"Put your things in there and wait for me in the living room," she said tersely.

Well, this is off to a fine fucked-up start.

Welcome to domination, sport.

Sam did as he was told. A barrel bolt and padlock on the closet door said anything inside would stay there. The closet was empty except for a large screw eye hook set into the floor at the back wall, the only hint of what she practiced. Sam put his gear in the closet, sat on the living room sofa, and tried to improve his attitude. A few minutes later, Lady Indigo emerged from her bedroom, a bit more awake and dressed in rumpled sweat clothes, the basic anti-dominatrix fashion statement.

"Get off the goddamned sofa!" she snapped. "You're not allowed to sit on the furniture."

"What?" Sam jumped to his feet, shocked and bewildered. "I didn't know."

"Well, you do now."

Sam simmered. Gone was the warmhearted Lady Indigo of a few weeks ago; a monster cold bitch had taken her place. In any other circumstance with any other woman, he'd be instantly out the door, no question. That option was still available, but at a cost he was not yet ready to pay. He stood by the forbidden sofa and resumed simmering. How could this turn so bad so quickly? The fucking furniture—how the hell was he supposed to know? He wished he could start this morning over. *Too bad life doesn't have a rewind button,* he lamented.

Lady Indigo had brought a large canvas bag from her bedroom. She reached in and withdrew a length of heavy chain and a large padlock.

"Strip," she said.

Sam did, acutely embarrassed and made even more so when he remembered that Danielle was somewhere in the apartment. She gave Sam the bag. "And put everything in here."

"Everything?"

"Everything means everything! Clothes, shoes, wallet, car keys, everything."

"Can I keep my glasses on?"

"Everything!" she shouted.

Sam sullenly complied. If Danielle was not already awake, she sure as hell was now.

"Bring me your cock ring."

Sam fetched his kit bag and gave her the cock ring and luggage lock. The spare key was in his car, just in case. Lady Indigo threw the lock into the garbage and took a larger and stronger padlock from a kitchen drawer. She dangled its key in front of his nose.

"Just in case you were planning something," she said, smiling.

Plan thwarted. He felt small and cheap for having had one.

"Kneel in your slave position," she said, looped the chain around his neck, and held the padlock to his face.

"Now listen to this," she said and clicked the shackle closed.

Although Sam knew what to listen for, the click did nothing for him.

"You are now Magic," Lady Indigo said. "Remember what that means. Remember why you're here. Focus!"

Lady Indigo tried to fasten the cock ring around his genitals, but she had none of the tattooed lady's expertise. She forced one testicle inside the ring but the other had crawled into his abdomen and wouldn't come out. He didn't blame it. Apparently, the woman had skipped Male Anatomy 101 in dominatrix school, or more likely slept through it. Sam tried to assist but got his hand slapped away. Lady Indigo continued fumbling around until she got it right and secured the strap with the new lock. The keys to his fetters went into her pocket.

"Get in the closet," she said. "That will be your cell while you're here. Now go write in your journal."

"About what?"

She said nothing, pushed him inside none too gently, closed and locked the door.

Typically, men were not supposed to be in touch with their emotions but this situation was not typical. Anger, confusion, humiliation, and a growing desire to slap the bitch senseless overwhelmed him. Not having the keys to his two collars concerned him—being locked in a closet even more so. Chastised. Captured. Humiliated. The contract mentioned none of this. What the hell? He stared at the blank page, fuming.

What's the matter, Magic? Writer's block?

I can't write that I want to slap the bitch senseless. She'd kill me.

294

Then why don't you write this: "Lady Indigo's strict reprimand about the furniture evoked childhood issues with my mother, and I appreciate the value of this lesson."

That sounds good to me.

It would. That's because it's crap.

The page stared up at Sam, taunting him with its vacancy. Sam set the pen to the paper, hoping his hand would come up with something. Nothing happened (no surprise). Through the door, Sam heard voices and movement in the apartment. Danielle was now up and about, increasing his apprehension. The cock ring, designed to stimulate and maintain an erection, now had the opposite effect, like a chunk of green Kryptonite turning Superman's junk to jello.

Sam sourly considered his assignment. He had plenty to write about all right, all of it hostile, but he didn't feel too cooperative at the moment—or slave-like. He finally made his hand move. "I don't like this" was all that came out. It would have to do.

About fifteen minutes passed. Not having his watch increased his disorientation. Lady Indigo finally unlocked the closet door and ordered Sam to come out on his hands and knees. Danielle was in the kitchen making coffee, wearing only a large white T-shirt that barely covered her buns. She could have been a pinup girl, petite and prom-queen cute, with her long brown hair hastily gathered in a bun. She regarded Sam briefly without expression and returned to her task. Sam cringed. Nudity had never felt so naked. The canvas bag containing his life had disappeared into the dark reaches of the apartment. *I most certainly don't like this.*

Lady Indigo's demeanor had softened by about a micron. She gave Sam a list of chores.

"You are to clean this entire apartment," she ordered, "top to bottom, and do it naked. The bedrooms are off limits."

Sam groaned at seeing her meager cache of cleaning supplies; the largest scrub brush was meant for fingernails. This would not be easy. Sam was unhappily learning that easy, like fairness, was excluded from the deal.

He started on the unbelievably filthy kitchen floor. Having seen two of Lady Indigo's homes, he understood that tidiness and domestic hygiene were not among her virtues. After an hour's scrubbing, the true color of the floor began to emerge. Lady Indigo gave it a thorough inspection and pointed to a few stains that were permanently welded into the vinyl.

"They just won't come out," Sam complained. He was tired and grouchy, which was exacerbated by being on his knees and having to dodge and defer to the two women as they walked around the apartment.

"No excuses. Get on your hands and knees, slave," she said and gave him several sharp cracks on his ass with a paddle. Danielle leaned her backside against a countertop and watched. All Sam could see of her were her pink toenails.

"So you say you don't like this?" Lady Indigo said. She'd seen the journal.

"No."

Whack!

"No what?" she snapped.

"No, Lady Mistress."

"Oh, so now you're saying you do like this?"

"What? No!"

Whack!

"Gaah! No, *Mistress*."

"Confused, are you? Focus!"

Whack!

Sam grimaced. The pink toenails walked away.

"Get back in your cell and write in your journal," Lady Indigo said. "Write about why you're here. You're probably thinking about that a lot right now. And write more than one sentence this time. And remember to focus, damn it!"

Lady Indigo shoved him into the closet and locked the door. Sam sat on his burning butt and fumed. The mindfuck she'd just run on him pushed him to the edge. Walking out of the contract was starting to look very good. Ripping her a new asshole on the way out looked even better. *My God, why* am *I putting up with this crap?*

Sex, of course. Is there any other reason?

But there's no sex! She's a dyke.

Then why are you here?

Good question.

That's why she asked it. I'd like to know, too, actually. Remember, focus!

Fuck focus. Focus would not unlock the door. Focus would not still his anger. He was trapped. Trapped and powerless. Since it was the only thing around, he focused on what being trapped and powerless felt like. It took perhaps two microseconds to conclude it really sucked. What a profound learning experience! He wrote all this down as it unfolded, including the asshole ripping. *The bitch wanted bottom-line honesty and by God she's going to fucking get it.*

After a few minutes he calmed down. *So why am I here? What is my intention?* He wrote that he really didn't know and was afraid he never would. *That* was bottom-line honesty too. He ended the entry with "Why are you being so mean to me?"

Lady Indigo finally unlocked the cell door. She was holding a leather waist harness and told him to stand perfectly still. She put him into it. One strap encircled his waist and another ran between his legs that held in a small butt plug. The plug made him feel like he had to poop, adding indignity to his discomfort. She secured the straps together with a padlock. Three locks he now wore, three keys she had to keep track of and possibly lose, and three times the difficulty to escape. This felt anything but sexy—just more humiliation to endure. Obviously, that was the point.

Lady Indigo retrieved the canvas bag with his clothes from her room and told him to get dressed. He could barely zip his jeans around the bulky harness and cock ring. Before he could button his shirt, she dangled a pair of nipple clamps on a light chain before his face and smiled. He didn't smile back. She snapped a clamp onto each nipple and gave the chain a sharp yank. He screamed.

"You'll get hell on earth if these come off," she said. "And I mean it."

Sam didn't doubt it. The clamps started to hurt... then *really* hurt.

"Breathe into the pain," she said. "And then release it. And remember to focus."

Sam concentrated on the pain. After a minute he noticed the pain was still there but didn't seem as unbearable. Curious.

"I have three tasks for you today," Lady Indigo said. "The first is to drive Danielle to her class at the university."

"What?" he said, stunned. "I'm supposed to go out in public like this?"

Lady Indigo's glare was her answer. Sam fiddled with the top shirt button to hide the chain collar. Lady Indigo slapped his hands away.

"Don't you dare!" she roared. "Is there something here you're ashamed of?"

God, the woman can be scary. "No."

"Good," she said and unfastened the second button. "Leave it this way."

Sam waddled and clinked out to his car with Danielle. He opened her door as any chauffeur-slave should, and she got in without saying a word. As he drove, embarrassment hovered around his body looking for a way in. He struggled to keep it out, which became even harder as he tried to drive in all his encumbrances. Working the clutch caused the harness straps to pinch his balls. He winced with every gear shift, as Danielle now noticed.

"Why are you doing this?" she finally asked.

That damn question just won't go away. Well, it was a reasonable one—she'd seen him naked, shackled, and beaten all morning. What should he say? What *could* he say? He was getting used to baring the intimacies of his life to strangers, so what was another? Why not give her the truth and let her deal with it? That was easier than trying to hide it, which was impossible anyway. *Focus.*

"I'm exploring my sexuality," he said, wondering why he hadn't told his journal that.

"Do you think this is sexy?"

"Yeah, I do."

"Well, from what I've seen, your cock doesn't seem to think so."

Ah, the problem with having a penis with a will of its own. But she was right. Arousal was nowhere around, although hearing her say *cock* lit a spark. What to say? *The truth.*

"Well, I'm turned on in my head," he answered. It was mostly true, but not at that particular moment.

"Being naked and beaten in front of me turns you on? How is that possible?"

Sam turned to her. "I don't know, Danielle. That's what I'm trying to find out."

Danielle looked straight ahead, her pink-glossed lips set in a thin, hard line. "I don't understand."

"I don't either." *Just don't ask me anything else.*

They arrived at her class building. Danielle got out without saying thank you or looking at him. *The hell with her.*

Task number two was a trip across town to the enormous home center. He was to purchase a one-inch-diameter wooden dowel and a package of screw eyes. For what purpose, Lady Indigo wouldn't say; she'd only handed him ten dollars and hinted that he'd find out soon enough. Sam crept through the cavernous building trying to hide the collar and muffle the clinking and creaking beneath his clothes. The store was out of one-inch dowels. *How could a giant fucking home center be out of fucking one-inch dowels?* he wanted to scream at the first fucking clerk he saw, if he could have found one.

Sam couldn't return without the dowel. He drove across town to a small neighborhood hardware store but had to park two blocks away. He was certain that everyone on the street knew exactly what was causing the odd bulges in his pants. Thankfully, the store had dowels. The young woman at the cash register glanced at the chain around his neck. The left nipple clamp suddenly slipped off and he winced.

"Are you okay?" she asked.

Oh, I'm fine except for these cruel steel jaws biting into my nipples.

"Tummy ache," he mumbled. She appeared to be convinced.

Coward. Is there something here you're ashamed of?

Sam was running late, but, despite her own temporal laxity, being late with Lady Indigo was unfairly unacceptable. He painfully reattached the errant clamp. She'd never know, and he sure as hell wasn't going to tell her. Working the clutch continued to pinch his balls and exacerbate his aggravation, as did hitting every red light the city owned. The traffic gods were obviously in league with the bitch. That, the afternoon heat, and the traffic congestion meant he returned to Lady Indigo's apartment sweaty, sore, and cranky.

She immediately knew something was amiss. He complained about the rigors and aggravations of his day, hoping for a little sympathy. Not a chance.

"Strip," she said.

As Sam removed his shirt, the left nipple clamp slipped off again, and he stifled a scream. Lady Indigo yanked off the other clamp and this scream came out.

"Get down on your hands and knees!" she shouted, obviously and inexplicably pissed about something. She picked up her paddle and cracked his butt hard.

"*Jesus!*" he jumped up and screamed, completely bewildered. "What the hell?"

"Get back down!" she screamed back and cracked him again, harder. "And focus!"

Sam focused on the only tangible things in his world: his burning butt, his mushrooming rage, his confusion about why this was happening at all, and Lady Indigo's magenta toenails. She continued to paddle him until she was sure the pain in his ass had replaced that in his head. Her intention finally became clear to him. *Paddling as a mood-altering agent,* he thought. *Brilliant!* If he weren't so sore, he would have praised the bitch for her groundbreaking therapy.

After a few more hard smacks, Lady Indigo ordered him to stand.

"Get in your cell, stew in your snit, and write in your journal," she snapped.

He heard the door's bolt thrown and locked. He sat on the floor, butt burning, harness still poking and chafing him. He swore he wouldn't stew in his snit as ordered, just to be defiant, but his snit wouldn't be denied. After staring at his journal for five minutes, he decided to write nothing and to hell with the consequences. Again, he was within a micron of bailing out.

You're getting it from all sides, aren't you? She runs your ass ragged then obliterates it. What would a twit do?

He'd walk out the goddamned door.

No, that's what a man would do. This is the price you're willing to pay, so pay it and quit complaining.

Yeah, you're right.

Of course I am. And the funniest part is you still don't know what you're buying.

It was true. In all of his fantasies, nothing even close to this was part of the script. *So, what* am *I buying?* He decided to stay until he found out—*if* he found out. He admitted it was a flimsy intention but the only one available at the moment.

A half hour later, Lady Indigo decided Sam's stew was cooked well enough and freed him from his closet cell. He gave her his journal without saying a word. She laughed at him and handed him the canvas bag. "Get dressed," she said. "I have another errand for you."

Great. He dressed, still locked in his leather accoutrements. His balls ached from their confinement and the pinching, the plug irritated his anus, his nipples stung, and his butt felt like it had been mauled by a belt sander. His cock, longing for any sort of attention, was feeling very sorry for itself.

For his third task, Lady Indigo gave him a roll of quarters and the key to her minivan and told him to take it to a self-serve car wash downtown.

"And I don't want to see a speck of dirt on it," she warned.

"Anything else?" Sam muttered.

"Yeah. Wax it as well."

"Anything else?"

"Do you want anything else?" she shot back.

"No… *Mistress*."

"Still stewing, huh? Well, you're going to get something else." She reattached the nipple clamps, adding to his misery. To make sure of it, she gave the chain a yank.

More anxious than ever, Sam drove through the downtown traffic, the harness pinching him at every turn. He knew his driving was being compromised, which ramped up his anxiety. He prayed he wouldn't have an accident. What would he tell the police and his insurance company? Was there an obscure city ordinance against driving while harnessed and butt-plugged? The traffic gods, in a rare moment of benevolence, gave him a long red light so he could try to adjust the harness. He couldn't.

The car wash was located in a high-crime neighborhood, a place Sam would be afraid to go even with bodyguards, let alone by himself and locked into leather underwear. He considered simply turning around, returning the filthy van to Lady Indigo, ripping off her smug face, and then scrapping the whole bloody deal. Ah, but she held the keys to his fetters. *Aha!* He did have a hacksaw at home. An escape plan took shape as he approached the car wash.

Thank heaven the facility was nearly empty. Sam put his plan on hold, pulled into the stall farthest from the street, waddled to the coin slot, and shoveled in the quarters. Mercifully, the other customers and passersby ignored him as he worked. Washing a van by hand, even a small one, requires a lot of stretching and agility—activities that leather harnesses, cock rings, and butt plugs are famous for hindering. The contraption continually abraded the already-sore flesh, and he dreaded the damage being wrought.

The worst was yet to come. As he was waxing the van, two scruffy-looking men across the street saw him and headed straight over. Sam felt the word *victim* emerging in blood on his forehead. One man was large and menacing; the other was short, scrawny, and had a severely bloodshot eye. The big man rubbed off a bit of wax from the door with his finger. Sam knew what was coming.

"Looks like you could use some help, man," the big man said.

"Um, I'm sorry, but I have to do this by myself," Sam said nervously, but as courteously as possible. *Please, please, please don't ask why.*

"By yourself? What is that shit?"

"Yeah, that's some fucked up bullshit," said the smaller man.

"I'm sorry," Sam repeated weakly, his voice becoming the first part of his body to die.

What could he tell them? Did they know what a dominatrix was? Did they know the word impeccability? Could they possibly understand why a man would want to be a slave? Would they sympathize with how hard life can be with a rubber plug up one's ass or why a person would choose to have it put there? Sam could feel the left nipple clamp loosen. *Oh God no, they'll hear it for sure.* It held, miraculously.

The big man pointed to the chain around Sam's neck. "What's that shit?"

Sam just shrugged. He was so going to die. He looked around the street for rescue. None was in sight. Strangely, the big man also glanced up and down the street, nervous as well.

The smaller man stared at Sam. His eye looked terrible. "What th' fuck you lookin' at?"

"Your eye," said Sam, fearing those might be his last words.

"Yeah. I got jacked last week, jus' right over there." The man pointed down the street. "They fix me up real fine 'cept for my eye. I need surgery, they said. But ain't no one gonna fuck wid my eye. Ain't no one gonna fuck wid me ever again."

The small man was losing himself to anger. The big man turned his attention back to Sam, his stare drilling into Sam's skull and pouring fear into his eyes. Through his paralysis, Sam noticed a small blue teardrop tattoo at the corner of the man's left eye. He knew this wasn't just decorative; it meant the man had killed another. Sam's fear skyrocketed until he felt a critical mass had been reached; it just was not possible to feel more distressed. The next moment would be pivotal, and he had no idea what it would contain.

The nipple clamp slipped off. Pain exploded in his chest. It took everything Sam had to block it—pain was now irrelevant compared to staying alive. *Focus, focus, focus.* He was still caught in the big man's glare, but the inner steel he needed to stem the pain in his nipple reversed the flow. Instead of fear flooding into his eyes, Sam felt fire streaming out of them. The big man blinked.

And like a switch had been thrown, Sam fell into a calm, the storm's eye. Time seemed to slow down. In that moment he saw something deeply profound: the difference between being a victim and not. He chose: he would *not* be a victim. Something shifted within him. He distinctly felt it, and so did the men. Was this Magic's doing? Was this compensation for his locks and fetters? No time to think about it; only time to act.

In that long, protracted moment, Sam saw he had another choice: conflict or compromise. His decision was just as clear—he would not win in a conflict. He looked at the van, shrouded in its wax haze. He looked at the two men, the larger again scanning the street, the smaller agitated with a throbbing eye, and neither sure what to do next. Sam did. He hauled out the remaining batch of quarters, about four dollars.

"This is all I have," he said, looking into the smaller man's one good eye. "And that's it." He turned to the big man. "Now, are you going to help me or not?"

The big man said something unkind about Sam's mother and walked away. Sam dumped the quarters into the smaller man's hand. Would he walk, wax, or shoot him? But he surprised Sam. As they rubbed off the wax, the man rambled on about his life, his failed dreams, and his daily challenge to find work and survive in a violent world so alien to Sam's. Sam felt petty for having feared the guy. It was an enlightening ten-minute conversation, but Sam was relieved when it was over. As the small man wandered away, Sam realized he was still wearing the harness.

He returned the glistening van to Lady Indigo. The miracle at the car wash buoyed him but couldn't compensate for the day's hardships. He was utterly famished, completely drained, and feeling thoroughly cheated. He'd worked his plugged ass off for six hours, almost gotten murdered, and for what? *If the goddamned bitch hits me again, she's toast.*

But Lady Indigo was kind and soothing and without a whisper of bitch. The woman was a surprise from one minute to the next, and Sam forgot about making toast. Lady Indigo delicately removed the nipple clamps. Blood returned to the tissue, waking up the nerves and sending more waves of pain howling through his chest. Now he was free to scream as much as he needed.

"There's no way around this," Lady Indigo said, gently massaging his dead nipples back to life. "You have no safe word with clamps. Sooner or later, they have to come off, and that's half the fun."

"Some fun," muttered Sam. He undressed, and she unlocked the harness.

"Clean everything up," she said, "and go take a shower. Then go to your cell and write in your journal. This evening will be reserved for your goodies."

Hallelujah, at last.

Sam let the shower run hot and long; it was her damn water bill, not his. He wrote about his long and trying day: his conversation with Danielle; clattering about the stores in his harness; his anger, frustration, pinched balls, and constant desire to jump ship. Despite the urge to crow about it, he said nothing about the car wash, the most important part of the day. And he decided he never would.

Well, the twit has finally done something intelligent in his life. Do you know what it was?

Dealing with those guys?

No. Not telling her about it.

Why?

Because you're the only one who should know. And me, of course.

Um, thanks for the help back there.

That wasn't me, Sam.

Lady Indigo prepared a dinner for him and Danielle. He ate sitting on the floor, as a proper slave should. The two women ignored him as if he were a stain on the rug. They were vegetarians and barely passable as cooks, as it seemed most vegetarians were. His arduous day had made him ravenous, which was the only way he could choke down the overcooked vegetables and undercooked pasta. He listened to the vapid, excited gossip between the women, understanding nothing of its content or appeal. Thank the stars he wasn't supposed to.

After dinner, Lady Indigo sat on the sofa with his journal and Sam kneeling before her.

"Do you know why I'm being so 'mean' to you?" she said. "Why I ran your ass ragged today, as you put it?"

He had a number of theories but wisely decided not to voice them.

"I needed to test your commitment," she said, after seeing he wasn't about to answer. "To see if you had an ounce of impeccability. To see if you would stay or run. You thought about running, didn't you?"

Sam nodded. "Yeah. I did. A lot."

"But you didn't." She laughed and kissed him on the forehead.

That simple gesture instantly negated the agonies and trials of his day, he noted with chagrin. *This what I'm buying? Yeah, but what is it?*

"Get up and get over here," she said. "It's goody time."

So this is what I'm buying.

Was it all worth it, twit? It had better be a damn good goody, right?

Damn right.

Lady Indigo led him into the hallway, where four large screw eyes had been solidly driven into the crown and baseboard molding. He'd noticed them earlier and correctly guessed their function. With leather wrist and ankle cuffs, she fastened him to the screws with padlocks, arms outstretched overhead and legs spread wide. On the floor she unwrapped a blanket that swaddled her array of floggers, whips, paddles, and other instruments with impact potential. Over the next hour, she used almost all of them on Sam's backside and butt, and, like their previous session, Sam flew away on Endorphin Airlines.

Danielle passed by and stopped to watch for a few minutes. She still would not look Sam in the eye. Lady Indigo offered her the whip. Danielle paused, shook her head, and walked on.

Sam was left to hang there for another hour while the two women watched television in the living room, some crime drama. He presented an obstruction on the way to the bathroom. Danielle was able to carefully maneuver by without touching him, as if his body was radioactive. Being so close to a naked man undoubtedly violated every article in the Lesbian Constitution. Lady Indigo had no such problem and squeezed by with a generous amount of body contact. Sam had long given up being embarrassed and was immensely enjoying everything, especially Danielle's discomfort. The stress of the day seemed years past.

Lady Indigo released him from his chains and told him to wash up. In the bathroom's full-length mirror he saw a naked man with a chain locked around his neck. His back and butt were covered with welts and bruises, and his nipples looked like giant mosquito bites. He remembered staring into the mirror of Mistress Morgaine, terrified and not knowing what he was seeing.

But Lady Indigo's mirror showed a different man, one who, surprisingly, stood unashamed and strong, not the weak, fawning weenie he feared he'd have to become. Was he now looking at Magic? What a day. *Yeah, it was worth it.* He wrote all of this down.

Sam returned to Lady Indigo's feet and gave her the journal. Danielle had finally gone to bed, leaving the two of them alone in their bubble of intimacy. Lady Indigo read the passages, bemused but approving.

"So you wanted to strangle me? Then rip me a new asshole? Well, at least you're being honest."

"Yeah."

"A good thing you didn't try," she laughed. "I'm taking kung fu lessons, you know." She continued reading. Then at last she said, "I think we can proceed. Now, I think it's bedtime."

In his cell, Sam unrolled his sleeping bag. Lady Indigo locked on leather wrist and ankle cuffs and padlocked one ankle cuff to the screw eye in the floor.

"What if I have to pee during the night?" Sam asked.

Lady Indigo frowned. She unlocked the cuff from the floor but not from his ankle.

"Is there anything else you need?" she said, more more out of irritation than hospitality.

"How about a bedtime story?" he grinned, pleased with his small victory.

"How about some blisters all over your ass?" she grinned back.

Sam thought better of it. He worried he'd have a rough night trying to sleep in fetters with a burning welt for a body. But he found the captivity surprisingly comfortable—even comforting, and he slept like a baby in its barred crib.

He awoke early, before the two women. Ten minutes later, he was lounging on the sofa, enjoying a stolen cup of Danielle's coffee, and feeling quite rosy about this strange little affair. Lady Indigo emerged from her bedroom in her robe, red-eyed, disheveled, her face sleep-bloated and looking like Medusa on a bad hair day with a mood to match.

"I told you not to sit on the furniture! Jesus Christ! What's wrong with you?"

He'd forgotten. He leapt from the sofa, stunned, having fallen from the clouds into a latrine in less than a second. Magic was instantly nullified, replaced by a five-year-old boy freshly scolded and growing furious. Both slid into a black sulk, unable to do anything else. Lady Indigo, now in full bitch mode, would have none of it. She made her coffee, snapped at him to clean up her mess, and went into her room. Sam just stared after her, furious, barely able to contain his inner incensed child from further eruption.

Thirty seconds later, Lady Indigo returned, set the canvas bag with his clothes and belongings on the floor, and put the keys to his collars and cuffs on the kitchen counter.

"You can free yourself any time," she said curtly, "and just walk out the door."

She mimicked walking with her fingers and went back into her room.

Sam thought about what had just happened, and it didn't take much thinking. The scolding had had all the symptoms of transference with his neurotic, moody mother. But the insight was old news and resolved nothing. *Focus*, he reminded himself. But focus did nothing except to show him his complete inability to focus. He picked up the keys. Such small items with such massive power.

He sighed. This daring new adventure had just turned sour—a house of cards beginning to collapse. He now saw the contract as nothing but a silly game to justify his obsessive hunger. Magic was nothing but another name for jackass fool. Lady Indigo was nothing but a crazy-ass dyke jacking him around. Nothing was all he had. *What the hell did I expect?*

What the hell did you expect? A festive visit to slave world?

Just look at all the shit I had to go through!

Pah! You've gone through a lot more with the ladies and gotten a lot less.

But nothing this... this warped and weird.

You, of all people, are complaining about warped and weird? You weren't drafted into doing this, you know. What is your problem here?

I don't know, but I'm sure as hell having one.

Amen to that, worm.

Sam set the keys on the counter. Uncertain what to do next, he sat on the floor and waited for Lady Indigo, still wondering why. She finally emerged from her bedroom, looking more like a human being and minimally acting like one. She seemed pleased he was still there.

"You're still here," she said. She didn't ask why, but Sam knew it was a question. He couldn't give her an answer because he had none.

"Do you know why I was so angry?" she asked.

"Because I screwed up? I sat on the furniture?"

"No. Not because of the furniture. It's because I knocked you flat on your ass and you couldn't figure out how to stand back up. That's what pissed me off. That's impeccability, or, in your case, the lack thereof. Do you understand?"

He nodded.

"Good." She knelt beside him, looked into his eyes, and unlocked his collar. Unexpectedly, the sharp click brought him back to Magic and the five-year-old back to an adult. The adult was astonished how one little click could do all that and he couldn't.

He dressed while Lady Indigo watched. The silence between them felt pregnant with tension and uncertainty. He started to speak, but she shook her head.

"Write about it in your journal," was all she said.

At least the contract was still on. Sam gathered up his belongings, his journal, and his remaining wits and left Lady Indigo's apartment dungeon with a week to think things over.

24

LESBIAN TITS

THE MORNING OF SESSION TWO BEGAN like the first. Sam arrived precisely at ten, and for once he and Lady Indigo were in the same time zone. Now a little wary of the woman, he put his belongings in his cell, stripped, and placed his clothes in the canvas bag. He knelt before her in the proper position, smooth and easy, like the experienced slave he was trying to become. Lady Indigo was not impressed. *Why do I even bother trying to please this woman?*

Because pleasing women is your job in life. And that's what the contract stipulates. Jeez! Where have you been lately?

Then why isn't it working?

What do you think "working" will get you? A pat on the back? A fuck?

Well, I'll get, um...

Still don't know, eh? And besides, it is working. You're still trying to please her.

Lady Indigo looped the chain around his neck, inserted the padlock shackle, and paused. She didn't have to tell him to listen. The click jerked Sam out of one life and into another, and this time it showed. Lady Indigo smiled. She locked him into the cock ring, this time a little more skillfully, and told him to proceed with his housecleaning. But she added a twist.

"Today you are forbidden to make eye contact with me," she said. "Under no circumstances do you break that rule."

Sam thought it was an odd rule but one that seemed easy enough to follow. At least he already knew what his tormentor looked like—not like a Mistress Morgaine facial void. But now he suspected that odd things around this place were more than what they seemed.

An hour into his housecleaning, Lady Indigo told Sam to dress and sent him to the minimarket for groceries. Mercifully, he was spared the harness, but not the nipple clamps. Driving unrestrained and unpinched was heaven, but the escalating pain in his nipples was not. Worse, the left clamp kept slipping off, which meant he had to keep reclamping it and enduring the agony. He tried switching the clamps, but it made no difference. His left nipple simply wouldn't have it. He'd always thought his nipples were identical, but apparently not. S/m was indeed proving to be a journey of discovery.

At the market, Sam waited in the checkout line, more embarrassed by Lady Indigo's junk food being in his basket than by his exposed collar. Maybe she thought her holy vegetarian ways would cancel out this crap. The left nipple clamp again slipped off and the chain clinked. The middle-aged woman ahead of Sam turned and saw his chain collar.

Oh shit. He was now exposed in public as a deviant, with no excuse and no place to hide. What to do? Stand there and cringe? Or stand tall? *Focus. Choose!* He did. Surprisingly, the collar now felt sexy and daring. *Yes, ma'am, I am a certified deviant. I'm not hurting you, am I?* The woman quickly looked away, but the cashier kept glancing at it. She rang up his purchases and avoided his eyes like there was something inside him she didn't want to see. There most certainly was.

Sam gave Lady Indigo her bag of pseudo-groceries, feeling quite pleased with himself and properly slavish. To create a wide no-look zone around her face, he focused on her toenails, which were now alternating turquoise and orange. What would a slave do without toenails to examine while he was on the floor or on some other screwy jag?

He prayed the left nipple clamp would hang in there a little longer, and it complied. At last, Lady Indigo gently removed the clamps and massaged the tender flesh, as if being gentle would make a difference. It didn't, and, as always, the pain caused by her kindness was far worse. What was this damn thing she had for nipples? She ordered him out of his clothes, which were again bagged and hidden.

Lady Indigo brought out the materials Sam had obtained the previous week. According to her instructions, he sawed the dowel into two eighteen-inch sections. Into each end he drilled and inserted a screw eye. That was it. He couldn't quite figure out its purpose.

"You'll soon see," smiled Lady Indigo.

He didn't have to wait long. She put him in leather wrist cuffs and padlocked one end of a dowel to each cuff. That simple no-eye-contact rule was now becoming more difficult to follow, and he still didn't understand its purpose. She locked the other end of each dowel to the cock ring, creating an unusual predicament.

Lady Indigo told him to resume his housecleaning chores, which proved insidiously awkward while locked in this contraption. Vacuuming was not much of a problem, but scrubbing the floor on his hands and knees definitely was. And washing the windows provided the neighbors next door with a most interesting show. Lady Indigo and Danielle greeted his clumsy domestic gymnastics with amusement. Danielle seemed to be getting more comfortable having a naked man rattling around the apartment. Sam admitted he indeed looked ridiculous, and his antics made it even more so. Perhaps that was the idea, and he joined in the fun. And fun it was until he had to figure out how to urinate.

Lady Indigo interrupted Sam's cleaning and pulled him into his cell. She sat him down and snapped three clothespins on each of his freshly inflamed nipples. The dowels prevented him from reaching the clothespins or anything else of interest.

"You have one hour to cook in your own juice," she said and turned off the light, then closed and locked the door.

The closet was tomb dark; the only sensory input came from his nipples. After fifteen minutes, as he reckoned in Lady Indigo torture time, the pain subsided to a bearable dull ache. He was not sufficiently immobilized and not tormented enough to make it fun, so what was the point? He wished she'd snapped clothespins on his pouting and neglected cock. Unbelievably, he again was in danger of becoming bored right in the middle of a fond fantasy come true. Outside the city was reveling in a warm, spring afternoon and he was spending it locked in a dark closet and trying to cook in his own juice, however one did that. *How utterly sick can sick get?*

"You chose this. So quit whining and focus."

Sam startled. Was Lady Indigo in the closet with him? It sounded like her voice but he really wasn't sure. He looked around the space, unable to see past his nose. "Lady?"

Nothing.

"Lady Indigo?"

Sam strained to detect any sound in the absolute blackness but heard only his own breathing. *Her damn words are inside my head again.* Even in her absence she was still there riding him. He calmed himself. Then he heard another voice, then two, soft and feminine. He peered into the void, trying to locate the source. It definitely wasn't Lady Indigo and Danielle. Was there someone else in the apartment? No, the voices were also coming from within him. As if that was their cue, the voices turned into light and spirited laughter, with him as the spectacle on a stage. Sam knew he was hallucinating.

Then the ordeal became much more interesting and more difficult. The ache in his nipples ramped up. The clothespins grew claws and glowed red hot. He focused on the pain. And pain it was, blooming into a nuclear fireball. The laughter became louder, almost jeering. He felt fluid running down his chest. Was it sweat or blood? Maybe one of the clothespins had torn open the skin. He struggled to reach them and couldn't.

Then he heard drumming, distant at first, then growing louder and more insistent, adding a primal backdrop to the stage. Was it blood pounding in his ears or was he eavesdropping on a tribal ritual from elsewhere and ages past? He knew hallucinations could happen in a sensory deprivation chamber, so why not in a sensory stimulation chamber with burning nipples as the focus? *Focus.* That word again. At least he was no longer bored.

The drumming gradually faded into white noise. Lady Indigo finally unlocked the door. It could have been an hour or a day, as he was still adrift in time. She roughly yanked off the clothespins and it felt like parts of his flesh as well. She massaged his nipples, making the agony far worse as usual, and freed him from his restraints.

"Have a nice trip?" she asked.

Sam couldn't speak. He nodded. Avoiding her eyes was now becoming a pitched battle.

"Good," she said. "Lie down for a while and then write about what happened in here. Write a story for me."

"A story? About what? Why?"

"This is not a request." Lady Indigo closed and locked his cell door.

After about thirty minutes in slave Magic time, this emerged in his journal:

Once upon a time magic was born. He came into being the moment She said his name. You are magic, She said, the warrior who will lead his children home. But how can I be a warrior while I'm naked and chained?

magic said. You have no power, they said. Your bag of tricks will not work here. Warrior is not for you. Magic looked in the mirror. Was he seeing the body of a warrior? But what is a warrior without a weapon? Then voices, ancient, millennia old, cried out as one: we are waiting for you, magic. You suffer pain and abuse but you still remain standing. Your sword is your intention. Your shield is your will, and no one can ever disarm you.

Sam suspected there was meaning hidden in the words, but he had no idea what it was.

That's because there is nothing there. Just more hallucinating.
I'm not so sure about that.
How can you be sure about anything right now?

Lady Indigo unlocked the closet cell and told Sam to come out on his knees, eyes down. She knelt in front of him and held his face. "Now look at me."

Sam did and felt an immediate jolt, like a massive voltage surging throughout his body. He had no idea why, only that he was caught in a riptide of relief, joy, and tears. Lady Indigo just smiled, as if she had known exactly what would happen.

"The eyes are the windows to the soul," she said. "We've been together all day, we've been very intimate, but you've had no way to communicate or express it. So how do you feel?"

"Like I want to completely ravish you from head to toe. And then eat every last morsel. And it still wouldn't be enough." His steady gaze said he meant it. "But you know I won't."

Lady Indigo held the eye contact. "I know you won't. But I understand the sentiment. That's a nice gift. Thank you."

She hugged him, and longer than he expected. "Now it's playtime," she said, soft and low.

Playtime found Sam again chained up in the hallway. He was hungry for the whip and couldn't wait to be fed. Lady Indigo went into her bedroom and returned wearing black stretch pants and a skimpy red leather vest that laced up the front, revealing most of her breasts. She was a well-built woman to begin with, and her slinking around in that outfit diverted Sam to horny in a hot hurry.

She stood on a chair in front of him to adjust his chains, with his nose and lips an inch from her chest. It might as well have been a mile. Sam stared at the flesh bulging against the laces of her vest and beckoning to be devoured. Ogling was nowhere near enough. Lesbian or not, contract or not, he had to do something. He strained forward and stuck out his tongue, its tip writhing like a snake hot after prey. Lady Indigo moved slightly back, keeping her breasts just out of reach. He groaned. She laughed and sang an impromptu ditty:

"Lesbian tits, lesbian tits! You'll never touch these lesbian tits!"

Sam had heard something similar once before in another dungeon. The two lesbian tit owners couldn't be more different, but the teasing still burned his brain and inflamed parts lower. Indeed, his penis couldn't inflate any further and threatened to start popping its capillaries. Lady Indigo saw this, smiled, and inched her breast within a micron of his tongue, which was stretched to the point of dislocation.

Once again Sam got hijacked, this time by a fourteen-year-old boy with acne and beat-off blisters, trapped in unrequited sexual heat. Lady Indigo's breasts became Miss Miller's breasts, then all the breasts of all the girls and women who used them to tease and torment him for the past thirty years. An angry knot tied his guts.

"Lesbian tits! Lesbian tits!" again chirped Lady Indigo. She lightly grazed her breast across the tip of his tongue and hopped off the chair. The gut-knot grew tighter.

Thirty years had changed nothing except for thirty years' more fury. He struggled to remember about what Judith had said about desire and choice, but his anger wouldn't give it any room. Was it Buddha who said that attachment to desire was the cause of suffering? *That's well and good,* thought Sam, *but was the fat man ever chained up in a dungeon?*

"Ah, yes, I was," Buddha said. "I've been chained up in a very deep dungeon indeed, the deepest of them all: the illusion of the self, the illusion of control. What we have here, blessed one, is a fine opportunity to experience your attachment to those illusions. This is very good."

"No, this isn't very good. I want to experience boobs, not my attachment to them."

"Well, you can't have boobs," Buddha said. "Instead, you can have the experience of suffering in their absence. Do you know what alleviates suffering, Sam, my child?"

"Yeah. Boobs."

Lady Indigo turned up the voltage, pressing and grinding her lesbian tits into his back and then across his chest. Worse, Sam knew she was enjoying every damn second of it. He wanted to hate her and demolish her and fuck her, but he could do none of those things. He stared at Lady Indigo's laced-up breasts. They were so beautiful, so luscious, so full of life and burgeoning with feminine essence. Why did he want them so much? They were just tits, for God's sakes!

Nice eye candy, eh, twit?

Yeah.

Can't have any, can you?

No! This is horrible! I hate it!

What's so horrible about it?

You just said it. I can't have it.

No, you can't. But look at what you do have.

Like what?

Like your cock, dimwit! Look how nice and hard it is. Isn't that a wondrous miracle of nature and hydraulics? Look at what it's giving you.

It's giving me nothing!

I disagree. It's giving you suffering and lots of it. And that's giving me a good time.

Good. At least one of us is happy.

Suffering. Sam remembered what the fat man had said about it. Lady Indigo stood before him, hands on her hips, smiling, self-possessed, her breasts rising and falling with her breathing. Did she know what she was doing to him? Of course she did. He knew it as well. His turgid cock. Her beautiful breasts. The dominion of sexual desire. They were all miracles, and it made no sense to rage at any of them. Did he rage at his stomach for getting hungry? Now his anger seemed foolish and juvenile, and besides, what would it get him?

"Nice tits," Sam said, not caring how that would be received. She just smiled.

She indeed had changed. Her mischievous teasing was just that. He could not rage at the woman for being a woman, for having breasts as all women do, despite hers being agents of caprice and her being a royal pain in the ass. Suffering simply wasn't worth the bother.

After making sure his chains were secure, Lady Indigo grasped her largest and heaviest flogger, a many-tailed monster almost four feet long. She didn't warm up with lighter whips, as was her custom. After a few practice strokes to determine the range, she let loose with a single, hard blow. It was like being hit with a refrigerator.

The fridge hit him again and again. The thunks of the flogger echoed throughout the apartment. Flogging, especially with one so heavy, was definitely an aerobic exercise, although medical science had yet to recommend it. After a series of particularly savage blows, Lady Indigo dropped the flogger and stopped to catch her breath. She massaged Sam's flesh, now glowing bright red. He hung there in absolute bliss. She firmly pressed her breasts into his back in that annoyingly seductive habit of hers.

"Now it's poetry time," she whispered into his ear.

"Poetry?" he could barely mumble.

"You bet. You have five minutes to compose a poem for me."

Sam struggled out of his cloud bank. "Now? Are you serious?"

She picked up the flogger and gave him her answer.

"But I can't write a poem. I'm, I'm—"

"You are going to compose a poem, period, so stop complaining. It doesn't have to rhyme or even be a good poem. Five minutes."

After another hard crack to his butt, Lady Indigo left to take a shower.

Sam's list of laments grew like a toothache. Endorphin trip aborted. Shoved out of his body and into his head, the very last place he wanted to be. To make it worse, he had to write a fucking poem. Writing poetry in Miss Miller's class had been agonizing enough, but at least he hadn't had to do it chained up and naked. Now he was in a different kind of classroom. What would Miss Miller think of all this? Maybe she should use this technique with her students. Maybe she has. The memory of his first dominatrix with her unbuttoned blouse and seductive smile gave him a tingle.

Now back to business. Sam focused on the popping points of light skittering across the inside of his eyelids. Remarkably, a distinct image coalesced: a small island in a dark and troubled sea. There was a solitary figure on the island that Sam sensed was trying to tell him something. *Please let it be a poem*, he hoped. He strained to look more closely at the creature. It was thin and dark, only about two feet tall, and curiously had no face.

Lady Indigo returned. "Is the poem finished?"

She was wearing a different pair of pants but no shirt. *Goddamn that woman.* He stared at her big lesbian tits and the metal rings through their tips and sighed.

"Well?"

"Not yet," said Sam, knowing he had nothing coming but her retribution.

Still topless, Lady Indigo resumed beating Sam as hard and fast as she could. He twisted at the chains, screaming and sucking in huge gobs of air and trying to escape with all sincerity.

"Safe word?" she asked.

"Never," he said and got five additional lashes. She dropped the flogger and held him. *What irony,* he thought. *Naked boobs on my back but all I feel are burning welts.*

"I'm giving you another five minutes, so you'd better damn well have that poem done," she said and went back into her room.

Sam hung there, trying to catch his breath. He thought about those nineteenth-century English country gentlemen poets, leisurely composing verse amid the fields and flowers under the warm springtime sky. *Try writing poetry while hanging in chains with a blistered ass and a five-minute deadline imposed by a half-crazy, half-naked dyke witch, you foppy bastards.* The fops had no comment.

Sam confronted his deadline. Lesbian tits, lesbian tits, he kept repeating her goofy song. *I will never touch those lesbian tits. I will never have any power. I will never have what I want. Never, never, never.* A ragged poem emerged:

There is a place called Never, where dwells a beast with no face.
Your future is forever denied to you, it said.
You are never and will always be never.

Three lines, no rhyme, but it would have to do.

"It's called The Beast with No Face." Sam recited the poem to Lady Indigo, who was now mercifully wearing a T-shirt. The poem was beyond lame, which concerned him. Oddly, being naked and restrained felt far less embarrassing than turning in a weak assignment. But she seemed satisfied and unchained him. They sat on the floor close together.

"That beast is your personal saboteur," she said. "It keeps whispering 'never' into your ear to the point where you define yourself by your limitations and failures, rather than by your potential and accomplishments."

He nodded. Now the poem made sense, although his brain was running on fumes.

"What did you do with the beast?" she asked.

That stopped him. He hadn't done anything but would now.

"I took it into my heart and embraced it," he said, not really knowing why that, of all things, had come out of his mouth. "I will give it a safe home." Judith would have creamed over that.

Lady Indigo smiled. "Good," she said. "Very good."

The dominatrix as a therapist. Despite Judith's warnings, Sam decided that there was something to this after all. Lady Indigo had gone where no therapist dared tread. She had literally beat a demon out of him where it he could see it, name it, and begin to free himself from its insidious grip. Trying to coax it out of hiding by blubbering on a therapist's couch would not have worked, and therapists usually didn't chain up and whip their clients. Perhaps they should. He tried to imagine Judith with a whip and couldn't.

An hour later, Sam sat in his cell trying to tell his journal what happened with his faceless beast when he heard a man's voice in the hallway. He froze. Lady Indigo whisked into the closet and quickly shut the door behind her, flushed with concern. Apparently, Danielle had forgotten he was there and brought home her date.

"Her date?" Sam said, stunned. "I thought she was, you know…"

"The word is bisexual," Lady Indigo said, her sour tone suggested this had been an issue between them. "She's confused."

"Aren't you two, um, together?" Sam asked, for the first time suspecting perhaps not.

"What we are is not your concern," she snapped. Then she softened. "I'm really very sorry about this, Sam."

Hearing Lady Indigo apologize was just as jolting as one of her refrigerator hits.

"It's a serious breach, a violation of your safety, and I ask your forgiveness," she said as solemnly as he'd ever heard her.

Sam gloated. *Now I'm the one holding the whip and she knows it, oho, oho.*

Lady Indigo didn't wince or shrink but just solidly stood there in her culpability, waiting to see what he'd do next. Sam remained silent, a common passive-aggressive trick.

"You have a choice," she said. "You can use your safe word and go home, or wait until they leave. Danielle said they'd be gone in a few minutes, so *decide.*"

Now how the hell had she snatched that whip back? Sam realized he couldn't win here if he'd brought an army of ninjas.

"I'll wait."

Lady Indigo nodded and left the closet.

Sam sulked. The magic of the day had vanished, torpedoed by the newly heterosexual Danielle. Even torture by poetry had been scuttled. *What would a warrior do?*

Why don't you just walk out there naked?

I'm thinking about it.

A half an hour later (a few minutes in Lady Indigo time), Danielle and her alleged beau left the apartment, the man apparently none the wiser. Lady Indigo had set up her massage table in the center of the living room. She told Sam to get on and gave him a back massage. He wondered if this was atonement for the security lapse. He asked if it was.

"I won't say," she said.

That felt like a slap. "Why not?"

"Sometimes you need to keep things close to you. Keep them unspoken."

"Isn't that called withholding? A kind of power game?"

"Sometimes, but not with me and not now," Lady Indigo said as she worked. "You must be very careful about who you reveal yourself to. You make yourself vulnerable. That sets you up to be fucked with and abused, especially if that person is not trustworthy."

"Are you saying I'm untrustworthy? Gee, thanks."

"Oh, get over it. We're not equals in this contract, and you know it. It's been that way from the beginning. You must always be transparent to me, and I must remain opaque to you. That's the only way this thing can work."

"What?" Sam said. "I have to open myself completely and be vulnerable so you can fuck with me all you want? Is that your idea of how this thing works?"

"Basically, yes."

"That's crazy. That's totally unfair!"

"You're absolutely right. I told you that fairness will not apply here. Do you remember? And I'll continue to fuck with you as much as I want. That's what my domination is all about, as you've probably figured out by now. And keep in mind that not only are you allowing me to fuck with you, you're also paying me to do it. Why? Do you think I'm trustworthy?"

"Well, yes."

"Are you sure?"

Sam had to think about it.

"Ha!" she shouted. "You really have no way of knowing that, do you? You want me to be trustworthy so I'll be your honorable and wise teacher and take care of you, right?"

"Well…"

"What if I'm not trustworthy? What if I'm actually batshit crazy? Maybe I'm fucking with you because I get off on it and really don't give a damn about you. A little bullshit here and a little abuse there. What will you do about that, huh?"

"I can walk out the door."

"You sure can. And go find someone else you think is trustworthy? Someone you can manipulate into taking responsibility for you?"

"But I'm trusting you not to hurt me," Sam cried.

"You're *paying* me to hurt you!"

"You know what I mean!"

"I know what you mean, and I refuse to play your game. Go read our contract again. Especially the part about protecting your sacred being. You do know you're a sacred being, don't you?"

Sam sulked in his thoughts.

"Look," she went on, "I will not become a saint for you. That's a horrible, awful job. What a burden! I'm presenting you with another way, a better way."

"Which is?"

"Impeccability!" she roared, almost startling him off the table. "Haven't you heard me mention the word? Then trustworthiness becomes irrelevant. Then what a person says or does makes absolutely no difference. Even if that person is me. You're still able to protect yourself. You're still standing. You're keeping your center. Haven't you gotten that yet?"

"I'm trying. I'm really trying."

"Well, let's hope that trying becomes doing."

Sam remained silent. Lady Indigo slowly ran her elbow down either side of his backbone. That felt great. His head didn't.

"If you learn nothing else here, Magic," she said more softly, "learn that."

Although he wasn't sure how, Sam knew Lady Indigo was right. Again. She finished the massage and helped him sit up.

"Feeling better?" she asked.

"My body does."

"Yeah. You've had quite a day. Take a shower and go to bed. No cuffs tonight."

She hugged him and kissed his cheek. He just sat there staring at her. *How can I love someone and want to obliterate her at the same time? How can I love a woman when sex is not even possible?*

Maybe you can't, twit.

I'm doing it right now.

That's because you don't know what you're doing. As usual.

It was true. Lesbian or not, contract or not, Sam was in love with Lady Indigo. Of this he was certain. He was exhibiting all the symptoms: the mooning, the obsessing, the fantasizing, the plotting, and knowing none of it would lead to anything. But it was real and aching and too huge and growing huger just to sit on it.

Midweek, he called Lady Indigo to, well, just talk. It seemed she had known this was coming. She was cold and aloof, which crushed him. His sullen silence confirmed he hadn't been expecting that. It took some explaining from her.

"It's a boundary," she said, "and a very important one. I have no intention of becoming your friend, and certainly not your lover. That's not the purpose of the contract. We just talked about that. Weren't you listening?"

"I thought I was." Hearing this was like trying to swallow a pineapple whole, spiky end first. He felt more naked now than he had while prancing about her apartment in his skin. "I feel completely powerless."

"I know you feel that way," Lady Indigo said, "but you have to know it's not true. You have some powerful options before you. I'm holding open a space for you to identify all your games, all the manipulative tricks you use, and then release them. I'm giving you permission to project all of this onto me, no matter how immature, foolish, or conniving they are, and I promise not to punish or judge you in reprisal."

Sam let this in, surprised and humbled.

"Remember that a warrior can stand naked before his enemies," she continued, "naked inside and out, and still keep his balance and power. His sword is his intention and his shield is his will. You said that yourself, but do you understand it? Can you stand there naked?"

"I don't think so."

"You wouldn't be doing this contract if you could," she said. "I'll see you Saturday."

25

ATONEMENT

SESSION THREE BEGAN BADLY. DESPITE TRYING to pretend otherwise, Sam was sinking into a world-class funk. He arrived on Lady Indigo's doorstep infested with insecurities about continuing with the contract. He told her that. He said he was hooked on a confirmed lesbian with no hope of reciprocity or a relationship, and that really sucked. She just shrugged. He said he didn't know what the hell he was doing here. She nodded. He didn't tell her that he doubted if she did either. She probably guessed that anyway.

To make everything worse, he had the beginnings of an all-day pollen allergy headache that no analgesic could touch. Sam thought things couldn't get any fouler, but he was wrong. After the stripping and collaring rituals, above and below, Lady Indigo gave him two additional rules that he had to obey without question. He read them and groaned.

Rule One: On the quarter hour, he was to stop whatever he was doing, stand up, turn around three times, and sing the nursery rhyme "Mary Had a Little Lamb." This was to happen whether Lady Indigo was present or not.

Rule Two: On the half hour, he was to crawl across the floor on his belly and chant five times, "I will honor and obey my Mistress. Her every wish is my command." Again, he should do this regardless of her presence.

Sam was puzzled. The silliness of the rules was inconsistent with the oddball intelligence Lady Indigo had so far shown. He suspected there was something to this he wasn't seeing, but he wasn't feeling moved to find out. As his morning chores wore on, his mood was further darkened by following these foolish rules. The angrier he got, the more she loved it, to the point of raucous hysteria. She taunted him without mercy as he crawled, giving his butt an occasional swift whack with a riding crop. Danielle walked through the room and, in rare acknowledgment of his presence, just looked at him and shook her head. *The hell with her.*

As if that wasn't enough, Lady Indigo set down three pairs of mud-caked leather boots on the kitchen floor—hers and Danielle's. Sam was vacuuming the living room carpet.

"Magic!" Lady Indigo shouted. "Get in here!"

Sam didn't hear her over the vacuum. He suddenly felt his neck collar roughly grabbed. Lady Indigo switched off the vacuum. "Down on your hands and knees, slave!"

He instantly complied, confused and shaken. Danielle was in the kitchen, now seeming interested in the scene. Lady Indigo held out her hand to Danielle, who, without saying a word, handed her a paddle.

"When I give you an order, you'd better fucking obey it!" she hissed into Sam's ear and gave him a sharp crack on the butt.

Sam jumped. "But I couldn't hear you because of the—"

Whack! Whack!

He gritted his teeth but remained down.

"Now get into the kitchen on your knees, slave," she said, a micron calmer.

Sam heard that order and quickly obeyed. The word *slave* stuck in his craw.

"Hold out your hands," she said and locked handcuffs on his wrists. Danielle stood aside, watching. His headache hammered away. Anger at both women boiled in his guts.

"You are to clean and shine these boots," Lady Indigo said. "And I don't want to see a speck of shit on them."

He nodded.

"Did you hear me?"

"Yes, Lady."

"And remember your rules. If you skip them, you'll only be hurting yourself."

"Yes, Lady." *Eat shit, lady.*

"We'll be back in a couple of hours."

Lady Indigo dangled the keys to his collars and handcuffs under his nose then dropped them on the kitchen counter. He knew why but said nothing and just glared at her. Lady Indigo burst out laughing and took Danielle's arm, and the two women left the apartment.

With undiluted fury in his heart, Sam watched them step out the door. He stared at the filthy boots. This kinky little adventure he'd so eagerly sought out had just turned into another pineapple in his throat, but now the size of a Volkswagen and just as easy to swallow. He eyed the keys. They were becoming more and more attractive. *Maybe it's time to pull the plug on this... experiment.*

Poor twit. You're not enjoying your little, what did you just call it, experiment?

No.

Is that why you're still here, all naked and handcuffed?

No.

Then why?

Because... because of my commitment.

Commitment to what? Lady Indigo?

Yes.

Do you really think she's dragging you through this crap because she wants to be worshipped by a twit?

Sam's brain was caked with more mud than the boots.

Maybe it's my commitment to myself?

What a committed way to say that. What sparkling clear intention! And by the way, you missed song time.

Sam got up, turned around three times, sang about Mary and her fucking little lamb. He sat down and began to scrub the boots. The handcuffs were a bother but he could work in them. As he scraped and scrubbed, he became painfully aware of the many things he'd done in his life he truly didn't want to do, and for people he cared little for. Abruptly, he laughed out loud but could think of nothing that was particularly funny. The bitch's cackles still echoed in his head. Curiously, the laughter, his own and hers, slightly eased his mood. He finally finished the boots, grateful that at least she hadn't told him to lick them clean.

Lady Indigo and Danielle returned, prattling to each other, apparently a couple again. Sam proudly presented the shining black boots and was promptly ignored.

"Get in your cell and write," snapped Lady Indigo.

The closet door bolt was thrown and locked. *What the hell?* He'd expected a compliment. He'd expected some gesture of appreciation that he was even still there. He heard the gods of expectations laughing so hard they shit their drawers. He stared at the journal. Lady Indigo's face was on the cover, taunting him. His journal no longer seemed a book for his benefit but just another instrument of torture. How could any fool find this sexy?

An hour later, Lady Indigo unlocked the door and ordered Sam into the living room on his hands and knees, still wearing the handcuffs. She sat on the sofa and read his journal while he anxiously watched. He'd written a verbose apology for his pouting and resistance to her rules that ended with, "I should have trusted your wisdom and motives, and I ask for atonement."

He imagined atonement would be a nice, long, luxurious flogging, and hoping the pain in butt would alleviate that in his head. Lady Indigo closed the book and stared at him the way a batter looks at a fat, juicy fastball coming down the center of the pipe. Tapping her fingers on the cover, she made ready to swing.

"This is *crap*," she said, holding the journal under his nose. "This. Is. Fucking. Crap."

Sam was floored. Something had gone horribly wrong. Wrong thing to write, wrong attitude, wrong everything. He had never seen her so pissed. Why?

"Atonement? You want atonement? Okay, you got it. Get down on your belly."

Sam obeyed, wondering if this was what a fish felt like before getting gutted and fileted.

"You are to crawl from one end of this room to the other for a full hour," she growled. "A full hour! And you will chant your devotion mantra nonstop. *And* you'd better say it like you damn well fucking mean it!"

"Yes, Lady," said Sam's mouth. Sam was elsewhere, thinking escape, somehow.

"And focus, goddammit, *focus!*" she screamed in his face. The woman was spitting nails and absolutely seething.

Danielle came into the room to see what the ruckus was. He began to crawl, which was not easy in the handcuffs. "I will honor and obey my Mistress. Her every wish is my command," he muttered, still stunned by the scolding, confused by it even more, and all made excruciatingly humiliating doing this in front of Danielle.

"That's fucking lame!" Lady Indigo bellowed. "Focus! And remember your name!"

Lady Indigo watched him crawl for five minutes, scowling, occasionally cracking his butt with a paddle, and screaming "Focus!" in his ear. Again, she jingled the keys to his collars and the handcuffs and set them on the kitchen counter. She finally stormed from the room, taking Danielle with her. Sam returned to his task, now seriously thinking the woman indeed was batshit crazy and wondering where that would lead next.

After only ten minutes, Sam was exhausted and seriously doubted he could survive the next fifty. His arms ached, his butt burned, his elbows were sore, his wrists were chafed by the handcuffs, and his belly and cock had been abraded raw by the cheap shag. Worse, it had not been vacuumed. His face was flocked with carpet lint, dust, dirt, and God knew what else he was inhaling. He knew this wasn't doing his allergies any good. In fact, everything about this morning seemed deliberately designed for his undoing. Maybe it was.

But he persevered, more to show her he could do it rather than atone for his sin, whatever the hell it was. He was barely able to croak out the chant, let alone understand it. He'd crawled through acres of shit before to earn a woman's approval, or her body, or favor, or whatever the hell he thought she had that was worth crawling for, but never anything remotely like this. Was this the bitch's plan? Show him the price he was willing to pay to satisfy a need? *Well, excuse me if I don't feel like praising the bitch's wisdom right now.*

You're not supposed to be praising. You're supposed to be atoning, remember?

Fuck you.

Watch your language, slave. I've got a whip too, and mine can hurt a lot worse.

"I will honor and obey my fucking bitch Mistress," he said aloud. "Her every fucking wish is my fucking command." *If she hears me, good. Fuck her, too.*

The keys were still on the countertop, calling out to him. Lady Indigo returned, swishing her cane.

Shit! The cane! Sam gritted his teeth.

"Who is the atonement for?" she said.

"For you?"

The cane whistled down on his already burning butt. *Whack!*

"Gaah! For you, *Lady* Indigo?"

Whack!

"Goddammit!" he screamed into the shag. He caught his breath. "For me?"

Whack! Whack! Whack!

Sam almost exploded off the floor. Lady Indigo just glowered at him. Between gasps he caught sight of something. "For Magic?"

No whack.

"Yes! For Magic, not for some bullshit you wrote," she hissed. "It's Magic who needs your atonement, not me. Remember your name. Remember what it means!"

Whack!

"Fuck!" Sam screamed. Maybe she *was* batshit crazy. That would certainly explain all this.

Lady Indigo knelt by his face. "Think about this, *Magic.* How do you stand empowered in the face of disempowerment?"

Sam could say nothing, even if he had something. And crazy bats don't say shit like that. He'd never been so lost at sea.

Still fuming, Lady Indigo stood up and stomped from the living room. Sam resumed the crawling and chanting, his brain shut down and body on autopilot. He stared at the tiny twists of filthy yellow shag an inch under his nose. It was their fate to be walked on.

Well, look at this. You've gotten your pickle pickled real good by the ladies before, but this takes the prize. And I've got a ringside seat! Why, why, why are you still putting up with this?

Fuck if I know. I'm supposed to be learning something.

Like how to be a better victim? Maybe you're in this because of those big lesbian tits. You dream about them every night, and what she'll do to your weenie. And don't you deny it!

That's ridiculous! Lady Indigo is my… teacher.

Your teacher? You still think she's some kind of weird whore.

No! That's not true! I love her.

Is that why you want to strangle her?

No! She's… she's teaching me impeccability. Or something. Shit.

What's this stupid obsession you have with that word?

It must be important. Jesus, she keeps screaming it at me!

What do you think it will give you? The answer to all your problems? Strength? Power? A free trip to Hawaii? You still have no idea what it means.

But it's the damn focus of the damn contract!

Maybe it's just your lame excuse for doing this self-indulgent, twisted little caper.

God. You're awful! Why can't you just be on my side for once?

I'm always on your side, twit. You, obviously, don't know what side you're on.

I'm… on Magic's side.

Really? So how's Magic doing lately? He looks tired and pissed, kind of like you.

Sam resumed seething, crawling, and chanting. Yeah, he absolutely wanted to strangle the bitch. *That* he could be sincere about. As the ordeal wore on, he plotted how to exact revenge—a welcome diversion to his current misery. Kicking her ass was out of the question, as she was half his age, two inches taller, certainly a lot stronger, and a something-belt in kung fu. She was also smarter and quicker and had already proven how easily she could shred him into kibble with her tongue. Complaining would only send her into more fits of riotous cackling. There were only two ways out of this hell. One was to keep crawling and shredding himself to raw meat; the other was lying on the kitchen counter and growing more attractive.

Five minutes later, Lady Indigo appeared in the doorway, naked and glistening wet from the shower. She stood with arms and legs akimbo and ordered Sam to look at her body—her big, beautiful, queen bitch body with her lesbian tits and nipple and labia rings shining. Her timing with this malicious tease was impeccable.

An erotic response was unimaginable; Sam could barely lift his chin from the carpet. "Why are you punishing me like this?" he could barely croak out.

"Punishment? What punishment? You wanted atonement, didn't you? Do you understand the difference?"

"No." He laid his face back on the carpet, too tired to hold it up.

"I told you to chant with sincerity," Lady Indigo said. "I want to hear sincerity, damn it, and so does Magic. Not some bullshit mumbo jumbo."

Sam substituted growling through his teeth for sincerity, and Lady Indigo decided not to press the matter. She took her beautiful, naked, queen bitch body back into her room. The point of her blatantly sexual display was not lost on him, and he added it to his growing shit list.

He resumed crawling and growling out his chant, assuming nothing worse could happen… until Danielle walked into the room, stepped over him like he was a pile of dirty laundry, and retrieved a book from a shelf. She detoured to step over him again and returned to her room without saying a word. Sam had plenty of words for her but wisely kept to his chanting.

The hour finally ended—the longest hour ever in Sam's life. Even longer than Lady Indigo time at its worst. Sam was too drained and wasted to even swear. There was no triumph of an ordeal survived, no elation of an edge confronted, and no staggering epiphany to make it worthwhile. Only dark, sullen mud that could not be scraped off. Lady Indigo shoved him into the closet.

"Write!" She slammed the door shut and locked it. "And no fucking bullshit this time!" she roared through the door.

He was too wasted to even get angry, plan how to get even, or even figure out what to do next, other than follow her orders. He wrote, "What a fool I was for thinking I could fool Lady Indigo. Now I know atonement is more than apologizing. It is not punishment. Now I understand that magic is a warrior waiting for me." Sam looked at the words on the paper as if they were centipedes, ugly and repulsive. It was bullshit. He wrote that down as well and decided to add nothing more.

Later, the bathroom mirror didn't reflect a strong, unashamed explorer, but clearly showed him with every miserable inch what a victim looked like. His chest and belly were abraded red and flecked with carpet lint and filth. His cock looked even worse. His brain felt shredded and bleeding as well. Seeing the destruction in his reflection amplified his fury tenfold. Maybe this was why Viridian hated mirrors so much.

Victim. There was no mistaking the battered man in the mirror for anything else. Sam utterly loathed being a victim, as would anyone in their right mind. Yet here he was, obviously in the wrong mind, being a victim and getting ready for more. The mirror was trying to tell him something, but what? Being a victim sucked? He already knew that, but there was something else just beyond his reach. He didn't know what it was, and, even more puzzling, he didn't care.

He gave the journal to Lady Indigo, resisting the temptation to hurl it at her, which was impossible anyway in handcuffs. She read the passage without comment. Her silence disturbed him more than one of her screaming fits. She closed the book.

"Get back to work," she said, and nothing more.

The enervating ordeal did not excuse him from housecleaning, which again he was to do naked and still handcuffed. Every time he glared at

Lady Indigo, she burst out laughing. The angrier he got, the more she loved it. Danielle understood this about as well as he did and simply watched, bemused, as he bumbled through the chores. Sam managed to scrub, dust, and vacuum, but washing the windows again exposed his predicament to the city. Well, if Lady Indigo didn't care, neither would he. *Fuck them all.*

Lady Indigo was not yet finished with his head.

"Go into your cell and write another poem," she said, "about what a dominatrix is for."

Sam immediately had several ideas, all of them dead wrong and sure to invite more carpet swimming. He was totally depleted of energy and too depressed to even be angry, but he came up with this:

> *She is not her shiny leather, nor her silky breasts.*
> *She is not my wildest fantasy, where all desire rests.*
> *She is not a vicious whipping, nor crawling on the floor.*
> *She is not the queen of chaos, perhaps She's something more.*
> *She holds a door wide open and presents it to her thrall.*
> *He holds the gift in wonder and sees She's really not there at all.*

Warily, Sam recited the poem to Lady Indigo. Astonishingly, he got a smile instead of a snarl and a crack on the backside.

"Bingo," she said. "There's something very important in that poem. Now go find it."

"But what? Where?"

"Think about it. Think about what happened today. All this is really for your benefit, even the crawling."

Sam was dumbfounded. "Benefit? My God, how can this possibly be for my benefit?"

"Read your poem," she said. "Think about doors and a dominatrix."

Her words went in one ear and out his ass. Sam again read the poem, not sure what he was looking for, and was stopped by *She's really not there at all.* That was the key, he was sure, but it clattered down the drain, and he wasn't up to chasing after it.

After another dreary vegetarian silage supper on the floor, Sam cleaned up the kitchen and dumped the leftovers into the compost bin, presumably for their next meal. Lady Indigo dragged him into the hallway, removed the handcuffs, and chained his wrists up to the ceiling. She snapped clothespins on his nipples and flogged the tar out of the man. Sam was still too angry to enjoy the beating, and he miserably resisted it.

Without taking a break, Lady Indigo unchained Sam, led him into the living room, bent him over the huge television console on his belly, and secured his wrists and ankles to the console's four legs. Danielle sat on the sofa filing her nails. Lady Indigo lit a taper and dripped hot wax on his back and butt as he howled and struggled. Danielle kept filing, regarding the scene with as much interest as she would a credit crawl.

Lady Indigo left the room, leaving Sam stretched uncomfortably tightly over the console and growing increasingly unsettled by Danielle's silent indifference. Lady Indigo returned, carrying a stainless-steel tray bearing a bottle of hydrogen peroxide, gauze pads, and several dozen packets of disposable hypodermic needles. Sam had previously discussed his interest in play piercing, but this venue was not what he had in mind, as if anything around this loony place ever was.

Lady Indigo swabbed his entire back with peroxide and went to work. Sam closed his eyes and held his breath. To his surprise, the first two needles went through each earlobe. The intense pain startled him, and he yelped. *Jesus, is this what girls have to go through to get earrings?* Danielle stopped filing and was now paying close attention.

"Good," Lady Indigo said. "Very nice little ear studs."

She put a needle through a pinch of skin on the back of his neck and then another an inch lower. She repeated this procedure on either side of his spine down to his butt. After the first few needles, Sam's endorphins took over, each needle feeling like a tiny, electric shock, like a kiss from a very large and mischievous spider. Lady Indigo stepped back to admire her handiwork. She swabbed his butt and inserted the remaining dozen or so needles.

Sam remained bound and perforated like that while Lady Indigo and Danielle watched television, seemingly oblivious to the unusual decoration atop it. The program was a repeat episode of *Northern Exposure*, one he'd already seen. It would run for an hour. His outstretched arms ached and the needles began to burn, and he knew the next hour would not be pleasant.

It wasn't. For a distraction, he visualized the scenes as the dialogue ran, absolutely sure the habitués of Cicely, Alaska, had never had a bound, naked pincushion draped over their show. The television heated his belly, and he feared what the radiation might be doing to his gonads. He dared not move a muscle for fear of the needles tearing the skin. The clothespins on his nipples decided to bite down harder. His cock, which should have been relishing every second of this, was AWOL.

He thought of a *Monty Python* skit. "What's on the telly?" he snickered.

"Shut the fuck up," said Lady Indigo.

In his opinion, *Northern Exposure* was the only thing on television worth a hoot, but he was darn glad when it was over. Lady Indigo jerked out the needles and dabbed the dribbles of blood. She told him to shower, go to his cell, and write in his journal.

He didn't write a word. His anger precipitated into a cold, hard resolve. He swore he'd leave the next morning and never return. That gave him comfort throughout the night.

Despite himself and his steadfast vow, at midweek Sam called Lady Indigo, looking for sympathy, explanations, clues, anything to lead him out of the hellish turmoil and confusion the previous session had fomented. It all came out as one continuous whine.

"I didn't like Danielle watching me," he said.

"Tough tit," said Lady Indigo. "She lives here."

"I didn't understand those stu… rules I had to follow."

"I know. You're not supposed to understand them. You're supposed to follow them."

"And all the chanting and crawling. It was horrible. I hated it. I hated just about everything."

"Everything I do," she said wearily, "I do for a good reason. This is no game. I told you it's all for your benefit. You seem unable to grasp that."

Sam was floundering. "Grasp what?" He felt her patience growing thin, but so was his and pressed on. "I almost walked out. Several times. This is not what I signed up for."

"What did you think you were signing up for? Jesus! The contract couldn't have spelled it out any clearer."

Sam said nothing.

"Do you want to end the contract?" Lady Indigo asked.

Sam thought for several moments. She remained on the line, silent.

"No, I don't," he sighed. "But now I don't know *what* I signed up for. I thought I did, but it hasn't turned out that way."

"Just like life?"

"Yeah. Just like life. And I don't understand this contract any better."

Lady Indigo softened. "I think you do. Read your poem again. Ask yourself that question: what's a dominatrix for?"

Sam thought about it. *She wasn't really there at all.* "A doorway?"

"Bingo."

"Um, maybe Magic is a doorway, too?"

"Double bingo!"

"But a doorway to what?"

"You tell me," Lady Indigo said. "Again, how do you stand empowered in the face of disempowerment? Last week, I gave you disempowerment in spades. Being a victim doesn't get much worse, does it? Now what are you going to do about it, *Magic,* hmm?"

"I don't know. I don't even know how to find out."

"I'm not the one disempowering you," she said. "You are. See you Saturday." She hung up.

The pineapple in his throat said the woman was right. It was true; he hadn't a clue what she was trying to teach him. He felt like he was crawling around a dark room with a hammer, randomly banging on the floor, hoping to hit a nail.

Oh, you poor, sad, pitiful boy. Tell me, how many dykes does it take to screw in a twit's light bulb?

This isn't a joke!

Oh, but it is. You love playing the victim. It's comfy, isn't it? No responsibilities, no work, no thinking. All you have to do is lie down and suffer. How does that feel? Nice, right?

It sucks.

Sucks is an opinion, not a feeling.

I hate it!

Another opinion. Well, if you're feeling so horribly victimized, then why do you stay?

I'm in it too far to back out now.

That's a fabulous reason. Try that out on Lady Indigo the next time you feel like getting annihilated.

26

THE GODDESS

LADY GREY STOOD BESIDE THE LECTERN on the Planet S/M stage without any notes. At first glance she seemed more at home in an accounting office than a dungeon. She was around fifty and a little plump; had short salt-and-pepper hair; wore not a scrap of leather; and had hung her glasses around her neck from a band decorated with cartoon characters. Despite her schoolmarm visage, Lady Grey was a professional dominatrix and rumored to be a ferocious one who swung in every direction on the sexual compass. Indeed, she projected dominance like a lighthouse.

"The title of my talk tonight," she began, "is edgeplay."

Sam was one of a hundred people in the audience. He hoped this evening's presentation would address how to survive a crazy dominatrix with a poetry fetish, or something equally relevant to his current situation. He'd heard about edgeplay and how BDSM edgeplay fanatics looked down their pierced noses at everything else on the kinky menu. Sam remembered Lady Indigo mentioning she liked edgeplay. *So let's see what it's all about.*

"The kind of edgeplay I'll be discussing tonight," Lady Grey said, "is about self-discovery and growth. It's an intense spiritual exercise, a form of tantra. You pursue an extreme and possibly dangerous activity that gives you an opportunity to find and confront a personal limit and then break through it. That limit can be psychological or physical—whatever you've got. That's where you'll find the true transformative power and potential of s/m."

That magazine article about shamanism had said basically the same thing. Sam was now listening carefully.

"Each of us has a choice," she said. "Do we want to expand and be truly alive, or not? Do we want to read only X number of books in our lives, or have Y number of friends, or eat at Z number of restaurants? Or push ourselves beyond that? Pushing can be a lot of work. It can be difficult and scary. Sometimes we need something or someone else to push us, and that's what dungeon edgeplay offers.

"Pain is commonly involved in edgeplay, as few things get edgier than that. People choose to use pain in different ways. For some, it's the sheer enjoyment of pain as a sensation, such as a good flogging. Pain can also heighten sexual release; just ask any masochist. To other folks, playing with pain is about achieving a personal best, like how many needles, how many lashes, and how much weight they can take, and so on. And for a few of us, pain and discomfort become the vehicle for exploration, to see what's on the other side of their endurance. To see what's beyond their edge. That's what my talk is about."

Sam's recent experience on Lady Indigo's carpet made him wonder about this. He'd been on the other side of his endurance to be sure, and it had looked like more carpet, not nirvana. So where was this promised tantric reward?

"Some may question whether edgeplay is necessary for personal growth," Lady Grey continued. "Of course it isn't. There are many paths that lead to self-awareness, to enlightenment. And by enlightenment I don't mean sitting in a cave while you fly around the cosmos in your astral body. I consider anything new that you learn about yourself, no matter how profound or trivial, an enlightenment experience. You can go sit in a cave for years and meditate if that's what works for you. Or sit in an ashram. Or just sit on your butt, if you do it mindfully. Spiritual disciplines are just that—discipline. Practice and persistence. And that's just fine for some folks.

"But others need something faster, harsher, and more immediate, like a good swift kick in one's spiritual ass. That's what edgeplay gives you, if you're willing to bend over, so to speak. Earlier I used the word *tantra*. People think tantra is about having wild, uninhibited sex and lots of it, and say, 'Oh boy, that's for me!' *Not*. The practice of tantra advocates using any worldly experience as an opportunity for enlightenment in the moment. Sex certainly qualifies as a worldly experience, and so does BDSM play.

What you do is not as important as how you do it. And the more intense the act, the more likely it will provide a tantric opening."

Sam recalled that previous lecture on tantric yoga and had heard nothing remotely like this. Apparently Mauve hadn't either. He'd already discovered that intense acts were the main course for his contract with Lady Indigo, but was its purpose also this tantric enlightenment? Was that what she'd meant about magical s/m? And when's it supposed to happen?

Maybe when it wants to.

Do you know anything about this stuff?

What am I, a fucking guru?

"In an s/m scene you're doing something edgy anyway," Lady Grey said. "Usually you're playing with fear and pain. Then why not go a step further and use those elements to confront your hidden limitations? Fear and pain are fundamental human responses. They're absolutely necessary for survival. Fear tells you there's danger, and pain tells you there's been damage to the body. Any sensible person would respect those boundaries, and that's what safe, sane, and consensual play encourages us to do.

"But edgeplay pushes on that slogan, and that's what makes it so controversial in the BDSM community. There are plenty of guidelines and information about playing safely and responsibly, but not for edgeplay because of its very nature and because the play varies with each person. Violence is often associated with BDSM because that's what a lot of play looks like, but that's not always the case. Both tantra and edgeplay use violence as well, but not limited to physical violence. Violence is being done to one's preconceptions and beliefs, which can be far more jolting than a cane to the butt.

"Using fear, pain, and danger as tools for personal growth are not just confined to the dungeon," Lady Grey went on. "A man once asked me if edgeplay was limited to just s/m. 'What about rock climbing or skydiving?' he said. That was a good point. Edgeplay is everywhere you look, wherever there's a challenge. Edges can be physical, like the examples he gave. But just as risky is standing in front of a room full of strangers and giving a speech or a music recital.

"Physical challenges often involve pain, perhaps not from a whip, but from intense exertion. Pain is pain, no matter what the source. Although I've never done it, I imagine reaching the top of a mountain after an arduous climb can change someone profoundly. And I've recently learned about a way to get down from a mountain called base jumping, where you glide back to earth. Not for me, *thank you*! The same goes for skydiving. Gravity doesn't give you a safe word.

"Speaking of slamming into something," said Lady Grey, "edges are not subtle. It's like running into a brick wall at full speed. In fact, finding an edge is often called hitting a wall. You may not know what the wall is, or where it is, but you'll know you've just hit something and can go no further. That's your edge. And that wall is almost always fear. It could be a concrete fear, like the fear of needles—"

"That's called trypanophobia," volunteered a man in the back.

"Thank you," Lady Grey said. "It seems we have a phobia-freak in the house. Then there are abstract fears, like the fear of open spaces, called agoraphobia, and the fear of its opposite, enclosed spaces, claustrophobia. That one's a popular game in dungeons. My personal favorite is the fear of intimacy—"

"Aphenphosmophobia!" the man shouted.

Lady Grey put on her glasses and scanned the room until she found the culprit. Sam had never seen proverbial eye-daggers until now, and that convinced him never to set foot in her dungeon. The guy's smile, however, suggested his intention with Lady Grey was the opposite. Baiting a top was a common game for horny—and stupid—bottoms. *This guy must have a death wish,* Sam thought. *I can relate to that.*

"To continue," Lady Grey said, turning away from the loudmouth, "fear is necessary for a creature's survival, especially ours. It's there for a good reason. Our brains are actually hard-wired to fear. That's the reptile brain's job, to keep us constantly alert for threats. That enabled cave… persons to avoid being eaten by predators when we were first becoming people. Fear tells you there's danger—go no further and get your ass out of there.

"But some fears no longer serve us. True, we're no longer running from sabertooth tigers and dinosaurs and things, but being asked on a coffee date can be just as threatening to the reptile brain as being stalked by a tiger. In fact, for many of us, that could be the point! But there are also other fears—irrational fears—that we carry around from our upbringing that can unconsciously constrict our lives. Those are fears we've created for ourselves, or have been created for us, and for reasons we don't always understand. Some are called phobias, as was just pointed out, and can present some nice, juicy edges.

"In edgeplay, and most s/m play for that matter, fear and danger are tools that can be just as effective as a flogger or cane. The dungeon challenges our conceptions of safety and well-being. And challenges, as mountain climbers know, are where real growth happens. In a dungeon, you know that your top is not going to cut out your gizzard, but the fact that she *could* is the edge. We all have different edges, and if someone wants to do gizzard play, well, that's up to them. Edgeplay can illuminate our fears in very dramatic and unmistakable terms. What we do with that is up to us. Then it takes a courage, and a lot of it, to proceed. Is everyone with me so far? Any questions?"

A woman in front asked, "How do you know the difference between a fear that's necessary and one that's not?"

"Only you can answer that," Lady Grey said. "In edgeplay, despite the presence of danger, you'll be in a safe place to find out, as strange and contrary as that may sound. In addition to discovering what you fear, you're also presented with choices. You can see your edge, your wall, as a legitimate fear and sensibly back off. You can simply be afraid of it and run away. Or you can choose to break through and see what's on the other side."

"But that can be potentially damaging," the woman persisted. "You're opening yourself up to some pretty serious emotional trauma, and you only have, what, some unqualified, possibly unstable dominant to save you? That's… just plain stupid! My God."

"You're absolutely right," said Lady Grey. "Depending on the top to save you *is* stupid, and it takes a stupid top to believe she or he can do that. The foundation of edgeplay is taking responsibility for yourself, and that can be a powerful edge in itself. In fact, it commonly is. The top serves as a guide and no more. Some tops are perceptive and experienced enough to know how to guide you and where they're guiding you to. But there are no classes that teach this. There is no certification. So you must know how to protect yourself, and do it with impeccability."

That word caught Sam's ear.

"I still say it's stupid and dangerous," muttered the woman.

"Well," Lady Grey said, "that certainly counts as a valid edgeplay decision and worthy of respect. But you've raised a critical issue, and the rest of us would do well to think about that. Thank you, dear."

Lady Grey looked out at the audience. "BDSM, by its very nature, is dangerous. It invites edgeplay, and one should not go there lightly, because who knows what you'll find? Keep in mind that, unlike plummeting to earth while depending only on a thin piece of nylon cloth to save you, in a dungeon you can always stop the fall with just a word. That's an edgeplay decision as well."

Sam recalled his recent dance with fear when Carmine had hand-cuffed him. That qualified as an edge to be sure, though it hadn't been talked about that way. He had freaked, begged, and fled, but those weren't choices—they were the only options available. No edgeplay growth there. What should he have done differently? Flee sooner? Beg more sincerely?

His intimate evening with Morgaine had been a nonstop plummet into fear; his only intention had been to survive, and with all his body parts intact. Edgeplay and enlightenment were obviously irrelevant to the woman, although he did learn a great deal afterward, no thanks to her. Sam wondered what choices he'd make now if he were to see Mistress Monster again.

And now with Lady Indigo, it seemed like he was living in Edge City. He wasn't sure why, but tonight's talk seemed to promise a way through the smorgasbord of torments she relished cooking up. It was worth the risk to raise his hand. "What do you do when you find an edge?" he asked.

"Ah, that's the true gift of edgeplay," Lady Grey answered. "That's where the rubber meets the road, as they say. But there's no single answer to that question because there's a different answer for everyone. The best advice I have is to keep your head and trust you'll know what to do in the moment. And you will, with the help of an experienced top who's been there. Good question."

"Are you saying that edgeplay needs to be consensual?" asked a woman in the back.

Sam recognized the voice and turned to look. The question had come from a tall, statuesque woman with a blonde buzz cut standing in the back of the room. His diaphragm seized. He imagined her with a dark wig: Mistress Morgaine. He finally saw her face—she was achingly beautiful. Standing close to her was a smaller woman whose head was completely shaved and whose neck was encircled by a wide leather collar. Sam quickly looked away, fearing he'd be recognized. Fear again, just at the sight of her. What was his edge now?

"Absolutely," said Lady Grey to Morgaine. "You can't push your sub-missive off a cliff and then tell him 'Surprise! We're now doing edgeplay!' Even though you can't say where he'll find his edge, or what it looks like, he still has to know what the game is, and what it's about, and consent to it. Otherwise, there can be serious damage, as was just pointed out."

"I disagree," said Morgaine. "A domme is entitled to do whatever she wants to her slave. That's what he's paying her for. The slave has his safe word, and it's his responsibility to use it. He's there for my pleasure. I'm not there for his personal growth. His welfare is his own concern and not mine."

"You're right," Lady Grey said. "A domme is entitled to create her own rules and agendas. If her goal is to just demolish people—and there are some who want demolition and will gladly pay for it—that's her business. But if her goal is to use her dungeon to create magic, well then, that's *my* business."

Creating magic. That jerked Sam out of his Morgaine-induced whirlpool of worry. He surreptitiously eyed the woman, who was now intently focused on Lady Grey thinking God knew what. He was safe—for the moment.

Unruffled, Lady Grey continued her talk. Morgaine folded her arms across the balcony of her bosom and said nothing more. Sam decided to sneak out during the break, before she could identify him and finish his demolition right there on stage. He was fleeing again, but now it was a conscious choice, albeit a no-brainer. *This is an edge I can live without.*

As SESSION FOUR WITH LADY INDIGO approached, Sam began to think he'd finally gotten a handle on the woman's unorthodox curriculum. Dominatrices and doorways, at least hers, were finally making a smidgen of sense. Was this all about self-awareness and growth, as Lady Grey had said? Considering Lady Indigo's ongoing obsession with impeccability, the two dommes seemed to be in agreement.

But when Saturday morning arrived, he felt like he'd forgotten everything everyone had said. Sullen, insecure, and in a fog of despair, he stood at Lady Indigo's door wondering what was behind it. He was not looking forward to any more carpet crawling.

He was in for a surprise. Lady Indigo locked him into his neck collar and told him to kneel in the slave position.

"This session will be a little different," she said with an impish smile. "You will be entitled to receive three scenes of your own choosing and device."

Sam could hardly believe it; he had the run of the candy store.

"There are two rules," she continued. "One, you will have to beg me for the scene, and two, I have to agree to it."

"No problem," Sam drooled.

"No problem, eh?" Lady Indigo laughed. "And remember sex is O-U-T."

To emphasize the point, she was wearing a baggy sweatshirt and sweatpants she'd no doubt scrounged from a pile of Salvation Army rejects. Still, Sam knew what was underneath. Despite her thoroughly asexual wardrobe and stern warning, Sam was fired up and ready to go. *Ah, this is the sweet reward for enduring last week's mammoth mountain of shit!* But Lady Indigo's seemingly generous offer made him wary. Nothing about her or her unpredictable agenda was ever as it appeared, as he was repeatedly and painfully learning.

Sam burned through his domestic chores, happily preoccupied with designing the three scenes. Danielle was away for the weekend, leaving him and Lady Indigo alone together, finally. After completing his tasks in record time (a testimony to the power of proper motivation), he asked to be chained up and flogged, something he knew was mutually enjoyable.

Lady Indigo just stood there and stared at him. Sam stared back, wondering what the fuck was going on now.

"There were two rules," she said, "and you've forgotten them already?"

Sam dropped to his knees and repeated his request. Lady Indigo smiled.

"Up," she said and chained his wrists to the overhead screw eyes, stretching his arms a bit more tightly than usual. She attached a spreader bar to his ankles to keep his legs far apart.

"Um, ah, this is a little uncomfortable," he said.

"Tough shit," said Lady Indigo. "Remember, you asked for this."

"Wait a minute. This is supposed to be my treat."

"I'm giving you your treat. So shut up."

Sam darkened. *Just whose candy store is this?*

Lady Indigo then attached the cock ring in a way that painfully dislocated one testicle. Sam winced and said so. With a hard glare she ignored him and locked the ring. She dragged out her entire arsenal of impact implements and arranged them on the floor. Now both of his balls were aching, but Sam said nothing, fearing he would jeopardize the beating to come.

And it came, starting with the medium-sized flogger, warming up his back and butt with restrained blows. She switched to the larger flogger and used less restraint. The whacks turned into brutal and unwelcome thuds, which worsened the pain in his groin, and doubled his misery. He feared damage to the delicate tubules and blood vessels.

"My balls!" he gasped. "My balls really hurt."

Lady Indigo paid no attention and continued beating him.

"Please! No more!"

The flogger didn't comply.

"*Crimson!*" he screamed.

Lady Indigo immediately stopped and removed the cock ring.

"That's what safe words are for," she snapped. "It's your job to use them, not mine!"

"I'm sorry."

"Don't you apologize to me! You apologize to Magic!" Lady Indigo shouted into his face. "Remember what the contract said? You swore an oath! You swore not to abandon yourself, not abdicate your responsibilities. Don't you fucking see that? S/m is a very dangerous business. I've told you that a thousand times. Now do you understand why? Now do you hear me?"

Sam nodded. Getting scolded was bad enough in any circumstance, but while chained and naked, it surpassed intolerable. There was no place to hide, nothing he could say to defend himself as there was no defense. He felt like a little boy getting chastised, so he did what any five-year-old would do in this situation: he started bawling.

Lady Indigo waited for him to stop sniffling, then softened. "Well," she said, "it looks like I hit one of your hot buttons."

"Hot button?"

"Yeah. You went from a man to a child in a heartbeat, and you had absolutely no control over it, right?"

"Yeah."

"You're not a child anymore, yet you reacted like one. All it took was just a few harsh words from me."

"Just a few?" Sam said, struggling to get his adult brain working again.

"That doesn't matter. What's important is that one of your hot buttons is still alive and as potent as ever."

"I'm not sure what you mean."

"Some people call it a preconditioned response. Others call it karma. I call it a hot button. We get them from our childhood. They're programmed into you without your knowledge, and they hijack you when they're pushed. Just like now."

"They're, like, hidden?"

"Yeah, just like little booby traps. Look at what we've done. I've exaggerated one of your childhood situations to the extreme. I've chained you up, beaten you, and scolded you without mercy. Disempowerment doesn't get much worse, does it?"

"No." Sam thought about Miss Miller shaming him about the giant mole people. At least he hadn't been naked, but he'd felt like it.

"So how do you protect yourself? How do you keep a warrior's stance in the face of such a ruthless barrage?"

"I don't know."

"Impeccability!" she said sharply. "That's why you're here, damn it! That's why I'm doing this to you. We just found one of your hot buttons, and I'm going to keep pressing it all day long if I have to. I told you I was going to fuck with you without mercy, and now you know why."

She let loose with a laughing fit. "I swear, sometimes I like pressing hot buttons more than my own clit!"

Sam's back went up. "So this is all about fucking with me?"

Lady Indigo's cackling tapered off. "No, it's not, although I'm entitled to have some fun too, you know."

She let him sulk for a moment. "This is about disabling hot buttons. The way to do that is to keep pressing them until they no longer work. That teaches you it's only a button and not you. That's how you make a hot button go cold. It has to do with growing new neural pathways or something."

Sam remembered Judith had said something similar. It just may be true. "So how many hot buttons do I have?" he asked.

"Don't worry," Lady Indigo laughed. "You'll never run out of them."

Despite himself, he laughed too, accidentally snorting out a gibbet of snot. He was still chained and found the mess almost as embarrassing as his hot button. "Talk about being a child. I can't even wipe my own nose."

Lady Indigo cleaned him up. "Well, we don't chain children from ceilings and whip them, do we? Or, at least, we shouldn't. Remember that using your safe word is not an admission of weakness, or defeat, or cowardice, or failure. It's respect for your body and being. It's guarding your sacred being, remember? Feeling like a wimp is just your story about it, nothing more. Do you understand that?"

"I think so."

"Here's something else to remember. When you're restrained and vulnerable, like you are right now, you're incapable of protecting your body, but you still can protect your being. Be your own impeccable protector, right? You must create internal protection, a boundary that's solid and inviolable. And you have to make it out of absolutely nothing but your intention because that's all you have. Remember your story and what your sword was?"

That made Sam think.

"And a boundary need not be a walled fortress," she said. "It can be a conscious choice."

"A choice?"

"Yes! As simple as a choice! Look at what we just did. You can choose to receive the pain and enjoy it, or you can choose to stop it with your safe word, like you finally did. You can even disregard my scolding and say, 'What the fuck is her problem?' Now just imagine having *that* as an option!"

"That's what a warrior does," Sam said, thinking about swords and shields.

"Praise the Goddess!" shouted Lady Indigo. "The boy is finally catching on."

She picked up the large flogger and untangled its thongs. "I believe we have some unfinished business, wouldn't you say?"

Sam smiled and nodded. The refrigerator returned with a vengeance. Now it was welcome.

Midway through the flogging, Lady Indigo became overheated, stripped off her shirt, and resumed beating him. Her breasts and nipple rings bobbed and jiggled with each stroke. She seemed not to mind him ogling them in the least. Surprisingly, he didn't mind not being able to get at them, either. He noticed small bruises around both of her nipples and asked about it.

"Clothespins," she grinned. "They were whipped off with a riding crop. It hurt like the holy bejeezus. I really got my ass creamed last night."

"You? Bottoming? What?" This was inconceivable.

"Yep. To a totally vicious dyke at a women's party. It was divine. Then I did the same thing to Danielle."

"Danielle? Didn't you say she wasn't kinky?" Sam would have given anything to have been there and seen that.

"I said she was occasionally kinky. I'm corrupting her."

"Did she like it?"

"I liked it." Lady Indigo smiled.

After a rest, Sam begged for his second scene. He'd already outlined it in his journal.

"Since I finally know how to use my safe word," he said, "I want to forfeit it."

"Are you sure?" The tone in her voice implied he'd better rethink this. Sam nodded. He had thought and rethought about this, for all the good thinking did him.

"That's heading into edgeplay," she said. "Do you know what that's about?"

"I think so."

"You *think* so? Do you think you're ready for that?"

Sam thought about Lady Grey's talk. "Is anyone ever really ready?"

"Point taken."

"Take me to an edge," he said.

"Okay, cowboy. But remember, it's your decision."

According to his instructions, Lady Indigo placed a kitchen chair in the closet, sat him down, handcuffed his wrists behind his back, and duct taped his legs wide apart. Then she dangled a ball gag in front of him. His face went pale. This definitely was not part of his script.

"I can't tolerate gags," he said. "They make me gag. I don't want to drown in my own vomit." He'd heard this was possible in s/m play and couldn't imagine a worse way to die.

"Then why didn't you list it as a hard limit? That's what making the list was all about!"

Shit! It just hadn't occurred to him. What else hadn't? "I'm sorry. Please don't."

"I'm not the one you should apologize to!" She held the gag under Sam's nose. He stiffened and tried to pull away. He couldn't. "No safe word, remember?"

"But this wasn't in the plan!"

"No safe word, *remember?*"

The unforgiving reality of nonconsensual play began to sink in. Lady Indigo rolled the ball around his lips and against his teeth, increasing his anxiety. It worked. She finally dropped the gag, much to his relief. She tore off two strips of duct tape and slapped them across his mouth. Relief abruptly ended when she pinched his nose, cutting off his breath. He jolted and jerked at his bonds. Anxiety exploded into primal, desperate panic. After a few more seconds, Lady Indigo released her grip and smiled.

"How's life without a safe word, cowboy?"

Sam's answer was wide eyes and flared nostrils as he tried to suck in as much air as the narrow passages would allow. Lady Indigo waited until he finally caught his breath and calmed down.

"I warned you that s/m is dangerous," she said. "Now do you believe me?"

He nodded sheepishly.

"Do you want to continue?"

He hesitated, then nodded again. She tied a blindfold on him.

"You're going to damn well have to deal with this," she said.

Sam heard the clatter of instruments on a metal tray and knew what it was. One needle went through each nipple and one pierced the tip of his penis. Lady Indigo looped dental floss around the three needles and slowly drew them together so Sam could not sit upright without stressing the tissue. She removed the blindfold.

"I'll return in one hour," she said. "And not a minute before."

She closed and locked the closet door.

One hour in real or Lady Indigo time? It didn't matter. Seeing the needles turned him on. He tugged on them. That turned him on even more. Then he remembered his previous inauspicious visit to the candy store and became uneasy. True enough, the real ordeal soon emerged from behind him. His upper arms and shoulders began to cramp and ache from their restraint. He tried to adjust their position, but the handcuffs wouldn't allow it. The cuffs also sharply bit into his wrists, causing even more discomfort. He could ease the growing stress in one shoulder but at the expense of the other. He had two choices: pain or agonizing pain. The needles were quickly forgotten.

The distress could only get worse, and it did. Lady Indigo's distorted time sense now became an issue, and a damned important one. The fire in both shoulders was constant and unrelenting. Like falling dominos, the pain crept into his neck muscles, which in turn stressed his deltoids, then the big latissimus muscles in his upper back. The true meaning of edgeplay hit him like a wrecking ball. He could not escape from the pain, nor his bondage, nor could he cry out for help. He was stuck without a prayer and totally dependent on a time-challenged, capricious sadist for salvation. *Edgeplay. Brilliant move, cowboy.*

Pah! You're not stuck, twit. People dying of cancer are stuck. Women in labor are stuck. So are men dying on a battlefield. They don't have a safe word. They won't become unstuck in forty-five minutes.

Oh God, what do I do?

Suffer! What else can you do? Duh!

Sam remembered what Lady Grey had said about dealing with an edge: you'll know what to do in the moment. *So what is the moment?* Excruciating, intractable pain. That was his reality and would remain so until the hour's end. *Then what do I do other than suffer?*

Then it occurred to him: pain was causing the suffering; they were not the same. He could do nothing about the pain, but could he choose not to suffer? The nipple clamps had shown him this was possible. *Choice.* Lady Indigo's recent words about it were still alive. So was *focus*, as she continually kept screaming at him.

He did. He concentrated on the fire in his shoulders, exploring it, even amplifying it, trying to feel pain as pure sensation rather than unbearable torment. Focus slipped him into a trance. The pain was still there, but it seemed to be happening to someone else. To his astonishment, he was actually finding the experience engaging.

Even more astonishing, Lady Indigo returned precisely in an hour, real time. When she saw Sam was in genuine distress, she immediately freed him. She vigorously massaged life back into his arms, shoulders, and neck.

"How was playing at the edge, cowboy?"

Sam didn't speak, but his glazed-over eyes must have said something. Lady Indigo looked into them and laughed.

"Find anything out there?" she asked.

I'll be damned if I didn't. "Yeah, I did."

"Keep it close," said Lady Indigo.

That evening brought his third romp in the playground. According to his wishes, Lady Indigo stretched him on the floor to four eyebolts set into the hallway's baseboard, again a bit tighter than he wanted, and went into her room to change. And change was never so dramatic. What emerged stunned him: the frumpy lesbian was now a devastatingly gorgeous vamp dressed in that long black lace gown of hers, cut low in the bosom. She'd brushed her hair to shine like burnished bronze, applied exotic eye makeup and lipstick, and, as usual, wore no underwear.

"Safe word?" Lady Indigo said.

Sam shook his head. The vamp grinned.

At either end of the hallway, red tapers burned in their holders. Lady Indigo picked one up, held it waist high, and let a drop of molten wax fall on Sam's already-inflamed nipple. Her aim was off. The next drop was dead center, as confirmed by his scream. She got the other nipple after six tries, but target practice was not the point. Burning Sam was.

Lowering the candle greatly improved her aim as well as making the wax much hotter. She burned through the first candle and held the second even lower. She left no part of him unscathed; his body soon looked like a measles victim gone riot. At one point, the flame was only an inch above his body. Sam begged her to stop, but she would not stop. He howled and tried to twist away from the candle, but he could not escape, and she still would not stop. Truthfully, he wanted to be nowhere else.

Lady Indigo stood astride his head and continued dripping the paraffin lava. Her long legs and sturdy thighs rose above him like massive columns in a cathedral nave soaring upward to meet the ethereal vault of her vulva. Her labia rings glittered like Venus in the evening sky. Sam stared into her vagina. He thought he could discern the vague form of a wrinkled eye hidden amid the folds of flesh.

In the next instant, the eye jumped out of her vagina and into focus, so clearly and so suddenly he startled. It was the eye of an unbelievably ancient woman. It seemed to pierce clear through him and beheld him without a trace of judgment or malice, desiring only to see the man who would offer himself like this. Sam felt his heart open of its own will, and the eye flooded him with an abundance of love and grace, incinerating all traces of his doubt and fear. It was the eye of the Goddess. He knew this with absolute certainty; it could be nothing else.

The eye melted back into the pink folds of Lady Indigo's vulva. Before vanishing, it left him with a single word: *paradox.* The hot wax continued to drip; he didn't notice. *How on earth or in heaven could I have made this up?*

After his sojourn, after he was released, and after picking off hundreds of hardened wax droplets from his body, Sam told Lady Indigo what he had seen. She only smiled, as if she knew what lived inside her sex. *What else did she have up there?* he thought. He also thought it most curious that Lady Indigo never assumed the mantle of Goddess, as dominatrices and other like-minded women were so fond of doing. She only called herself a student, nothing more.

"The eye gave me a message," he said. "She said—"

"No," she said sharply. "Don't speak it. Keep it close."

"But—"

"Some things should not be spoken. Putting it into words will drain its power. Talking about it, even to me, opens it to judgement and can diminish its value. Let it incubate. Keep it close. Do you understand?"

"I think so." He remembered deciding to keep the incident at the car wash to himself. Now he knew why.

"You've had enough for one day," Lady Indigo said and kissed firmly Sam on the lips, leaving him stunned and the room swirling. He left the following morning ecstatically in love with all life, and especially with Lady Indigo. *She kissed me. On the lips.*

I know, and I am not pleased. Don't get any steamy ideas, twit. Remember the contract.

Why would she kiss me, then?

Maybe she's fucking with your head again. Figure it out for yourself for once.

Was that really the Goddess I saw?

What, do you mean the hallucination?

Sam spent the week thinking about goddesses, dominatrices, women in general, and Lady Indigo in particular. He knew there was a powerful, mysterious, and vaguely conspiratorial connection between them, unsettling as that was. Women, he conceded, did live in a special room in the mansion of life, a room no man could enter. One major reason being that men squirt out only a teaspoon of gooey fluid, whereas women can squirt out a whole human being.

What a staggering miracle! Its implications became immediately clear. No wonder women seemed magical, sanctified, and therefore so threatening. No wonder they've been oppressed and vilified throughout history. Now he could understand how envy, fury, lust, and fear consumed and drove the inquisitors, witch-burners, misogynist priests, and politicians. And perhaps himself as well?

Mistress Morgaine's ludicrous feminist manifesto came to mind. At the time, it had seemed to be another arrogant affectation of the woman's arrogant profession. But was it more than just a dominatrix posturing? Perhaps it was a reasonable, even necessary, stand to take in defiance of overwhelming and equally arrogant male dominance. Maybe she had a goddess in her vagina too, where a man might encounter a flame-throwing harpy instead of the bosom of compassion.

Sam could feel his cage of sexism being rattled. *Why can't I see women simply as women? Why must they always be something else?*

That's so you can be someone else.

Huh?

It's obvious. You need to make women perfect and wise so in return their approval validates your worth. That's the only way you can feel good about your twit self. That's why you're so addicted to your safe man fixes. That's called a racket, and a damn transparent one at that. What a wimp!

It's much more complicated than that!

No, it's not. Just think about it. If you dare.

He dared. He wrote in his journal: "The joy of connection inherently contains the despair of separation. If a woman is responsible for one, she must be to blame for the other. Her smile is heaven; her scowl is hell. Women must be perfect, yet I hate it when they are, and then defile them when they're not. The Goddess is both forgiving and cruel, seductive and unattainable, the creator and destroyer. Is that what her eye meant by paradox?" Sam stared at his words.

What did I just tell you?

But Sam wasn't quite ready to become a goddess worshipper, whether she lived in Lady Indigo's cunt or not. That's because he was a devoted brain worshipper, and it got right to work trying to demolish the goddess and her enigmatic eye. The most logical explanation *was* a pain-induced hallucination, a common experience during periods of extreme stress, and being burned by hot candle wax certainly qualified. He considered visions, hallucinations, and dreams a product of neurochemistry and nothing more. Brain vomit, he called it, just random discharges to clean out the visual cortex, like a janitor sweeping the factory floor for the next shift. And that was that.

Except for a few annoying questions—such as why there was the distinct and overwhelming feeling of a presence behind that ancient eye, loving and compassionate, which deposited that single word into his pile of brain barf? And why was this presence wearing the face of the goddess? Not the vitriolic, male-negative goddess embraced by the more strident feminists. Nor was she the condescending and reproving matriarch of Heart Feather and her flock. This goddess felt different, more compelling, and far more inclusive.

And why did he see the eye of a crone and not of Captain Nemo or Batman? Both were heroic and meaningful childhood figures, but it was unlikely either would be hanging out inside a pussy. Sam could readily accept male authority, as most men did, but not female—most men couldn't—despite his fixation on dominatrices. Was this another learned sexist bias, or did it run deeper? The question seemed unanswerable, so he dropped it. He decided to declare the contract to be a game, an unusual experiment, and he, a man, not Magic, a weenie, would remain at the controls. And that was that, again.

Almost. But why was that presence unmistakeably *female*? Well, his brain said that since women had been playing ping-pong with his identity for decades, it seemed right that a feminine apparition should stop the game. The symmetry pleased him. He couldn't do this himself because he didn't believe in himself or his abilities. Lady Indigo couldn't do it because she was a woman and therefore part of the problem. But a Sam-centric, pain-induced vision of the alleged goddess delivering the message? An end-run around his male ego? Acceptable, and that was that, debate over. Period. His cage was again safe.

Absolutely brilliant, twit! That was a world-class exhibition of thinking. Now, what did all that get you?

My power and control back.

Oh? That sounds like more brain barf to me. Power and control are just your illusions, just like the fat man said.

Maybe you're an illusion, too?

Really, Sam. Do I act like one?

27

THE MUMMY

SAM STOOD AT LADY INDIGO'S DOOR the morning of session five and knocked, expecting more romps in the candy store. Instead, he strolled into the teeth of a furious lecture and got another ass kicking.

"You're just not getting submission," Lady Indigo hissed, again in blazing bitch mode. "You're not truly in the contract, and I'm getting goddamned tired of this!"

My God, where the hell did this shit circus come from?

Well, it's true, isn't it?

But how the hell did she know?

Why don't you ask her?

Because that would confirm his crime. It seemed like Lady Indigo had spies hidden in his head, and he kept forgetting that. Sam picked up his freshly kicked ass, stunned by the volatile unpredictability of the woman who was now staring at him like he was a pimple needing to be popped. That did it.

"What the fuck?" he shouted back, throwing caution out the window. "Haven't I done everything you said? I've been following all of your goddamned screwy rules! I've been doing everything you tell me! Just look at the bullshit I've gone through! What more do you want?"

"That's not good enough! You're still treating this like it's a game. Well, it's not! This is dangerous, really dangerous. It's real, so don't you fuck around with it!"

"Yes, ma'am." *Whatever the fuck you say, ma'am.*

"Did you just say 'ma'am'?" she screamed into his face.

"Lady!" He glared at her.

She outglared him back. Sam still hadn't a clue what the bitch was talking about or why she was so steamed, and she knew it. They were at a wall, the dimensions of which eluded him, and both of them had multiple head bruises. Lady Indigo waited to catch her breath.

"Go into your cell," she said, like a teacher disciplining a brat. "And write five pages on this subject: how can there be honor and value in submission? Five pages and not one fucking word less! Is that clear?"

Sam nodded. Lady Indigo ordered him out of his clothes, locked on his collars, shoved him into his cell, and slammed and locked the door.

"How long do I have?" he shouted through the door.

"Write!" came the answer.

Bitch!

But the bitch was again right. He was only acting submissively and would go no further. And why the hell should he? What was so damned special about submission? It fueled his fantasies but made for a living hell here on earth. He was at a wall all right, and paradox was written all over it in blood. *Paradox! Koans! Shit!*

He imagined that ancient eye looking over his shoulder—another damned woman to please. The other damned woman had told him to write. *Okay, I'm locked in here so let's do it.* Paradox. If the point of paradox was to be a pain in the ass, then it was working. How could he honor and respect himself while crawling on her filthy carpet? How could he be a strong man in control and a weak, pussy-whipped weenie at the same time? And always hovering about was her vexing, unfathomable question: how did one stand empowered in the face of disempowerment? The opposites swirled around as if he were peering into a smoke-filled kaleidoscope. Five pages? Not possible.

He stared at the closet wall through the bars of his own inner cage of sexist self-imprisonment. He could hear submission singing to him from the other side: "Mary had a little lamb, whose fleece was white as snow. And everywhere that Mary went, the lamb was sure to go."

Sam knew a message lurked in that mindless nursery rhyme, but he'd have none of it. Something inside him had to die, he concluded, something noble and vital, so he could crawl into the weenie world of submissive men who were slaves to their crotch, following Mary wherever she went. He just could not do this. He saw the contract going down in flames. Honor and value in submission? *No fucking way.*

Are you sure there's no fucking way?

Yeah. Absolutely.

Then why don't you leave?

Because the goddamned closet door is locked, that's why!

Oh? Has your safe word expired?

No, he'd give it one more try—maybe for the last time. The first page he wrote was pure drivel: "Some submission is acceptable. Certain situations demand it. We submit to traffic cops and the IRS. We submit to drill sergeants and schoolteachers. A child submits to his parents. A worker submits to his boss. A slave submits to his dominatrix."

The list went on, until Sam saw that submission was an endless row of pineapples he'd have to swallow every day and from everyone who handed them out. *Submission really sucks*, he concluded but did not write. It turned a man into an impotent, insipid shadow of himself until he could take no more, grabbed an assault rifle, and made his tormentors and anyone standing nearby submit to hot lead. That was probably how that atrocity happened; it was as good an explanation as any. Strength, value, honor, and submission clearly did not belong on the same page or even in the same book.

Then Sam stumbled onto the word *surrender*, and a light, albeit only one watt, went on. That gave him an idea—and a squiggle of hope. He rephrased his assignment: how can there be honor and value in surrender? That gave things a slightly different spin. Surrender didn't have to mean defeat, shame, or weakness. It wasn't about groveling at someone's feet. There was another kind of surrender, one where respect and honor flourished—even nobility.

He thought about yogis, nuns, monks, and lamas prostrating themselves before their deities, and another light lit up. The bedrock of their devotion was surrender to the will of God, Goddess, Allah, the Almighty, or whatever they chose to name it. And wasn't surrender to a higher power the essence of twelve-step programs? "Let go and let God"—is that what they said? No, he wasn't giving up his manhood, only its assumed, hubristic entitlements.

Entitlements. If Sam wasn't already sitting, that would have knocked him on his ass. The pursuit of male entitlement—an elemental universal force that rivaled gravity in its power and purpose. *We've made it into a religion,* he thought. *We'd rather die than give that up. My God!* For the first time, Sam saw his cage door begin to swing open.

More lights went on and things less drivelly started to appear on the page: "A student surrenders to his ignorance and submits to the wisdom of his teacher. The soldier surrenders to the reality of battle and submits to his officers. A father surrenders to the needs of his family and submits to a supervisor. A man surrenders to his libido and submits to a Dominatrix. A man surrenders his entitlements and submits to the will of his higher good.

"These situations demand that choice be exercised, for the individual's good or not. No one can truly make you do anything, despite how it may appear. There's always a choice. Accept the terms of your reality, and surrender is transformed into a place of grace and dignity. Humility replaces humiliation, and the real value of submission emerges."

What will she think of that? But it didn't matter. The words kept coming.

"We unconsciously submit to a tyrant within, our own ego, which is far more insidious than the most devious of our oppressors. The ego rules and imprisons us with its lengthy list of unreasonable demands, petty grievances, vain aspirations, addictive behaviors, and moronic notions about how to get all those things. We submit to a 24/7, year-round, lifelong, merciless Dominatrix who lets us believe that we are running the show.

"The dungeon is a classroom where you can't be saved by the bell. Despite its strange appearance, rules, tools, and activities, it teaches cause and effect in terms that are impossible to ignore. Adopting roles in a dungeon can illuminate and exaggerate what submission and surrender truly feel like, and how we use, are used, and are abused by these dynamics in our daily lives.

"A power gradient eventually emerges in almost all personal interactions; it has to. If you want something from another person, that fact gives them all the power. Knowing which end you're on can make or break a deal. If the deal is confusing, it could be because the gradient has not been clearly defined or is in contention.

"Knowing that you're being submissive gives you a clear choice whether or not to be. Unconscious submission invites a lifetime of abuse. Conscious submission allows us to function, function smoothly and with less conflict and more compassion. All other creatures have worked this out eons ago."

Lady Indigo read the five pages and seemed satisfied that Sam was at least in orbit around something. Sam felt like he'd just dodged a speeding bus. He had and didn't know it.

Then she locked him into that irritating leather waist harness and made ready to attach the nipple clamps. Sam told her about the left clamp always slipping off. She thought for a moment, went into her bedroom, and returned with stronger and, of course, more painful clamps, and roughly snapped them on. *I should have known.*

Lady Indigo sent him on two errands. The first was back to that kinky sex shop to buy a vibrating butt plug, larger than the finger-sized item that currently dwelled within him. The little plug was not arousing, more of an insult and annoyance than a torment. But a larger item loomed far more menacingly, and it worried him.

Sam crept into the store, his restraints creaking and nipples on fire, certain the sales staff had seen it all before. Alas, tattooed lady was not there. He located the anal accessory department, which seemed to be half the store, and grabbed a generic-looking rubber plug from the shelf. It was pink and vulgar, and everyone knew where it was going.

I do not believe what you just did. Oooh, I just can't wait for this!
What do you mean?
You'll see. Whoop!

He scuttled over to the cashier counter. A heavily pierced and tattooed Goth man stood behind it. He regarded Sam, who had not a sliver of metal through him or a speck of ink on him, as a tourist from Squaresville who had no business being there. To demonstrate otherwise, Sam plunked down the plug as casually as if it were a can of soda pop. The man looked at the plug, then at Sam, shook his head, and rang up the purchase without saying a word. *Fuck him.*

The second task was a more mundane purchase: shaving cream and a disposable razor. Lady Indigo said he was to shave off all his body hair below the neck, and she emphasized *all.* There would be an inspection afterward, and any stray hairs would be yanked out or burned off. *Yikes!*

Sam entered a convenience store, collar and clamps clinking and the harness betraying itself with every step. At the cash register, he kept rubbing his beard stubble to convince the cashier of his true intentions. The lady at the register noticed his collar and decided not to notice anything else.

Back at Lady Indigo's apartment and freed from all devices, Sam began the depilation. Lady Indigo pulled a chair into the bathroom, popped open a can of her ubiquitous Diet Pepsi, sat, and watched. Sam balanced uncomfortably on the icy bathtub rim and lathered up his legs. He knew that women shaved their legs all the time, but he had never actually seen it done. He was ill-prepared to negotiate all the complex curves and hollows, and soon the bathtub resembled the one in the film *Psycho*.

His confidence sorely shaken, Sam went after his crotch. It was tough going, scraping and hacking through the bush, but only a few red dots bloomed in the aftermath. Lady Indigo sat there, saying nothing, just watching and sipping. Next in line were his balls.

Danielle walked by the bathroom, saw what was happening, and stopped to watch. The two pairs of eyes made Sam's nervous grip on the razor even shakier, especially considering its target. He proceeded very carefully and finished with as many testicles as when he'd started. Danielle shrugged and walked away. *What was she expecting? To see me neuter myself?*

You'd need something better than a disposable razor. Why don't you go out and buy an Elasticator for our amusement?

Why don't you give me some peace?

Because this is too much fun to watch, that's why.

Sam then went after his arms and the sparse tundra on his chest. Shaving his armpits made him edgy, what with all the subaxillary nerves and veins running so close to the surface. But if girls could do it, then damn it, so could he. He rinsed, toweled himself off, and beheld a hairless person in the mirror. His skin felt very smooth and very sexy.

Now, isn't this interesting? Yeah, I'm totally cool with body shaving.

Lady Indigo was not; she immediately sensed something was off. She'd warned Sam that shaving the body hair, especially the pubic area, could have dramatic emotional repercussions. But the totally cool-with-body-shaving Sam stood confidently as she made her inspection with tweezers in one hand and cigarette lighter in the other. To his relief and her disappointment, she found it unnecessary to use either.

She leaned back and frowned. "What's with your anger?"

"What anger?" He was genuinely mystified.

"This anger." She poked his balls.

Sam looked down. And there they were: a grown man with little boy's balls, small, shriveled, and hairless. He'd never felt more naked. This was not smooth and sexy. This was very emasculating. And a woman had made him do it. Now he understood Samson's pickle.

"Yeah," he said. "I'm pissed all right, and getting more pissed. And I don't know why."

"Think of hair as your protection, your shield," Lady Indigo said. "Animals have it and we don't. We lost it long ago. But the body remembers it and how important it is."

"But why am I so angry about it?"

"You're feeling more naked and vulnerable and unprotected than ever, aren't you?"

"Well, yeah."

"That would piss off anyone," she said. "Now you need a shield in the worst way, right?"

"Yeah."

"So, Magic, where are you going to find one, hmm?"

He knew but didn't want to say.

Lady Indigo laughed. "If it's any comfort, it'll grow back. And besides, now you won't be screaming anymore when I pluck off candle wax, right?"

Despite himself, Sam laughed as well.

Lady Indigo withdrew the butt plug from the shopping bag and her jaw dropped. She held the package up to his face. "*This* is what you want?"

Sam's jaw dropped too, and so would his anus's, if it had one. During his hurried and nervous foray into the sex shop, he had unknowingly bought the largest plug in their stock, wider than Carmine's Rhinoceros and even more frightening. No wonder that Goth sales creep had looked at him askance.

Sam's ashen face delighted Lady Indigo, but she mercifully allowed him to return to the store to exchange it for one of more humane proportions.

"Next time, look at what you're buying," she admonished.

Sam dreaded what the Goth creep would have to say about this. But, oh joy, the tattooed lady was there instead. Even more joyous was that she remembered him and gave him a wink. He anxiously placed the item and receipt on the counter. She looked at the plug, then at him.

"Is there a problem, dear?" she smiled.

"Well, uh, yeah. Could I possibly please exchange this for—"

"For a bigger one?" she laughed. "Or one with spikes?"

"Oh no, no, no. Please?"

"Well, the package hasn't been opened," she said. "Go ahead, sweetie, and find your size."

After a little more prudent shopping, Sam picked out another plug, this one made for a smaller rhinoceros. The tattooed lady examined it and smiled.

"A good beginner's plug," she said. "But I'll hold the other for you, just in case, okay?"

Sam said nothing; his face said *oh God no.*

She laughed and finished ringing up the sale. "Have fun with it, sweet thing."

"Put it in," ordered Lady Indigo, "and you'd better use plenty of lube." She was sitting on the sofa next to Danielle. Each woman had a can of pop and was anticipating what was to come with undisguised glee.

Sam had complied with some humiliating tasks before, some with enormous reluctance, but he had soldiered them out. This, however, went far beyond the pale. He regarded the two women with unbearable embarrassment, and the plug, slick with lube, with apprehension. *Be a soldier again, cowboy.* He examined the plug more closely.

"It's too big," he said.

"It's not too big," said Lady Indigo. "Bend over and put it in."

He gave it a tentative poke. "I can't. It's just too big."

"I told you it's *not* too big. It'll go much worse for you if I do it. Just relax and push."

He tried; it wouldn't go in. *I'll get you for this*, growled his sphincter.

"Push!" Lady Indigo shouted.

One last mighty shove and *yow!* up it went. Lady Indigo yipped and clapped with joy. Danielle, eyes wide, covered her mouth and stifled a gasp. Sam was immobile, stunned by the sudden, rude intrusion. Lady Indigo handcuffed his wrists behind him, dragged him into his cell, made him sit, and locked the handcuffs to the eyebolt in the floor.

"You're going to spend the next hour like this," she said. "So deal with it."

She turned off the light, then closed and locked the door.

Sam knew he'd have to deal with it as he couldn't stand up to eject the thing, if that was even possible. He began to worry it might not be. After the initial shock of the penetration, he found the plug was not all that uncomfortable. But it didn't do much for him either. Maybe the thrill was in the idea of the invasion rather than the sensation. He thought about Carmine and her slave boi shackled and pegged at the dungeon party. She obviously had a thing for pegging, and the guy seemed to like it just as much. Well, some people liked broccoli, too.

So Sam sat, delicately. He could have enjoyed this classic scene in the BDSM repertoire, complete with captivity, impalement, and pressure on his prostate. But he continued to worry. Would he be able to get it out? Would it permanently stretch his asshole? Would he have to wear adult diapers for the rest of his life? What if Lady Indigo suddenly died and the landlord found his rotting, handcuffed, and buggered body seven weeks later? What would the autopsy report say? He knew that these things could and did happen, and no matter how remote the possibility, he would be the exception.

You could give a clinic on paranoia, you know.

But it could happen.

Why? Because you deserve it? Because this is perversion? A sin?

Yeah.

You're absolutely right. You're sitting handcuffed in a dark closet, naked and hairless, with a rubber plug up your butt. There's nothing particularly unusual about that. People do far stranger things to themselves all the time.

Just look at me! This cannot be right.

I am looking at you, and so what? You've been given a rather unique life experience, so experience it! And be glad it's not your head up there for once.

Okay. Focus settled in his head. Being locked, cuffed, and pegged in a dark closet was certainly giving him an appreciation of Lady Indigo time at its most irritating. He'd previously experienced time-dilation ordeals, such as waiting for a work shift to end or suffering through TV commercials during a close football game. Temporal elasticity was a common perception, and perhaps the quantum physicists were onto something. Sam wondered how a butt plug would impact their theories, assuming the eggheads would bend over.

He shifted his focus to his other end, concentrating on his distended sphincter muscle, and feeling it trying to relax and accommodate the intruder. He admired the anus's resilience and forbearance of such an unnatural guest. The asshole's job was pretty gross and thankless, he mused. Consider the ensuing horror if it stopped working or disappeared altogether.

That gave him a perverse idea, as perversion was his immediate world at the moment. People should respect and honor the asshole, he thought, instead of ridiculing it. And stop abusing its name as an insult. There should be a National Anus Appreciation Day. Friends could send each other N.A.A.D. cards with the puckered brown ring on the front and "Thinking of you!" printed on the inside. *I'll design it*, he decided. *It'll make a million bucks.* Visions of fame and wealth became his universe for the remainder of the hour. It was better than obsessing over adult diapers and autopsy reports.

Lady Indigo finally unlocked the cell door, switched the handcuffs to his front, and set him to housecleaning. The butt plug was to remain in, and Sam was amazed he could proceed. Danielle, normally ignoring Sam and his antics around the apartment, now was paying close attention, especially to his rear end. And Sam, normally ignoring Danielle ignoring him, found her interest becoming acutely uncomfortable. No matter what he was doing or where, she moved her view accordingly.

"Now go take it out," said Lady Indigo after Sam's very long, tiresome, and impaled day. Her smile unnerved him, as if she knew something.

She did. She dragged a chair into the bathroom to watch, this time without her Pepsi. Sam worried that after being forced open for so long, his anus might not be able to close again, and a true living nightmare would ensue. He hoped he could simply eject the plug with just a squeeze. Not so, and not with a harder squeeze.

Now he began to worry. He awkwardly grabbed its base and pulled. Nothing but searing pain, and he backed off. Lady Indigo found the attempted extraction just as entertaining as its insertion. Danielle stood at the doorway, equally amused. He wished the both of them would just go off somewhere and die.

Sam bore down hard and the plug stubbornly bore back. Now he worried a lot, seeing himself lying in an emergency room, waiting for his impending plugectomy while the medical staff snickered. He bore down again and pulled even harder. The pain said "no way." The ER and its laughing nurses loomed closer. Then he squeezed and yanked with everything he had and the plug shot out, sending him into blinding agony and Lady Indigo into hysteria. Danielle just stood there with a wide grin on her face. Sam could take no more.

"What the fuck are you looking at, you goddamned skanky cunt?" he hurled at Danielle.

Lady Indigo's laughing fit ramped up two notches. Danielle darkened and fled into her bedroom.

"Oh, shit," said Sam. "I'm in trouble, aren't I?"

Lady Indigo caught her breath. "Clean yourself up," she said, "and wait for me in here. And you don't know the first thing about trouble, cowboy."

After the intense pain subsided, Sam apprehensively tested his sphincter. To his relief and undying gratitude, it still worked. He shuddered thinking about the rhinoceros-sized plug he'd first bought and wondered what kind of GI tract could accommodate such a beast.

Then he thought about Danielle and what he'd just said to her. He'd never erupted at a woman like that before, especially such an attractive one, and never so spontaneously. Even more remarkably, he didn't regret doing it. At the moment her attractiveness counted for nothing. Once cuteness was deemed irrelevant, who was really behind the face? He had no time to ponder that question, as Lady Indigo entered the bathroom, her face hard and resolute. His comeuppance had come due.

"Get down on your hands and knees, *slave*," she hissed, "and crawl into the living room."

He did as he was told. Danielle stood in the center of the room, wearing only a brief white camisole and panties and holding one of Lady Indigo's paddles—the small, really nasty one, he noted with dread. Danielle's thin, delicate lips were set stone hard, and her usually gentle and winsome blue eyes now glowed in fury.

The irony of the moment struck Sam as hard as that paddle would. Semi-naked and prom-queen-pretty Danielle, with her pert breasts and pink toenails, was about to administer well-deserved justice. It was a page ripped from *The Chateau of Cruel Bondage*, one of his beloved fantasies about to become real, and his only desire was to rip apart her smirk and cunt, burn the pieces, and to hell with her prom night tiara.

"I didn't consent to this," he muttered to Lady Indigo.

She knelt beside him. "Yes, you did. I can give you to others, remember? And that includes Danielle, who has every right to be here and be pissed."

"The contract wasn't meant for this."

"It's meant for any damn thing I want!" Lady Indigo barked.

Sam stared into the carpet shag. Danielle, Miss Miller, and the vast array of beauties and sylphs he'd ever fantasized about, lusted after, and goblin-tortured were now coming for well-deserved payback. How could he have ever found this erotic? This was unthinkable.

"I do not consent to this," he said more loudly through his teeth.

"That is your right," said Lady Indigo. "Do you want to terminate the contract?"

Sam remained silent, thinking hard. Danielle, still not saying a word and gripping the paddle, quietly positioned herself behind him.

"How do you stand empowered in the face of disempowerment?" Lady Indigo said softly into his ear.

"I can end the contract," he said.

"Yes, you can. That's one way. Are there any other ways, Magic? You do remember your name, don't you?"

Sam did and didn't care. He saw himself walking out the door but down a road that led into darkness and defeat. It flooded him with profound sadness. Ahead he saw another road. He didn't know where it led, but it had to be a better place.

The prom queen can beat and humiliate my ass, but not me.

There's no difference, twit.

There sure as hell is one now.

"I will stay," Sam said. He firmly resolved that nothing Danielle could ever do would chase him out that door. He steeled himself for what was to come.

Danielle gently laid the paddle on his back. Thoroughly astonished, Sam didn't know what to think.

Lady Indigo placed the paddle on the floor. "Stand up," she said.

Sam stood, and Lady Indigo surprised him with a long, warm hug. Even more surprising, Danielle approached him, lightly placed her hands on his chest, and laid her ear over his heart. She listened for about a minute. It was the first time she'd actually touched him. The scent of her hair wafted through Sam's mind and sent him into further confusion.

"Does he have one?" said Lady Indigo.

Danielle nodded and stepped back. Her eyes were wet.

"I think your ass has had enough for one day," Lady Indigo said to Sam. "Take a shower and clean everything up. Then go into your cell. Read again what you wrote about submission and think about it. Danielle and I are going shopping. You are to stay in there until we get back."

Sam walked to the bathroom.

"Sam?" Lady Indigo said.

He turned around.

"Thank you," she said, then quickly looked away.

An hour later, as promised, Lady Indigo and Danielle returned with several full shopping bags. Among the organic vegetables, granola bars, diet sodas, and potato chips was a box of plastic food wrap and two rolls of duct tape. At a Planet S/M demonstration, Sam had learned about an intense bondage practice called mummification and wrote in his journal that he couldn't wait to try it out. Lady Indigo held up a roll of duct tape and gave him an evil smile. Sam saw the mummy rise from its tomb in the gloom.

It took two people to make a mummy, not including the lucky corpse-to-be. First came the insertion of the butt plug, batteries included, which made it an electric mummy. Sam stood completely still with his arms at his sides. Lady Indigo wound the plastic wrap tightly around his body until it was completely encased, leaving only his nipples and genitals exposed. Danielle held his shoulders, steadying him. Her touch felt surprisingly electric, even through the plastic.

Before she wrapped his head and face, Lady Indigo stood close and looked hard into his eyes in a way that told him he'd better listen. "Once this goes over your mouth," she said, "you'll not be able to use your safe word. Do you understand?"

In his mummy hunger, Sam hadn't considered this. He nodded.

"If you get in trouble, scream through your nose. I'll hear you."

He nodded again.

"But keep in mind, it'll take time to free you," she said. "You must be vigilant. You must be absolutely impeccable. Or you could find yourself in very deep, dangerous shit. Got it?"

"Yes, Lady."

"Good! Those are the last words you'll be saying for an hour. Maybe longer."

Lady Indigo wrapped his mouth shut, leaving his nose exposed, then tightly wound the duct tape around his entire body, head to toe, layer after layer, with Danielle keeping him from toppling over. Lady Indigo used up both rolls, almost two hundred feet. Very carefully the two women laid the mummy on the floor on his back.

The immobilization was complete; Sam couldn't see, hear, or say a thing and the only muscle he could move was his diaphragm. He was as entombed as a body could get without first becoming deceased. Panic began to lick at him, but he was quickly distracted by clothespins snapped on his nipples and genitals. The plug's vibrator was turned on.

"Have fun stewing in your own juice," Lady Indigo shouted. Sam barely heard her through the wrappings.

Stewing meant spending an eternity in Lady Indigo time in another inescapable sensory stimulation chamber, this one a plastic and duct tape womb. He feared this might awaken any dormant claustrophobia, but he found the total encasement safe and surprisingly comforting. He focused on the escalating pain in his nipples and genitals until it became the endorphin joy ride, much to his perverse pleasure.

Until midway through the ordeal, when he felt much stronger alligator clips replace the nipple clothespins. The sharp pain was as startling as it was excruciating. The steel jaws felt like they were biting clear through to the spine. The butt plug was switched to high. There was not a thing he could do but suffer. *No.* He remembered he had a choice between pain and suffering. *Focus. Surrender.*

Sam did. After a few minutes, the agony in his nipples subsided to barely manageable, then to just an intense sensation, and finally back into the calm waters of Lake Endorphin. He fell into a deep trance, seeing no visions and hearing nothing but the sound of small waves lapping the sand.

At the hour's end (or had it been several?), Lady Indigo cut open and peeled away the shell of plastic and tape. She was wearing a long, white, clingy dress and looking every inch an angel from some weird alternate heaven. Sam emerged from the cocoon a sweaty, melted mess and still in free fall into the black hole of mummification. Lady Indigo gently toweled him dry, creating a deeply intimate moment between them. In that moment, Sam felt he would have gladly died for the woman if she asked it of him, right then and there.

Does this mean I finally, finally *understand submission?*

Lady Indigo suspected as much. She sat on the sofa and ordered him to kneel in his position before her. She held his face and looked into his wide-open, glassy eyes as if trying to find him hidden somewhere in their depths.

"Do you remember your atonement of a few weeks ago?" she asked. "The crawling and oath chanting?"

He nodded.

"I want you to do it again for me."

For her. Without hesitation, Sam dropped onto the carpet and began to crawl, this time with pleasure, with devotion, without the bitter rancor and confusion. The memory of that previous ordeal paled in the light of his newfound enchantment with submission and his absolute thrall to Lady Indigo.

The chant came forth effortlessly. "I will honor and obey my Mistress," he said, his still-mummified brain cradling and cherishing each word.

"Her every wish is my command." The oath seemed like a beacon in the night, guiding him home.

Lady Indigo sat on the sofa, intently watching and listening. One pass on the carpet was deemed sufficient. "Kneel before me," she said.

Sam rose from the carpet, knelt, and simply gazed at her. Nothing need to be said; nothing could be said. Lady Indigo bent down, held his face again, and kissed him on the lips, long and deep. Seeming unsatisfied, she kissed him again, this time thrusting her tongue deep into his stunned mouth.

He hadn't seen that one coming. What did it mean? *Yes, I will gladly die for this woman.*

Die for her? Twit! What the hell are you doing?

What I should have been doing all along.

"Talk to me, Magic," Lady Indigo said.

It took a few seconds for Sam to shake off his kiss-induced stupor. "Talk?" was all he could manage to say.

Lady Indigo smiled, stood, and helped him to his feet. "Go into your cell and come back to earth," she said. "When you do, think about submission, think about what happened just now. Write about it in your journal."

"Think? Write?"

"Jesus, you *are* zoned."

She led him to the closet, gently pushed him in, and closed and locked the door. Sam sat on the floor and stared at the black book in front of him. The intense moment of intimacy with Lady Indigo, her kiss—unexpected and provocative—and the introspective chanting had deepened his mummy trance, immersing him in euphoria but also profound disorientation. He felt he'd crossed a point of no return. But on his way to... where? Something had definitely changed. Was it between him and Lady Indigo, or just within himself? Did it even matter?

It matters to me, you little worm, it matters a lot! You think you got yourself a new queen? There's room for only one of us around here!

I don't know what's happened or what I've become.

I sure as hell do. A twit went into his cocoon and came out a weenie. Not your standard weenie, but a submissive slave weenie with a rubber plug up his ass.

But you don't understand! Submission is beautiful. It's a wonderful place.

I'll bet it is. Submission sure is a nice place to visit, but do you want to live there?

Why not? It's peaceful. There's no more fighting with myself.

Yeah? What will it be like an hour from now, hmm?

You can't ruin this for me. Don't even try.

I won't have to. You'll do it yourself.

Sam picked up the pen and played with it, oddly fascinated by the clicking mechanism. *What is submission?* He'd written about it before, but he'd also never felt this way before. It seemed he was back to square one—he hadn't a clue what to write, but he suspected where he might find one. He again considered the words of the chant. He rolled them around in his mind, seeing them as precious, radiant jewels. "I will honor and obey my Mistress," he spoke out loud as he wrote, believing in every cell of his body that submission was his natural place in life.

"Knowledge and wisdom flow down a natural gradient," he wrote, now silently, "teacher to student, master to disciple, dominant to submissive. As long as a thing is learned, what difference does the source make?" He remembered he'd earlier written that submission was a form of surrender. Onyx had said the essence of s/m was complete surrender to the goddess. He'd been there. Now he knew. Lady Indigo, that splendid bitch, was onto something.

Sam picked up the pen and examined it. *What is submission?* he asked it, imagining the answer lurking somewhere inside its barrel—all he had to do was coax it out. "Her every wish is my command," he wrote. "Surrendering to a teacher's will is the sincerest form of humility. If one understands and fully embraces submission, then he knows its purpose is service, not subservience and degradation. Then resentment and resistance disappear, and one's will aligns itself to a greater purpose."

Like to a dominatrix?

The dominatrix is a door!

A door to what? Another dominatrix?

No! To higher learning.

And what do you learn? How to obey your dominatrix better?

You don't like this, do you?

At last, the twit has learned something!

Sam stared at the rest of the page, waiting for more words to appear. He kept clicking the pen, hoping that would help. It didn't. He continued to write without its wisdom. "Obeying commands is simply the dues one pays to be a submissive. Everything comes with a price, and the greater the price, the more valuable the object becomes. But if one's desire for domination disappears, so would one's submission, and then who truly commands whom?"

He reread the last sentence and became vaguely uneasy, as if it threatened his flight through the cloudbanks of submission. Prior to this afternoon, he'd thought he'd finally nailed down submission until Lady Indigo once again turned everything inside out, as was her damned nature. What was she trying to get him to see now?

What is submission? he asked the pen one more time. Click, click. "C'mon, goddamn you!" He put the pen to the paper, hoping this would encourage it. "Submission is being…" it wrote and then ran out of ink. Sam stared at the three words on the page and smiled. "Well, well, well," he said to himself. "Perfect." He held the pen up to his face. "You clever little fucker."

"Submission is *being*?" Lady Indigo said, looking up from his journal. "Being what? What does that mean?"

Sam knelt before her in his "present" position, the proper position. He held it proudly. How could he have ever resented this?

"It means that being submissive is just that—pure being," he said. "Pure absolute being-ness and nothing more." To him it made perfect sense—sublime sense.

But not to Lady Indigo. She sighed.

Sam knew he'd gotten something wrong—again. That was the last time he'd let a goddamned ballpoint pen do his thinking for him. But he knew what he really wanted—*that* was diamond clear—and philosophizing about it would not make it happen. *Say it, damn it, just say it!*

Sam took a deep breath. "Lady Indigo, I want to become your submissive," he said formally. "The kind of submissive I'm supposed to be, what you're training me to be."

She regarded him for a long moment. "You're *already* my submissive," she said. "What is it you're really asking for?"

He was suddenly reluctant to speak it. No, he was terrified to speak it.

She did it for him. "Do you want to change our arrangement? Do you want this to be permanent? Are you asking to become my full-time, 24/7 slave?"

He nodded and exhaled. "Yeah, I am. That's what I'm asking."

There. Now it was out and too late to to take back. Lady Indigo's face became unreadable. That unsettled him. "But isn't that what you want, too?" he said.

She closed the journal and set it down. "What I want is for you to do everything I tell you to. Pretty simple, right? It's all there in the contract. It can't get any clearer than that."

"But that's not what I mean. What do you *really* want from all this?"

"What I *really* want from all this is not your concern!" she snapped. "Jesus, we've already been through that. I must remain opaque to you, do you remember me saying that?"

"But the contract—"

"Is not a test for our compatibility or a dry run for a relationship. It's not some kind of prenuptial agreement or whatever. It says nothing about the future, only about what we're supposed to be doing in the present. You seem to have forgotten that. *Focus,* remember?"

Sam well remembered, but now it simply wasn't enough.

"But the kiss!" he cried. "Doesn't that mean—"

"It means lesbians have hearts, too! Take the kiss as a gesture of my affection and nothing more. And keep in mind, I don't give them away to just anyone."

That was no comfort. He swallowed hard. He was back on earth and didn't like it one bit.

Lady Indigo let him sulk. "Do you *truly* want to be owned by someone?" she finally asked. "To be a pain junkie, like Onyx, wandering through life like a zombie, waiting for her next fix, and totally dependent on Liz to supply it? Onyx is stuck on submissive. She'll go no further and she likes it that way. Is that the way *you* like it?"

"No," he said, although now he wasn't so sure. That worried him. He also didn't know who or what Onyx truly was. She still frightened him. Maybe because he feared he'd end up like her, carpet tacks and all. Maybe this was how it began.

"What do you think being a full-time submissive is all about?" Lady Indigo continued. "Walking around all day in a mummy bubble of bliss? Getting flogged every twenty minutes? Do you want to be dressed up like a little sissy maid and serve tea and crumpets to me and my friends? Oh, wouldn't you look adorable in frills! Or maybe I'll lock you into a chastity cage and let you come once every six months—*or not.* That kind of submission sure looks great while your hand is in your pants, doesn't it? But then you come and submission goes bye-bye, right?"

Despite himself and his pout, Sam had to laugh. "Yeah."

Lady Indigo laughed as well. "Oh, I know all about that one, too. All those things happen to submissives, by the way, and worse, much worse. Did you ever consider that in your plans?"

Sam remained silent. How could his perfect answer suddenly become so wrong?

"The city is filled with damaged souls," she said, "who use submission like a drug or an escape pod to avoid dealing with the real world. Is that your path? Is that what you want?"

Sam stared down at the carpet. It seemed to be permanently filthy, no matter how many times he had vacuumed it. "No, it isn't. But I just don't know what I want. Not anymore."

"Well, maybe you should start by thinking about what you *don't* want. That should be easy."

"Easy, you say?"

"Did you like crawling on the carpet for an hour and being beaten? That should be pretty easy to figure out. That's also part of submission, you should know. It's not all lovey-dovey all the time. Sometimes it's damned hard work—and painful work." She lightly tapped him on the head. "Up here as well as on your ass!"

Sam had run out of questions, answers, ideas, energy, and hope—everything. Lady Indigo sensed his despair. She laid her hand on his journal and thought for a moment.

"Do you remember what the last line of our contract said?" she asked.

"Um, no."

She cleared her throat and looked into his eyes. "'In return for observing, complying with, and executing the above clauses and provisions, I will be shown the possibilities of submission, slavery, and mundane and magical s/m.' Do you remember that?"

"Yes."

"Well, you've been given the mundane in spades, to be sure, and also the magical, but you're not seeing it."

Sam was kneeling upright, but inside he felt slumped. "No, I guess I'm not."

"Submission *is* magical s/m. You've witnessed its magic. It's a gift that has other gifts it passes along. It's given you some incredible insights and visions, right? It just gave you a nice trip to mummy land. It opens you up and lets you see possibilities you never knew existed. There are many other things submission can do, ways it can change you. Try looking at submission that way instead of wanting it to be some kind of cosmic sexual thrill, or a kinky fairy tale adventure with a fairy tale dominatrix. *Or* an escape pod."

Sam was quiet for a minute, then brightened. He thought of a line from his earlier poem about the dominatrix. "She holds the door wide open," he recited, "and presents it to her thrall." He looked up at Lady Indigo. "That's it, isn't it? That's submission."

"Praise the goddess!" she said, beaming. "Now think about this. What's on the other side of that door? After you walk through it, what's left?"

Sam smiled. "I'll be sure to let you know."

She reached forward and hugged him fiercely. "And besides, if you want to be *my* full-time submissive, you'll first have to lose those boy parts and then grow a cunt and some tits—big ones, preferably!"

He laughed. "I'll get right on it."

"Good! Now go take out that plug before you forget it's in there."

An hour later, Lady Indigo chained Sam up in the hallway and thoroughly cooked his backside and butt with her entire arsenal: whips, canes, floggers, quirts, crops, and paddles. Danielle sat on the floor in front of him and watched. The beating blessedly returned him to his earlier trance. Each strike of the whip felt like a whole-body kiss. Then Lady Indigo gave him a real one, again with tongue included. He didn't mind Danielle witnessing the beating and the intimacy with Lady Indigo. In fact, he found it curiously thrilling. Sam was back in his cocoon, except now with two others, and he felt his heart open to embrace them both.

Ack! I think I'm gonna puke.

Then puke.

28

THE SAMINATOR

SAM REFLECTED ON THE PAST REMARKABLE six weeks, especially the last one. The difference between that time span and what had preceded it was clear. Previously, his life could always be described as having a common and predictable rhythm: Mondays through Fridays he worked as a scientific illustrator. On Saturdays, he cleaned house and ran errands, and on Sundays, he'd relax, morph into a couch potato, and perhaps watch a game on TV.

Now the rhythm of his week was basically the same, but the particulars had changed—some markedly. Saturdays he still cleaned house, but the house belonged to someone else, and he did it while naked and shackled. He also ran errands, but not for himself, and did them wearing collars and clamps. During the workweek, his mind was not on his job but on the coming Saturday. Fortunately, that didn't matter because drawing variations in ladybug spot patterns didn't take much of a mind. And on Sundays, relaxing meant finding a comfortable position to sit with a sore ass. Not the sort of week he'd want to have forever, but not a boring one either.

When Sam was out on the street, he was certain no one suspected he had another life, or if they did, they certainly didn't know what it could possibly be. He watched people on the sidewalks and in stores going about their daily business and wondered how many of them had secret lives as well, and whether theirs be any stranger than his. And did they wear unusual appurtenances under their clothes? Although Lady Indigo's chain collar was absent during the week, he still felt it circling his neck and accepted its authority. Oddly, that pleased and comforted him. He had to admit he'd never felt so alive, so solid, and... focused? Was this all due to the contract?

The contract didn't affect his social life because he hadn't had much of one to begin with, as a result of his introversion. And that was perfectly fine with him. Saturdays with Lady Indigo provided more than enough social interaction, although some of it was less than fine. Despite the enormity of his excursion into the kinky unknown, it was not something he could share with any of his friends. Although Lady indigo was technically not his friend—she declared she never would be—she had more than sufficed as one, and Sam found he could share everything with her. In fact, he was required to. Wasn't that what friends were for? Indeed, the details of his adventure were so far removed from everyday life that none of his friends would have believed them anyway.

That week he ran into precisely this situation. He was invited to a birthday party for the coming Saturday for Peggy, a friend he'd known since high school. They'd never dated, which meant they were still friends. Normally he would have accepted the invitation, albeit reservedly, hoping to fake his way through the event and survive, as was his habit. But now Saturdays were no longer normal, and he declined. Peggy was not one to accept no for an answer easily.

"What's so important," she said on the phone, "that you can't be there for my forty-fifth? We're not getting any younger, you know."

Sam knew he couldn't talk his way out of this one. *And what's so special about forty-five anyway?* But he had to give Peggy something, so he silently ran through the introvert's list of standard excuses.

Tell her you'll be tied up that day.

Funny.

"Sam?" Peggy said.

"I have a... previous commitment."

"Oh? To what?"

He remained silent.

"Are you seeing anyone?" she asked.

This was the first time he'd been in this bind, and he kicked himself for not being better prepared. Lying wouldn't do because one lie led to another, and then another, and soon everything would get gnarly and out of control. Besides, Peggy was a good friend who deserved the truth, which he had always provided through the years without a problem. Until now.

"Yeah," he said quietly. "I am." It was not a lie.

"Really? Who is she?"

The bind was getting tighter. No one dates a woman called "lady something" and he didn't know Lady Indigo's real name. What name should he make up? Then it would be a lie, whatever he chose.

"Ah, you wouldn't know her," he said, hoping that would satisfy her.

It didn't. "C'mon, Sam. We've known each other thirty years. You can tell me."

It seems she doesn't know you at all.

"Well, we just met," he said. "On Saturday we're doing this all-day workshop on, um, sexuality." It was still true, sort of, and the ice he was standing on didn't seem to get any thinner.

That immediately caught Peggy's interest and she dropped her interrogation. "Sexuality? You? Well, I just can't wait to hear about this!"

"Yeah, sure. Happy birthday, Peggy."

He relaxed. The crisis had not been averted but simply put off. *What the hell am I doing?*

A good question. Sam was thinking about the contract now in terms of being in service and submission, rather than chasing after his chimeric sexual fantasies. He knew that service was the heart of many spiritual disciplines, so why shouldn't this, despite its weird affectations, qualify as one too? Admittedly, it was a stretch. He imagined himself as a monk or lama humbly doing the dharma, also a form of submission, though on the fringes of spiritual expression.

Lady Indigo's question haunted him. What was on the other side of the door? What, or who was left after you walked through it? He couldn't imagine. He thought of the Zen saying: "Before enlightenment: chop wood, carry water. After enlightenment: chop wood, carry water." He didn't quite understand the adage's meaning but noted it didn't say that one should be wearing clothes while doing all that chopping and carrying.

Just what goal was the mad monk Magic pursuing? Enlightenment was not explicitly stated in the contract, nor was its pursuit central to his regular life. Sex with Lady Indigo was, of course, out of the question. Acting out his s/m fantasies was proving to be problematic, disappointing, confusing, and on occasion involving the wrong kind of pain. The visions and hallucinations had been engaging, even instructive, but where were they leading him? What *was* left? To live in an escape pod forever as Lady

Indigo's slave? Perhaps he'd find out. Perhaps not. But he vowed he'd see this crazy contract through.

SESSION SIX BEGAN EARLY IN THE morning in his apartment, specifically in the bathtub—the Altar of Depilation, he'd ordained it—for the body shaving. In this sanctified space, he discovered he could nick himself bloody just as easily trimming stubble as mowing through the bush. Thank heaven for styptic pencils. The unhurried procedure induced a light trance: a slow, gliding descent into submission. The term was called *going under*, and that was exactly what it felt like: a descent into another realm, one that was unknown, a little dangerous, and yet intensely magnetic. What dwelled in that subterranean labyrinth called submission that called out to him so persistently?

He was definitely going under, all right, but to whom or what? Lady Indigo had made it quite clear it wasn't her. Perhaps he was going under something else, something vast and immeasurable that he knew should remain unnamed, no matter how loving was its vagina-eye. He thought about his hair being a warrior's shield that went unnoticed until it was gone. *How do I stand hairless in the face of disempowerment?*

He expected no answer and, of course, none came.

On Saturday morning, the submissive, hairless warrior knocked on Lady Indigo's door at the appointed time feeling strong and confident. *It's simple. I'm a submissive. All I have to do is please Lady Indigo. That's what a submissive does. So what if she has an attitude? That's just her nature.*

Sammy, I'm hurt. I have an attitude, too, you know. Don't you care about pleasing me?

My God, you're impossible to please!

Very astute, twit. That is my nature.

Sam knocked on the door. No answer. *God, not again.* He'd wait one minute in warrior time. He knocked again. No answer. Was she not home? Had she forgotten? Knock. Wait. Knock. Wait. An irritated, impatient little boy hijacked the warrior, and that's what Lady Indigo saw when she opened the door. Sam's view wasn't any better. Lady Indigo looked like she was ten feet past the end of her rope. Her hair was a matted mess; her eyes were red-rimmed and swollen, and her face was frozen into an acidic frown.

"I overslept," was all she said. No apology. No respecting the warrior. "Make me some coffee," she snapped.

Sam bristled at the order. So much for the sacred act of hairless submission. His bubble of bliss from last week's session popped so abruptly he wondered whether it had actually even happened. Whatever place he felt he had gone under *to*—the goddess, the eye, or the groggy, testy bitch now standing in front of him—disappeared as well. Danielle stumbled from her bedroom, looking not much better than Lady Indigo. Without acknowledging either of them, she went into the bathroom.

What the hell kind of night did they have?

"Get the fuck out of your clothes," said Lady Indigo, clearly spoiling for a fight.

Fuck you, cunt, said his face.

"Oh? Fuck me, is it?" said Lady Indigo. "O-ho, that'll be the day!"

Damn mind reader. More unfairness. Sam stripped, knelt, and accepted his two collars with his nose an inch from her crotch, which she intentionally put there.

"Fuck me, fuck me! The boy wants to fuck me!" she sang.

Wouldn't it be fun to rip out those lovely rings with my teeth?

Apparently still reading his mind, Lady Indigo quickly backed away. She handcuffed his wrists in front of him.

"Get on with your chores," she said. "Fuck me, fuck me! The boy wants to fuck me!"

In the early afternoon, Lady Indigo pulled Sam into his closet cell. Scattered on the floor was every restraint in the house: leather wrist and ankle cuffs, another set of handcuffs, a black leather hood, the waist harness minus its small plug, and the new vibrating plug. The candy store was open, but the owner was in a black, irascible mood.

"Bend over," she said. She lubed and not too gently inserted the plug.

"Stand up."

She locked on the harness and the four leather cuffs. She wrestled a leather hood over his head and tightly laced it up, leaving him partially deaf, totally blind, effectively mute, and barely able to breathe through the two small nose holes.

"On your belly."

She locked his wrist cuffs behind his back with one handcuff and the other locked his ankles together, leaving him hog-tied and helpless on the floor.

"See you later," Sam heard through the hood.

"When's later?" he grunted. He heard no response, only the closet door being shut.

Never mind. He was hog-tied and in hog heaven. He managed to roll over onto his belly and cock, trying to work up some excitement, and his cock happily complied. But would it be wise to leave a puddle on her carpet? He tried to cool off, thinking about baseball, England, Danielle's smirk, anything that would deflate the growing tumescence, but the boner would not debone. Inducing an erection was the whole point of cock rings, but now its timing was unfortunately impeccable. He rolled back onto his side and grappled with the restraints, but to no use. He was captive and deprived of all sensation except for the frustration of an unreachable erection.

"Ohh, my kingdom for a blowjob," he moaned into the rich, redolent, leathery darkness of the hood. "Or a hand job. Shit, I'll even settle for a finger job. Damn dyke bitch!" *If she'd only come in and–*

Whack!

A riding crop came down hard on his cock, and he shrieked into the hood. He hadn't heard anyone enter the closet, and that made the blow twice as jolting. *Was she there all the time?* Lady Indigo had obviously seen his erection and would have no part of it.

"If you come, you'll have to lick it up," she shouted. "Every last fucking drop!"

That he heard. He thought about carpet lint and dyke dirt covered with a creamy semen sauce and repressed a gag. Lady Indigo rolled him back onto his belly, squashing and further exciting the engorged organ.

"You stay on your belly," she growled. "And by the way, the damn dyke bitch heard every damn word you said."

She gave him five more sharp cracks on his butt. "Don't move or else!"

Sam heard the closet door close. He shifted to adjust his cock's position and got whacked again. *Damn it!* She was still standing over him.

"Do. Not. Move. A. Fucking. Muscle," she hissed through the leather hood. "Especially this one!" She jabbed the side of his cock with the crop.

Sam again heard the door being shut but not locked. He didn't know if she had left or was still standing there and waiting for any opportunity to whack him again. Maybe Danielle was there as well. The uncertainty was profoundly unsettling.

As any man knew, once the ejaculation sequence was initiated, there was no abort button. That was half the fun: anticipating what was to come, literally. But for the first time in his life, Sam dreaded having an orgasm. The countdown had started and was approaching the point of no return. Lady Indigo was already angry, and his orgasm would certainly send her into a paroxysm of fury and him into the street, most likely dressed as he was.

The pressure on his erection was hot and constant, and he dared not move. Was she still there and watching? The only thing worse than coming would be coming in front of her. He thought about gooey carpet lint and stifled another gag. But erectile nerves kept firing, his penis kept swelling with blood, pre-orgasmic electricity had seized his testicles, and he was no longer at the controls. *Oh yes, oh no, oh yes...*

He heard Danielle suddenly scream in the next room. Silence, then another loud shriek, followed by her pleading for mercy. What the hell were those two doing? She screamed again. Was she bleeding to death or coming? Then all was silent. Sam strained to hear more through the leather hood, but that seemed to be the end of the show. Miraculously, the distraction had somehow aborted the emission—no doubt a male physiological first—and he and his cock, ass, and stomach had been mercifully hauled back from the precipice.

A few minutes later, he felt Lady Indigo undoing his restraints, the hood coming off last. She led him, wobbling and bleary-eyed, into the living room. Danielle was sitting on the sofa wrapped in a thick robe. He saw no blood, visible welts or marks, or bone splinters protruding through the skin. Her eyes were red and face tear-streaked, but she seemed happy as a newt in mud, as if she and Lady Indigo had just chatted pleasantly over tea.

"God, what happened in here?" Sam asked, absolutely dying to know.

"None of your fucking business," said Lady Indigo. "Or any other kind of business!"

He knew better than to pursue the issue.

Earlier in the week, Sam had attended a Planet S/M demonstration of suspension techniques used in advanced dungeon play. The presenter was a large, hairy, dominant man, appropriately called a "bear" in the gay BDSM culture. This bear was an experienced rope top, and soon his cub bottom was trussed and suspended in an elaborate rope harness. Sam had read that suspension greatly increased the victim's helplessness, as it deprived them of stable footing and induced a disconcerting loss of control. People who've been through severe earthquakes speak of how profoundly unnerving such gravitational uncertainty can be.

Unnerving the victim can be the entire point of suspension play, although many enjoy the sensation and liken it to flying. Sam had seen pictures of all the various ingenious ways there were to dangle someone above the floor. But it was not without risk, because when suspension was done improperly, disaster could occur. Blood flow could be constricted, nerves damaged, joints dislocated, muscles stretched, ligaments torn, throats strangled, heads concussed, and necks broken.

Some heavy bondage enthusiasts actually invited this danger as an element essential to their experience. Knowing the Reaper was just a step away could ramp up the excitement—for some to the point of aphrodisia, assuming the players know how and when to step back. If something could possibly hurt the body, as Sam was now seeing, someone would invariably try it, and hopefully the first time wouldn't be the last.

Sam was not quite ready to die in a dungeon accident. At the presentation, he'd also seen a relatively safe suspension device called stirrups: two wide leather straps that hung in loops from chains attached to an overhead beam. The thighs went through the loops to comfortably support one's body in a seated position. The wrists were locked upward toward the chains, or behind the back, rotating the body forward to present one's butt and business on a plate. Then one's comfort was rudely disregarded at the whim of the tormentor, as the bear had demonstrated with a cane on his boi.

Sam had built a set of stirrups for Lady Indigo—or for himself, technically—and had eagerly brought them along for their session. She was just as eager to use them on him. He affixed two large screw eyes to an overhead joist, attached the stirrups, and sat in loops to test the contraption's security. She ordered him to stay there and locked his wrists upward, and he hung there like a sack of oats.

"Comfy?"

"Oh yes," he smiled.

"I'll fix that." Lady Indigo snapped three clothespins on each of his nipples, making him wish he'd been less honest. She blindfolded him and let him dangle. He heard motion in the room and strained to discern what was causing it.

The blindfold was removed. Lying on a blanket in front of him was Danielle, face down and naked from the waist up. Lady Indigo knelt beside her with a stainless-steel tray containing a bottle of alcohol, some gauze pads, and a mysterious packet. Lady Indigo donned surgical gloves, swabbed Danielle's left shoulder with alcohol, and peeled open the packet. It was a scalpel blade. Then, to his horror, Sam was ordered to watch Danielle receive a cutting.

Sam remembered his wooziness while watching the young man at the dungeon party whose chest had been streaked with red rivulets. Later that evening, he'd seen a woman's breasts that looked as if they'd been in a fight with an alley cat and lost, which added to his distress. Everyone got cut accidentally, and he'd had his share, but his stomach could always handle it. The dangers were obvious: loss of blood, infection, septicemia, and ligament and nerve damage. But being sliced up intentionally? Sam now found himself getting just as queasy as he had on that long ago evening.

"If cutting is so risky, then why the hell do it?" he'd once asked Lady Indigo.

Her eyes glazed over. "Cutting is very popular with leather dykes in general," she sighed dreamily, "and me in particular."

She removed her shirt and showed him a pattern of scars on both of her breasts, so thin and faint he hadn't noticed them before.

"I don't get it," he said.

"Men can't get it," she said. "It's about blood and pain, and men can't deal with either. Women can; we have to every month. Seeing our blood lets us know we're alive and what it feels like to be alive."

"Then I don't want to get it," he said, not caring a whit about hearing his gender's problem with pain and gore. "Cutting utterly terrifies me. No fucking way, ever!" The instant he blurted that out he regretted it.

"Is that so?" Lady Indigo said with a hint of a smile.

And now she was forcing him to watch one. Sam constantly had to remind himself to watch what he said to the woman; he frequently forgot that rule.

Danielle had a previous cutting on that shoulder, a geometric mandala the size of a tennis ball that she wanted recut. Without any hesitation, Lady Indigo lightly ran the scalpel across the skin. Danielle gasped, Lady Indigo smiled, and Sam winced. A thin red line quickly emerged, barely visible, beading with blood. Lady Indigo continued to cut, slowly and carefully, until the design oozed into being. Danielle moaned and sighed as her endorphins surged ahead.

Sam's stomach turned over. From all his groaning and squirming, one might have thought he was the one being dissected alive. When the cutting was finished, Danielle lay still as a corpse on the blanket, having melted into a leather-dyke blood trance.

Lady Indigo unlocked Sam's handcuffs and relocked them so that his arms were behind his back, causing him rotate forward and expose his butt, which was then given a thorough flogging and paddling with an occasional whap on his cock. Danielle came back to life and turned on her side to see what was happening. After applying clothespins everywhere on his genitals, Lady Indigo sat down with Danielle's head in her lap. The two women watched Sam hang in escalating discomfort and greatly enjoyed the show.

Sam did not share in the entertainment, nor did he enjoy finally seeing Danielle's small, firm breasts. The flogging set him swinging in the stirrups and was edging him toward vertigo. He was already queasy from watching the cutting and felt the stirrings of nausea.

"Um, Lady, I think I'm going to puke," he said weakly.

"If you puke, you're going to eat it off the floor," was her response.

That did little to calm his guts, but he tried to tough it out. Like ejaculation, once the urge to vomit was switched on, it became very difficult to switch off. After a few acidic burps, Sam yelled "Crimson!" and in a flash Lady Indigo was loosening his bonds. He sat on the floor in the spinning room until the nausea subsided. Danielle got to her feet and staggered into her room.

When she was certain Sam wouldn't barf on her, Lady Indigo embraced him.

"You did good, Magic," she said. "That's what a safe word is for. That was a warrior's act. That's impeccability, right?"

Sam nodded. The compliment was nice to be sure, but it wouldn't save him from the agony to come. He gingerly started removing the clothespins, one blazing stab after another. Lady Indigo slapped away his hands and finished the job herself with a lot less ginger.

The following morning, as he was preparing to leave, in an unbelievable gesture of trust, Lady Indigo gave Sam her own journal to read. He was floored, humbled, honored, and dying to get at it. Upon returning home, he immediately devoured the entire book.

One year earlier, he read in the journal, Lady Indigo had undertaken her own contract, one that had been similar to his: submission to a pair of Old Guard leather dykes who had subjected her to all manner of hell and misery, far worse than what he was getting. Sam wondered if the pair were Liz and Onyx. The journal included a photograph of slave Indigo, naked, shaved from head to toe, complete with nipple and labia rings. She stood firm like a fierce Amazon warrior, proud and tall, daring the viewer to say something untoward.

Sam was particularly impressed by one passage in her book: "Exploring one's soul through s/m is a raw, brutal, and messy business. Trying to look good while doing it is not only impossible but also counterproductive." He could definitely relate to that. Another page struck home as well: "Being forced to do something that goes against your very nature also forces you to find your true inner strength, and if you have none, then you must create it then and there. That's the only way to survive your test of fire."

Test of fire? Was one waiting for him as well? Sam had the uneasy feeling that the trials he was reading in her journal would foreshadow his. Where did they take her? Her journal didn't say and it ended inconclusively. But when he put it down, he felt a deep kinship with the woman and an abiding love for her. It was a love that would not exist, he freely admitted, if he'd been trying to get into her pants. Weird whore or not, Lady Indigo was, he could see now, an extraordinary and miraculous gift that had been set before him.

A gift, is she now? Last week she could have owned you. Gifts don't do that.

Whatever I do here is wrong, isn't it?

You don't expect me to approve of this nonsense, do you?

You don't approve of anything!

That's not true. You just don't like what I approve of.

At midweek, Pauline called Sam.

"Hey, hon, there's a dungeon party this weekend at the swinger's club. Can you make it?"

Sam hesitated; the contract strictly forbade him playing with others. But that wasn't quite true. He could still play, but he would need permission from Lady Indigo. Would she give it?

"Sam? Can you come?"

"A party? Well—"

"How can you possibly not? There's someone here who wants to see you."

Sam was rapidly warming to the idea, but his uncertainty was just as rapidly cooling it. But it wouldn't hurt to hear a little more.

"Yeah?" he said. "Who?"

"Katy. Do you remember her?"

Oh my. Beautiful, sexy Katy. "But isn't she, uh, Herb's, you know…"

"She still is," Pauline said. "Herb just had rotator cuff surgery, and it will be months before he can lift a whip, let alone use it. Katy understands, but she is still very hungry. Herb will be fine to just watch."

That clause in the contract had said nothing about him playing the dominant role, fine print or not. He could feel the pieces falling deliciously into place.

"Well," Sam said, "you know I'm not very experienced at this sort of thing."

"You're experienced enough. Katy asked for you. She wants to wear you out."

"Pauline, listen to me. I'm not a top. I don't know the first thing about it!"

"Just do what you did before, hon, and you'll be fine."

"But what I did before destroyed Katy and almost put me in the nuthouse!"

"Sam, now you listen to me. Katy was far from destroyed, and you know that. And tell that goblin of yours he's not invited." Pauline was not one for excessive processing.

Not invited? As simple as that? "Well… okay," he said.

"Fabulous!" chirped Pauline. "I'll tell her. You can stay with us. See you Saturday, hon."

Pauline hung up before he could waffle or wimp. But then he remembered: Saturday was to be session seven, the final one with Lady Indigo and the most important. *Shitfire and damnation!* He should call Pauline back and cancel. But Katy and her beautiful butt and breasts. He could tell Lady Indigo that he was… that he had… that he couldn't because… *shit!*

"Thank you for being honest with me," Lady Indigo said to Sam on the telephone. "That's what's truly important. Of course, you have my permission to play with Katy. We can reschedule seven for the following week. Let me know if you want to borrow some of my gear."

Sam had not been expecting that at all. But before he could enjoy his relief, he was again abruptly brought to a halt: he knew next to nothing about being dominant and was now committed to cream a heavy and ravenous bottom who apparently chewed up tops like a whale plowing through krill.

"But I'm not a top!" he said. "I'm terrified!"

"Terrified?" said Lady Indigo. "I don't see anyone coming at you with an ax or a whip. What are you afraid of? Who is your enemy here?"

"Um, Katy?"

"Katy will be tied up. She can do nothing to you. You're obviously feeling disempowered, but by what? Again, who is your enemy?"

"Fear," Sam said.

"Good," said Lady Indigo. "What does your fear look like?"

"Katy. But it's not really Katy. It's my fear of failing her. Of disappointing her."

"Excellent! That's huge. You're afraid of disappointing a woman. It's the end of the world if you do, right?"

"Pretty close to it."

"Let Katy be responsible for herself," Lady Indigo said. "Her feelings and expectations are her problem, not yours, and let her take care of them. Your responsibility is to be mindful of what you're doing and take care of her body the best you can. And to take care of yourself, too. Do you understand all that?"

"I believe I do."

Then something else loomed ahead of him. "So how do you top somebody? I don't want to screw up and look like a fool."

Lady Indigo laughed. "You've been screwing up and looking like a fool for almost two months! So what's different now?"

"What's different is I'll be the one holding the whip."

"It's not just holding a whip. It's how you hold it. Dominance is not something you can fake, especially with an experienced bottom."

"But I'm not a dominant!" he cried, remembering Liz's admonitions about it.

"And you're not a submissive either!" Lady Indigo said. "You're a person. Dominance and submission are choices you make; some are easier than others, but you can still choose. Do you know what I think about when I'm flogging you?"

"It seems like you're not thinking at all."

"Right you are! But when I do think, I think, 'This is how *I* want to be flogged.' Let that be your guide, your inner top, and you'll do fine."

Sam tried to let this in.

"Katy wants the real you," said Lady Indigo, "not her fantasy of you. So what do you want? If it's to please her, you're going to fail, guaranteed.

Let her please you. That's her job as a bottom. She'll pick up on that and melt into you."

"But what is my job as a dominant? To *be* dominant?"

"Good. You're finally catching on. Simply said, being dominant means becoming your intention. If you're crystal clear about what that is, then your confidence and authority naturally follow. What is your intention? What do you want? What pleases you? Hearing Katy screaming and begging for mercy? Seeing her come? Seeing her blood?"

"Well, that's what part of me wants," Sam said, thinking about the goblin and its hunger for a brutal feast. "And I really don't want to indulge that. But I don't know what else there is."

"Yes, you do. You've felt it with me. Many times, as I recall."

"Huh? What?"

"Intimacy. Not romantic emotional intimacy, but a more immediate and tangible kind of intimacy. A connection can happen when you're whipping someone. A very personal and intense connection, if only for a few minutes. That's because you're both being completely open and honest with each other, not with your words but with your bodies, and unlike words bodies don't lie. Then something truly special can happen. It may not look like intimacy, but it definitely feels like it. You know what I'm talking about."

"Yeah, I do. Of course I do. And that all sounds good in theory."

"It will sound even better when you do it," she said. "And you will."

Sam had only five days to graduate from the BDSM School of Bottom Creaming with a master's degree in Mastering. Maybe it would help to assume an alias, a *nom de kink*. He tried on Master Sam and it wouldn't fit. Sir Samuel sounded even more ridiculous. Maybe something ferocious and a little scary. Black Dragon was already taken. Yellow Yeti and Flogzilla were still available, with good reason. The Prince of Pain? Tops-R-Us?

Sam had heard that circus clowns create their own faces and put them on a national registry, ensuring ownership and originality. He thought that self-proclaimed s/m masters, a different kind of clown, should do the same with their monikers. That would probably turn Black Dragon into Black Dragon 5127. Sam decided if he needed an alias, he was in the wrong business anyway.

A common nightmare of college students was that one in which you're sitting naked in a classroom, waiting to take the final exam of a class you didn't remember enrolling in. Sam had had his share of those. Now he saw himself standing naked in the center of a dungeon he didn't remember entering, holding a whip he didn't know how to use, and pretending to be dominant while everyone pointed and laughed, especially Katy, who'd spit him out bloody with the rest of the krill... *the Goblin!*

That yanked him out of his waking dungeon nightmare. The Goblin was the perfect alias, sinister and scary indeed. And totally appropriate because it was true. But maybe it was too true. And maybe that might set him loose and out of control and maybe—

Oh, gag me with a spoon.

Oh, fuck, what is it now?

Just listen to yourself. Oh no! There's an awful goblin inside me making me do awful things. The shame, the shame! Am I depraved or am I decent? What drama! What crap!

But I don't know how else to—

Pah! There's no goblin and there never was. And believe me, I'd be the first to know.

You saw what happened with Amber that night. How do you explain that?

Going schizoid was your way of handling it. Your evil goblin is nothing but a cop-out. You're just lazy and a coward. That's why you keep him around. He takes all the blame so you can pretend you're virtuous. This is getting mighty old and mighty juvenile, Sam. It's time to let that go and grow up."

Maybe I don't know how.

Maybe you don't want to. Now, where's that spoon?

On Saturday night, that beautiful, naked woman was tied to a column with her wrists high above her head. The rest was now up to The Saminator, the alias Sam had chosen, though he'd never reveal such silliness to a soul. Herb, with one arm in a sling, directed Sam and Pauline on the knot tying. Pauline needed a stepstool.

Sam dressed for the party in basic dominator garb: a black T-shirt, black jeans, and his too-tight, side-zippered black leather boots. Lady Indigo's riding crop hung from his belt along with a pair of her handcuffs, a folding knife in its sheath, and keys on a long chain—accoutrements he'd seen other male tops sport as they prowled about their prey. On him they made a fine Halloween costume, one that would surely break the needle on the dweeb-meter. At the last minute, he decided to scrap everything on his belt and especially to lose the tarsal-crushing boots. *The Saminator wears running shoes, so deal with it.*

A small group of people gathered around the trio to watch. Beautiful, naked women seemed to be a dime a dozen at this particular party, but Katy's reputation trumped them all. As he and Katy had earlier agreed, there would be no negotiation between them prior to the event, as one of her thrills was the spicy danger of submitting to a stranger. Although Sam was not a complete stranger, he vowed to be as strange as possible.

Sam looked at Katy tied to the post—eager, expectant, and quietly waiting for the dance to begin. He was waiting as well, but for what? The goblin to drop by and get him unstuck? No, not this night. Katy would not be its brutal feast. He thought about the other possibility, that intense, transient intimacy Lady Indigo had talked about. Katy looked over her shoulder at him, as she would an anticipated lover. That would be him.

He tried to imagine himself as Lady Indigo, hungrily regarding her prey before she attacked. *Intention. Focus. What do I want?* The picture was getting clearer. He stood close to Katy and lightly ran his fingertips along her sides and down her back. She closed her eyes and shivered. He reached around, caressed her breasts, then massaged her nipples. Her hips began to gently rock. He pinched her nipples and she gasped. He remembered pinching Amber like that until she'd cried out.

Katy is not Amber, and I'm not cowering in the corner. There are no goblins here.

Then who is here?

Get lost.

Sam released Katy's nipples and withdrew a medium-sized flogger and a length of rope from Herb's equipment bag. He circled her waist with the rope, drew the line taut between her legs and crotch, back to front, and tied it to the post, firmly immobilizing her hips.

"Mmm, nice," she hummed.

Sam started whipping her upper back with a steady rhythm, mild strokes at first, then building in strength. *Focus. Intimacy, not savagery.* Tonight there was no arm holding back his. The strokes came easily and boldly. *This is for me, not her.* Lady Indigo was right: Katy was turning into a puddle at his feet. He continued his pace, now flogging her with progressively harder strikes. He stopped to caress her reddening back and buttocks. Her skin was burning hot and seemed to caress his hands in return. He reached around and pinched her nipples hard and held them. Katy gasped and the puddle turned to steam.

Sam switched to Herb's heavy flogger, the one he'd used at the previous party, and repeated the pattern. Katy's body was now crisscrossed with welts. Her hips, pinioned to the post, did their best to escape. He took a break from the beating and massaged her back and butt. He looked into her face. Eyes half-closed, lips half-parted, she seemed to be enveloped in a cloud of bliss light years away. *Good, I'll fix that.*

He pressed himself against her back and whispered into her ear. "Maybe I should have brought my other flogger, my dear, the special one."

"Hmm?" said Katy, smiling in her trance.

"Yeah. The one with the carpet tacks embedded in the ends."

Katy's smile fell to the floor. "Carpet tacks? You have *got* to be kidding."

"I never kid," said Sam and laughed like Mr. Hyde. Now it was okay do that.

"You motherfucker."

"Motherfucker, am I? That deserves ten more, lady."

After those ten lashes, and then another ten even harder, Sam was winded. Pauline took the flogger and went after Katy like a mad maid beating thirty years of dust out of a rug. *My God*, thought Sam, *those two women are not human.*

Sam felt a tap on his shoulder and turned. Behind him stood an attractive woman of about forty wearing a black lace bustier, thigh-high black leather boots with spiked heels, and nothing else. She was slightly overweight, and her full breasts looked like they'd been glued into the garment's cups. Her long blonde hair was tied back in a ponytail. Around her neck was a wide leather collar adorned with metal studs and a padlock.

The huge, hairy-bellied biker dude Sam had seen at the previous party stood behind her. He was dressed head to booted foot in black riding leathers. He nodded to Sam and grinned. Without saying a word, the blonde bent down on one knee and offered Sam a riding crop. Sam took the crop and nodded back to the biker as if he knew what the fuck was going on.

Then he had an inkling. "Present!" Sam said crisply to the woman.

She immediately stood up, put her hands behind her back, placed her feet apart, thrust out her bosom, and looked down. *Well now.* Sam took careful aim and gave the top of her right breast a sharp crack with the riding crop. She winced but stood firm.

"Thank you, sir, may I please have another?" she said softly, still with her eyes down.

Well, well, well now, indeed.

Sam gave her left breast a crack, this time much harder. She yipped, recoiled, and then returned to her position.

"Thank you, sir, may I please have another?" she said even more softly and breathing heavily.

Sam lightly traced the border of the rising welts with his fingertip. *She asked for another. How many does she want? No, how many do I want? Focus.*

"Look at me, dear," Sam said to her. She raised her eyes.

He looked into her blue eyes, open, excited, and without a trace of artifice or posturing. The eyes, the windows to the soul. In that moment, Sam felt as close to another human being as he'd ever been, never mind he'd been with her less than five minutes and didn't know her name. *Did she feel it too?* Then the connection quickly dissipated. Transient intimacy—a thing to be embraced then released. The alternative to the brutal feast.

"I think not," Sam said to the blonde with no name. "That's all I have left in me tonight. You did very well, my dear."

She relaxed and gave him an unexpectedly heartfelt smile. Sam handed the crop back to the biker. His transient submissive knelt down and kissed the top of his running shoes. He wished they smelled better, but they were the Saminator's shoes and due their respect. The woman rose, smiled, and again said "Thank you, sir," and the biker led her away.

Now how the hell did I know how to do all that?

Not from me, that's for damn sure.

Sam turned back to the whipping post. Pauline had finished beating the now dustless rug hanging limply from its bonds and floating somewhere beyond the orbit of Rigel Seven. Herb was caressing Katy's neck and back with his good hand.

"Well, look at you, mister," Pauline said to Sam. "You're not very experienced, isn't that what you said?"

"I'm not," Sam said. "This was… a fluke."

"Mistress Desmonda didn't seem to think so."

"Mistress who?"

"The blonde whose tits you just basted."

"What? She's a dominatrix?"

"Most Mistresses are, hon. She's also a switch, as you now know."

"What's a switch?"

"Someone who likes being at both ends of the whip. And Desmonda doesn't let just anyone touch her."

"But why me of all people?"

"Because she knows us," Pauline said. "And she probably got wet watching you do Katy. You did fabulous tonight, Master Fluke. Now come over here and pet Katy for a while. It takes her forever to come back to earth."

Sam did as he was told.

Well, Master Twit, did you have a good time whipping Katy?

Yeah. The best.

Did you feel strong and powerful?

Oh, yeah.

Did you feel even more strong and powerful when you smacked that blonde on her tits? And a dominatrix, no less!

You bet I did.

It feels good to feel powerful, doesn't it?

Oh, yeah.

Do you want to feel powerful again?

Well, of course I do!

But then what happens when you run out of Katys and Desmondas?

29

THE TWO DOLLS

"So how was the dungeon party?" Lady Indigo asked on the telephone. "I want details. Lots and lots of details."

Sam recounted everything but names. What happened in the dungeon, Pauline had said, stayed in the dungeon. But Lady Indigo had an insatiable appetite for gossip that found ways around the rules. "This, ahem, submissive blonde dominatrix you're not allowed to name. Was she with a biker with a big hairy belly?"

Sam said nothing. That was all she needed to hear.

"*Desmonda*? You whacked Desmonda on her boobs? I don't believe this."

"Do you know her?"

"I'd be breaking confidentiality."

"Well, you broke mine," he said. "And besides, who am I going to tell?"

"You know that vicious dyke who creamed my tits a couple of weeks ago?"

"It was Desmonda? How can that be? She was submissive to that biker guy."

"She's bi and a switch to boot. And she was the one I was thinking of giving you to. Well, that sure ain't gonna happen now. I just do *not* believe this."

"Oh, no. Oh, shit. Is the whole leather scene this secretive, incestuous, upside-down, and screwed up?"

"Pretty much," she laughed. Then she turned serious. "Tell me something, when you were whipping Katy, did you feel powerful?"

Hearing that question again spooked him. "Um, yeah…"

"It sounds like you're not sure."

"Well, it *felt* powerful."

"*It* felt powerful? There was an *it* somewhere feeling powerful?"

Sam paused. "No, I was feeling powerful, or I thought I was, but now I'm confused."

"Did you feel empowered?"

"I'm not sure of the difference."

"What do you think power is?" Lady Indigo asked.

"The ability to get what you want?"

"Like sex? And a woman to whip?"

"Yeah."

"And that means someone else has it and you have to get it from them, right?"

"Uh, yeah."

"And that means tricking or begging or bullying them until they give it to you. Or maybe just grabbing it. Right again?"

Sam had to think about that. "Yeah. Shit."

"So just how powerful do you feel when you're doing all those dances? How well is it working for you?"

"Not very, actually."

"Not at all, I'd say," she said. "Sorry to rain on your parade here, but that kind of power is the ultimate irony. You're depending on someone else to make you feel powerful, aren't you?"

"Shit again."

"That's not power, that's its opposite—*dis*empowerment."

"Well, then, what is empowerment?"

"If I were to tell you, that would negate its, uh, power."

"Can't you at least give me a hint?"

Lady Indigo sighed. "I just did."

THE CONTRACT HAD ALSO SET FIRE to Sam's easel. His new paintings reflected the new place s/m occupied in his life: no longer a dirty secret but a noble, albeit unusual, adventure that was due all the respect he could muster. And he did. There were other artists to paint tableaus of crystal mountains, not the monsters dwelling beneath them. He worked almost every day, abetted by a waiting room filled with pixies, goblins, their victims, and their lovers. Every time he completed a piece, another pixie whispered in his ear.

Soon he had a menagerie of artwork begging to be released into the world, but where? Clara and her Galerie Outré preferred outsider art, and he suspected that kinky erotic art was too outside for her tastes. And besides, he was now probably too skilled an artist to qualify. Pauline and Herb's enterprise was definitely an option, but he was tired of the six-hour round-trip drive that each visit cost.

Sam finally decided to exhibit the work not in a gallery but as a narrated slide show, as he'd been diligently photographing his art from the very beginning. Meredith at Planet S/M eagerly agreed to host the event, and a date was set. The audience, most of whom were far kinkier than Sam ever could imagine, would be as safe as they come. But like all audiences, they would still expect an entertaining show, and he had better deliver. He thought this would be the perfect test of what he'd learned under Lady Indigo's quirky tutelage, as if he needed another one.

The challenge would be simple enough: to stand before his artwork with impeccability, like that Amazon warrior in slave Indigo's photograph. The problem was he'd been flunking Impeccability 101 since day one. But in compensation, he was acing graduate-level Paranoia, which he habitually felt before any art show, erotic or not. He wondered if his decision to give this presentation was a subconscious death wish, although he could think of better—and worse—ways to die.

He remembered his Galerie Outré debut, and how frightened he had been displaying those three relatively tame, below-the-waist pieces. He'd been braver at Pauline's gallery with the Viridian series, but he still considered it soft-core. The core of this show couldn't get any harder. He'd be revealing everything, no matter how twisted and violent. But his greatest dread, the one shared by all artists and performers, was of being boring.

The evening had arrived. Seeing two hundred chairs in the large, empty room flattened Sam with acute stage fright. A performer, as he well knew, had no safe word. Comedians often spoke of dying up on stage. This could be total annihilation. Sam set up the slide projector and the screen and rehearsed his introductory speech. He looked in a mirror every thirty seconds for a stray booger or zit. A person's fly didn't normally unzip by itself, but he nonetheless added that to his list of anxieties. Compared to what he was about to expose, a rogue cock head peeking through his pants would be trivial.

The audience trickled in, some as singles, most in couples. A few groups defied description, suggesting unusual families bonded by their love of BDSM and other intimacies. Sam seemed to be the only person in the room not wearing leather or fetish gear. Exposed female skin was rampant, threatening distraction everywhere Sam looked, and he sure looked. He kept silently chanting "Focus," which only accentuated his complete lack of it.

As if invited by the imp of the perverse, Viridian and Gareth walked into the room and took their seats. Sam nodded to them, and Viridian politely nodded back. Gareth started looking around the room to see who else was there, his head on a swivel. Sam had already survived one Viridian appraisal of his artwork and didn't want to press his luck. But this was a public event, and public meant everyone, welcome or not. At least his geek stalker wasn't there. Yet.

Lady Indigo and Danielle sat in the front row, keeping their coterie with Sam a secret. He found their presence to be the only point of comfort in the room, an amusing reversal of their normal circumstance, and tonight it was immensely appreciated. As usual, Lady Indigo wore no underwear, as her low-cut, side-split, clingy black gown revealed. Sam feared he'd forget everything he'd learned in her school, fearing even more she'd leap up on stage, whack his butt, and scream "Focus!" in his face. At least he wasn't wearing the plug, not that it wouldn't have occurred to her.

As was her custom, Danielle was dressed in pink. Her dress was more modest than Lady Indigo's but not by much. She looked utterly stunning. If the prom were held tonight, she'd be instantly crowned queen. In a departure from the aloofness she'd previously shown Sam, her eyes were now glued firmly on him, watching his every move and adding to his stress. One of her heels dangled from her toe, in sharp contrast to Lady Indigo's black army boots. *What a pair.*

It was showtime. Meredith introduced Sam with such praise he wondered if she might be confusing him with someone else. She'd earlier asked him for an artist's statement that she could send out to her mailing list. After ten drafts, he'd come up with one. Not wanting to go through the agony of self-promotion again, his introductory speech was to simply read it.

"For the past fifteen years my day job was as an illustrator and fine artist, specializing in scientific and wildlife artwork. But at night I turned into a pornographer. For many years I kept this artwork secret. I've only recently brought it out of the closet, and tonight you'll be seeing all of it. I view my work as photographs of what's roaming around my libido. None of the art has been censored, and all have had messages to give me, and tonight, perhaps to you."

Sam retreated to the back of the room and the slide projector. Meredith's freckled slave girl turned off the house lights. Sam turned on the projector and began the show. A few people shouted "Focus!" Sam smiled and turned the focus knob on the slide projector, and the screen came alive with his secret portfolio of sex, the one he'd sworn would forever remain hidden, the one that was now on public display.

The first slide was his first erotic piece, that portrait of his penis. The moment became supercharged with absurdity. "Behold, here is the artist's cock," the projection screen declared. Sam's stomach seized and couldn't feel his knees. *What the fuck was I thinking?*

It's obvious you weren't, twit. And this is a hell of a place to begin.

Please! This is the worst time to start in on me!

I can't think of a better time.

Impeccability, focus, impeccability, focus. Sam repeated the words like a mantra, but his brain, breathing, and heart rate didn't seem to be getting the message.

"The Wheel" was next on the screen: a naked man, clearly himself as the model, was chained to a huge rotating wheel and suffering torment that exceeded all common sense. The actual size of the painting was only twelve inches square, but projected on the screen, his balls were the size of dinner plates. Sam teetered on the edge of a cliff, his missing knees threatening to send him careening over any moment.

Focus. Mercifully, his hand clicked to the next slide. The painting showed a tightly bound man being lowered by his cock into a pit filled with giant spiders. *Great.*

"What medium do you use?" came a voice from the audience, a common question when someone doesn't know what to say about a painting but wants to say something.

"Watercolor and acrylic," Sam replied, relieved to be on safer ground.

"Do you ever paint with your own blood?" another voice asked.

"No."

"Someone else's blood?"

"No."

"How about semen?" asked another.

"No, I paint in watercolor and acrylics," said Sam. *Safer ground?* Next slide *now.*

Sam was hanging in a clock tower with a two-hundred-pound bell chained to his balls. *Shit, I forgot I'd included this one.*

You forgot a lot of things, besides how to think. Like your sense and sanity. And here you are, shriveling up on stage like a newt on a hot griddle, and right in front of Lady Indigo and Danielle to boot. This is just fabulous!

Oh God, it can't get any worse.

Oh yes it can. Go to the next slide.

Viridian had nailed Sam's cock and balls to a tree stump while a line of more Viridians, each holding a hammer and a nail, waited their turn.

You're right. It's worse.

The next slide showed a dominatrix with her whip regarding her slave hanging from the rafters, his back and butt crisscrossed with red welts. A scene not so far removed from reality, as the actual dominatrix was present in the room. Lady Indigo turned around to look at Sam, her face unreadable in the dark. Had she winked, snarled, or mouthed "focus"?

It didn't matter; the reminder was enough. *I am the top here. This is* my *show. This is* my *audience. Focus!*

Like the incident at the car wash, a presence ballooned within him. Was it Magic? Had the Saminator shown up? Who or whatever it was took charge of the show, and he began to speak with confidence, spontaneity, and incidental humor. The audience, now *his* audience, responded with laughter, applause, and lewd comments, abetting his impromptu fling with show business. He noted that the artwork also changed, moving from sewers of unbearable shame to gleaming monuments dazzling all who beheld them.

And dazzle they did. Over the whir of the projector's fan Sam didn't hear the gasps, wows, and "oh my gawds" that continually punctuated the show, as he later learned, but, ironically, he did manage to hear someone yawn. After the slave girl switched on the lights, people gathered around the stage to ask him questions, make comments, and display their body modifications. Sam found himself playing the celebrity without apologizing for its rank egotism.

Lady Indigo, still in her seat, was beaming. Sam knew why. Danielle just stared at him without any expression. Curious, but that was Danielle.

Viridian extracted herself from Gareth, who was standing close to a pair of Goth girls with his large, hairy arm around the waist of one. Viridian approached Sam; he noticed her collar was absent. His hand unconsciously went to his throat; his felt absent too. *Well, how about that?*

"How did you like the show?" Sam asked her. Now her answer wasn't that important—another surprise.

"I liked it," she said. "Do you want to know why?"

"Sure."

"It was honest. Not like some other people I know."

Sam knew all about this little drama and wanted none of it. He felt someone take his arm. It was Danielle, holding him close. *What on earth?*

Viridian's brow furrowed. "Who's this? Your next model?"

"Everyone is my model," said Sam, without thinking.

Viridian said nothing. She looked at Danielle, then turned toward Gareth and zeroed in on him like a hawk after a rabbit.

"Well, this is a surprise," Sam said to Danielle.

"Not half as surprised as I am," she said.

"But, why—"

Danielle put a finger to his lips. "Keep it close," she said and held his arm captive.

Sam looked over at Lady Indigo. She just shrugged. Another mystery.

It was written that vanity was one of the seven deadly sins, and now Sam was getting why. Sinning had never dissuaded him from doing anything, clearly, but negotiating vanity was tricky. Tonight, he'd seen that vanity was a place in which you found yourself without realizing it, and when you did, it was a bugger to leave. Even trickier, once in thrall to vanity, you'd best play it well or the whole act would collapse, and all you'd have left would be a presumptuous fool sitting amid the rubble.

As if on cue, vanity revealed its price. A very kinky-looking couple approached Sam: a man leading his date by a leash attached to her chain collar. The woman was tall, made more so by tottering on six-inch heels. Chained cuffs hobbled her ankles, making her tottering even more precarious. Sam had no idea what she looked like, as she was completely encased head to foot in black latex with her arms bound behind her. The only visible flesh was that of her eyes. *Well,* he thought, *at least she saw the show, although she's unable to talk about it.*

Sam had noticed the pair earlier and recognized the guy as Derek—or Daddy Derek, as he was known in the leather and literary worlds. With a minimum of writing skill and not a whit of propriety, Derek wrote and sold bondage fantasy books, making himself quite a reputation as well as a ton of money. He also acquired a stable of utterly gorgeous women as bondage models and sex toys. And one was standing right there, ripped from the sticky pages of his novels. Sam had read some of his work and found it mildly stimulating but had quickly gotten bored when it became clear that one chapter read much like the next.

"She's beautiful, isn't she?" Derek asked.

"Uh, well, her eyes certainly are," Sam replied.

"Yeah. Hey, I'm working on my latest novel. It's called *Bondella*, a kind of Cinderella story, except the wicked fairy godmother changes Bondella into a sex slave instead of a princess. Bondella gets dragged to the dungeon party ball in a hearse, and Prince Charming chains her up and whips her. But at the stroke of midnight, Bondella magically turns into the dominatrix from hell, and they live horribly ever after trying to decide who's the top. Great idea, right?"

"Yeah. Weird." Sam decided to add *Bondella* to the bottom of his reading list.

Derek turned to Danielle, still on Sam's arm, and brazenly swept his attention up and down her body.

"Now you'd make a nice hot princess, wouldn't you, doll?" Derek said.

"She's not available," said Sam evenly. Danielle squeezed his arm.

"Right-o," Derek said. He peeled his eyes from Danielle's décolletage and turned to Sam. "Anyway, I'd be honored to have you to illustrate *Bondella*."

Sam had seen this coming and knew he wanted nothing to do with Daddy Derek, his literature, his crude behavior, or his rubber doll.

"I'm sorry," Sam said, "but I'm extremely busy and overcommitted."

Committed to what, Sam didn't say, but he sure as hell would come up with something. What he didn't say was, "I think your writing is the literary equivalent of a french tickler, and I'm loath to have my artwork be part of it."

But Derek wouldn't take no for an answer. He dangled his doll's leash in front of Sam as if it were the key to the Xanadu of kinky sex, and perhaps it was. The lady's wrappings could not hide the size of her bust.

"Would you like her?" Derek asked.

"What?"

"Tonight, she's all yours," Derek said, completely disregarding Danielle. "Please consider it an advance."

398

It? Sam wondered how the rubber-coated woman felt about being an "it" and used as wampum. Maybe it was actually her idea. Maybe *she* was really a *he*. In this bizarre scene, anything was possible. Sam also wondered what sort of irresponsible jerk would give away his girlfriend to a stranger. But in the leather world Sam had seen this was done routinely to both parties' excitement. The presumed lady winked at Sam, her only means of expression, which did nothing for him.

"Sorry," said Sam, "the answer is no."

Despite his coarse conduct and gall, Derek had enough sense and good manners not to press the issue. Bad manners would undoubtedly be reserved for his latex doll later that evening. The pair walked (and tottered) away.

Danielle finally released Sam's arm and took that of Lady Indigo, who'd been standing aside and watching the exchange with Derek. Her face was still radiant.

"So," Sam said, "how'd I do tonight?"

Like Danielle, Lady Indigo put her finger to Sam's lips and whispered, "Let's keep it close."

Sam was not going to get anything out of those two, which was no surprise. But he knew what he'd done this evening, and their approval was now irrelevant. He really liked that.

So did Lady Indigo. She embraced him hard and kissed him on the lips. Danielle hugged him even harder and eyed his lips but kissed his cheek. Both kisses left him lightheaded.

"I believe we have some unfinished business to discuss," Lady Indigo said.

"Yeah," said Sam. "Our last session." The word *last* brought up a surge of sadness.

Lady Indigo caught it and hugged him again. "I'll call you this week." The two women left the room.

Vanity was not yet finished with Sam. As the audience trickled out, a few remained to praise the show and the artist. He received one overt sexual proposition, another one that was coyly implied, and an offer from a stunningly attractive Seraphina wannabe to pose nude and in bondage. But all he could think about was Danielle. What a night.

What a night indeed! Vanity sure is fun, isn't it? So how does being a celebrity feel?

The best.

Like a drug? Are you now addicted? Do you want more?

Just leave me alone with that shit.

Not a chance.

I did great tonight and you're still on my ass! Jeez, I need a stroke now and then!

Then get it from someone else. That's not my job. Go have yourself another show and stroke away!

Don't spoil my evening, you hypercritical hag.

Don't spoil your life, you overinflated twit.

As promised, a few days later, Lady Indigo called Sam.

"In our final session," she said, "I suggest we do a ritual. Something that will incorporate everything we've done together. To tie it all together. Would you agree to that?"

"Sure," said Sam. "Like what?"

Lady Indigo laughed. "You tell me. You create it. This is your ritual."

"Shit! I don't know anything about making up rituals."

"Then this is the time to learn. Like you just said, make something up."

"Shit."

"Here, I'll help," she said. "Think about a ritual as a passage from one place to another. You decide what those places are. The ritual is to consecrate that passage and make it real for you. Go back and reread that magazine article on shamanism."

"Yeah, okay."

"And think about these passages as gates, four of them, each representing an aspect of yourself you need to confront and resolve. Make some kind of mask you'll wear that symbolizes these aspects. Write a short poem about each."

"Torture by poetry just won't go away, will it?"

"Not in my house!" she laughed. "Now, here's the most important part. Each gate will be guarded by a physical ordeal that you'll have to survive and pass through. That will be my part in this. That will solidify the ritual and make it meaningful. Bantering about affirmations and such just won't cut it. Do you understand this?"

"Now I do. Well, this is s/m, isn't it?"

"You bet it is," she said. "This is what s/m is all about."

"And I have three days to do all this?"

"Two and a half. The pressure's on, right?"

"Yeah. Thanks a lot."

"You are so welcome. Has anything in our adventure ever been easy and pressure free?"

"Well, no."

"And so it will be until the end," she said.

"Lady?"

"Yes, Sam?"

"What's going on, you know, with Danielle and me?"

Lady Indigo paused. "Let me put it this way. Magic has his adventure, and now it seems Danielle has hers, and apparently you are part of it."

That gave him a jump. "I don't understand."

"She told me she's never seen a man before."

"What on earth does that mean?"

"She'll explain when she's ready. Tell me something, have you ever seen a woman before?"

"I don't understand that either."

"I think you do," Lady Indigo said. "In the meantime, you have other things to understand, don't you? See you Saturday, Magic."

30

THE ARENA

THE NIGHT BEFORE THE LAST SESSION, Sam was visited by another portentous dream, a logical bookend to the jetliner crash dream that had come before the first session. Again, death was the message, but instead of being vaporized in a fireball of jet fuel, he found himself enveloped in breathless rapture, swiftly skimming above the diamond whitecaps of an infinitely deep blue-green ocean toward a point on the far horizon. An iridescent web of light overlaid an electric blue sky, shimmering through the visual spectrum and beyond. Sam knew he'd die when he reached that distant point. A death in peace and a life fulfilled.

On awakening, Sam grappled with its implications, despite the dream's euphoric cast. Like the other dream months earlier, the specter of death was a player. As he often conjectured, Lady Indigo was indeed facilitating a death—the death of the old to make way for the new. A very comforting thought. But also in that dungeon was an invisible elephant lumbering around, one that no one ever wanted to think about: the Grim Reaper, who was always just a defibrillation away.

Sam stood at Lady Indigo's door, intoning focus and impeccability, as if the words were magical spirits he could summon for strength. *What would this day bring?* He brought four gaily colored cardboard masks he'd hastily thrown together for the ritual. They looked like a third-grader's idea of a budget Halloween costume, but they'd have to do.

Lady Indigo appeared at the door on time for once. She was dressed conservatively—no makeup, no sexy gowns, and no fetish wear. Danielle was nowhere to be seen. In his journal, Sam had written the details of the ritual and handed it over. Lady Indigo read it without comment, then closed the book.

"So you want to be taken to an edge?" she said. "You do remember what that's like, don't you, cowboy?"

"Yeah, I do."

"You understand that edges have an unappeasable nature," she continued. "You plan on one thing and something else shows up. Something you didn't expect."

He already knew that. She knew he already knew that. *So why the lecture?* "Yes, I know."

"And then you deal with it, right?"

"Yes."

"Is Magic ready for that?" she said.

"Yes."

"Bullshit!" Lady Indigo shouted so loudly he jumped. "No one is ever ready for an edge. That's what makes it an edge! Got it?"

Okay, that's why the lecture. This was not going the way he'd planned, as if anything around here ever did. Sam saw his sacred warrior ritual turning to shit in a hurry. Lady Indigo, back to doing the mercurial bitch act she did so well, was right. He definitely was not ready. Not for another round of her craziness.

"I guess so," was all he could say.

"You *guess* so? That's a fine demonstration of impeccability, Magic!"

She stood with her hands on her hips and glared at him, at the warrior now flat on his unimpeccable, metaphorical ass. Sam had no idea what to do next, so he glared back.

"Today there's a new rule," she said soberly. "If you use your safe word at any time during the ritual, everything will immediately stop and you will leave my home and never speak to me again."

"But, why—"

"Because it's the damn rule!" she barked.

That was a hard slap, unexpected, brutal, and bewildering. Sam had no intention of using his safe word, but why banishment? That possibility flooded him with deep sadness. And questions: why was she so angry? What had he done, or not done? And what on earth would she be doing to him today?

"I understand," Sam said, not understanding a thing.

"You understand nothing!" she snapped.

"I agree to the rule," Sam said.

"That's better," Lady Indigo said. "Now undress and kneel."

Sam did. She looped the chain collar around his neck. "Today there will be no bonds or restraints. Your commitment is what holds you here. Nothing else. Do you understand *that?*"

He nodded.

She stared hard into his eyes and locked the collar. Its click seemed louder than usual. Lady Indigo opened the door to her bedroom and led him in. Sam had never before been in the room, and this lent an even more unearthly cast to the ritual. Indeed, he felt he'd stepped into another world, a temple like no other. An array of whips, floggers, canes, and paddles hung on one wall; a shaggy bison hide covered another. Red candles in ornate escutcheons burned in each corner. A huge kettledrum and a padded bondage bench dominated the room's center. The bench was a surprise, and Sam wondered why he'd never seen it—or been on it.

Against the far wall was Lady Indigo's altar. Sam knew she had one but had not seen it until now. It could have been a tableau in a natural history museum: a low table covered with animal bones and skulls, antlers, feathers, shells, and other mundane objects made magical in the flickering candlelight. In the center, an abalone shell held a bundle of sage incense. At one end of the table lay an ornately painted gourd rattle. An old tarnished hunting knife, called an *athame* in pagan practice, guarded the other end. Its blade was keen and glinted in the candlelight. The athame was supposed to have its edge dulled, but not this one, he noted.

Sam knew that knives were common objects on pagan altars for several reasons, all of them ceremonial and mercifully symbolic. He also knew knives were popular in heavy s/m play, a favorite for masochists who feared having their body parts unceremoniously cut while they were lashed down and helpless. He shuddered, remembering Mistress Morgaine and her knife, and wondered if this one would used likewise. But he knew Lady Indigo well enough not to fear mutilation and thought any edgeplay with a knife would be lame.

Lame? When have you ever seen lame around this place?

Just leave me alone, will you? I really don't need your help right now.

And you're certainly not going to get it. I'm so going to enjoy watching you, the twit who would be warrior, doing his would-be warrior dance.

Sam put on his first mask and stood at the east wall, the first gate. He'd cut the eyeholes wrong and stumbled—not exactly the strong, confident gait of a warrior and hopefully not an omen of what was to come. Lady Indigo lit the sage and passed the smoldering bundle over and around him. Soon the room was foggy with the blue pungent haze, which didn't improve his vision or help his lungs. Between coughs Sam recited the first poem to the element of air:

"I leave behind the voice of fear

Snapping in the air below me.

I take flight into the electric blue sky

Of imagination and mystery."

Sam knew enough New-Age poetic phrases, so stringing a few together was no problem. He had to admit that composing poetry while not being savagely beaten was a lot easier but not as inspiring. Lady Indigo bent him over the bench.

"You are to hold yourself perfectly still," she hissed into his ear, "no matter what happens to you, do you hear me?"

"Yes, Lady."

Holding nothing back, she struck his butt with her smallest and most painful paddle.

"*Gaah!*" It was everything Sam could do to keep himself steady.

"Now repeat after me," she said. "I am the impeccable keeper of my sacred being."

Sam said the words but heard them only as words.

"You'd better pay attention, *Magic,*" said Lady Indigo, inflecting his name like a sneer. "Every time I hit you, you must swear this oath. Every time! No matter how hard I hit you, swear it loud and remain steady. And swear it like you damn well mean it! Got it?"

"Yes, Lady."

Whack!

"*God!* I am the impeccable keeper of my sacred being!"

"I said say it like you mean it!" she screamed.

Whack!

"Goddammit!" He remained still, caught his breath, and repeated the oath.

Whack! Whack! Whack!

"Three times!" she screamed. "Swear it!"

After a dozen more strikes and a dozen more screams and oaths, Sam struggled mightily to keep himself still without bonds, a far more difficult task than he'd ever imagined. If you can't get something through a thick head, her logic apparently went, try the other end. Neither end was given any respite. And where were those damned endorphins when you needed them?

"Stand up," said Lady Indigo.

He did so, unsteadily. He cautiously looked at Lady Indigo. Her face was contorted into a scowl that would have frightened the most stalwart Samurai. He'd never seen such a face on the woman. It wasn't anger, but what?

Lady Indigo ordered him to the next gate, accompanying it with savage pounding on the huge kettledrum. The noise echoing around the small room was deafening, and Sam prayed that her neighbors were gone for the day. He put on the second mask, and, still reeling from the savage beating, stood at the south gate, the Earth, and recited:

"I leave behind the guilt of pain

To those I've caused harm.

I take refuge in the bosom

Of forgiveness and mercy

And fully loving all those I love."

"Stand absolutely motionless," said Lady Indigo. "Do not move a muscle."

She produced four large gauge needles and went to work. One needle went through each nipple, one through the tip of his penis, and, after pausing to think, she inserted one just below his lower lip. Despite their size, the needles were not particularly painful but made him nervous and vulnerable, which was the point. Four gates, four directions, four elements, and now four needles. *Pagans and their fucking fours.*

Once again, Lady Indigo bent him over the bench, resumed her brutal paddling, kept screaming "Impeccability!" into his face, and demanded he keep swearing his oath. Sam thought he'd seen everything in the woman's bizarre behavioral repertoire, but nothing had been so uncompromising and ferocious, as if she'd mutated into a raging, possessed demon.

Indeed, she seemed no longer human—perhaps appropriate for this event. Sam knew the kinky underworld was infiltrated with the unstable and the unhinged, and maybe this was how they acted before they attacked. He uneasily thought about multiple personalities and madness, and now the athame on her altar assumed a more sinister feel. Fear entered this unearthly temple as the fifth element.

Lady Indigo roughly yanked out the needles and loudly drummed Sam to the west gate. Blood oozed from all four wounds and speckled the carpet. She didn't seem to care, but he worried: *what about her damage deposit? What kind of spot remover would remove blood? Would salt work? Should the stains be removed now before they set? Does she have any salt or spot remover? Maybe her neighbors will have spot remover. But wait, her neighbors will be furious because of the horrendous racket. What should I do?*

Sam caught himself obsessing over this trivia. It was an absurd reaction, he knew, an attempt to flee from something far more absurd and infinitely less trivial. Surviving this ritual was his concern, retrieving her damn damage deposit was hers. *Focus.* For once, he did. He jumped back into the arena, and, wearing the mask of fire, spoke:

"I leave behind the anger of past hurt.

I withdraw the flaming sword from my belly.

Let my fire erupt onto creation's canvas

And light my way home."

Nice poem, he conceded. The ordeal by fire was, of course, hot candle wax. Sam stood motionless in virtual bondage while Lady Indigo dripped wax on his shoulders and chest. In the subdued candlelight, he could not distinguish the wax drops from his blood. Now he was elated. Everything was going perfectly. This truly was a warrior's rite of passage, grueling and painful. *Yeah, I so got this.*

Lady Indigo again savaged his rear end with another round of paddling and oath-swearing. He sailed through the beating, owing more to his butt nerves having gone numb rather than his spiritual resolve. She then turned her fury on the kettledrum, and Sam strode to the final gate, the north—the element water. His eyes were indeed watery and blurred from the incense fog, but at least he'd cut the eyeholes right. Ears numb and brain reverberating, he spoke:

"I leave behind all the poison

That rots my body and mind.

Let my heart beat unburdened,

Let me cherish all that flows within."

Lady Indigo told Sam to stand still in the center of the room and left to summon Danielle, who'd been holed up in her bedroom, quiet as a flower and listening to the mayhem. Danielle entered the temple barefoot, wearing only a white, sleeveless shift with her hair down and loose. She could have been a sorority girl on her way to bed or an acolyte preparing herself for a heathen sacrifice.

A sacrifice wouldn't be far from the truth, he thought, although here the sacrificial object would be him. The two women quickly mummified Sam with plastic wrap and duct tape, leaving only his head with the mask exposed, and, surprisingly, his genitals safe and protected. They gently laid him on the floor on his back.

"This will not be a nice, pleasant little vacation like before," said Lady Indigo. "This time you've got some work to do. You're to journey back in time to meet with your ancestors and retrieve their wisdom. Is that clear?"

My ancestors? Sam knew he had to have them, but who were they? And where on earth were they from? Caves? A steppe? The suburbs?

He nodded. She and Danielle left the room and shut the door.

Sam took inventory of his situation. There was no sensory deprivation; he could hear and see perfectly well through the mask. The mummification was not that constrictive; he could wriggle out and escape if he wished. But that was not the point. The point was getting wisdom, but from his basically clueless family?

But here he was. He focused on the candlelight patterns dancing on the ceiling and let the cocoon work its will. The paddlings, the deafening drumming, and the smoggy haze had worked together to drive him halfway out of his body already, so it didn't take long. Soon he felt himself falling inward, and a few moments later floating upward. Appearing through the mists of his mind's eye was a small fishing village on a wide river, of all places. Sam knew with certainty he was in nineteenth-century Czarist Russia. Was this a genuine transpersonal phenomenon or a scene his mind had dredged up from *Fiddler on the Roof*? No matter, at least something was happening, and he thought he'd better make the most of it.

Sam hovered over the village and saw a heavyset, bearded old man, looking suspiciously like Reb Tevye, gazing up at him as if astral tourists were a regular event. The old man was his grandfather's grandfather, this Sam also knew, but how? And how did he know his roots stemmed from a fishing shtetl in Russia?

Sam always presumed ancestor worship was important only to people of color and in poverty, those who had been marginalized by the soulless behemoth of western progress. People who had comforted themselves with quaint beliefs and strange traditions to make living at the margins survivable, even joyous. White people like himself, it seemed, needed no help from the past, wouldn't know where to look if they did, and would have no idea what to do with the information anyway. That was Sam's ancestral heritage.

But here he was, and there was that fat, funny old man, still looking up and awaiting a question as if he'd been waiting for centuries. Sam knew he was still embedded in skepticism. He decided to simply drop it and see what would happen.

Okay. What am I supposed to learn from you? Sam asked his great-great-grandfather. *What have you to teach me?*

"My name," the old man said, "is Wolf. It is a good name, a Russian name."

That Sam wasn't expecting. Wolf? Strange. That was his paternal grandfather's middle name. Now with growing interest, Sam looked at the old man, still patiently standing there. *Is there anything else you have to tell me?*

He expected the old man to cough up a nugget of wisdom, as was the job of ancestors, or what was the point of having them? But the old man just smiled. Then he and his village abruptly vanished, and Sam was back in his own century in the duct-tape time machine. His mission had been accomplished, but what was it? Just a single word. What could he possibly do with that?

Sam thought about his grandfather. In 1908, he'd arrived on Ellis Island, a fourteen-year-old refugee, alone and huddled with the rest of the masses fleeing famine and the pogroms, and knowing not a word of English. Yet he'd found a job and a wife, sired and raised three children, and modestly prospered. He'd made an epic hero's journey, in his own small way.

And now, here was Sam, his progeny and heir, bound in duct tape, bleeding from his dick, and freshly returned from a chat with an illusion. What would his grandfather make of this?

Then why don't you just astral travel back in time and ask him?
What? I thought you weren't going to help me.

I'm not, dummy. Do you really think that fat old man is your ancestor? Maybe he's another one of your brain-barf hallucinations.
No. It was more than that. It has to be.

Then where's that nugget you were supposed to get? Was he fresh out?

Not sure what to do next, Sam lay there in the fading remnants of his trance and waited. Lady Indigo and Danielle returned. They cut him free of his shell with scissors and gently toweled him dry. Lady Indigo knelt on one side of him, Danielle on the other.

"How was your journey?" Lady Indigo asked.

Language still eluded him. She patiently waited.

"I was in Russia," he finally said, "in a fishing village on a big river." He was forcing out the words, now unsure about what had really happened.

"Go on," said Lady Indigo.

"Okay. I met an ancestor, my great-great-grandfather, I think."

"What did he tell you?"

"Only his name. Wolf. He said it was a good name. That's all."

"It is a good name," Lady Indigo said. She looked at Danielle and nodded.

Lady Indigo stood, and Danielle remained kneeling by Sam. He rested on the floor, watching through the eye holes of the mask as Lady Indigo bustled about the room. Then she knelt down beside him with a metal tray. On it was a bottle of disinfectant, some cotton balls, and *oh holy mother of shit,* a scalpel blade.

Sam instantly froze. Danielle's cutting still bled in his mind. He knew what was coming. Lady Indigo thoroughly swabbed his chest with the disinfectant. *My God, my entire chest!* His throat constricted, his mouth went dry, and he felt like a cockroach trapped in a jar, panicked and scuttling around in circles—hardly how a warrior initiate is supposed to feel.

This wasn't what I wanted!

It's what you're going to get.

I'm freaking! I can't stop freaking!

What did you think was going to happen? Another massage? A blow job?

For the next ten minutes, while he writhed, howled, and sobbed, Lady Indigo slowly and exactly cut into Sam's chest. Knowing what was happening to him was much worse than the actual pain. He could feel his skin spreading apart and blood trickling down his sides. Trying to remain absolutely still took enormous effort, fearing the slightest twitch would cause the blade to jump and sever something important. He felt his heart slamming into his ribcage as if desperate to escape the carnage.

Lady Indigo ignored his shrieking and squirming and calmly continued to cut. Danielle sat very still and watched. After an eternity, it was over. Lady Indigo laid a sheet of handmade paper on his chest and lightly pressed down on the wound, blotting it. She carefully peeled the paper away and showed it to him. There, in mirror image in four-inch-high letters, written in his own blood, was *Wolf.* Lady Indigo smiled.

Sam didn't. He sat up, flung off his mask, and beheld the butchered mess of his chest, shaking and stunned. Crude letters carved into his flesh. Rivulets of blood running down his sides and belly. Sliced open. Scarred. The staggering, irreversible enormity of what just happened hit him like a howitzer shell.

He heard a grief-stricken wailing begin in the distance. His breathing became ragged and labored, like that of a dying elephant. He stared at the two women, eyes blank with shock, face contorted into a grotesque, simian mask. Lady Indigo seemed to have expected this. Danielle did not, her own face turning ashen. The two women rose and silently walked out, leaving Sam to suffer alone.

Welcome to the real world, twit. It's about time you saw it.
You go to hell.

I'm already there. With you. Just look where you are. God, what a scene!

Sam looked around the room. As if a veil had been lifted, everything turned black and ugly. In this harsh and heartless light, he saw the room as if for the first time. It was not a magical neo-pagan temple, not a chamber for shamanic ritual and transformation, but a dirty, trash-strewn bedroom in a seedy, low-rent apartment in a block of shabby buildings slated for urban renewal.

Do you like what you see? Look some more.

Lady Indigo was not a wise shaman or a goddess incarnation, but a crazy lesbian witch who had scarred him for life. And the contract had been a lie all along, just a vapid game pretending to be something more. A game for children too self-absorbed, misguided, and immature to find themselves a place among the adults.

Now look at yourself.

A naked man with a bloody chest collapsed on the floor. A one-hundred-sixty-pound slab of shit reeking of fear and shame, the victim of a perverted scene paying the pervert's price, and facing a lifetime of unrelenting remorse and misery.

Inert and in shock, Sam stared at his mutilated chest. The deed was done. *Sickness* had been indelibly and permanently stamped onto his body for everyone to see, judge, and ridicule. The wailing grew louder. *Oh my God, how did I get here?*

You walked through the door, twit. How else? Now you know what's on the other side. This is where your magical journey into submission has brought you.

I'm so scared. I'm... just so scared. What do I do now?

Go find another dominatrix to fuck you up. Maybe the next one will cut off your cock. Maybe you don't deserve one. Why not give Mistress Monster a call? She'll gladly do it.

His cock. He looked down at the small bundle of flesh like it was a parasite, a revolting, blood-swollen leech that had attached itself to his groin. He couldn't bear to touch it. He lifted his gaze to the door. Just beyond it he imagined an interminal, convoluted furrow that this mindless, sex-obsessed leech had dug through his years chasing after women and their bodies. A ditch that had led him to this room.

And now it's too late! Too late!

The knife on the altar caught his eye. The glint on its blade transfixed him. The nullifier of pasts and annihilator of futures—his future. He could not look away from it. Razor sharp and just two feet away. Now he understood what *nullo* was about.

What are you going to do now, twit? Cut off your own cock? That'll sure fix everything.

She cannot get away with this.

Hey, why don't you carve "bitch" into her tits? And with her own magical knife, no less! Or get a lawyer and sue her. Maybe never speak to her again? Oh, that'll show her.

Goddammit! She can not get away with this!

Of course, she can. They all can. They've been getting away with this all your life. And it's because you wanted them to! You asked them to! Wake up!

Sam delicately touched his chest. It stung. The letters were now thin red lines dotted with beads of dried blood. Letters without substance or meaning that he must wear for the rest of his days. He could never again go swimming in public, enjoy a hot tub with anyone, get a massage, or be naked with a normal, healthy woman. His life lay in ruins.

The wailing storm arrived in its full fury. Sam no longer had room to feel anything else, so he began to weep. The cries turned into sobs, raw and guttural, then into bestial howling. *If they hear me, good! If they're terrified, good. Fuck them all completely to hell.*

What a noise! My God!

Are you happy now?

Immensely. Just look at Magic, the mighty spiritual warrior. He's fallen and he can't get up. So he's throwing a tantrum, poor baby.

I don't want to hear any more out of you!

What's the matter, twit? Am I too close to the truth?

I said shut up!

No! I'm here and always will be. Accept that! You've failed in your little spiritual quest. Accept that! Just fucking accept it and grow up!

Just accept it. Those words beckoned to him, promising resolution and peace. He knew it well—the asylum found in defeat, surrender, and complete, unquestioning acceptance of one's lot in life. Was that submission? Was that what waited for him on the other side of that door? How could he ever have thought submission was something more, something even beautiful?

Then acceptance it would be. Sam folded himself around his heart and closed his eyes. A cool breeze washed over him, and he felt cradled in the lush bosom of sweet relief, blessed relief. He'd finally found his place in life. A dark and sorrowful place, yet it was a *place,* familiar and comforting. His struggle to be someone else—just to be *someone,* was finally over.

Now come home to me, Sam.

He lay on the floor, exhausted and empty. He felt like he was floating, as if the scalpel had also cut him free from his body. He again surveyed the room. Candlelight spattered the walls and ceiling with restive, menacing shadows, evoking demonic faces moving in and out of focus. Drops of blood and candle wax speckled the carpet. Whips hung on one wall, a moth-eaten bison hide on another. The discarded shell of plastic and duct tape were shoved into a corner. A bloodstained sheet of paper lay on the floor, a bloody scalpel blade on a tray. The room resembled a surreal gladiatorial arena with the loser lying crumpled in the center, bleeding, utterly vanquished, and vomiting up tears and remorse. Sam saw the life that lay ahead of that body, the life he was about to embrace.

"But that life really, *really* sucks!"

Sam startled and turned, expecting to see Lady Indigo behind him whispering into his ear. But he was still alone, desperately alone. It was just a hallucination added to this grim nightmare. Lady Indigo and her fucking submission—look where it had gotten him.

"That's *resignation*, not submission!"

Now he sat up, attentive but puzzled. That was *not* Lady Indigo's voice, and definitely not the other's. It was his own.

"Submission is a door, not a place," he said slowly and clearly. A frisson darted up his spine—this was *him* speaking, not anyone else.

Was his craziness returning? Now crazy was okay—even welcome—and God knew he had just cause. But this was something else; this craziness felt... saner. The athame on the altar again caught his eye, its blade shining in the candlelight. Then he looked at the scalpel, its edge blotched with dried blood—his blood. Blade edges. Edgeplay.

"What do I do when I meet an edge?" Sam asked himself aloud. He answered his own question: "I'll know what to do in the moment."

What is the moment? he thought. *Suffering. Despair. Defeat.*

"Do I truly want that?"

Oh God no!

More words came forth, seemingly of their own will: "How do I stand empowered in the face of disempowerment?"

Lady Indigo's question. He didn't know the answer but felt it was close, very close, swirling about him, almost within inhaling distance.

"Poor slave Magic. That poor, submissive little weenie." Sam kept watching his words speak themselves. He had no idea what they'd say next.

"Poor Sam. What a sad, pathetic story he is."

A story?

He jolted.

"A story." Sam said the word as if he understood it for the first time. Still floating, he looked down at that victim lying on the floor. But it wasn't himself he was seeing—

Then what am *I seeing?*

"Just my *story* about the slab," he said, sensing he was onto something.

What a miserable story. It sickens me.

"Well, who wrote it?"

I did.

"Why?"

So I could be somebody.

"Even if the story sucks?"

It wasn't supposed to suck. It just... turned out that way.

"Then why do I keep it?"

Because I didn't know it was a story. It was all I had. I thought it was–

414

"Me?"

Sam's brain skipped a beat, grasping the difference between the two. The difference was clear, startling, astonishing, profound, and utterly liberating. It seemed he'd been living in two separate worlds at the same time. *Fuck me.*

"So… ," he began, his words now coming, slow and measured, "if *I'm* not my story… this sad, wretched story… then why on earth have one?"

Because how can anyone exist without a story? How can I? Who would I be? That's just not possible!

"I exist right now, don't I?"

But if you take away the story, what's left? Who's left?

"*I* am."

In another beat, the slab vanished and was replaced by a man sitting upright, alert, and thoroughly alive. The squalid, desolate furrow in which he'd been wallowing rose up and surged into the future, splitting into a thousand wondrous directions. None led to a story. All led to possibility. It was his call. It always had been. He heard the fat man laugh.

Sam calmed himself and breathed deeply, feeling his lungs electrify his body with oxygen. He willed himself back into his story, and then back out again, just to make sure he knew how. All it took was a decision. It was surprisingly easy, like he'd just discovered muscles that were previously undetected and unused. He'd never felt so empow—

"Fuck me," he said, dumbstruck. "Well, fuck me." He started laughing like a madman and couldn't stop. He didn't want to. *If they hear me, good. If they think I've flipped out and gone bat shit crazy, good!*

Sam! Stop laughing! Stop laughing at once!

Why? I've never felt so good in my life.

I disappeared! I was suddenly gone, and I don't know why. I've never been so frightened!

And now you're back? Are you the piece of me that went missing? That's a riot!

This is not funny! Please don't ever, ever do that again!

The hell I won't. I'll be doing it a lot more now. And as often as I possibly can.

Please, no, I beg you. Don't send me away like that!

Why not? You've been absolutely horrible to me—and enjoying every second of it. God, you're a mean, despicable cunt!

Sam! I'm supposed to be that way! That was the job you gave me!

Me? Why would I do that?

Because you needed me. Who else would love you with your craziness and perversions? Who else would understand and accept you? You needed a place to feel nurtured and safe.

Safe from what? You?

No! From yourself. From your own folly, your recklessness, your delusions, and your monumental stupidity! So show me some damn gratitude, will you?

I'll show you the damn door, now that I know where it is.

Listen to me, Sam, you're just—

Quiet! Not a word!

Now don't you tell me to—

I said not another fucking word!

Sam sat motionless for a moment in the silence—the pure, sweet, invigorating silence. He sat with the stories of Magic and Wolf for a time, and then made them disappear. Then Sam's own story joined him, and soon that one had to leave as well. Stories certainly had their uses, he admitted, as long as he knew what they were—and were not.

"Here's to slave Magic, the hairless submissive weenie!" Sam shouted at the cocoon. Then to the door: "Did you hear that, you absolutely magnificent, beautiful bitch!"

Ten minutes later, utterly drained but at peace, Sam walked into the living room wearing only his new name. Lady Indigo and Danielle sat on the sofa, both quiet and subdued. From all the screaming, sobbing, and hysterical laughter, they had no idea what would emerge from the bedroom. But Lady Indigo knew something very important had happened in there, and she was, as always, correct. Sam thought of telling her, but as she'd once cautioned, words would taint his triumph.

"I need to keep this close," was all he said.

Lady Indigo nodded. "Kneel in front of me." With an air of solemnity, she unlocked his collar. The small click said the contract was over, its terms fulfilled. Magic was no longer needed. Sam wondered if he'd miss him.

He took a long, hot shower. In the mirror, he examined his chest. The dried beads and streaks of blood washed away, leaving the thin lines of the letters clearly visible. They still slightly stung. Like it had on the sheet of handmade paper, *Wolf* read backward.

"It all depends on which side you're standing," Sam said to the mirror. He thought about wolves and warriors and then Wolf. "Here's to you too, you fat, funny old man."

416

It was time to go. Sam dressed himself carefully so as not to break open the cutting and stain his shirt. He nodded to the man in the mirror and walked back into the living room.

"Magnificent, beautiful bitch, am I?" Lady Indigo said, her eyes smiling.

"Yeah," Sam laughed. No paddles now.

"And so the gift has been passed on," she said.

Lady Indigo embraced him, deeply and warmly, for a long time. Danielle also held him with what seemed more than just a farewell hug. Sam collected himself, gathered up his masks, journal, belongings, and that bloodstained sheet of paper that had so thoroughly traumatized him barely an hour earlier, and left Lady Indigo's dungeon for the last time.

31

A Real Woman

Sam lay in bed and watched Danielle get dressed. She sat on the edge of the bed to slip on her shoes. He reached for her.

"C'mon! I'll be late for class," she said.

"Then use your safe word."

She stood up and placed her foot between his thighs. "Use yours," she smiled.

"Okay, okay!"

She leaned over and gave him a kiss. "See you tonight, babe."

So, twit, do you think you finally found yourself a real woman?

See for yourself.

Don't get smart with me!

What will you do? Be mean to me? Oh, I'm sooo scared.

You should be!

I've never cared much for "twit" either.

Sorry, twit, I just can't help myself.

I like "babe" a lot more, you know.

Pah! What do you think she'll do when she sees all your sickness and your shit? Do you think she'll put up with that?

She already has, she is, and she doesn't care. Jeez, still the mean bitch, aren't you?

It's what I do. You know that.

Yeah, I do. That's what makes you so handy when I'm horny.

You little prick! You know that's not all I'm good for!

I know what you're bad for. That's real clear. You don't like being a story, do you?

I'm just as real you are!

You bet. As real as my other stories.

But I'm the most important one! Just look how much time you've spent with me, especially at night! And I did what stories are supposed to do, didn't I?

What? To insult me? To criticize everything I do? To make me feel like total shit? Incompetent and worthless?

That's what you wanted, Sam. That's all you know. And that's what you deserve, do you remember? I worked my ass off to give you all that.

That place stinks. I'm not going back there. I don't have to.

So where will you go now? To another dominatrix to stomp on your dick some more?

I don't need that anymore either. And when I do want to get stomped, I'll know who to see. And you know what happens when I get tired of that, don't you, hmm?

Hold on here. We really need to talk about this.

I know what to do with stories now.

Sam! No one will ever love you like I have.

Thank God! Now it's my turn to have some fun.

No! Don't you dare! Don't you even think of trying anything!

I think I'll go get a big, greasy omelet for breakfast.

You can't just pretend I'm not here!

With a side of bacon.

What are you doing? Stop! Stop right now!

And coffee.

Now you're really pissing me off, twit! You'll never have a safe word with me! Never! And you can take your pathetic

THE END

ACKNOWLEDGEMENTS

I AM A FUNCTION OF MY experiences, as are we all. I've been affected to some degree by everyone I've ever known and met. I acknowledge you all, whether you have been a friend of many years or are someone with whom I briefly spoke on the street who told me something new. I'm sorry that I don't remember all of your names, but I give you a heartfelt thank you—or a hard kick in the butt, whichever would be appropriate for our circumstance.

But the genesis of this book is another matter. I give my thanks to Simon for being the vessel into which I could pour this story.

To my courageous and steadfast readers, Michelle and Jo.

To Rick, Gary, and Bill, who remind me that not all men hide their hearts.

To Sarah for being my other.

To Rebecca for being impeccably Rebecca.

And especially to Jessica, who can see the gem in a lump of coal.

www.ingramcontent.com/pod-product-compliance
Lightning Source LLC
Chambersburg PA
CBHW072255020726
47501CB00002B/278